THE TEMPEST RISING COMPANION NOVEL COLLECTION

Storm and Sparks

Wind and Wings

Ember and Flames

Steel and Fury

Elliott VanDruff

Belle Rose Press

Books by Elliott VanDruff

Tempest Rising Series

Beyond the Shroud

The Last Dusk

A Gilded Cage

Empire of Dust

The Tempest Queen

Tempest Rising Companion Novels

Storm and Sparks

Wind and Wings

Ember and Flames

Steel and Fury

TABLE OF CONTENTS

STORM AND SPARKS

Tempest Rising 1.5

Destrian's Story

Elliott VanDruff

Belle Rose Press

Dedication

This book is dedicated to all of my readers who have believed in me and enjoyed the stories.

Map of Lyrica

Chapter 1

THE WELCOME MY FATHER planned for me in Morgania was worth slogging through the war-torn desert. We'd been drinking and carousing and partying for days by the time I'd realized that Master Gillius's visit was overdue and that I should probably be worried.

Why did Gillius insist on coming anyway? When Lord Alexander and I unexpectedly met the sorcerer in the capital, I'd been surprised but not overly concerned—even when he'd insisted on traveling to Morgania and to expect him before the spring melt.

The spring melt was a week ago.

But it was hard to be worried with all the diversions my father had planned for me. I'd thrown myself into them with abandon. It was sickeningly easy to forget the war I'd witnessed on my quest to retrieve my gem, like slipping off my dusty tunic and slipping on the overcoat that depicted me as nobility. I had my gem now. A ruby, exactly like the one my grandfather had, and his father had before him, and so on and so forth in the long line of fire sorcerers, my ancestors. As my father's heir, it would grow our prestige in the Western Empire. Not that we needed it.

I couldn't deny that my life seemed to be moving along a track of undeniable fortune. I had found my gem, a quest that had been in no way assured. My position as the sole heir of my father, the consul, meant that one day, I would inherit the position, stepping into the role as naturally as Sol rises in the east. It was a role I had been groomed for since birth. The thought was almost dizzying in its enormity, and grueling in practice, but it was a position I was ready for.

And then there was the matter of my wealth. As the richest nobleman west of the sea, my coffers were filled with more gold and precious gems than most people would see in their lifetime. I had fruitful lands under my name, the finest castle in the region, and a retinue of people ready to fulfill my every command. Materially, I wanted for nothing. I'd even managed to catch the eye of the daughter of one of the most prominent families in the empire. She was smart, beautiful, and accomplished - the epitome of an ideal noble lady. Her presence by my side further elevated my status, painting a picture of a future that seemed almost too perfect to be real.

Yet, I wasn't naive enough to believe that my

position came without challenges. The political land-scape of Lyrica was a place where power, cunning, and ruthlessness were the key to survival. I would have to fight, with every tool at my disposal, to secure and maintain my seat among the vultures waiting to pick at the carcass of the weak. But at that moment, with the taste of success fresh on my lips and the promise of a prosperous future in sight, it was hard to feel anything but satisfaction. My life was far from simple, but it was pretty damned perfect.

So, when Gillius turned up on the night of one of the feasts my father had thrown, I was filled with relief, having only just realized I should have been worried.

"Gillius, what took you so long!" I shouted with a grin, standing and rushing toward him in welcome, all the while hiding the guilt that I'd forgotten about him. "How was the journey? We hope you had no trouble on the road. Father has tried to make the going safer, but you never know with the Morganites." Depending on the season, Morganites could be an annoyance on the road, though they mostly targeted trade wagons and supplies. Still, it was early, yet, for them to be raid-ing.

"When they told me you'd traveled here with a mountain heathen, I'd not dared believe it." Father's voice carried behind me.

The relief was immediately replaced by apprehension when I noticed that very person standing beside him. I looked back at Gillius. "You have a companion?" The girl was slight, like a shadow, her face twisted into the most beautiful scowl I'd ever seen. Her hair lay in a thick rope over her shoulder, so inky black it seemed to drink in the light. Her stormy blue eyes carried a defiant spark as she glared at me. On the corner of each eye a crescent tattoo winged out, the symbol of the Morganites who still bristled under the empire's reign.

"Gillius?" I asked, turning my eyes to the older sorcerer as he strode toward my father, a determined look in his eyes. The girl studied me as though she found me wanting.

"I know that you weren't expecting me to arrive with anyone, but the girl will need to accompany me to Solridge to be tested," Gillius said, his voice low. He handed Father a parchment, which he opened, and I read over his shoulder.

The Articles of Clemency state that any person who displays an affinity for magic will be granted safe passage and proper boarding while seeking instruction and control of their skills to be used for the betterment of the Lyrican Empire. All banners who hold oaths to His Imperial Majesty are required to harbor and assist these individuals in attainment of training, either at Solridge Academy or the Academy of Somme. Any banner who does not comply with this order will be subject to penalization by the Emperor's Council.

Any stray magical renderings that occur from an untrained sorcerer by accident will be granted leniency under the Council of Five.

Signed,
Duke Agramon of Solin
High Seat of the Council of Five

I glanced at the girl, who still stood back at the door, now looking awkward and angry about it. She was clenching the sword at her waist as though she were ready to pull it out and start lopping off the heads of our dinner guests. Alongside her sword was a dagger with a hilt as black as her hair. I glimpsed the outline of a marking on her neck, a sign that she hailed from a clan. Some Morganites had tried to conform under Lyrica's reign. They still marked themselves with imorets, but otherwise they tried to work within the rules and laws of the empire. Clansmen, on the other hand, were the dregs of society. They insisted on living outside of my father's rule, thieving and pillaging whenever they saw fit. My father had been battling them for dominance for years and still hadn't seemed to bring them to heel. Sometimes I wished the army would just come and take them out, once and for all. Maybe then we'd have some peace.

My gaze settled on Gillius. As the son of the consul, I was expected to maintain a respectful and polite countenance when it came to the sages at Solridge—they were my teachers after all—but the thought of this Morganite angered me. What game was he playing? It was an insult to me and my father to drag her into our hall and put her defiance on display for all our subjects to see.

"My Lord Consul, may I present Rowyn Blythe of Espiria," Gillius said, holding out his hand to present the girl and waving her toward us. She marched forward, now glaring at Father. If Gillius was brandishing the Articles of Clemency, that meant she was a sorceress. I saw no gem, so she was still untrained, but I worried about how she looked at Father. You never knew with magic. I wondered if she could kill someone with a blink of an eye. It looked like she wanted to. Despite my misgivings I was curious. Curiosity quickly morphed into concern. We'd never known Morganites to have sorcerers before. What did that mean for the clans? Had they become more formidable in my absence at school? How would we control them with magic added to their arsenal?

"You must be mad, Gillius," Father said with a frown. "She's hardly fit to enter our halls."

I couldn't agree more. Though our castle was not without coarseness, we were still nobility, still the wealthiest consulship west of the sea. We had *manners*. Our women certainly didn't prance around in worn tunics and breeches with patches over the knees. I hated the way her clothes clung to her, making it impossible to ignore the curve of her hips, the slender strength in her arms. I looked away from her, pushing back those unwelcome thoughts.

"My Lord Consul, Rowyn of Espiria is under my care, therefore she is protected under the Articles of Clemency. You understand the consequences if you don't treat her with respect. Do you accept the terms or not?" Gillius asked, his voice stern.

"I don't make it a habit of hosting traitors in my castle," Father replied.

I nodded, affronted by Gillius's manner. He had told me that he was coming to visit Morgania. He'd said nothing about dragging mountain traitors into our halls and forcing us to harbor and entertain them! The only Morganites in the castle were those in the jail where they belonged.

"I don't think you want to ignore my warnings, Consul. She's in your care for her time here."

"Was that a threat?" Father asked.

"That's a warning, Consul. You should consider the person giving it. The Council of Five isn't known for granting leniency to those who break their laws."

"What of the countless laws she's broken?" I snapped, hating the way Gillius was speaking to my father, as though schooling him. Father was a consul. Gillius, though I respected him as a very talented sorcerer and healer, was still a commoner. He had no business lecturing us about the laws of the empire. My family had sat in the seat of Helena since the Western Conquest over a hundred years ago. "Espirians are known traitors to the emperor."

Gillius glared at me. "The Articles of Clemency protect Rowyn, just as they protected *you*." I froze at Gillius's implication. Sure, I'd had mishaps with my magic. When I was younger, I had a hard time getting my temper under control. Accidents always happened with sorcery. It was a part of the deal. Magic could be useful—it could make you wealthy and powerful—but it all came at a cost. A cost usually paid in your youth. But I was past that now.

Gillius went on. "Since she is now under Solridge's tutelage, the only ruling body that can try her is the Council of Five."

Father considered Gillius. "Blythe, you say? That's

the name of the chief, is it not?"

The girl, Rowyn, turned her icy gaze back to Father. She raised her nose straight into the air and spoke so forcefully that I almost took a step back. "Chief Weldon was my father."

By Sol above. The girl that Gillius insisted on dragging into my home couldn't just be any old mountain traitor. No, she had to be the daughter of the veritable king of traitors. We would have to increase patrols in the hallway tonight just so that everyone could get a good night's sleep and not worry about having their throats slit in their beds.

"*Was* you say? Could it be I'm finally rid of the man?" Father asked.

Rowyn hesitated. Something flickered in her eyes, some spark that wasn't the anger nor the caution that had lurked there in her introduction. "He died over winter."

Father smiled. "You bring good tidings then. In that regard, I suppose I can offer you safe quarter . . . for a few nights, at least."

Gillius's eyes were on me. He raised his brows in silent question. I pointedly looked away. How dare he ruin what was supposed to be my grand homecoming. I'd been at Solridge several years now, away from home, away from my father who I knew sank into his vices and ailments in my absence. Gillius interrupted what precious little time I had with him, before I was to leave for school again, with this Morganite business. I was angry. Angry for myself. Angry for Father. Angry at Gillius to presume to involve us in such a farce.

Father motioned to the table. "I'm required to let you stay, but you aren't allowed to leave the castle unless you have a chaperone, either Gillius or a guard."

The girl bowed, her back stiff, angry defiance written in every movement. "My lord, as a humble Morganite, I've heard of your hospitable nature. Know that I'm grateful for your protection, and the manner it was given."

I couldn't believe the audacity of this girl. My father was going against every instinct of his nature to allow her to stay, and she openly mocked him? I could feel my fingertips growing warm, the temper I'd tried so hard to control for most of my life brewing beneath the surface. I shot a furious look at Master Gillius. How dare he do this to us.

Rowyn and Gillius took a seat farther down the table, blessedly away from me. I tried to ignore the girl as much as possible, but I couldn't help but sneak a glance every now and then. My eyes lingered on the marking on her neck, the faint outline of black peeking out from beneath her hair. I wondered what it was. I secretly hoped she would shrug her braid off her shoulder so I could see, but she was too tightly wound for little movements like that. She was looking around as though the ladies and men sitting in silk beside her were going to start shooting arrows.

Not likely, though a few would've liked to. This wasn't the Morganite wilds; this was Helena, and we had standards of behavior. And yet, even as I thought it, I felt a strange pull. We had just met, and already, she was under my skin. I swallowed the strange sensation, forcing it down, trying to ignore the feeling, and her, for the rest of dinner.

As the candle wax began to drip on the tables, Gillius nodded to me and gestured toward the door. I knew it would come to this. My father was known to be stubborn and pigheaded. By Sol above, all of us Everetts were. But he would listen to me. He always listened to my sisters and me. Gillius would use me to try to appease him. I was all the more angry at him for it.

I followed Gillius into the hall, feeling righteous indignation with every step until we rounded the corner and Gillius turned to me.

"Why?" I growled. "Why did you have to bring her here? You know how we feel about the Morganites. You know what they've done, and you brought her here and just shoved her in our face! What is the meaning of this, Gillius?"

"Rowyn will die without help," Gillius murmured. "She needs protection. You must make sure to ward her, every night."

"And who will protect us from her?" I snarled, thinking back to all I'd seen of the Morganites. Their ruthlessness. Their lack of honor for laws and justice. "The wards fail if she leaves! What if she goes wandering the halls in search of silver or gold to steal?"

"She brings the rain, Destrian. She controls the weather, and her control is as volatile as I've ever seen. She's in trouble."

"So?" I scoffed. "I don't see how that's my problem! Why didn't you just go back to DarkPort and sail to Solridge if she's in so much trouble. It would've been faster!"

Gillius sighed. "Did you not just hear what I said? She is a volatile sorceress whose emotions influence the weather. You think it would be safe to take her out in open water on a ship? You see how angry she is. We would have been at the bottom of the sea within a day's time."

He had me there. "I still don't see why you had to bring her to Helena," I ground out. "My father is extremely displeased with this. How can you ask him to harbor an infidel? It borders on treason!"

18

"That's why I need your help, Destrian," Gillius pleaded. "We have to make sure Rowyn stays safe until we get to Solridge. You can't even comprehend how much is at stake."

But I was angry. I could feel the burning from the gem on my brow—the sparks alighting on my fingertips. I had come hoping to have a peaceful visit with my father, and Gillius was threatening to ruin it all. "No . . . she may be a child, but the law is clear in this matter. She should be put to the sword with the rest of the barbarians. Furthermore, Sol will fall from heaven before my father willingly harbors a traitor."

Gillius's voice turned hard. "Are you so willfully blind that you don't see how much you and your father already owe this girl?" he asked. "How can you think it a coincidence that Morgania was the only land in the empire spared from the drought?"

His words brought me up short. We were lucky was why. We were farther north and by the sea. Perhaps it was our proximity to Horan, and to the Others who dwelled there. After all, they were known magic users, too, with powers that we were still ignorant of. Any number of things could've been the reason why Morgania remained the most fruitful part of the empire. It didn't have to do with a girl, barely the height of my chest, and her petulant feelings that I cared nothing

19

about. "You can't mean . . ."

"I do. The Consulship of Helena owes this girl all the wealth you've gained in profit for your land. This is no *jest*, Destrian. You might as well hold the sword to your own throat if you let something happen to her. For when she falls, Morgania will fall with her. The drought that has plagued the empire will finally reach Morgania, and you will be to blame."

Footsteps echoed in the hall. I turned and found the scowling girl behind me.

Gillius held out his hand. "Rowyn, may I present Lord Destrian Everett, heir consul to Helena and the lands of Morgania."

This had to be some cruel joke of the gods. I watched as she made a vague attempt at a curtsy that nearly sent her to the floor when the point of her sheath met with stone. "Really? And you expect her to get along at Solridge?"

"I ask this of you all the same," Master Gillius answered.

I sighed. Obviously, I would not have a choice in the matter. All of our talk meant nothing when the Articles of Clemency were thrust in our faces. The only thing to do was be a nobleman and fulfill my obligation. No matter how distasteful it was.

"As you're in my home, I vow to defend your honor

and person to the best of my ability. Please forgive my offensive language, as Gillius has made me aware that it's beneath my rank to say it, and yours to hear it."

She met my glare with her own icy gaze. "You're a cad, aren't you?"

I bristled at the slight. This little mountain wretch called *me* a cad?

"Rowyn!" Gillius gasped. "Apologize at once!"

"Oh, please, it's not like he really apologized," she muttered.

I couldn't help but laugh. Clearly Rowyn agreed with our sentiment about her presence in Helena. She didn't want to be here either. "Keep your hose on, Gillius. It's no matter." I turned and led them down several corridors until we reached the guest wing. "You may stay here," I said, then warned, "Mind my father's orders, though. Don't leave unless you're being accompanied, and *don't* make a fuss, or you'll see how far my father's hospitality will get you."

Rowyn still looked extremely put out when she replied, "Thank you for your kindness, my lord. It won't be forgotten."

I shrugged, then Gillius nudged my shoulder. "I'll ward your room so that, gods forbid, no harm should befall you."

She barely thanked me before slamming the door in

my face. I placed my hand on the door and let my power flow into it before turning to Gillius. "You're making a mistake with her."

As I strode to my own room, I thought back to the pleasantries and laughter I had shared with my father during the precious few days I'd been allowed to relax in my homeland. The elaborate parties, the soothing rhythm of my daily life—all were about to be disrupted by Rowyn's arrival. This was no trivial matter. I had just been rejoicing in the splendors of my seemingly perfect life, and now, it was being threatened.

I let out a sigh of frustration. It wasn't just about my life being disrupted. I was being forced to play the role of protector for a person who threatened to ruin everything I'd been working toward. The irony of it all was almost laughable.

I could feel the heat from the gem in my forehead intensify as my emotions threatened to burst. A part of me wanted to reject it all. Yet, another part of me, a part I wasn't fully willing to admit existed, understood the implications if Gillius turned out to be right. Life as I knew it had taken an unexpected turn, and I couldn't help but feel a sense of loss. It was as if the dream I was living was slowly fading away, being replaced by a reality that was far less pleasant.

Chapter 2

I WAS STARTLED AWAKE, the crash of steel and smell of blood still lingering in my mind as I blinked at the morning sunlight. The dreams always felt so real. As if I were back in Yliria, riding with Lord Alexander as the army swept through the desert encampments that had been foolish enough to remain in our path. It was the crisp mountain air that rescued me from the nightmare. I let out a breath, lingering in the hazy warmth of the furs, willing away the remnants of my dream.

With a resigned sigh, I pushed the covers back and padded barefoot across the cold stone floor. Picking up a small bone pick, I began to scrape my teeth, a habitual routine I'd always done but never truly appreciated until my days in Yliria.

Moving to the window, I looked over the city of Helena as it began to stir from its slumber. The city was waking up, the distant hum of activity growing slowly but surely. People were moving in the streets, vendors were setting up their stalls, and the aroma of freshly baked bread was beginning to permeate the morning air.

Helena was home—it always had been, and it always would be. Seeing the familiar sights, the people, the streets—everything about it dimmed the horrors that I had witnessed in Yliria.

The sun cast a gentle light on the distant mountain ranges that bordered the city. They were a harsh, untamed frontier, much like the people who inhabited them—the Morganites.

My thoughts shifted. I picked up the small copper pitcher of water filled with crushed mint leaves and gargled a swig of it. The cool water did little to dispel the bitter taste of last night's surprise.

Rowyn. I couldn't help but glower at the distant peaks, a reminder of the headache that had been forced upon me. The peace I'd been enjoying since my return from Yliria was shattered now and the tranquility of my morning soured. Just the thought of her irked me, her presence in Helena like a stone in my boot. An irritant brought right into the heart of my city by none other than Master Gillius.

I spit into the basin as my mind replayed last night's confrontation. Gillius, with his blind eye for potential and misplaced faith in the savage clans, had thrust Rowyn into our civilized world without a second thought as to the implications.

I glared at the distant peaks as if they, too, were

responsible for my torment, then noticed clouds beginning to gather in the sky. They rolled in, gray forms casting a veil over the city, slowly overtaking the early morning light and replacing it with a more somber atmosphere.

I frowned, my fingers drumming against the stone window ledge. Could the girl, Rowyn, really be responsible for Helena's wealth? It seemed too convenient to be a mere coincidence. I considered the past several years. How rain came more often and storms more violent, while the rest of the empire watched us with increasing envy.

It was disconcerting to think that a single individual could hold such influence over the elements. I found myself shivering slightly despite the warmth of my room.

Either way, it was Gillius's problem, not mine. We'd agreed to harbor the girl and feed her meals and not kill her, but that was as far as my duty, and patience, would go. I didn't need to spend my last few days in Helena wallowing in anger and self-pity because Gillius hadn't thought of my feelings when he'd gone foraging in the forest and found a stray. Rowyn was not my problem.

With that resolution in mind, I got dressed and went out, determined to enjoy my day.

THE MORNING'S CONTEMPLATION and irritation gradually dissipated, replaced with a renewed sense of responsibility.

The first item on my list was a review of our trade agreement with Gryse. The meeting threatened to sour my mood; both my father and I were aggrieved by it, yet the empire had essentially intervened, imposing terms that were in no way favorable to us. It's hard to ask a fair price for what you had when everyone around you was penniless and starving.

Seated at the table, I found myself faced with my father's adviser. A man of considerable influence, he was a well-oiled cog in the imperial machine, ever ready with a smarmy smile and a wheedling tone. As I looked at him, my discontent grew. He was the figurehead of everything I loathed about the empire's overreach into our lands.

"We must consider our duty to the empire, young sir," he started, laying out documents and charts before me. "Gryse is in a bind. They can't possibly pay full price for the produce and grain we send over. It would cripple their economy—leave their people destitute. The empire . . . people would starve."

26

His words echoed in the room, leaving a bitter aftertaste. The sanctimonious emphasis on *duty* and *empire* grated on my nerves. My fists clenched under the table, hidden from view. The reality of the situation was clear to me: Gryse, for all its plight, was being used as a pawn by the empire to leech away our resources under the guise of imperial duty.

I held his gaze, letting the silence draw out. His smug smile faltered, his eyes flicking away nervously. I didn't respond, didn't argue, only watched him squirm.

After my frustration with the trade meeting, I sought refuge in the one place that could soothe my rattled mind—the forge. The clangor of hammer on metal, the roar of the furnace, and the malleability of raw iron under my control seemed to temper me back to even ground and clear my thoughts.

Inside, I stripped off my outer layer, rolled up my sleeves, and pulled on thick gloves.

I had been trying to crack a particular problem for a while—the formula for bitter steel. A type of metal rumored to withstand the harshest cold, it would be an invaluable asset for our soldiers on the northern borders. The formula, however, remained elusive. It was a delicate balance between the amount of iron, carbon, and a third component I had yet to identify.

I pulled a piece of steel from the furnace, glowing a

fiery orange, and began to work. I pounded, letting my frustrations out on the metal, the rhythm of my hammer against steel echoing in the vast room. I quenched the blade in oil, the sizzle and hiss of cooling metal the notes to a ballad of the Everett line.

The result was a blade, sharp and strong, but still not bitter steel. It lacked that unmistakable sheen. Still, I examined it with a critical eye, searching for any signs that might lead me closer to the elusive formula.

Frustrated, I returned to my rooms, washed up, and readied for dinner. Father had insisted on a feast almost every night that I was in Helena, as though he were trying to celebrate all that had passed while I'd been away at Solridge.

I stepped into the hall relieved that Gillius and Rowyn hadn't arrived yet. I'd had a blessed day free from thinking of the little Morganite and all the issues that she carried into my home, uninvited, and I was hoping to hold on to that feeling a little longer.

Sol granted my wish. The hall gradually filled with friends from the city. Well-wishers who'd watched me grow up came to admire the new gem that marked me as my grandfather's heir. Father was being a good sport about it. He drank too much, but I knew he was anxious about the Morganite. We all were.

So, when she slipped into the room, everyone

turned to look. It made me feel better that I wasn't alone, but in the end, it didn't matter what the others would've thought if they'd seen. I couldn't tear my eyes away.

The night before, her hair had been braided back severely. Now, it cascaded loose over her shoulders, completely softening her features. It looked so…intimate. I involuntarily thought of running my fingers through her hair and my heart seemed to stutter to a stop. I shouldn't be thinking anything of the sort.

Rowyn scanned the room like someone who was worried about getting jumped in a tavern, sharp, blue eyes marking every single blade worn by the others in the hall. Her eyes lingered on the guards the longest.

But that wasn't the most riveting thing about her. No, it was the fact that she was wearing a traditional Morganite gown. I recognized it immediately for what it was, though I'd never often seen them. Only out in the farms to the west of Helena, where peaceful Morganites who lived under our banners worked.

The gowns that I was used to seeing my sisters in, the style that Lyrican nobility wore, tended to be made of silk and gems and any pretty thing you could think of that would remind you of delicacy. Traditional Morganite gowns were made to be stiffer, with incredibly detailed and fantastical embroidered designs stitched from the neck to the feet.

"They were allied with the Woltari, you know," Aunt Maureen had said when I pointed out a dragon embroidered on a girl's dress as we watched a summer solstice celebration when I was younger. Perhaps I remembered it so clearly because it was the first time I realized that they were different. I'd asked for imorets, too, which my father smacked me soundly for.

"The Others?" I'd asked, using the shortened form. There were so many different ones, it was impossible to name them all.

Aunt Maureen nodded. "They're both children of Imor. That's why they always got along. Imor created the Others, then Sol challenged him to create a people as noble as his, so he brought the Morganites into the world."

I looked back at the embroidered pattern. There were sprites and sirens, giant birds, and horned creatures painstakingly stitched all over the fabric. I almost feared the embroidery thread because I imagined an old, frightful Morganite grandmother cursing and magicking a stitch within an inch of its life to get it to perform and create such spell-binding pieces.

Rowyn's was a work of art, obviously made just for her. The color was the exact blue of her eyes. The sleeves and hem were the perfect fit and there wasn't much wear. The embroidery was done all in variations of black. Some threads had a sheen, others a glimmer. I'd bet money it was someone close to her to put that much work into the dress. Roses and shadow panthers, falcons and unicorns, all hidden in darkness as though trying not to draw the eye. As if any of us could help it. There was no ignoring the little Morganite princess, bedecked in the traditional attire of her clan, head held high looking down on us mere Lyricans. As though she belonged here more than we did.

And the markings. My curiosity was finally sated. I could see the tattoo on her neck now, a rose pattern that matched the detailing of the gown. She had another that sat just above the swell of her chest. It was the outline of a star with the damnable crescent that they used to mark absolutely *everything*. Rowyn met my eyes as though challenging me, her brows raised in question.

I felt stupid because I merely stared at her.

I shook my head. For Sol's sake, get ahold of yourself.

Ingrid Byrne was the most eligible lady of the west. I was a lucky man, to have caught her attention and maintained it for as long as I had. She was far more beautiful and lovely than any Morganite wildling.

Rowyn and Gillius finally took their seats down the

table, blessedly away from my father and me, and I tried to ignore her the best that I could at dinner until her voice broke through as I was taking a bite.

"My lord."

I looked up and met her expectant eyes. "The lady Morganite addresses me?" I asked, trying to mask my discomfort with aloofness. I didn't want her to know how rattled I was by her. The girl should fear me, not the other way around.

"If it pleases you, my lord, I'm in search of a book. If I could but read to pass the time."

"You can read?" I was more surprised by her request than I'd meant to show. Father had talked about providing more schools to the farming communities and smaller villages around us but hadn't prioritized it. It was a project I planned to begin once I got home from Solridge for good. As a result, only the wealthiest and more prominent people of Morgania could actually read.

My reaction had clearly displeased her. "By my lord's pleasure," she said dryly, glaring at me as though I'd gone out of my way to embarrass her.

"Nothing would please me more than to hang you Morganites from the gates as a warning to other rebels. It's favor enough that I let you live. Ask for any more, and I'll mark you for impudence."

Rowyn looked at Father, her eyes flashing. I braced myself for a biting remark, but she merely said, "I'm forever indebted to my Lord Consul for your hospitality." Her eyes flickered back to me. "The book, my lord. May I borrow one, if it's not too much trouble?"

I could feel Father stiffen next to me. He wanted me to say no, but Gillius was looking at me expectantly. "I'll escort you to the library after dinner."

Rowyn smiled and something surged within my chest. I stopped breathing for a moment and clenched my teeth, scrabbling for a hold of the feeling and pushing it back. Whatever it was, it remained wholly unwelcome and unwanted.

I wondered if that was how she intended it. The Morganite gown seemed to be a well-planned assault on our company. Was she planning on using her pretty smiles to sneak through my castle and cause mischief? I began to wonder if there was a scheme here that Gillius wasn't seeing. Did the Morganites offer her up to him? Plead with him to deliver her to my city? To protect her? Gillius would be a fool to take her in on that claim alone, and I didn't know Gillius to be a fool. Then again, countless good men had been swayed by a sweet face and a sob story, and Rowyn was incredibly striking.

"Thank you, my lord," she said softly, the ferocity

gone from her eyes.

I looked back down to my plate, unable to concentrate on Alexo's story. He went on beside me, not catching that my mind lay elsewhere.

Rowyn went back to eating, this time sharing her smiles with Sir Bernard who I was increasingly becoming irritated with for allowing himself to be turned into the biggest mark. He was paying far too much attention to her for an old soldier.

Was she flirting with him? I wouldn't put it past a clan girl to befriend a Lyrican soldier to try to get information. She was probably sent to spy, a little girl whom no one would view as a threat. She could read and probably write as well. I wondered if she was recording things in her room. How often someone walked past her door. Where the guardsmen were posted in the castle.

The hackles on the back of my neck rose. I was sure that there was some underhanded plot afoot.

Very well, Morganite. I would find out her secrets.

Chapter 3

I WATCHED ROWYN OUT of the corner of my eye as she walked next to me. I didn't know what I was waiting for. I supposed I was expecting her to try to wheedle her way into my graces like she was doing with Sir Bernard, but the girl was strangely silent.

Not willing to endure the awkwardness any longer, I spoke. "So . . . you're going to be attending Solridge?"

She shrugged. "Gillius spoke favorably of the academy. If I can learn control of whatever power I have, I can return and help my people."

Exactly as I suspected. She wanted to return to her clan and make life a living hell for me and my family. I wondered what information she was able to glean from her stay until now. Had she been able to send a message out? Would they wait for us to leave for Solridge before launching a strike? Or would they sneak in under the guise of night while she was here?

I clenched my teeth, seeing the outline of a blade in her sleeve. Was she going to try to kill me? I was heir, after all. The clansmen would love to see my demise. What they didn't know was that there was a line of far worse men than me, ready and willing to take my place.

Still, they thought a little girl, Morganite or no, could gain the upper hand over me? Amateurs. That was why they still hid in the shadows of the mountains instead of wresting control from Lyrica. "Do all Morganite women fight?"

"Many do. Those who choose to, anyway."

"I hadn't realized the Espirians sent their girls into battle; when did your clan stoop to such low measures?" I scoffed. I wondered if she minded being used by them in such a way. She probably had been so brainwashed by her clan that she was proud to take up any scheme to further their ends, no matter how many people she hurt.

I could practically feel her temper rise to match mine. All pretense of politeness dissipated with her next words. "When you Lyricans stooped to poisoning children."

Her answer surprised me. I was expecting her to try to calm me, to encourage me to let my guard down by appeasing my views. Rowyn did none of those things. Instead, she glared at me with naked hostility. If Rowyn really was sent to Helena to get in our good graces and let our guard down, she was doing a terrible job of it. We were all very wary of her. "I've no idea what you mean."

Rowyn stopped, her eyes narrow and sharp as a blade. "I think you do, my lord—throwing plagued bodies into our river? We found out too late, of course, after they made their way downstream. It was an evil trick done by evil men."

Father had written that the plague had passed through Helena late last summer and fall, but he'd made no mention of the Morganites. Did they think they should be immune to famine *and* plague? I wondered if she was parroting something her clan had told her. Perhaps she believed it to be true. We never knew with the Morganites. I could see them lying to their own if it furthered their ends.

"What are you talking about?" I glanced out of the window behind her and saw clouds building in the sky. I tried to hide my disappointment. I hadn't wanted Gillius to be right.

"Your father dumped plagued bodies into the river. My mother and grandmother both died from it, along with many of the clan: women, children, dogs. It's a miracle any of us survived."

Father had never said anything. Women and children? She didn't know him at all. He might hate the Morganites, but I didn't think his hatred would take him so far as to poison the river.

No, Father would never do that. What if it had hurt

our own? "You Morganites and your lies."

"May Imor strike me if I lie," Rowyn retorted. "It doesn't matter if you don't believe me. Everyone will be punished for their actions in the afterlife."

She certainly felt righteous in her anger. I wanted to ask her more about the accusation but didn't want to give her the satisfaction of knowing that she had rattled me. "What do you know? You're nothing but a cut-throat."

"That's a harsh accusation, but you're free to kill me if it pleases you. I'd expect nothing less from a Lyrican lord."

Ha! She shouldn't tempt me with such an appealing offer. Instead of enjoying myself at the feast Father had thrown in *my* honor, I was dutifully escorting her through the halls of my home, where I hadn't wanted her in the first place. "You and your clansmen have terrorized the forest for far too long. I'd burn the lot of you if I could." I couldn't keep the venom from my voice. She'd come here and was actively ruining *everything* I'd planned for my stay.

Rowyn scowled, racing after me as I sped through the halls. "Then why don't you? What's stopping you from wiping us all from the face of the earth?"

I scoffed, but she just kept right on going. "We're the poor and struggling, the hungry and weak. Is this how you would treat the people needing your help the most?"

The audacity it took to preach to me! As though the Morganites weren't the ones trying to steal our food and resources from right under our noses. "If those who follow you are really struggling and helpless, they should come to Helena and seek services here," I snapped. "No, those who follow you are traitors to the empire, nothing more. As such, they deserve a traitor's death."

Rowyn's voice shook with frustration. "People come to us because they don't have a choice. They've pleaded with your father, but your family isn't the most welcoming."

I could feel the heat burn within my gem and my fingertips. My temper was about to get the better of me. Then again, maybe Rowyn deserved to see what happened when I was crossed. "What do you know of such things? You're just a mere girl-child from the wild who knows nothing of the world."

"How could you understand?" she snapped. "You, a spoiled consul's son who only knows the comforts and opportunities of life in Lyrica. I know brutality when I see it. Men, women, even children have come to Espiria with missing hands or tongues. For the smallest of infractions, no less! Is this the world you speak of!"

Foolish, impudent girl! She dared try to lecture me in my own home? "A ruler has the responsibility of keeping order and enforcing the emperor's laws. What you see as brutality, we see as justice."

"What you see as justice, we see as tyranny," she retorted.

"You should watch your tone when you speak to your betters," I growled, still amazed at her presumption that I cared what she thought.

"Tell me, my lord, how should I behave that's to your liking? Should I sit silently among my betters while your father insults my family and honor?" She threw up her hands. "Just tell me what you wish of me, and I shall do it!"

I turned at the library doors and studied her with my arms crossed. Her chest was heaving, eyes ablaze with anger. "You'll never fit in at Solridge if you keep this up," I mocked. If she was even trying to make it that far. My guess was that she would sneak away at the border and return to the mountains, ready to spill a wealth of information from her time within our walls.

"Don't you think I already know that?" She threw up her hands in frustration, and I almost burst out laughing right then and there. I couldn't help but feel vindication that I was getting under her skin as much as she was getting under mine.

Actually, it gave me pause. If Rowyn *was* sent as a spy to get me in her good graces, she was doing a terrible job of it. The girl couldn't hide her feelings, and I didn't doubt that every word she uttered was true. I'd never met someone who was so brutally and inescapably honest.

"I don't know how to behave like a courtier," Rowyn spat, looking altogether like a hissing cat. "I was never taught! But forgive me if I refuse to take advice from someone as unchivalrous as you. How you let your father speak to me like I were the lowest vermin. Degrading me before your court and insulting my virtues. So, I apologize if your words of warning mean nothing to me! Now, if it pleases you, *my lord*, I'll survive as I know best, by my wits and charm. And if that doesn't work, then by my bow and sword."

The laughter burst out of me before I could stop it. She frowned and I was granted a reprieve from her snarling her feelings at me. By Sol above. Did Gillius know what he was getting into? I could just imagine what Ingrid and Lisbet would say.

"What's put you in such a humor?" she asked, the frown deepening.

"They won't know what to think of you," I said, wiping my eyes. "Are all Morganites so temperamental?"

"Are all Lyricans so bothersome?"

"Yes," I said before breaking out into laughter once more. Her bottom lip jutted out, and the wrinkle above her nose sent another surge within my chest, sobering me. Maybe she *was* getting to me. "Come, let's find you a book."

I held open the door and lit the room with my magic. Rowyn brushed past, absorbed with the ball of fire that hovered in the air beyond. As she walked by, I caught a whiff of her hair, and the feeling within my chest surged again, even stronger than before. She smelled like rain. Not the smell of coming rain when awaking to gray skies. No, she smelled like a meadow after a morning shower. Wet and sweet, laden with flowers and the piney aroma of the forest. It was a scent that lingered after she passed, rooting me to the spot. I fought to control the rushing feeling within me. I was glad she was fascinated by the fire because I needed a moment to collect myself.

"Well, let's get on with it," I said finally, impatient to be away from her and for this feeling to abate.

I kept my distance as she walked down the aisle, looking over countless titles. I began to worry that she would keep me there all night, and I was anxious to get out of that space, to get away from her. I'd been wrong.

If Rowyn really was a spy, she was doing her job well enough to cause me to second-guess myself.

When she put back a book for the twentieth time, my impatience got the better of me. I grabbed a worn lesson book I'd been forced to read as a youth and walked over to her. Gillius *had* told me to help her.

"The Intricacies and Customs of Lyrican Court," Rowyn read out loud when I'd handed it to her.

Hmph. She *could* read. A part of me still expected her to be lying. "This is the book my tutor used. You may find some useful tidbits here and there, although it's as dry as the wells in Adair." I found myself smiling at my own joke.

Get ahold of yourself. Her little machinations shouldn't be working. Not on me.

A slam sounded on the other side of the library, then it seemed to echo when Rowyn dropped the book in response. Damn it all. I'd missed many things from home, but certainly not the spirit of the woman who lurked in the library. When I was a child I'd tried to hide within the shelves when my sisters were being especially cruel. I remembered seeing a woman's face in the window, watching me. I'd hidden under the table, my heart racing, until my aunt found me an hour later. I'd pissed myself in terror, afraid to move for fear the ghost would come snatch me.

When I'd gotten older, I refused to be frightened by her presence. I would come to the library, then sit and read as an act of defiance against my previous fear. Every once in a while, I would feel her over my shoulder, or see a reflection of her in the glass, but she'd never actually done anything cruel or malicious. She simply was there, and there wasn't anything I could do about that.

So, when I strode toward the sound, I hoped it wasn't her. She'd never moved anything before. More likely it was a rat or some other vermin eating the pages of the books that stood in neglect due to servants unwilling to stay long in the haunted room. But I heard no pitter-patter of little feet, or scratching, or any other signs that another creature lurked in the dust and shadows with us as I came upon the book lying in the middle of the floor. It was too far from the shelf to have simply fallen. It had been thrown.

"How did it fall?" a voice whispered behind me. Rowyn had followed me, standing far too close for my comfort. The scent of her hair wafted up and I stepped away. She looked around, her eyes on the cobwebs. "Why does no one come here?"

I wondered if she was frightened. The gods knew I was. Still, I couldn't help the niggling suspicion at the back of my mind that anything I said or gave away would be used against us by the Morganites later. "It's no business of yours," I said, brooking no argument on the matter. She might be able to weasel information about us from the others, but she wouldn't do it through me. I strode over to the book and snatched it up before Rowyn could say another word. I turned and nodded to the other aisle where she'd left my manners book just sitting on the floor. "Will that title do for the remainder of your stay? If so, I'd like to be gone from here."

Rowyn held out her hand expectantly. "May I see it?"

"No." Good gods, the nerve of this girl.

Rowyn scowled and turned, stomping off to get the book.

"Thank you for letting me intrude upon your evening, my lord," she said when she'd joined me again.

As we walked down the corridor, I could feel her eyes on the leather cover under my arm. I kept shifting it away from her gaze, and the wrinkle above her nose deepened. She was glowering by the time we reached her room. As soon as Rowyn recognized the door as hers, I turned, practically racing to my own quarters to see what the ghost of Helena had insisted I study.

Chapter 4

I EYED THE TOME ON MY DESK, running my finger along the worn, leather cover, my mind drifting back to the library. Was it Rowyn's presence or mine that had precipitated the ghost's action? What was she trying to say?

Flipping through the pages, a chill coursed through me. They recounted the gruesome tale of the last king of Morgania's reign. Theramon's family, butchered at the hands of the Lyrican Army when they took to the sea and invaded Morgania. The images, graphic and vivid, etched themselves into my mind. Women and children, innocent victims of a brutal conquest. It was a bloody chapter of Lyrican history, one that I had known but never truly understood. My great-great-grandfather had been instrumental in conquering Helena. Fire rained down on the city, burning parts of it to ash before the Morganites finally fled to the mountains.

I stumbled upon a hand-drawn portrait of Theramon's wife, the queen. My heart pounded in my chest as I noted a familiar rose tattoo. The same design that adorned Rowyn's neck.

I leaned in closer. Morganite tattoos all had some meaning attached to them. Some showed lineage, others retold part of a person's history, and others communicated a person's profession or trade. I knew a little about them, but not what individual tattoos could mean, and there were hundreds, if not thousands, of them.

Why did the ghost choose to drop this book? Why did Rowyn bear the same marking as the Morganian queen?

I turned to the death logs, my brow furrowed in thought. Among the names of the family that I'd seen, one stood out—Rhoswyn, Theramon's youngest daughter, who was around five at the time of the conquest. According to the record, she was in Eslin during the invasion, but her name was conspicuously absent from the death logs. I felt a cold sense of dread creeping into my gut as I looked back at the name. Rhoswyn, so like the name Rowyn. The rose marking. Could the youngest princess have survived?

I ran a hand through my hair, feeling the tension knotting my muscles. If I dug deeper, I risked unearthing truths that could put my family and my position as the future consul at risk. It could ruin everything.

The Morganites were already on the brink of open rebellion. There was no telling what they would do if they found out that one of their own royals was freely walking around Morgania with the Articles of Clemency protecting her.

Letting out a gust of frustration, I looked at the fireplace and set it ablaze. Blue flames consumed the oxygen in the room. I got up and opened the window to let in more air. I'd learned young that the fire and I both would be in trouble if the air ran out in a room. I paced, sending more and more energy into the fire until I was spent.

Too often it felt like the world was crushing my shoulders and slamming me to my knees. My powers had made growing up incredibly difficult, even in a family with lots of resources and knowledge about sorcery. I made mistakes, as children did. The problem was that children's mistakes with magic could be catastrophic. It was not uncommon for untrained sorcerers to have deaths on their hands. I was one of them. Every Everett had killed others when they were young. It was just a matter of who it would be and what would precipitate the situation.

I couldn't imagine the fear of our serving staff. They never spoke to me, not after three had died in my presence. I'd get angry about something childish and stupid, and I would lash out. One time I incinerated a room. Only my grandfather was protected from me.

It was strange, though. I was a walking menace but treated like a prince. Ancestral magic was highly prized and protected among families. The promise of power for future generations was quite a lure, and most noble families within Lyrica had some magic in their bloodlines. They would just pop up irregularly. That's what made the Everett line so enticing. We cropped up in every generation except for my father's. None knew why he was skipped, but when I'd shown the trait, he was relieved. He never wanted me to have his life. Nor did I.

Then my grandfather stole me away from him. I was the son he'd always wanted, and I'd eaten it up. He protected me from every single accident. My father stepped back, thinking that he was doing the right thing, and it had broken him. He remained close with my sisters though. Onora and Ilisa took good care of him when they were home. When they'd gotten married and left, as daughters tended to do, he began to drink more.

I'd had to take on more and more at Helena while I was at Solridge, and managing the wealthiest consulship in the west was not an easy thing to do from leagues away.

I sat in my study, gripping the book tightly as my mind raced with suspicions and unsettling thoughts.

The image of Rowyn's black rose tattoo lingered in my mind, a symbol of the old royal family, a connection to a lineage that once held power over these lands. What did it mean? And more importantly, what were her true intentions in coming here?

Did Rowyn seek the seat of my family's power, a land coveted by other houses in the west? Ayastaren's hunger for control was palpable, and I knew Duke Roland wasn't the only one seeking to claim the consulship. The families of the Fens were cunning, inching their way closer, their eyes fixated on our gold. We could not afford another enemy encroaching on our reign.

It wasn't just the gold though. An ally of Helena was an ally to the whole of Morgania. The people had always been that way. Adair and the Fens were plagued by infighting. Most moved separately, but Morgania had always been different. One thing the first Lyricans who settled here took from the Morganites was their sense of duty and loyalty. We moved as one . . . always.

But it wasn't just the western nobles I had to worry about anymore either. The allure of Helena's riches would soon attract attention from the eastern houses as well. They would see the potential, the power that lay within their grasp. The consulship—the legacy of my family—was in jeopardy.

I'd tried to hide my father's weaknesses for years at Solridge, but the cracks were starting to show. He accumulated money and refused to spend it. Our guard was a skeleton crew, barely able to contain the rebellious Morganites, let alone defend against an attack from another consulship. The entire empire had watched us grow wealthy while their reserves slipped away from them. They were angry, they were hungry, and those seeking power were all looking to my father's weak position, and mine.

The only smart thing Father did was make good matches for my sisters, though I didn't think he could claim much credit for them. Onora and Ilisa were not without wit and cunning. They'd pretty much brokered the matches themselves.

Though I loved my father, I wasn't a fool about him. He hadn't always been a terrible leader, but he was now. If I had any hope of retaining our position in Helena, I needed to ensure that I kept Ayastaren happy and off our borders. I needed to ensure that Gryse had no reason to sail across the sea and claim our resources in the name of the emperor. I needed to make a good match with a house whose privilege, army, and political clout rose above Helena's. I had the burden of the consulship on my shoulders already, and if I wasn't careful, I would lose it all.

As if I didn't have enough to worry about with the rest of the nobles, now I had a little Morganite to fret over. Seeing the marking in the book only increased my wariness of the girl. My mind strayed to the image of her in our great hall, the traditional gown making her look altogether like the lost princess I worried she was. Were the Morganites preparing to break away from the empire? How much would her magic, which now I was sure she had, assist her in wresting control of my lands from me?

As I contemplated the possible scenarios, a knot formed in my stomach. I stared out of the window, watching the sun dip below the horizon as it cast an amber glow over the rooftops of Helena. The city seemed blissfully ignorant of the storm gathering in the distance.

Chapter 5

I AWOKE TO POUNDING on my door. My eyes snapped open.

"Lord Destrian!" a voice called out. "You are needed immediately."

I'd fallen asleep in my tunic and breeches. I pulled on my boots and flung open the door. The guards' faces were tight with apprehension.

"Someone attacked Lady Rowyn in her quarters. Master Gillius has asked for your presence."

My eyes darted to the window. Rain was beating down, pooling on the sill and leaking into the room. Was she attacked? Or had she attacked somebody?

I gritted my teeth as I led the way to her room. Master Gillius might be under her control. Some sorcerers had other gifts that came naturally to them. Manipulation was a common one. I wondered if it was a guard. Would she have some story ready? Would she just thin my forces while we slept?

As we approached Rowyn's room, I noticed the door ajar and the chaos within. Guards were arguing and looking out of the window. Gillius stood in the middle of the floor, his face stormy, his eyes filled with worry. He turned at my approach, his relief evident.

"Destrian," he breathed, "thank the gods you're here."

"I heard what happened," I said, my gaze flicking around the room. The disarray spoke of a struggle. There was blood. A lot of it. My heart twisted in my chest.

I realized the guards said she'd been attacked. They never said if she was all right.

"Where is she?" I asked.

"She fell," Gillius said, his hand on my arm, leading me to the window. My eyes widened. The breath froze in my chest. She'd fallen out of the window?

I looked down. A little figure was huddled on top of one of the large stone gargoyles. I recognized the black hair, now twin rivers down her shoulders.

"We got a rope," a guard—Tod, I thought—offered. They all looked at each other.

"I'll go." I nodded at Gillius.

They began securing the end of the rope while Gillius and I looked out of the window again. It was hard to see in the rain, but it looked as though Rowyn had scooted with her back to the wall.

"What happened?" I asked, ducking my head back into the room.

"Someone attacked her on the road here. She

wouldn't have lived if I hadn't healed her," Gillius confessed.

I glared at him, feeling heat in my fingertips. "She was attacked on the road here and you didn't tell me?"

"I asked you to ward her room," Gillius snapped. "How did he get past it?"

I opened my mouth to say something, then immediately shut it. I cursed. How could I've been so thoughtless? That stupid gods-be-damned book!

Gillius's eyes widened. "You didn't place the ward, did you?"

"We're ready, my lord," a guard said, stepping forward. I didn't look at Gillius as I wrapped the rope around my midsection and tied it into a knot. I stepped up to the window and nodded to the guards. Hoisting myself onto the sill, I gripped the rope and slowly lowered myself.

I quickly regretted volunteering. The rain made the going almost impossible. After a gods-blessed eternity, I reached the gargoyle, soaked to the bone.

Rowyn had scooted back as far as she could, so I stepped onto the gargoyle and lowered myself in front of her. She looked up at me, her eyes inches from mine. The surge rose in my chest, and this time it didn't go away.

"Are you all right?" I asked, realizing her arm was

soaked in blood. The surge intensified. I grappled with the rope and tied it around her waist.

"My arm is hurt," Rowyn mumbled.

Done with the rope, I lifted her arm and saw a large gash. "By Sol above, what happened?" I asked, the surge coming in waves of anxiety. Gillius. We just needed to get her to Gillius and she would be all right. He'd already said he healed her before.

I felt the gargoyle tremble. Without thinking, I wrapped my arms around Rowyn and gripped the rope. "Hold on!" I yelled as the stone crumbled beneath us, smashing into the courtyard below.

Rowyn stiffened from the jolt of the rope. I worried I was going to cause her further injury. "Hold on to me," I ordered. Finally, she cooperated, wrapping an arm around my neck and her legs around my waist. She looked down, apparently not as afraid of heights as I was. Her slick hair was cloaking my face, and I could do nothing but breathe in the intoxicating scent. My mind went a million places at once. I hoped to all the gods she had no mind-reading ability. Her body was soaked and pressed entirely too close to me in all of the wrong places, and I thought I was going to burst into flames from either embarrassment or frustration.

After a millennium, I handed her off to a guard. My body wanted to follow, but my mind stayed me for a moment to get myself together. Shame began to bubble to the surface, and I was half tempted just to let myself fall. Shame for not warding her room as I should've. Shame for the thoughts that sprang into my unwilling mind as I clasped her in my arms. Shame for feeling anything in the first place. She was not only a likely enemy, but at the moment, she was a guest. And she was injured because of me.

After deciding that smashing against the cobblestones was not the death I sought, I accepted a hand and was hauled back into her room, which still looked like a bloodbath.

Master Gillius was at Rowyn's side, and I let out a relieved breath.

"How did he get in?" Gillius was asking.

She pointed to the window and said as much. "The man came in through the window."

"How?" I asked. "No man could climb this without a rope, and I didn't see any evidence of tools." I'd actually made a point to check while I was slipping over the stone.

"It doesn't matter how he got in. What matters is that he did. I told you to ward this room," Master Gillius seethed. "Rowyn was almost killed for your carelessness!"

I met Gillius's eye. He saw the shame there. Shame

and regret. I hoped he saw nothing else.

Father stepped in. "Don't you dare raise your voice to my son. He just risked his life to rescue the whore, and I'll not have you abuse him further."

I froze at the insult. Rowyn had not done anything to raise that sort of implication, though rumors were swirling about her and Gillius. I would've wondered that myself if I hadn't known Gillius better, but to call her a whore?

The guardsmen quieted, their eyes on Father.

I opened my mouth to say something but snapped it shut. I couldn't rebuke my father in front of his own guards. It was a dangerous thing, to undercut someone's power like that in front of their men. It was imperative that the guards remain loyal and thought nothing amiss. Our hold on the consulship was tenuous enough.

Master Gillius rounded on me, refusing to be put off by a consul who ruled only in name. "I told you of the consequences if harm should befall her. You didn't take me seriously before, but mark my words now. Under no circumstances should she fall to harm in your city, or you will find your rule here short-lived."

"It was an accident," I said, bristling at his words. Words that I'd been ruminating over for half the night. I glanced back at Rowyn, trying to look apologetic, then stared. Her gown . . . the rain . . . it had turned into nothing more than a veil, the curves and outlines of her body visible through the wet fabric. I ripped my eyes away as the warmth from before came thundering back. I adjusted my hands, trying to look aloof.

"My lords, the man is gone," Sir Bernard said, stepping into the room and tearing me from my shameful thoughts.

"But he fell . . ." Rowyn said, going back to the window and looking down. I took an involuntary step forward, not wanting her anywhere near that cursed opening.

Bernard cleared his throat. "Mud again, Master Gillius."

Rowyn whirled on Master Gillius as though that meant something and stepped away from the window. I let out a relieved breath. "Who is he?" she demanded.

"Yes, Gillius, what evil has followed you here?" Father added.

Gillius only shook his head. "I can't say. But I assure you it's only Rowyn he wants."

"Well then, I want her out of my city," Father ordered. "By first light, take that girl, and the evil that follows her, out of here."

It was hard to register what he was saying, but my mind began to catch up and I met Gillius's eye.

Whatever was after Rowyn was incredibly dangerous, and whether I liked it or not, Rowyn was an invaluable asset to Morgania. That much was clear.

I wondered who had sent the creature. Was it another noble trying to hurt my family by taking away the cause of our fortune and wealth? If so, why was Gillius keeping their secret? A sorcerer had to gain mastery before being trusted with any real information about how the empire was run, and allies among sorcerers were common. Still, Gillius was asking for Helena's help in protecting the girl without divulging *any* information about who we were protecting her from, why they were after her, and what their plans were.

Gillius opened his mouth to say something, but Father held up his hand. "No, Gillius. I'll take no argument. I want the lot of you gone."

I stepped forward. Despite my anger at Gillius, and myself, I knew what I'd have to do. There was too much at stake, and if I put myself in a position to protect Rowyn, then I would also be in the position to find out more about what she was after, and what this other person might want with her.

Furthermore, it would strictly be about my duty as the future consul and had nothing to do with whatever churning was going on in my midsection. "I must go too. Father, I must return to the academy."

"But you just got back!" Father exclaimed. I knew I was hurting him. He'd lost so many moments with me, and with his lifestyle, there might not be many moments more. But if Gillius was right, and Rowyn was the reason we'd become powerful, then I had a duty to protect her. Even if she used that protection to stab me in the back later.

"I'm supposed to return with Master Gillius and Rowyn." My heart fell at the look on my father's face. I hated disappointing him. "It can't be helped. Would you have me travel alone?"

"I'll send an escort with you. It's no matter!" Father offered.

I shook my head, my mind made up. "What of our tribute to Duke Roland? No, I must go with them when they leave."

"Fine, you may stay till the end of the week. But if there's any more evidence of this . . . this . . . thing, then you'll be out for good. Am I understood?"

"Thank you, Consul." Gillius turned to me. "Help me take her to a new room and get her into bed."

My body responded immediately, my arms itching to wrap around her once more.

Rowyn shoved me away. "I can walk myself to bed. I'm not helpless." She turned to hold onto Gillius.

I frowned, worried that Rowyn sensed my inner

turmoil. She stepped on something that must've been sharp because she immediately raised her foot and started limping. Grinding my teeth, I followed them into the room across the hall and watched Gillius lower her onto the bed.

"Do you see now what I speak of? I expected careless disregard from your father, but never from you," Gillius said, surprising me.

I'd agreed to do what he wanted, hadn't I? And all for what? A girl who would sooner slit my throat than honor my claim to the consulship.

I glanced at Rowyn and immediately felt shame. Gillius was right. She'd gotten hurt under my roof. Still, I couldn't shake the anger I felt in suspecting that there was more at play than Gillius was letting on, and I wanted to know why—and what. Who was he protecting? Because it wasn't just Rowyn and it sure as the gods wasn't me. He'd put me in an impossible position, and it was his fault I was floundering in it.

Rowyn rolled into bed, and Bernard pulled the blanket over her in a fatherly gesture. I should've been the one to do that, I thought, then cursed at myself. No, I still wasn't entirely convinced she wasn't a Morganite spy. Gillius had always sided with the common folk of the realm. Was he working against me? Sure as gods felt like it!

Gillius held up Rowyn's arm as though to brandish her wound in front of me. I didn't need his help feeling bad.

"Fine, I apologize," I said, nearly shouting. "I'll ward her, but you can't make me accept her."

"Destrian!"

My frustration began to boil over. If I wasn't careful, I'd start a fire. I'd already been feeling overwhelmed before Rowyn came to Helena, and now it felt like my tenuous control over the city was ripping at the seams. "No, I'm done with this. The Morganite doesn't belong here, and you know it!" I strode out of the room and slammed the door behind me. Throwing both hands on the wood, I shoved my power into the walls and felt it slide away.

I was doing everything I could, and it always felt like it was never enough. Like the gods were testing me and I kept coming up wanting.

Chapter 6

THAT NIGHT, I STAYED AWAKE long after the castle had fallen back asleep, attuned to the ward, making sure nothing prodded or poked where it shouldn't. While I stared at the canopy above me, I replayed the night, feeling as though every awful emotion I could experience was wrung out of me in front of an audience.

My mind ricocheted from one memory to another. The threat of the creature. Gillius's anger at my failings. The rose marking on Rowyn's neck and the repercussions of what it could mean. The intoxicating perfume of her hair. My father's disappointment that I was siding with someone other than him. The guardsmen's marked looks when my father spoke. The feeling of the girl's slick skin on mine. The way the gown had revealed her curves.

I hated myself as I lay awake, unable to sleep and trying to get my mind off the girl. Rowyn of Espiria was a threat, nothing more. A threat that had to be contained since she also could be integral to my rule. A threat that had to be protected since it was obvious that someone else knew that. But a threat, nonetheless.

Father and I went hunting with a small party the next morning. It was fun, though I had other obligations pressing on my mind the entire time. I needed to appoint a judge for the lower district. Helena's tribute for Ayastaren was not adequate, and I would have to direct the changes. Several letters needed to be written to update the empire on Helena's standing in terms of military and resources and then I would have to get Father to sign it, which always started an argument. He would insist he could do all those things, which was true. But he didn't. He'd become absent-minded and put off every little duty, letting the consulship fall into disarray.

Despite all the tasks filling my plate in the short time I was in Helena, I relented and went on the hunt. I struggled to say no to Father when I felt so much guilt for how my grandfather and I had treated him when I was younger.

I ended up glad to have gone. Father had always enjoyed hunting and hadn't had a single drink while we rode through the forest that bordered Helena's walls. Though the sky was cloudy, there was no rain. The air warmed as the day went on, and it was pleasant just spending a day enjoying everybody's company.

Since hunting ran long, there was no grand feast that night. Father and I planned to eat in the morning room that doubled as our study. I still liked to refer to it as *our* study, even though Father rarely went in there anymore without me, but when I entered the castle, I remembered my duties.

Sir Bernard was standing to leave so I hailed him to me. "Anything happen here while we were away?" I asked, trying to sound casual.

Sir Bernard shrugged. "There still in't a sign o' that person from last night. A man who lives near the wall mentioned seeing some shadow slink up it, but it was dark and he din't seem the most reliable person."

I nodded. Since there was no more excitement that night, it appeared that Gillius was right, and my fire ward did keep whoever it was away. "And the girl?"

"I dunno." Sir Bernard shrugged, glancing at the door. "She din't come to dinner."

I frowned. Gillius would have attended her during the day since she was injured, so if something were amiss, I was sure he would let me know. He'd been very vocal in his displeasure at my lack of hospitality up to that point.

"Have Daisy bring a plate to her room," I said, re-adjusting my pack.

Sir Bernard nodded. "I was goin' check on her, jus' in case."

"I'll go," I said, turning toward her hall. "I have to place the ward again anyway, but can you keep an eye on her hall tonight?"

Bernard nodded and I turned, striding through the halls until I came to her door. I knocked and waited, hearing rustling inside. The door cracked open, revealing Rowyn standing there in a worn tunic and breeches, her sword at her side.

My words escaped me when I saw how worn and tired she looked. The spark that I'd seen the night before was gone. My worries about her spying in my castle and stealing my family's seat dissipated when I considered that she may be more injured than I'd previously known.

"Yes?" she mumbled, breaking me from my thoughts.

"I was just making sure you were in your room so I could set the ward." I looked back down to the sword. Rowyn hadn't relaxed her grip when she'd seen it was me. Something clenched within. "I heard you weren't at dinner, and I wouldn't want to go to all the trouble of putting a ward in place if you'd been roaming the castle."

"I was told to stay in my room," Rowyn said, her

eyes narrowing.

I nodded, trying not to act too concerned. Any weakness I showed Rowyn, she would use against me later. "Bernard will keep watch outside your door tonight. He said just to give a shout and he'll come running."

Rowyn nodded. "Tell him thank you." She shut the door, finishing our conversation.

I tried to push aside the temptation to linger. To knock again and make sure she really was all right and the blade hadn't been poisoned or anything. I warded the room as fast as I could and strode away. I couldn't afford any other distractions.

Chapter 7

THE DAYS PASSED IN A BLUR as I attempted to resolve the issues that had piled up in my absence. A new contingency of guards was hired and began their training. I scheduled a goods transfer with the Consul of Rudin. I approved the plans for a market held outside the city gates.

Not everything I tried to accomplish was a success though. I failed to perfect the recipe for bitter steel. I failed to gain any information about the person who had attacked Rowyn. I failed to make inroads into whether or not the Morganites were mounting a larger initiative against me. And night after night, I failed to keep myself from wondering if Rowyn would join us for dinner. She didn't, but that didn't stop my eyes from straying to the doors on the off chance that she would slip in.

The first night I chalked it up to her injury. Sidling up to Gillius, I tried to sound apathetic as I asked, "How is your patient?"

"Rowyn is healing well," Master Gillius had said, though I saw the weariness pulling at his eyes. For the thousandth time I wondered what the full story was behind her presence in Helena. "Thank you for increasing your diligence in warding her. I think the guard helps to keep her mind at ease, too, especially at night."

"So, she is sleeping well?"

Gillius nodded. "Yes, well enough. Her body appears to suffer from bouts of insomnia, so I worried the attack would put her off sleep, but she seems to be doing all right."

Something twisted in my chest. I frowned and involuntarily glanced back at the door. That night, I asked the guard who'd taken Bernard's place if she was in her room and the guard nodded.

"Hasn't left, m'lord. She has a maid now. *That* girl's been coming and going."

I hesitated at Rowyn's door, ready to knock, but then thought better of it. What was there to say? The guard had already told me she was in her room, and I could feel the man watching my back. There was no desire to have a conversation with an audience. So, I placed my hand on the door and pushed my power into it, letting the wood and stone absorb the magic. When I finished, I turned, nodded to the guard, and left for my chambers. There was too much to do anyway. I didn't have time for idle conversation.

But when the next night was the same, and the night

after that, I found myself staring at the damned book in the study, my mind at war. I'd been so sure she was here to spy or cause mischief, but hiding in her room for days on end was not conducive to either nefarious activity. I ground my teeth, second-guessing my convictions. Perhaps that was just what she wanted—for me to let my guard down. I couldn't afford to let my guard down. Not with her. Not with how my body reacted every time she was near. Not with Helena on the brink.

FOR MY LAST NIGHT in Helena, Father had planned his grandest feast yet. Though I was irritated that he refused to spend money in my absence to bolster our military or provide more services in the city, I played my part as the dutiful son. It wasn't hard to enjoy myself. Father had the cellars emptied, and all the accomplished cooks of the city came with a variety of masterpieces. It was fun, with folks from the city and castle alike, laughing, and talking, and wishing me well on my journey back to school. All of them whispered the same wish in my ear. They hoped that soon, I would return home for good, while glancing at Father out of the corner of their eyes.

It always made me feel guilty, how much faith they'd lost in him and put in me. I could tell everyone was just waiting for me to come home, to fully take over the responsibility of the consulship. I hoped their patience would last a little longer, and they wouldn't seek help from others outside of Helena. The gods only knew there were plenty who wished to step in.

I tried to spend some time with each group clustered around the tables brimming with delicacies. I kept glancing at the door as the merchant council wished me well and assured me that their offerings to Ayastaren would appease Duke Roland's demands . . . for now at least.

The Solston caught my ear for a while, speaking earnestly about the need for more assistance and money for hiring more caretakers for the temple and for outreach. I nodded while craning my neck to see past the group of people who had congregated at the entrance, but I made no promises. Father hated spending money on the temple, and that request would have to wait until I returned for good.

Finally, I relaxed in the company of the young knights that Grandfather had me train with while growing up. Hector slapped me on the back in greeting before tousling my hair. I laughed, trying to smooth it back down, when I saw Alexo nudge Vince and nod toward the door. My head whipped around.

Rowyn had walked in on Gillius's arm, and it felt as if time stood still for a moment. She was a vision, her hair woven around her head in a regal black halo. Her gown was cut in the Lyrican style but shared hints of blue with her traditional dress. My gaze traced the contours of her body, the low neckline, the gathering at the waist. My mind lurched back to the night of the attack. Of everything I'd seen through the sheer fabric of her chemise. A wave of self-reproach washed over me, and I was sure my face was red. I clenched my fists, fighting the warmth that started to gather at my fingertips.

I hated the way my heart stirred at the sight of her. I hated myself for admiring her, for being so captivated. She was a constant reminder of my own vulnerability, my own desires that threatened to overshadow the duty that bound me. I knew I shouldn't be drawn to her, shouldn't allow myself to be entangled in her presence.

With a heavy sigh, I tore my gaze away from Rowyn, forcing myself to focus on the affairs of the evening. There would be time to contemplate my feelings later, when the weight of responsibilities didn't loom over me so heavily. But for now, I needed to bury those emotions deep within, to focus on the duties that awaited me as the heir to the consulship and the fact that Rowyn was more enemy than ally.

Still, I tracked her through the hall, telling myself that it was in case her attacker snuck in to make a move. I half-listened to the knights around me, focusing more on drinking my ale and watching Rowyn out of the corner of my eye than on their jokes and jibes.

Rowyn sat at the table, with Master Gillius at her side, and began eating with a few others from the city. When Bernard came in, he said something that caused Rowyn to smile. The surge came thundering back. She looked damnably radiant when she smiled, and it didn't seem to happen often.

I watched them as they talked, her drinking wine and tilting her head with a grin as though she and Bernard were old friends. My jaw hardened, and I wished I could hear what they spoke of. They seemed to be in a good mood, but mine was getting fouler by the second when she laughed. What in the gods had he said to make her laugh like that?

I was so absorbed in watching Rowyn and Bernard's conversation that I missed Hector shoving Alexo into me and jostling my ale. I glared up at them as the other knights began to chant.

"Duel . . . Duel . . . Duel!"

The demand echoed throughout the room until the

entire crowd was saying it. Alexo looked over to Hector with a mischievous glint in his eyes.

It took no time at all for my father to order the center of the hall to be cleared, allowing space in the middle for a fight. It happened often enough, a knight challenging their friends to see who could best who, and putting it on as a show for everyone else's entertainment. I'd even fight if the mood struck me. The knights would make it a game to test me, to see if I was worthy of their loyalty. I always won, and not because they let me. Grandfather ensured I knew everything about swords, not just how to make them or care for them, but how to wield them as well.

I kept my eyes on Rowyn as she leaned closer to Bernard, presumably to hear him better over the noise. If she'd been a smart little spy, she would've lingered with others in the room, getting information from the wealth of people present who could give away any number of important facts about how the city was run and how close my family was to losing Helena.

But no, she did not speak to any of the other guests. Now it looked like Bernard was whispering in her ear. *Whispering.* At that moment, Rowyn met my eye and raised her brows, seemingly at my expression. I looked away, trying to school my features but feeling altogether like a fool. I shouldn't be paying attention to her beyond what duty required. She was safe, she was contained, and that was what I needed.

I kept my eyes on the match but didn't really watch it, keeping my mind on the duties at hand. I still had to pack and gather the materials from the forge that I planned to take to Solridge with me. It was necessary to take a guard with us to school, especially because we were passing through Ayastaren. I found myself thankful that Sir Bernard wasn't going with us.

When I heard clapping, I wrenched my mind back to the present and dutifully clapped as well. I think I even managed a smile as Alexo hugged Hector and then looked around the hall. His eyes found mine and he raised his brows in silent question. "Is there another challenger? I might still have a round or two left in me!"

"Fight the Morganite!" Sir Merrel said from next to me. I elbowed him sharply in the ribs, but someone else took up the call.

"Yes, the Morganite!" the crowd shouted, and my heart sank.

Rowyn was looking around, that little line above her nose scrunched together. But the spark in her eyes was back.

Gillius was already losing his mind. "No! I must insist Rowyn not participate in any kind of dangerous sport." He looked to Father for help, but I think it just spurred him on.

"I disagree, sorcerer," Father said. "I think it would please me very much to see a show of skill from the girl."

Master Gillius seemed at a loss. He looked at me. "Surely you forget yourselves, my lords. It would be unchivalrous to put the poor girl through such a display. She's been recently injured after all."

I opened my mouth to intervene, but Father cut me off.

"Seems to have healed up well enough, Master Gillius. You do a discredit to your skills." Father looked at Rowyn with a challenge in his eyes. "I wish the girl to duel, and so she shall . . . unless she's frightened of Lyrican brawn."

He'd always known the best way to get under a Morganite's skin. Rowyn's accusation the other day still plagued my thoughts, but I'd not had the courage to ask Father about it during our time together. He was so fragile, I didn't want him to feel as though I thought less of him. He already hated himself; he didn't need my help to send him over the edge into full-on depression. I needed him to function while I was away.

"Very well," Rowyn said, rising from the seat that Bernard had pulled to the side of the match area for her. She began walking to the doors, her gown trailing on the stone floor behind her as the whispers and excited murmurs picked up with the prospect of the upcoming match.

Gillius's eyes were pleading with me. I turned and strode after her, my head ducked, refusing to meet my father's eye as I went.

She'd made it out of the door by the time I'd reached her and was walking fast. I grabbed her elbow, conscious of how thin her arm was.

Rowyn seemed to stop herself from drawing her dagger as she spun, then froze when she saw it was me. I wondered who she'd been expecting. "You could refuse. No one will blame you," I told her. Even if it displeased Father, I would make some excuse about why the girl couldn't fight. I was admittedly curious to see her skill myself, but I had an entire journey to Solridge and then schooling to see how good she was with weapons. It didn't have to be now, so soon after she'd been hurt. It didn't have to occur in a hall surrounded by people who would be rooting for her to fail. I didn't need to like her to respect her dignity.

Something flickered in her eyes. "It's all right, my lord. I wouldn't want to be seen as a coward," she said, not a hint of nervousness or trepidation evident in her tone.

The Morganites were known as some of the fiercest warriors in the empire. The army *loved* it when my father sent them Morganite fighters, whether they were willing or not. The Morganites had a reputation for being bloodthirsty, strong, fast, and clever when it came to fighting on difficult terrain. They were known for bravery as well. Morganites would sacrifice themselves to grab the injured if need be. They were ferocious people, terrifying really. I wondered if that was why the Helenian Guard never seemed able to best them. If we were all truly honest with each other, we'd admit that we were afraid of them.

"People call you many things, Rowyn, but a coward is certainly not one of them," I murmured as the crease above her nose smoothed and she stepped back.

"My lord, is that a compliment?"

I realized my misstep too late. She seemed to see something in my face. A tell that I'd been thinking of her far more than I should've. I ignored the warmth rising to my cheeks. I needed to get away from her before I revealed anything else. "Take it as you will," I said, turning to escape from her gaze.

When I reentered the hall, Father was glowering at me. I strode toward him, knowing that he'd be angry that I tried to interfere.

"Is she getting ready," he asked, "or is she running

away?"

"She's preparing." I took the seat beside him. "You can't expect her to fight in that dress, can you?"

"Good." Father took a drink and watched the excitement from the crowd. I looked for Gillius and found him next to Sir Alexo. He looked as though he were practically pleading with the man. I leaned back, unworried about Alexo's part in all this. He wasn't a bad man—he'd not try to hurt her.

Still, I bit my lip, worried about Rowyn—not that she would be injured but about how she'd feel when she lost. Alexo was one of the few swordsmen at Helena who'd come close to beating me. I hoped she wouldn't be too upset about it. I hoped the spark in her eyes wouldn't go out.

I chided myself. I shouldn't be thinking about that.

"I hate that Gillius is putting you in this position on the road," Father said next to me.

I frowned. "What do you mean?"

"She's going to try to kill you," Father said. "Now that her father is dead, it could be she's the new chief of Espiria. Did you ever think of that? She could just be sitting back, like a snake in the grass, biding her time before she strikes."

"I don't think she's after me." Although Father's words echoed my concerns, I didn't want to cause him worry by agreeing with them.

"Just watch your back," Father said. "You've been away for so long, you don't know how it's been with them. They are building to something. I just know it."

I tried to keep myself from rolling my eyes. Father was always convinced the Morganites were building to something, but they'd only ever been a nuisance. They never tried to mount a full-on assault on Helena, or any other consulship of Morgania for that matter. They didn't have the numbers for a full-scale takeover, which was incredibly lucky for us, because we didn't have the numbers to defend against an attack of that magnitude without reaching out for help.

I rose from my seat and rejoined the other knights, claiming my mug of ale and taking a deep swig.

"I'd more prefer to have her on her back than in the fighting rink," Sir Merrel said next to me.

I turned, sparks dancing unexpectedly from my fingertips. "Why don't you say that closer to my father?" I snapped. "Let him tell you what he thinks of that thought."

Sir Merrel shut right up at that. It was distasteful to fraternize with Morganites, not that they were interested in us romantically either. Not the clansmen anyway. One or two of the guards had married a Morganite girl, but they had been from the city. Peaceful, law-abiding citizens who caused no problems. Still, even those Morganites were looked upon with a wary eye.

The door to the hall opened, and Rowyn stepped back in, this time in a new tunic and breeches. She crossed the hall and accepted a practice sword, her eyes on Alexo as he jumped around, performing his usual intimidation routine. Even with Alexo's experience, he did have a significant disadvantage. Rowyn had watched Alexo's fight closely. I knew because I was watching her. Alexo, on the other hand, hadn't yet witnessed Rowyn's skill, nor had the rest of us. Despite my worry, which was minimal, excitement began to build, and I leaned forward as they bowed to each other.

My heart quickened when Alexo began with a series of blows that came fast and hard, a disarming tactic that he used often. Rowyn seemed to expect it, and I marveled at her ease in blocking the onslaught. The clack from the wood swords reverberated through the hall, but her movements were swift, fluid, and seemingly effortless. Alexo looked as surprised as the rest of us, and he twisted away, abandoning his attack for caution.

Rowyn's focus was unwavering, her eyes fixed on her opponent. Her movements were confident and graceful. There was nothing of the girl from before, who stumbled when she curtsied and glared daggers at the dinner guests over the table. The blade was clearly something she knew. It was obvious that she was good at it too.

I realized in that moment that she'd been confident in her skills against Alexo before she'd agreed to the match. I felt confidence in my own skills begin to waver. I'd never seen a Morganite woman fight before. I knew they did, of course, but I'd never actually witnessed one. Seeing Rowyn keep up with Alexo, the best of our knights, gave me pause. I wasn't alone. Sirs Merrel and Hector muttered and shifted uncomfortably as they watched.

I schooled my face to impassivity, not quite deciding how I felt about it. Rowyn was good, I'd give her that. Not as good as me, but better than most people in the empire for sure. I was betting Sir Merrel regretted his comment about her. Had they actually met on the battlefield, he wouldn't stand a chance. He always found an excuse to skip training sessions, so let this be a lesson to him.

As the duel continued, I marveled at the way Rowyn handled herself, the way she danced with her blade. It wasn't until Alexo got a hit in on her back that she began to waver, that her concentration seemed to break as she rolled to the ground. I sat back, convinced that

Alexo had her and feeling slightly better about the fact that she'd held out so long against one of our best knights.

I shouldn't have counted Rowyn out so soon. She leaped up, wiped her forehead with her sleeve, then blocked Alexo's lunge. A prickle crawled up my neck. Rowyn moved as though she'd seen active battle, and often. That meant that she was either incredibly lucky during a fight, or she'd been trained young. From her footwork I would guess the latter. Rowyn began a lightning-fast assault, her sword whipping through the air, switching from one hand to another. I rose, my eyes glued to the match, trying to follow her movements as Sir Alexo retreated to the edge of the ring.

A gasp of triumph escaped Rowyn and her sword stilled at his throat. Naked joy danced across her face. I tried to look as though I didn't care about the outcome of the fight, but it certainly gave me pause.

I supposed her skill was what came from being the chief's child. I remembered back to the meeting my father had called years ago to bring peace to Morgania. It went worse than expected, but Rowyn's father had shown up. The man seemed like a giant, with thick arms covered in tattoos and wild, black hair. I recognized some of him in Rowyn . . . the wildness . . . the ferocity in their blue eyes. In fact, I saw so much of him in Rowyn that I wondered what her mother had looked like.

Alexo dropped the wooden practice blade and grinned. He said something that I couldn't hear because the knights around me all began to talk at once. I didn't engage with them anymore. I sat back in my chair, lost in thought. If Rowyn, at her skill level, had been nearly killed by an assassin twice, then whoever was after her was powerful indeed. I didn't think that any noble or consul on the western shore had the resources to obtain such a person. The nobles in the east could, though.

Sir Alexo offered Rowyn a mug of ale, and I ignored the protest in my head. There were more important issues at hand. I tore my eyes away from Rowyn and directed my attention to the candles that lit the room. I fed my power to them. At once, all the flames brightened. I concentrated, letting the flames leech the magic away. I didn't like to keep too much on hand, just in case I lost my temper, which seemed to be more volatile these past few days. I'd learned young to keep my reserves low.

It was hard to judge the extent of Rowyn's powers at the present. Sure, it rained, but I couldn't really tell how far her powers reached. The more powerful a sorcerer, the more they could do from a distance.

I bided my time at the party, sitting back and watching everyone else throw themselves into the revelry, but as soon as Rowyn and Gillius retired, I left. I thought of following them but tossed out the idea.

I was angry at Gillius and didn't wish to be scolded in front of Rowyn again. Besides, her maid still needed to help her to bed, so I would put my ward on later, after I finished my research and Gillius was well out of the way. If he failed to offer the answers that I sought, I would find them out myself.

I let myself into the study and went to the bookcase built over the castle stone behind Father's desk. I scanned the years of record books and pulled five off the shelf. Walking over to the table in the corner, I moved my father's pipe and leaf off the map of Morgania that lay there. Taking the marble lid off a small bowl that helped hold down the parchment, I took out a small stone. I opened one of the record books, read, and began to place stones on the map. Finishing the first book, I opened the second. Some stones I left, some I replaced with a different color, then I placed new ones. Over and over I did this until I finished the books I'd pulled and stepped back.

There were stones over almost the entirety of Morgania. To the south they stopped right at the river, at the entrance over the Ayastaren border. To the north, the Nightlands, and to the west, Rudin. The crop yields from the record books showed that the farmlands to the west of Rudin were still struggling all the way to Horan. And Horan was known to be dry. I ran my hand through my hair and tried to calm my thoughts. For someone without a gem, Rowyn's range was massive.

I poured myself a drink and sat at my desk, my head in my hands. The history of magic and nobility was complicated, but usually there were a handful of powerful sorcerers every generation. Since the bloodlines were difficult to predict and not at all regular, different powers cropped up at different times. My grandfather taught me to think of it in cycles. Most of the noble bloodlines carried at least one variation of sorcery. Some, like the Marendeslys, had numerous skills attached to their name. Within a cycle, the family with the most powerful skills available usually had immense control over things that happened in the empire. They controlled the rest of us.

My grandfather had been one of them, and his grandfather before him. Our influence ended for my father's cycle, and now I was working to reclaim it, at least on the western shore.

I took a sip of wine and stared at the map. I'd already tried to suss out the major players for my own generation's cycle, but it was proving difficult. I didn't know the sorcerers at the capital very well—I'd only met them in passing—but there was a time render from Maryse and a materials manipulator who showed promise.

The sorcerers of the west had their own cycles, of course, rising and falling with the east's, sometimes merging, sometimes separating. The most promising of us, though the others would refuse to admit it, was Fin. General Ivar would've faced a heavy penalty from his family for letting that one get away. Once a skill ran rogue, it could be hard to get it back, especially if loyalty was in question.

But now there was Rowyn. The noble families were used to working together. We knew what to expect from each other and how to best use the powers around us. We were even used to dealing with rogues, like Fin, and others who cropped up in the community. Skills that remained latent over time until they were lost. We were *not* used to dealing with someone like Rowyn. She was a traitor, and she was easily the most powerful sorcerer of our cycle.

Gillius had mentioned Morius the Black, so I pulled a book I found on him in the library and glanced through, trying to glean what I could from her presumed ancestor. He lived almost three hundred years ago. When magic lay fallow for that long, it could build, but it still would've needed some kind of catalyst for it to pop up in Rowyn. Usually that's what happened with rogues. A certain magic met with a needed blood catalyst, and the ability would assert itself. That's why sorcerers liked to marry each other. We were already blood catalysts, though it was still unpredictable.

My eyes went back to the map. Rowyn's extensive reach required a lot of magic. The magic kept building for three hundred years, waiting for its catalyst.

I put my finger on Espiria and shook my head. The shroud must have absorbed some of it. The shroud was put in place by the Others of Horan when they ruled over the forests of Morgania. But the magic could not have maintained itself for that long, even by their standards.

I rose to ward Rowyn's room, now regretting what the morning would bring. I had to assist Gillius as he escorted the most powerful sorcerer of our cycle out of my lands and to a place where she would learn to harness it all.

Chapter 8

I WATCHED ROWYN AS WE RODE south from Helena. Her eyes were attuned to the forest. She spun in her saddle at every odd sound. I gritted my teeth, wondering if she was planning some sort of attack on the road with her fellow Morganites, but when no attack came, I realized that it was far more likely she was looking for the assassin.

We stopped at an inn for the evening. Gillius took the room across the hall, leaving me to take the one next to Rowyn. Though he didn't say it, I guessed it was an extra precaution against intruders. Gillius didn't use weapons.

I dumped my pack and stomped downstairs to eat, famished after a long day on the road. Gillius came soon after, and the innkeeper brought us some bowls of stew and large, frothy mugs of ale.

Gillius asked after my work on bitter steel on the pretense of being polite, and I filled him in on what I'd read and tried already. Gillius was nodding, interested, but with little knowledge of the topic, he could offer little advice or thoughts on the matter.

Rowyn came down a little later. She'd washed her

face, and her hair fell over her shoulders. I tried to resist the urge to stare, but Rowyn caught me admiring her. I hastily looked away.

Embarrassed, I tried to come up with an explanation that would explain my wandering eyes. The last thing I needed was for Rowyn to find out how my body reacted when she was near. How my thoughts seemed to rebel against me. I willed myself back into enmity. "I've always wondered, why do Morganites continue marking themselves if it leaves you open to discovery?"

Rowyn seemed put out by my question. The wrinkle above her nose appeared, and a spark lit behind her eyes. "We don't shrug off traditions of the past so easily, my lord."

I smiled, enjoying her reaction as she ate her meal. She was offended. That was good. The more I offended her, the less likely it was that she'd discover the thoughts that I'd been trying to keep hidden. I went on, espousing the rhetoric that I'd grown up with around Father and Grandfather. It wasn't hard. I'd been around it my entire life. Besides, she'd thought it well and good that she share her views of me and *my* family. Why should I not repay her in kind?

"But surely, it's a new age. Lyrica is an empire now. Don't you see that survival lies in taking up arms with the emperor? It's the only future for your people now."

The wrinkle above Rowyn's nose deepened. She was obnoxiously pretty when she scowled. "A dog or a horse doesn't forget freedom, no matter how much their masters try to beat it out of them. The memory of what we once had still burns in our hearts to this day."

I shrugged and looked away, willing myself to stop admiring her. "I see no sense in it."

Rowyn lowered her spoon to her bowl. "Considering you rule over people who were once Morganites, maybe you should try."

"You've done little to deserve any sway within our lands, raiding our convoys and such." The ladies at Solridge, my sisters, all had been raised to tamp down their anger, to be a calm and obliging presence. Rowyn might've benefited from that instruction because she let everything show. If I was honest with myself, a small part of me enjoyed it. It wasn't often that anyone lashed out at me, let alone a *lady*, though that may have been too generous a term for what Rowyn was. "Why should I seek to understand such barbarism?"

"People do many things to survive, my lord," she snapped. "Surely you can't begrudge a person that."

"Indeed," I said, "and do all the girls dress as men where you live?" How could the Morganite men stand it, seeing the ladies' curves all the time? It was distracting in the worst way.

"No," she said, taking a sip from her drink. "However, I can tell you, hunting in a dress is a somewhat difficult task."

Gillius laughed. I smiled, seeing her relax once more. But I wanted to see the scowl again. The spark. "Are the men where you live so deficient that they can't provide for their women?" I challenged.

Rowyn's expression grew fierce and wild as she rose. "When disease comes, and it does, it hits with force," she said. "It spreads quickly. We can't afford to be so scrupulous."

I wiped the smile off my face and tried to look as though I'd not intended to rouse her anger. "You're the one who said I should learn about the people I'd one day rule. I was only asking." That only seemed to infuriate her more. If she only knew how pleased that made me.

"Sit down, Rowyn," Gillius admonished. "By all the gods, you're so dramatic. To more important matters, I've heard there's a rebel group on the road south of here. We will probably need to head east and sail out from the port after all. It would be safer."

I almost rolled my eyes. If Gillius had wanted to take DarkPort, we should've gone east from Helena.

Perhaps he was trying to avoid Espiria again. My thoughts went back to my suspicions of Rowyn using the guise of her sorcery to try to ensnare us. Raiding season would start soon, and the Morganites in Espiria would love to capture me. "That's leagues out of our way, and we have to stop by Ayastaren before heading to SeaPort."

"What kind of rebel group is it?" she asked, shooting a glare at me before taking her seat. I tried to stifle my grin. Getting under her skin was proving to be fun.

"Morganites," Gillius said. "Not Espirians, but some other clan that claims the hills of the south. Apparently, they've been there all winter."

Father had mentioned that when he'd apprised me of the goings-on at Helena. The band of Morganites had attacked two merchant caravans, but there was no loss of life in either case, and they'd only taken food and a bit of gold. Still, I was the heir to Helena. I was surely not wrong to think that they'd love to leave my bones scattered along the road. I appreciated Gillius trying to protect Rowyn, but now he was putting me in danger to do it.

"Well, I can help us cross then," she said with authority. "I am a Morganite, after all." I raised my brows. Apparently Rowyn was used to giving commands. I narrowed my eyes at her. The Morganites were usually not united in their schemes. Perhaps when I'd been away, that had changed. Had the Espirians allied with this group to the south to capture us?

Gillius shook his head. "No, Rowyn, I don't want to risk it." I wondered if Gillius thought the same way as I did. I was reluctant to share my suspicions. After all, Gillius had done very little sharing with me.

"Why not?" The crease above Rowyn's nose returned. "It wouldn't even be a risk; just let me ride at the head. They wouldn't dare attack our group then. This much I know."

I tried to ignore the worry crawling up my throat. Why would she want to put herself at risk after just being attacked? "How can you be so sure?" I asked. "Rebels are unpredictable. Why should they care if some maiden rides at the head?"

Rowyn turned her steely gaze to me. "Despite what you think, there's honor among Morganites. They wouldn't attack me—I'm sure of it."

I met her eyes. She seemed so certain, and I wondered if it was worth the risk. Either way we were in danger of an assault, whether Rowyn was working with this new clan or not. Still, we needed to go south. I turned to Gillius and shrugged. "It would save us days of travel."

Gillius sighed. There really wasn't much we could

do, no matter how distasteful the road forward was.

VALOR WAS RESTLESS beneath me as I waited for Rowyn and Gillius in front of the inn with our guards. My sword was at my side and my bow and arrows ready. I grew nervous when I thought of the road ahead. It seemed as though there were too many conflicts that aligned against me. That morning I hadn't leached off as much power as I normally did—I wanted a larger reserve of magic just in case things went south with the clan. I didn't believe for a second that Rowyn riding in front would do us any good. She was either in cahoots with them, which put Gillius and me in significant danger, or she would be an easy target as well. It wasn't uncommon for the heads of rival clans to go after each other for more power, and Rowyn's father had led the strongest band of Morganites we knew of. She seemed pretty naïve about the honor among her own people.

All thoughts of danger escaped when Rowyn emerged from the inn and strode to her horse. She'd put on her traditional dress and a cloak bearing Morgania's old sigil. It was hard not to take it as a personal attack. Especially considering how good she looked in it.

I clenched my teeth, wary of her as she mounted and trotted her horse up to mine. I tried not to admire her. At least, not obviously.

Gillius rode to Rowyn's other side, and our party followed her as we passed into the hills and forests that made up southern Morgania. I wondered if Gillius was picking up on her range as we rode. He'd never asked me for information about Morgania's resource output. He was probably waiting to test how far her magic reached in Solridge. At least I had some information that I could lord over him in my mind.

"The plague ran its course here a while back," Gillius said, pulling me from my thoughts. "It might be that their numbers are low, much like Espiria."

I clenched my teeth, wondering how much Rowyn revealed about her home to Gillius. How much more they were keeping from me about the state of her home and clan. Gillius hadn't actually been inside Espiria . . . had he? I shoved the thought away. There was no way that the Morganites would let a Lyrican behind the shroud. Still, Rowyn must've said some things to Gillius, which meant that she trusted him far more than I did. If Espiria's numbers were low, it could be that they would hold off raiding this year. That would be a welcome blessing for the merchants and travelers on Morgania's eastern road.

"If it did, then they'd be more desperate," Rowyn whispered, quashing my hope. "That only makes them more dangerous, not less, so keep a watchful eye."

The guards were glancing at me from behind their helmets, clearly affronted at her presumption in giving orders. I tried to school my face to impassivity and instead watched the trees for any sign of movement.

Suddenly, Rowyn reined in, twisting to look around at the trees that bordered the road around us. I held up my arm to stop the guards, then followed her gaze. "What is it?" I felt the hairs on my neck rise.

"They're here," she murmured.

I gripped the bow behind me and slowly unclasped it from my saddlebag.

"I knew this was a foolish idea," Gillius growled.

Rowyn shushed him and squinted into the trees to the right of us.

"No!" Rowyn yelled as she barreled into me. The bow slipped from my hands as I went tumbling into the road with her on top of me.

I was still trying to reclaim my thoughts when Rowyn scrambled up, grabbed her bow, and shot an arrow into the trees. I looked in time to see someone fall from a branch.

The soldiers around us were shouting and pulling out their swords while circling the wagon where Rowyn's maid, Ena, sat with the tribute to Ayastaren. Ahead, a large Morganite stepped from the trees and planted himself directly in front of us holding a Morganite quarterstaff covered with all sorts of lethal accessories.

"Peace, sister," he shouted to Rowyn as I rose and grabbed my sword. She stood her ground, an arrow aimed at him. All thoughts of Rowyn betraying us slipped away as I looked to where she'd shot and saw a man struggling to get up with an arrow shot clean through his hand. You tended not to shoot people you colluded with.

"My lady, why do you travel with Lyrican dogs snapping at your heels?" the Morganite asked, his smile barely visible through a wealth of facial hair.

Rowyn lowered her bow and I almost cursed. They'd already tried to kill her once, and here she was, giving them the chance to do it again. "Our business is our own," she shouted. "Will you let us pass, brother?"

Brother? I glanced at Gillius whose arms were held out in peace as he watched the scene. This was foolish. I needed to grab Rowyn and retreat with her into the circle of guards. The look on my face must've betrayed my intentions because Gillius shook his head.

The Morganite nodded. "I will, sister, if you treat with our chief a moment."

Just as I thought she must be out of her damned mind, Rowyn stepped forward. I grabbed her wrist, ready to toss her over my shoulder if I had to. The clan was probably trying to separate us. They would take Rowyn captive and kill the rest, including me. They might even kill Rowyn too. We were fools for agreeing to her plan. "Rowyn, don't!"

"He only wishes to talk," she said, yanking her arm away from me. "It'll be fine. You'll see, my lord."

"They just tried to kill you!" I whispered exasperatedly. They were going to do something awful to her, I was sure of it. Morganites were bloodthirsty fighters. I didn't see how her being one of their own would matter when it came to the fact that she was with the heir to the consulship. They could easily see her as a traitor to their ways.

Rowyn was studying me. "It wasn't me they were aiming for." She walked toward the Morganite while I stood stupidly, processing what she'd said.

"Do you promise no harm will come to a member of my party?" Rowyn asked loudly.

The Morganite nodded, barely registering our presence. His eyes were on Rowyn's gown, her cloak, and her sword. I took another step forward, but Gillius's hand shot out and held me back.

"Calm down," he hissed, seeing the sparks alight from my fingertips. "If you don't, we really *will* see a battle today."

"You're just going to let them take her?" I growled, flames dancing over my fingertips.

I looked back to the trees where Rowyn disappeared. A handful of Morganites had stepped out, their hands leisurely placed on their weapons as they watched us, me in particular.

I turned toward them, pushing the anger back and the flames away. I ground my teeth as we waited for far too long. I glanced at Gillius, and even he was starting to look concerned.

Finally, I'd had enough. "Stay back," I ordered our guards, then, with my hand on my sword, I let the excess of my power seep into the blade, which grew hot within the sheath. I strode toward the Morganites. "Where is she?" I asked through clenched teeth.

"The lady is meeting with her own," one of the clansmen said, stiffening. "She will return to you when we are done with her."

"When you're done with her?" I growled, staring the man down as I stepped forward, fists clenched. "What are you planning?"

"Funny," another Morganite said, coming to stand

next to his brethren. He tilted his head to the side and palmed the short sword at his waist. "We were wondering the same thing. What could the Lord of Helena possibly want with a Morganite girl?"

"Yes," said the clansman in front of me. "If you think we're going to let the consul return to abusing our women, you will see the full fury of Imor from our blades. We are not your *whores*."

I let go of my sword and swung my fist at the Morganite, riding the wave of fury. My knuckle connected with flesh before the other man grabbed my arms and wrenched me away.

I caught a glimpse of Rowyn through the trees, standing with an older woman. She had her back to me and was talking animatedly.

I elbowed the Morganite holding me and flung him down, but another one was there to quickly take his place.

"Rowyn!" I shouted, using all my strength to try to twist out of their grip.

Rowyn looked back at me. Nodding to the older woman, she began making her way back carefully through the underbrush. As she approached, the men let me go. Turning away from them, I straightened my coat and tried to ignore their glares and the implications in their words. I was on the brink of losing control. I let out a cooling breath as I strode over to Rowyn and resisted grabbing her arm and dragging her back to our guard. "What did you and the woman speak of?"

"She was making sure I wasn't a prisoner," Rowyn said, her hand going toward her belt. She seemed to catch herself and moved her other hand to her sword hilt. I clenched my fist. The ebony dagger was gone.

"You lie."

"It's the truth."

I glared at her. "Perhaps, but you were gone a moment too long for me to believe she was simply asking after your well-being."

"She inquired after my father, and I told her the truth."

"A likely story," I said, feeling a rush of resentment. Not only was I obligated to protect her, but I had to do it under the pretense of some cockamamie story from her and Gillius about where she came from and what her intentions were, and have her brethren insult my honor in the worst possible way to boot. "And that ebony dagger of yours is missing."

Worry flashed in Rowyn's eyes. I celebrated a small victory that I'd finally caught her on the wrong foot.

She must've read something in my expression, because she stiffened. "Do you challenge me when I'm

103

the reason you're still alive? I wouldn't fret over my blade. I've plenty of others."

This girl was going to be the death of me. I fought to get myself under control. There was no reason to linger on the road, surrounded by enemies, just because my honor had been insulted. "Thank you . . . for what you did," I said through my teeth. I still hadn't quite grasped the fact that she'd saved my life. Especially when Gillius had made it clear that it was *my* duty to protect *her*, and not the other way around.

"You're a member of my party. I'm sure you would have done the same given the circumstances, my lord," she said, then added, "Maybe."

Rowyn's *maybe* threw me. I was a noble . . . a gentleman! I frowned as I put my hands on her waist, about to lift her into the saddle to show her that I was, in fact, chivalrous.

Rowyn shoved me away. "I can get up myself, thank you very much." She then leaped into the saddle and looked down at me as though I were a pebble in her shoe.

My pride wounded, I glared at her. "Many a lady at Solridge would deem it an honor for me to help them into their saddle."

"I'm not a lady of Lyrica, Lord Destrian," she said airily. "You can keep your honors to yourself."

My temper flared. I clenched my fist, trying not to explode in anger as she nudged her horse forward. I took a deep breath to calm myself and swung into my own saddle. Valor shifted uneasily beneath me, sensing my mood.

"Farewell, Rowyn, and safe travels to you!" someone called from the trees. I glared at the back of Rowyn's head as she waved back.

Chapter 9

I DIDN'T FEEL LIKE TALKING to Rowyn as we made our way to Ayastaren. The clansmen's accusations about my intentions had lit something within that made me uneasy. Was that what Rowyn thought of me? Was that what she feared?

I couldn't stand the thought of it. I wasn't some monster that preyed on helpless women, though Rowyn was far from helpless.

By the time we reached Ayastaren, I was feeling all sorts of put out. My time with my father had been cut short, Rowyn had made some deal with the clan on the road—I was sure of it—and I was back to thinking that she was involved in some underhanded scheme to steal my family's seat. Of course, we'd just entered the territory of a man who I knew for a fact was scheming to unseat me. I betted that Duke Roland and Rowyn would get along just fine on the "I think Lord Destrian is a terrible person and crap leader" wagon.

All my thoughts shifted as we rode through the city streets. It had been a year or two since I'd last been to Ayastaren, and I didn't remember it being so . . . desolate.

Our party was obviously unsettled by the way the peasants' faces turned away from the road, unwilling to be seen. I looked to the white marble towers of Ayastaren that rose ahead of us, trying to sort my thoughts for meeting with Duke Roland.

This was the part of nobility that I hated the most. Rubbing shoulders and speaking graciously to the same people who would slit my throat and steal my seat the first chance they had. And Duke Roland was the worst of them. Father had rejected his offer of Onora's marriage to one of his sons, which was no small feat. Ayastaren could bully their way into the beds of other bloodlines if they saw fit. That's what they did to the Tores. Their daughter was killed within a year. I was glad Father stood up to them. How long after the marriage would I have been involved in some sort of "accident," leaving his son as the only option for an heir? For all of Father's faults, he did an excellent job of protecting my sisters and me.

A scream tore through the street, wrenching me from my thoughts as we rounded a corner. A woman was bound to a post in front of an abandoned shop, her back bared and a soldier poised with a whip in hand. A group of men in uniform cheered him on as he dealt a brutal lash across her skin. The woman's screams and pleading cries echoed, her face streaked with mud and tears.

My jaw clenched in disgust, my eyes scanning the scene, landing on a tax document in the hands of one of the soldiers. I recognized the paper. It was a tax summons from the emperor. The same request that I'd resolved during my time in Helena. Her apparent crime was clear—failure to pay. It was a despicable spectacle, but it wasn't within our power to intervene.

The woman jerked away from the whip as it lit upon her back. I flinched, but when Rowyn reined in, my gut sank.

"What has she done to deserve this?" she asked.

Fucking Lyons. "They're holding a tax document. She must've failed to pay."

Rowyn looked up at me, her blue eyes bright between the black imorets that lined them. "Will you do nothing?"

I wanted to do something, anything, but to go against Duke Roland in his domain was not a battle that I would win, and certainly not one I wanted to fight, given my tenuous hold on Helena as it was.

But the way Rowyn had looked at me. The surge was back and I hated every moment of it. "Don't be absurd," I attempted to reason. "What the duke does to rule his lands is his own business." I looked away. I couldn't stand the sight of her anymore. I'd watched her for days, but she did nothing. Only watched the road and looked over her shoulder.

"We've no authority here, Rowyn," Gillius said sadly.

Rowyn looked back at the woman, the spark alight in her eyes. She kicked her horse forward and rode toward the soldiers, drawing her bow from her saddle.

I probably should have done something, but I was frozen to the spot, watching as she shouted, pulled an arrow from her quiver, and shot the string in two. The woman's arms fell to her sides as she gasped with relief. Rowyn's actions were bold, perhaps reckless, but there was a certain sense of admiration in me for her courage. Then again, courage without foresight would easily get her killed.

Gillius, acting the mediator, rode to her side, validating her statement. The standoff ended with the soldier releasing the woman and Rowyn offering her sword as payment, a gesture that shocked me. This was a woman who valued justice above personal possessions. Her actions were rash, impulsive even, but there was a raw honesty to them that I found admirable, albeit begrudgingly so.

I led the guardsmen over to Rowyn and Gillius. Looking ahead at the castle, my heart began to sink. Mellan Lyon, one of Duke Roland's sons, had told me everything I needed to know about his father when I'd been in Yliria. Rowyn was the exact type of person that Duke Roland loved to break. Kind-hearted, passionate, with entirely too much courage and entirely too little common sense.

I nudged Valor closer to the girl, studying our surroundings as we rode through the castle gates, wary and uncertain. Thankfully, I recognized the young man limping down the stairs.

"It's Pawl, the fifth son," I whispered into Rowyn's ear after she'd dismounted. The scent of her hair enveloped me, and I involuntarily breathed deep. Rowyn looked up at me, those blue eyes filled with surprise, though surprise at what, I couldn't tell.

"Well met, Gillius and protégé, well met," Pawl was saying. I tore my eyes away from Rowyn and nodded at Pawl's greeting. "We expected you yesterday, but it's no matter. Your rooms are waiting, and dinner should be ready soon."

Pawl led us into the castle and through a series of corridors. He stopped outside one door and motioned Rowyn toward it. When her maid, Ena, closed the door, Pawl turned and kept walking.

"Where are we going?" I asked, confused. There was a line of doors, giving off the appearance of a guest hall.

"Your rooms are this way," Pawl said, stopping at the end of the hall to wait for us. Gillius and I looked at each other, but there wasn't much we could do at that point. We followed Pawl to the end of the hall where he turned and kept going until we were across the castle, as far away from Rowyn's room as the duke could put us.

"We hope you don't mind sharing," Pawl said lightly, swinging the door open. The room was lavish enough, with two large beds separated by a side table, but I didn't miss the intended slight. I was nobility. My station meant that I received my own room. I didn't mind sharing with Gillius, but I did mind Duke Roland playing games with me, and I sure as the gods minded the distance he'd put between us and Rowyn.

"Thank you," Gillius said quickly as I turned, about to say something.

Pawl had already shut the door and I cursed. "You can't tell me that this is acceptable for you." I clenched my fist. "This isn't an accident. What if whoever came at her in Helena tries again?"

Gillius sighed. "I don't like it either. Had Rowyn not made a scene in the market, we probably could've demanded closer quarters without much fuss, but she ruined any latitude we might've had with her thoughtlessness. You can still ward her room. That's just as good as our presence."

"Rowyn wasn't being thoughtless. She was guided by her conscience," I said, throwing my pack on one of the beds and pulling my tunic off. Ayastaren was dry and my shirt was caked with dust. I refused to sit through an Ayastaren banquet looking like anything less than nobility. I went to the washbasin and began to scrub up, my mood souring the longer I stewed on the issue.

It wasn't just that I was worried about her safety. There was something about her. The way my body reacted—I hated it. I was hyperaware of her every time she was near. I would subconsciously move closer to her. My dreams had even betrayed me. More than once I'd woken up in a sweat, imagining how she'd felt in my arms when I rescued her from the wall in Helena.

Some women had gems that made them more alluring or attracted those they desired to them in ways that were hard to explain. Jewelry like that was passed down from mother to daughter, a way to secure marriages and maintain bloodlines. It was all magic, a ruse, and I again doubted Rowyn's intentions. Did she have one of those? It wouldn't surprise me. If what I suspected was correct, then she was from the royal Morganite bloodline. Was she trying to entrap me? Make me weak? Find out my vulnerabilities? It would make sense.

If she was going to all that trouble to defeat me, then why didn't she just allow the arrow in the woods to fly true? Why had she insisted on saving me?

I stewed about her all while getting ready for dinner. I followed Gillius down the hall, memorizing the route to her room until we came upon her door and Gillius knocked.

The maid answered, her face apologetic. "I'm sorry, I've only just gotten her dressed. She's not quite proper."

"What do you mean, she's not ready?" Gillius snapped.

I elbowed him and he shot me a grumpy look. There was no point in yelling at her maid. If she wasn't ready, then she wasn't ready.

Over Ena's shoulder, I watched Rowyn hastily shove blades up her sleeves, trying to hide the movements. I smirked. Rowyn didn't wear jewelry, but she did have knives. I wondered if they were enchanted to entice wary nobles to her affections. The very thought stoked the fires of my temper.

"Up or down, my lady?" Ena asked while Gillius and I took a seat at the table that had been placed in the middle of Rowyn's room.

"Down please, Ena. Thank you," Rowyn said, her

voice unnaturally prim. I couldn't help it. I laughed. The girl who just stared down her arrow shaft at a bunch of Ayastaren guards was now trying to act like a proper maiden? For the love of the gods.

"Something about me amuses you, my lord?" Rowyn asked, twisting in her chair to glare at me.

My smile deepened. She had that spark in her eyes again. The one that danced about, refusing to be tethered. Something happened to me every time I noticed it. I just wanted more, more fire, more wildness, more of everything she had that I'd not seen before.

"If you're trying for the innocent look again, it won't work," I goaded her, enjoying the scowl that briefly appeared on her face before she wiped it away. "You fool no one."

Rowyn turned up her nose at me and twisted back to her mirror, letting her maid get on with her work. "It doesn't hurt to try."

"It would do you well to resist speaking at dinner," Gillius told Rowyn. "The Lyons are highly conscious of a lady's presence and ask that they defer to men at mealtime."

I had to hold back a chuckle at the dark look Rowyn shot Gillius in the mirror.

Rowyn's maid was still trying to get her long hair to behave, so I leaned back, propping my feet on the table, my favorite dagger spinning on my fingers. "My father's tribute might placate him," I offered. It wouldn't resolve any of the issues he currently had with Helena, but it might distract him from Rowyn.

"And if it doesn't?" Master Gillius muttered, echoing my thoughts.

"Well, let's be open-minded," I said lightly, not wishing to worry the girl. "Maybe he'll forget the slight if she calls the rain."

"I'm sitting right here," Rowyn snapped. Her maid jerked her head to the side, and Rowyn made a face like it had hurt.

"Hush." Master Gillius turned to me. "That might work, although she's never tried to bring it on herself. It's triggered by an emotional reaction."

"I could stab her for you if you like," I offered, anticipating her reaction.

"If you so much as touch me, I'll gut you."

There was that spark again, brighter than I'd ever seen it. I shouldn't feel smug about it, but I did. I liked making her feel something, even if it was just anger. If nothing else, it meant that I held the advantage.

"Maybe it won't come to that," Gillius murmured. "The tribute might be enough."

I softened my voice to a whisper. "Honestly? I don't think we should reveal her skills."

Gillius checked to make sure Rowyn wasn't paying attention, then turned to me and nodded. "I just want to lie low until we can get out of here. Don't give anything away to the brothers at dinner."

I nodded, pleased that for once, Gillius and I were on the same page.

"Finished, my lady," Ena said, stepping back and helping Rowyn rise.

We made our way to the great hall and waited until we were each announced. I strode in and immediately met the eyes of Duke Roland who was looking at me with a bemused expression. As though my very presence was entertaining to him. I tried to resist clenching my fists. It was clear that he enjoyed toying with me.

"Well, well, well, Lord Destrian Everett, we are so thrilled to have you grace our halls after so long." Duke Roland's voice dripped with sarcasm. Nobody liked to visit Ayastaren unless they had to.

"Greetings from Helena," I said, my voice easy. It wouldn't be wise for him to see me upset or angry. It was just cannon fodder he could use later.

I heard Rowyn step into the room behind me, and I motioned to one of our guards. He produced the chest of gold and opened the lid with a flourish. Duke Roland just waved me aside, and my heart sank as his gaze sharpened on the girl walking past me.

"So, this is the wild girl," Duke Roland said, rising and stepping down from his chair to get a closer look. I stood behind Rowyn, my hands clasped behind my back as I tried to mask my discomfort. The duke stepped right up to her, his hand on her chin, so near her throat.

I stiffened, my eyes on his fingers.

"Tell me of your new charge, Master Gillius," Duke Roland ordered. "Are you sure she'll fit in at the academy?"

"To be sure, Your Grace, she's a unique student," Gillius said beside me.

I was glad Duke Roland appeared to be baiting him and not me. I didn't want his attention focused on me more than what was warranted. I would give myself away.

Gillius went on. "Espiria isn't cultured, so I apologize for any offense you took in her callow behavior. I ask that you excuse her ignorance."

Duke Roland nodded, and his hand went to Rowyn's neck, running his fingers through her hair as he brushed it off her shoulder.

Rowyn was silent, with her hands balled into fists at her side. Her back was rigid. I wished I could see her eyes.

His fingers lifted to the roses etched into her flesh.

117

I unclasped my hands behind me and sent my power to the fireplace where a steady fire burned. It brightened for a moment, just enough to take the edge off before I lost it completely and took out the room.

When Duke Roland's hand finally dropped, Rowyn stepped back, into me. I grabbed her arm, resisting the urge to shield her from the duke.

"Are there many Morganite clans who roam your lands?" the duke asked, his eyes on my hand that still gripped Rowyn's arm. I released her.

"There are several large ones in the wilderness, but most live peacefully under our banner." I knew that he would already have that information. The more I tried to conceal, the more it would trigger his curiosity.

"Your father must stamp out this rebellion. He's coddled them for long enough as it is." Duke Roland's head tilted to the side.

I tried to laugh but was afraid I sounded foolish instead. It took everything I had to keep my voice steady. "I'll be sure to tell him."

We joined them at the table, me sitting next to Elias and Seith. By the gods I hated those two. I was forced to play nice and be sociable at Solridge, considering they were the sons of my closest liege lord, but they were the worst of men. They were crass and drank too much and made the ladies at Solridge insanely uncomfortable with their lingering eyes and wandering hands. Ingrid especially had a hard time with Elias. I'd already spoken to him about her and was met with derision. I'd hate to think what he'd say if I spoke in Rowyn's favor. So, at dinner I played nice and responded to the Lyons' questions in an affable manner, trying to show that I was calm and relaxed, and not at all fearful.

Teilo Lyon got up about halfway through dinner to deal with some issue. Duke Roland took the opportunity to further press about Rowyn's presence.

"One of my men heard from your guards that the girl brings rain," the duke said, turning to Gillius and me. "Is that true?"

Heat pulsated in my fingertips. I put my hands in my lap.

"She's shown promise in weather work, yes," Master Gillius said begrudgingly.

"Would you care to sell her?" Duke Roland asked, his eyes on me. My stomach fell at his implication. Already it had begun. It took everything I had not to glance at Rowyn. I had no wish to see how she was looking at me. "I could use the rain here. We've very nearly turned to desert under the hot eye of Sol. I'll pay handsomely to take one rebel off your hands. As she's already a traitor to the empire, you could consider it a prison sentence."

I couldn't help myself. I looked over, hoping Rowyn wasn't in tears. She wasn't. She was glaring at me as though she could will arrows from the sky and kill every nobleman in the room. I was glad she was angry. Better angry than hopeless. Better lively than broken. It made the next words out of my mouth come easier. "She's untrained, Your Grace. I fear in her current state, she'd be of little use to you."

Duke Roland nodded. "Perhaps when she gains her gem, you'd be willing to part with her. Morgania is already fruitful after all."

"Perhaps," I said, looking down at my plate. Not a fucking chance.

I watched Rowyn out of the corner of my eye as she silently ate her dinner, staring into her bowl as she stirred her soup angrily.

A pang of regret stuttered through me. Was her light so easily dimmed? I should've stood up to the duke. I should've said something to him about keeping his damned hands and greedy thoughts to himself.

I walked behind Gillius and Rowyn, making sure no one followed as we walked Rowyn back to her room. My fingers were blazing with heat. I was about to lose my mind.

Rowyn had the same thought. When we reached

her door, she whirled, the spark back in her eyes, this time directed at us.

But Gillius held up his hand and shook his head. "No, Rowyn, not here. Tomorrow we leave and can talk more then. Destrian will ward your room, so don't leave again tonight." Gillius shoved Rowyn into her room and shut the door.

"I don't want to leave her," I hissed, sparks dancing from my fingertips.

Gillius glanced over my shoulder and shook his head again. "They have spies in their serving staff. Get it together and ward the door."

I slapped my hand against the wood and thrust my power in harder than I intended. The glow was bright, and I hoped Rowyn and Ena weren't touching the walls because they would've been burned for sure. Once the glow faded, I followed Gillius back to our room, looking over my shoulder all the way.

"You have no idea what you are doing, do you?" I snarled as Gillius shut the door.

"Duke Roland was only trying to provoke us. It's important that we don't rise to the occasion."

"He had his hands all over her! Why is she so far away?" I yelled. "He's planning something."

"Keep your voice down. You don't know that for a fact." Gillius shouldered off his robe and hung it on a hook near the door. "The duke is well-versed in the Articles of Clemency."

"I'm going to demand that they move us," I said, striding toward the door. "You're gambling with her life and you, of all people, should know better than to gamble against a Lyon."

"Do you really want him to see our weakness?" Gillius asked, his hand on my arm, stilling me. "What do you think he will do to her when he finds out?"

"He already knows," I growled.

"We cannot act unless we know for sure."

I shook my head, furious at how cavalier he was about Rowyn's safety. My mind went back to my musings from Helena. Rowyn was going to be one of the greatest sorcerers of my generation's cycle, and she was from the land I ruled. Gillius was the one who insisted that I was responsible for her safety. "You cannot make a mistake with her."

"I know," Gillius whispered. "Greater men than you have told me as much."

I met his eyes, my brow furrowed. Gillius turned as though nothing important had occurred. "Tomorrow is another trial. We need to get some rest."

I looked back to the door, feeling that surge return. I'd warded her. I could feel it in my mind, the pulse of magic in the walls. She was safe for the moment.

Perhaps Gillius was right. Duke Roland was just testing us.

I LURCHED AWAKE, my gem pulsating with a searing burn.

"The ward!" I roared, grabbing my belt and securing it before pulling on my boots and taking off for the door. Gillius tailed me down the hall as I sprinted toward Rowyn's room, my heart pounding in sync with my feet hitting the stone floor as I gripped my sword tightly.

There, in the hall ahead. Rowyn and Ena were outside, attempting to put out the fire on two burning men. Rowyn looked up at me, her eyes brightened by the flames. I extinguished them, relieved that she appeared unhurt.

"What happened?" Master Gillius asked, kneeling to one of the men on the ground. I glared at him. He knew perfectly well what had happened.

"I don't know," Rowyn said. "Ena and I just heard them yelling."

I checked the man on the other side of the hall. He wasn't moving, his eyes lifeless, his mouth twisted in a scream. I checked his pulse anyway.

"Is he?" Gillius began.

"Dead," I told him as I went up to the door. A key had been inserted into the lock.

Guards approached from the other hall and I shook my head, wondering who the duke would send to clean up his mess.

"What's the ruckus?" Teilo Lyon asked, turning the corner.

I glared at him, hating the way his voice dripped with false innocence. How Mellan told it, Teilo was the worst of his brothers, though they were all pretty terrible. He did mention that Teilo was the one who would leave small, mangled animals around the castle to scare the serving staff. "They tried to break past my ward."

"Did they?" Teilo asked in mock surprise. "Well, my apologies. We don't tolerate robbery in Ayastaren." He drew a dagger from his belt and slit the throat of the man Gillius was tending to without a second's pause.

"We don't even know what they wanted!" Master Gillius rose.

I held back my frustration. Now he was getting upset? Where was this attitude hours earlier when we could've prevented this very thing from happening?

"My father doesn't tolerate those who endanger our

guests." Teilo shrugged, his eyes shooting to me. I tried to mask my anger, but I was unsuccessful. I'd not been to school with Teilo Lyon, but I'd certainly heard about him. There were several girls from SeaPort who had accused him of assault, and probably several more who never said anything so as not to invoke the Duke of Ayastaren's ire.

I saw the apprehension in Rowyn's eyes as she watched Teilo clean his dagger on a blanket, Ena crying beside her. Rowyn had obviously seen death. She just stood there, watching Teilo and stepping away from the blood that crept toward her.

"On behalf of my father, I apologize for this disturbance," Teilo said, his eyes on me. "It won't happen again."

I didn't acknowledge Teilo's words. I didn't even look at him.

"Come," Master Gillius said to the ladies. "I don't even care what people say, you'll sleep in our room tonight. And by all the gods, nothing will keep us in Ayastaren tomorrow. We'll leave by break of day."

As I stepped into Rowyn's room to retrieve their things, I checked the door. The key was gone. Shaking my head, trying to push back my anger, I grabbed the bag, stuffed the girls' things inside, then quickly went back into the hall and caught up with the others.

"You and Ena can share my bed," Master Gillius was saying when I entered the room behind them. Rowyn was holding Ena around the waist, supporting her as she continued to weep. I set the bag down on the floor and watched Rowyn, searching for any signs of fear. Rowyn's expression betrayed nothing. Instead, she focused on helping Ena into bed. As she grabbed the covers and pulled them to the maid's shoulders, a hiss escaped and Rowyn began to tremble as she looked at her fingers.

I stepped forward. Rowyn *had* been injured.

"Sit here, and I'll work on your hands." Gillius sat on the edge of the bed next to her.

I strode to the door, making sure it was locked on the inside with a key still in the lock.

"What was that all about?" Rowyn asked, looking from Gillius to me.

I glared at Gillius, but he refused to look at me.

"It was the duke," I said, my hand on the door as I fed the ward through.

"We don't know that for a fact. We've no proof," Gillius said.

"And we'll never get any either. Teilo has seen to that," I retorted, going to my bed and pulling off my boots. I cursed Duke Roland a second time for placing me in a room with Gillius.

"You can't just make wild accusations, Destrian."

I scoffed. Gillius was a commoner—and begging me to act like one in front of Ayastaren. He had no right to tell me what to do. Again, I regretted not demanding that we room closer sooner. At least it would've saved the maid a traumatic experience. "All right. But why didn't Teilo question the man? If it were me, I'd at least ask how they managed to get into the castle."

"Why would he want to kill me?" Rowyn asked, her face oddly lit with the green of Gillius's magic. "Surely not because of the woman in the market."

"Who said they were trying to kill you." Had she really not put two and two together? "My guess? The duke was going to make it look like you'd run back home, then keep you here to bring rain to Ayastaren."

"Well . . ." Rowyn stopped, the crease above her nose returning. "I guess I'm just used to everyone wanting me dead."

I didn't know why I laughed. But the moment I realized that she included me in the "everyone" she spoke of, I quieted, feeling altogether too queasy. She didn't think . . . shit.

The memory of all I'd said to her in Helena came roaring back to me, and I felt like the biggest fool. Why had I said those things? Why had I been so needlessly cruel? I'd thought her views of nobles were outdated and false, yet I acted exactly how she accused me to behave.

Gillius finished with Rowyn's hands, the green light illuminating the room.

Rowyn was an enigma. Gillius was convinced she was some lost soul, separated from everyone who knew the inner workings of magic. Initially, I'd counted his feelings false, sure that she was a spy.

Despite my suspicions, I'd started to reconsider. Rowyn didn't act like someone with a mission. She acted like someone who was trying to survive. She stayed in her rooms, followed orders, didn't wander. Only looked over her shoulder as though waiting for a blade to strike.

Did she really have no training before Gillius? The Morganites would never send a princess as a weapon that nobody knew how to use. Had they lost her due to desperation? Who would've been there to show her the way?

Lyrica was always systematic when it came to conquering. They destroyed the sorcerers first. Having several generations of magic wiped out decimated the area from sorcery for an extremely long time. Sometimes it took upwards of a hundred years for the cycles to start again. Sometimes they were lost entirely.

I thought back to that day on the road, when Rowyn had thrown me out of the saddle to save me from an arrow. I'd worried that she was involved in some nefarious scheme with the Morganites, but we hadn't been bothered since that altercation and had left the borders of Morgania quite peacefully.

The Morganites had no sorcerers and therefore wouldn't have known how to help Rowyn with her magic.

By the gods, no wonder she was so sporadic. She'd been trying to suppress her magic instead of control it. That was a common reaction among people where magical abilities seemed to pop up out of nowhere. I thought Rowyn too powerful than that. Just looking at her with a blade told me she knew discipline.

That was the worst thing to do with magic. She had to learn to funnel it . . . manipulate it and use it up. Magic cried out to be involved in our world, and if we didn't listen, it lashed out. Rowyn didn't seem to have any control over her skills. Everything responded to her emotions and those she couldn't bury. Rowyn wore her heart on her sleeve. She was one of the most open people I'd ever met.

A thought. One that I immediately wished would've never entered my mind.

I looked at Gillius. He saw her as the key to ending

the drought. But how long had she been suppressing her power? How long had the magic been building? Could Rowyn not only be the *solution* to the drought, but the *cause* of it?

I'd never known about her, yet she dwelled within my domain. I couldn't track magic like Gillius, but I knew when it was happening. I wondered if the very magic that had absorbed into the shroud also protected her from our sight. Rowyn had grown up sheltered, completely separated from our world, living in a cave city and only sneaking out to steal gold and bread.

The searing burn in my chest returned with a vengeance. I watched her, the imorets around her eyes making her look otherworldly. She stretched her fingertips, looking up at Gillius with a smile, her black hair hanging loosely down her back.

I seethed at Gillius. It was his fault she'd been put in that position in the first place. Did she even know the danger she was in? Did she even realize who she was? I glared at the ceiling, trying to calm the burn. Why was I constantly thinking about her?

But I knew. There was a stubbornness about her, an unwillingness to bow to anyone, including me. It was infuriating. And yet, that very quality was part of what made her so . . . magnetic.

I doused the light. I was in for a sleepless night

listening for noises in the hall and Rowyn's breathing. I rolled to the side, already feeling my temper rise.

"Thank you for your ward," Rowyn said in the darkness. My heart skipped a beat.

"You're welcome," I managed. "An eye for an eye as they say."

Chapter 10

I COULDN'T HELP THE PLEASURE I felt when Rowyn chose to ride next to me. Of course, if my other choices were two Lyon brothers and a grumpy healer, I would probably choose me too.

I kept close, wary that the duke would try something else as we left. He didn't even show up to see us off, which, hopefully, meant that he'd been stymied.

Still, as we passed through the streets of Ayastaren, I kept a watchful eye. The people seemed in even lower spirits than when we'd arrived.

Perhaps it was because Elias and Seith rode in front of us. The Lyons were not well-loved in their city, and more than one rebellion had happened over the years because of the family's poor treatment of the peasants. My father had even written to the emperor about it once, but the emperor wasn't ever concerned about western affairs. We were relied upon to govern ourselves. But Duke Roland Lyon was the highest of us.

I was so lost in my thoughts that I didn't really notice what was going on until a woman staggered toward Rowyn and I reined in. Looking up, I saw what had silenced everyone else.

A family hung on the wall, including two little bodies. Children. The sourness of bile filled my mouth, and I thought I would vomit. It felt just like Yliria. It felt like war.

The woman was screaming at Rowyn. I recognized the wounds on her back, but the rain had started, thunder reverberating through the marble streets of the city. The crowd was running, screaming through the gate as the rush of rain began.

I waited until Gillius got Rowyn riding away from the scene to bolt, knowing that Valor was already at his wits' end. Rain lashed against my face as I finally reined in, glad that I couldn't yet see our party. They were probably far behind me.

I held out my hands and called a giant ember sizzling from the rain determined to quash it. I fed it more and more power, trying to get ahold of my panic.

Yliria was behind me now.

I didn't have to fear it anymore.

But it wasn't Yliria I was afraid of, and this time I wasn't just scared for myself.

"CAN YOU JUST TALK TO HER?" Gillius asked, nodding

to the stairs that Rowyn had just stamped up after smacking the grin off Elias Lyon's face.

I was equal parts angry and amused. Elias Lyon definitely deserved what she did, but she needed my protection, and provoking the Lyons was not, in any way, helpful to me.

I trudged up the stairs, resigned to my fate. I already knew what was going to happen. She was probably going to yell at me a bunch and call me a terrible person.

Again.

I stopped outside her door and knocked, steeling myself for the argument to come. "Gillius, I'm not talking to you anymore about this . . ." Rowyn opened the door and stopped short when she saw it was me instead. I looked into her room. Her maid, Ena, looked to be packing her bag. Rowyn had strapped her weapons on as though she were going riding.

No.

This was not happening.

She couldn't just *leave*.

I shoved past Rowyn, sat in the chair, crossed my arms, and glared at her, trying to put my thoughts in order. Where did she think she would run?

"I don't want to talk anymore—to any of you!" Rowyn shouted at me. Yep, there it was. The inevitable yelling that Rowyn seemed to reserve just for me. The

134

storm outside mirrored her state of mind perfectly. The rain thrashed against the window while thunder punctuated her declaration. It was evident that she was at her wits' end, teetering on the edge of control. Rowyn took a deep breath as if to try to shove it down. She could only do that for so long before the magic shoved back.

Gillius had been right. She'd had no guidance whatsoever in how to control her powers. She was a walking, talking catastrophe waiting to happen.

"Leave us," I told Ena. If Rowyn was going to lose it, we didn't need a casualty. "You're a fool," I announced after Ena had left. Probably not the best choice of words for someone who was already teetering on the edge of control, but I was not a perfect person.

Rowyn went to the bed and began shoving clothes into her bag. The deep crease in her forehead had returned. "If you would excuse me, my lord, I haven't yet finished packing."

Rowyn always seemed to find a way to make my noble status sound like an insult. I was glad I'd already released a lot of magic because it was starting to get under my skin.

She threw her pack over her shoulder. I rose and strode to the door, blocking her from leaving. If she thought I would just let her march into Ayastaren by herself after what had just happened, she had another thing coming. She was going to get herself captured or killed.

"Going somewhere?" I asked, trying to keep my breathing calm and steady.

"Let me pass, my lord," Rowyn said slowly. "I don't belong here."

"No." I couldn't let her go.

Rowyn pulled the dagger from her belt. "Let me pass," she demanded, her eyes illuminated by anger.

I laughed, thrilled with the excitement of her standing so close. I had a death wish because I absolutely believed her when she said she would stab me. She knew enough about blades to aim for a spot that wouldn't kill me. At least, I hoped so. "What're you going to do? Stab me? My father will burn Espiria to the ground if you do." She shouldn't stifle her magic; she should be letting it go.

"If he could, he would've already, my lord." Rowyn stepped closer, brandishing her blade and bringing the scent of rain with her. I breathed deeply, the smell enveloping me.

"Why are you here?" Rowyn snapped when I refused to move from the door. "I'd think you'd rejoice at my departure."

So, she thought my opinion of her so low? "What will you do when you go back to Espiria?" I asked, knowing full well what would happen if she returned home. Either she learned to use her magic or it consumed her. "You need to be trained, or you'll pose a threat to all. The welfare of Morgania is very much my business, despite what you and your clan think."

"I can't stand it here—the woman's family!" Rowyn's voice began to break. "They'll forever be on my conscience if I stay. You know as well as any that I don't belong. I should be at home with my family and clan and the people who love me!"

The weight of her remorse hung heavily in the room. Those were not the words of a spy. My heart stirred at how lost she sounded, her voice tinged with vulnerability and fear. But I couldn't ignore the recklessness of her actions. "What did you expect? You had no business trifling in the duke's affairs. Consider it a lesson."

"So, you agree with the duke's actions?" she asked, a threat in her voice. There it was. She thought I was just like Duke Roland.

I'd been crumbling under the pressure of running Helena from afar, and now everyone seemed to find me wanting. From the Duke of Ayastaren, to the emperor, to Gillius, and now, to this little girl from the wild who wouldn't stop invading my thoughts. She thought me just as bad as the Lyons? What was the point of this ruse then? Maybe I should be the evil noble she thought me to be.

The burn of my magic ripped through me, and I had to send it somewhere, so I directed it to the dagger in Rowyn's hand. She squealed and dropped it, tears pricking her eyes. I kicked the weapon away.

"No, I would have strapped you up in the woman's place. You Espirians and your lofty ideas. You know nothing of what it means to rule."

Rowyn stood her ground, her hands clenched at her sides. "What you speak of isn't ruling—it's barbarism. I'm amazed, by the counsel you keep, that I would be deemed the savage!"

What a hypocrite! She spoke as though the Morganites were the pillars of peace and justice in the land, which was far from true if you looked at the number of soldiers they needlessly slew a year. "I've seen your people's raids, Rowyn, or do you forget that your clan terrorizes the road to Helena?"

"You think I'm like them?" Rowyn gasped. "When we raid, it's grown men we fight! Soldiers trained for battle!"

She really believed there was no difference. "Death has many faces," I said slowly. "It has many faces, but it's still death. The soldiers have families, their own children, who now have no one to provide for them."

Rowyn's expression softened. I saw a flicker of fear in her eyes. "Why should I stay?" she murmured, her voice shaky. "Why, if there is no one else like me?" The sound of the rain drumming on the eaves grew louder.

Her question was a desperate plea, and for the first time, I saw her for what she truly was. Lost. Afraid. Alone. I had to resist the urge to reach out, to touch her. Despite the centuries-long feud between our people, I couldn't help but feel a flicker of sympathy for her. "Your people have tormented my family for years, and although we've tried to scratch the itch that is Espiria, you seem to evade us at every turn." My anger dissipated as I looked down at this poor, broken girl from the wilds who refused to be tamed.

"Then why, in Philemon's name, are you here?" she asked, those blue eyes filled with something I couldn't place.

I looked down at her lips. I wondered what it would feel like to kiss them. Would I feel the wildness within her? I fought the urge that seized me, hoping to all the gods that she couldn't read what I was sure was written across my face.

I clenched my fists. "Because as much as I dislike your clan, Gillius is right. I can't ignore the signs. The drought has been going on for five long years now. People have prayed to the gods to send them rain, but instead, the gods sent you. Like anyone else, I'm curious to see what it all means. I don't think any of us, least of all you, will find out if you go back to Espiria."

Rowyn couldn't return to the shroud. Her magic was out now and ready for her to seize control. She needed us just as much as we needed her.

"Just give us a chance. Don't judge all the students of Solridge based on the actions of the Lyons. You may come to like it in time." I turned to the door, knowing that if I stayed, I would do something I'd regret, and Rowyn would never look at me the same way again. She couldn't see how weak I really was. "Do what you want. Just know that the gods are watching, along with the rest of us." I shut the door behind me and let out a long, slow breath.

My room was next door. It was small, with a bed pushed up against the wall, which wasn't nearly long enough, but I'd suffered through all sorts of poor housing during my quest to Yliria. I went in and pulled off my coat and tunic. I wasn't picky, unless you counted noble snubs.

Rowyn's words still roiled in my thoughts as I scraped my teeth and rinsed before collapsing on the bed. I heard her door open and mumbled voices that followed.

Ena had returned. I pressed my hand to our shared wall, sending my power through the cracks and eaves until it encompassed our rooms.

When I finished, I lay back, my eyes on the ceiling. Rain continued to tap on the shutters. Flames bloomed in the fireplace. I listened to the rest of the party return to their rooms along with the crackling of the fire. The Lyon brothers shoved against each other loudly until their door closed and the halls were silent. Thunder rumbled overhead, and I tried to get comfortable on the lumpy mattress and pillow.

Beside me, through the wall, I heard a sob. Something inside me broke, like a dam crumbling from wear. I scooted closer to the sound, not even feeling ashamed that I was trying to listen. I didn't hear any words spoken, though, just soft gasps as Rowyn cried. I reached out and touched the wall, wishing I could change something, anything, to make it easier to bear.

My grandfather taught me everything he'd known about magic, a wealth of knowledge passed down through the Everett line. Because ours cycled through so regularly, we were more knowledgeable than most lines who tended to scramble for their resources when sorcery did pop up. Grandfather had taught me, protected me, and helped shoulder the burden that we endured for generations.

Rowyn never had that. My heart quickened at the thought of how alone she must've felt. How afraid. I wondered what happened within the shroud. I'd thought she was being used as a weapon. Yet, that was clearly not the case. She seemed on the verge of losing control constantly. She was afraid of her magic, and I was not fool enough to think that her fear didn't come from somewhere. What did her clan do to her when they found out?

I heard another faint gasp through the wall, and an ache began to build in my chest. Gillius was right. Rowyn was my responsibility. It was my duty to protect her, and I wouldn't shove the responsibility off anymore. I told myself it was about Helena, about keeping my seat, but when I turned over, trying to will sleep to come, I admitted to myself the truth.

It wasn't about Helena anymore.

It was about her.

Chapter 11

OUR JOURNEY TO SOLRIDGE continued under an oppressive canopy of gray clouds that mirrored the tense atmosphere surrounding our small party. Mist clung stubbornly to the ground, the air carrying a damp, earthy scent. The landscape was as cold and unyielding as the silence between us.

Despite the chilling atmosphere and my uneasy companions, I kept my focus on shielding Rowyn from the worst of the Lyons'. After all, she was exposed on the road, and the brothers seemed to feed on the tension. Seith and Elias chatted and laughed among themselves, speaking with entitled arrogance, their jests and crude humor grating on my nerves.

I didn't think Rowyn noticed why I enticed the Lyons to hunt off the road with me or play dice with me in the evenings—all so they wouldn't get bored and turn on her.

At least Solridge awaited us at the end of the journey. Rowyn would be protected from the worst of the world we lived in. A world, I feared, she'd already seen too much of.

I glanced ahead, letting the Lyons' jokes fall to the wayside. Rowyn rode her horse like she was born on it, her back straight, her gaze focused on the path ahead. Her face was a portrait of composed anger, and it was clear she wanted nothing more than to be left alone. I respected her silence, keeping my own counsel and maintaining a polite distance. But I watched her, concerned by the storm that seemed to rage within—and above.

Finally, after days of traveling under the weight of gray skies and heavier silence, the formidable stone façade of Solridge Academy rose before us. The sight of the familiar castle was a welcoming presence. A strange mix of relief, apprehension, and anticipation filled me.

We handed our mounts to the stable boy and entered. I nodded to Lady Vianne, then headed after the Lyons, down the corridor to the boys' dormitory. I cast one last glance at Rowyn over my shoulder before leaving her to the care of the masters. She met my gaze with wariness.

The familiar sounds of the academy filled my ears— whispers of magic seeping through the cracks within the stone walls, the echoes of student chatter bouncing off the vaulted ceilings. It was where I'd been happiest, without the yoke of guilt and duty around my neck. In some ways, it felt like home.

Approaching the door to my quarters, I took a moment to collect myself. Behind the door waited one of the constants in my life, Lord Marc Trinidan of Korballis. He was a sorcerer, though a second son and therefore not heir to the consulship, but that did not lessen his commitment to honing his craft.

Knocking lightly, I pushed open the door. My bed had new covers, and the window and desk had been dusted. I looked over to Marc seated at his desk by the window. He looked up as I entered. A wide grin split his face.

"Des!" he exclaimed, leaping to his feet and crossing the room in a few strides.

I greeted him, then let my bag fall onto the mattress as I sank into a nearby chair by the hearth. Marc went to open a window and I held up my hand. Fire appeared in the fireplace, dancing and flickering.

"How was your quest?" Marc asked. A sorcerer's quest was always considered a major story in the history of the empire. Sometimes it helped with alliances; other times it started wars. The gem's quest was the first time a student ventured away from the academy walls and acted as a sorcerer. The Trial by Stone changed you. Mastery was even worse; you had to change the world.

Sighing, I leaned back in the chair. "Yliria was a

mess," I admitted. "We'd torn the place up. The locals almost turned us away."

I narrated my journey of how Lord Alexander and I had navigated through the devastated landscapes of Yliria, constantly on guard for danger. Alexander, with his water-summoning abilities, had been invaluable during our journey, often helping us out of tricky situations with his talent.

Our pursuit of my ruby had led us to rely heavily on the Ylirians. Despite the constant state of war they lived in, the Ylirians had shown immense courage and kindness, guiding us through their lands and sharing vital information. I expressed my admiration for their spirit and resilience, earning a thoughtful nod from Marc.

"And then, there was the ruby," I continued. The crimson stone glimmered in the warm light, casting a beautiful array of red around the room. It was a part of me—a testament to the journey, a symbol of the challenges overcome, the change within.

Marc listened intently, his eyes wide with interest as he hung onto my every word. When I finished, he sat back. "And now you're back."

I nodded. "There's something else," I said, pulling off my boots with a grunt. "There's a girl."

Marc's brows shot up. "A girl?"

"She's a Morganite Gillius found on the road to Helena. She controls the weather."

Marc's nostrils flared. "What is a Morganite doing with weather magic?"

"I don't know," I lied. "But I've seen it myself. Her range is . . . it's big, Marc."

"So, what happened? She's here? Now?" Marc rose from his chair.

"Yes," I admitted. "Her name is Rowyn. Just . . . don't make trouble with her . . . please. She's already put up with a lot on the way here."

"What do you mean?"

I told him about Rowyn and the Lyons. I didn't want to speak about the assassin. He hadn't shown his face on the journey to Solridge, and the wards placed around the school would require an army of sorcerers to dismantle.

"Good gods, what a mess," Marc said when I was through. "You know the Lyons are already looking for an excuse to get at Helena. You don't need to go out of your way to get on their bad side by protecting a traitor."

"I know," I agreed half-heartedly, studying my hands.

Marc smiled. "We should head to bed. Everyone will want to see you in training tomorrow, and I've caught a certain someone checking the road for you the past few days."

I smiled, pulling my tunic off. The wards around the academy would protect Rowyn, and the masters would help her gain control. I wouldn't need to worry about her anymore. At least, not so much.

Even so, I lay awake in bed long after Marc had fallen asleep, unable to shake the lingering concern that gnawed at my mind. What would the others say? Would the Lyons continue their jeering, fueling the flames of animosity? Would they turn the students against her?

As the night deepened, the room's shadows danced along the walls. In the stillness, I let myself think of her. The way my heart raced whenever she was close. The eyes that seemed to draw me in.

As sleep finally claimed me, I remembered back to the night outside Ayastaren as I listened to Rowyn crying through the thin walls of our rooms. My fingers on the wood paneling, wishing I could reach out to her. Knowing that if I did, she would only push me away.

Chapter 12

THE MORNING SUN STREAMED through the towering windows of Solridge Academy, casting long, golden beams on the smooth stone floor. The usual morning bustle of the young men coming in from weapons training and the ladies coming down for breakfast echoed through the halls, with students flitting to and fro, their jovial chatter blending into a vibrant hum. In the heart of it all, a figure stood out like a sunbeam amid the shadows, Lady Ingrid Byrne.

Ingrid turned and smiled at me, her golden hair, styled impeccably, gleaming under the sun and her dark eyes dancing with unrestrained vivacity. As I approached her amid the sea of students, my heart stirred with a sense of eager anticipation. Ingrid's attention was not something one took lightly—it was a seal of approval. I'd missed her easy smiles and witty conversation.

"Ingrid," I greeted, a casual smile curving my lips. She returned the gesture with a playful tilt of her head and a flash of her dazzling teeth, eyes brimming with a mischievous glint.

"Lord Destrian, I was quite bereft when you took so long to return," Ingrid said, holding her hand out for me to kiss. I smiled, bowing and placing my lips gently on her warm, golden skin. She smiled, a swirling eddy of charm, a gust of fresh air, effortlessly sweeping everyone within her vicinity into her aura. The way she charmed those around her, the confident flair she exuded—it was heady, infectious, a respite from the burdensome thoughts of my quest, and home, and Rowyn's presence. I allowed myself to bask in the easiness of Ingrid's company as we walked to the dining hall, letting her laughter wash over me like a refreshing spring, a stark contrast to the intense heat that Rowyn brought.

I was just about to enter the hall for breakfast when a voice called me from the masters' chambers. Lady Vianne's amethyst gem glinted in the same light that I'd used to admire Ingrid a mere moment before.

"The council would have a word with you before you eat," Lady Vianne said.

I thought my stomach audibly grumbled, but I shot a small smile at Ingrid as she looked over her shoulder at me and followed Vianne to Solridge's council chambers.

They were all there: Lord Alexander, Vianne's husband and my mentor for the quest, Master Haris,

Gillius, Lord Obi, and Lady Madeline. I nodded to them all as I took the seat in the middle of the room, ready to debrief about my quest to Yliria.

"First of all," Lady Vianne said, smiling at me, "congratulations on completing the Trial by Stone. Do you feel much changed?"

"I do," I replied, glancing at each one to make sure no one felt slighted. "I've been drawing more power that I've had to funnel a bit more, and a precision is there that I hadn't felt before."

Lord Alexander nodded. "You're a credit to your grandfather," he said, intending the words to be a kindness. I tried not to let my feelings show. I'd thought far too much about the old man lately, and my admiration for who he once was had begun to wane.

"Lord Destrian had already received a wealth of training before he came to Solridge, which made the journey easier. His skills have certainly improved with the gem, but his mastery was already well above what is required." Lord Alexander turned to the others, but Lady Vianne's head was tilted thoughtfully, her gem aglow as she studied me. "Honestly, the hardest part of the quest was the journey through Yliria, and even in that Lord Destrian excelled."

I smiled, grateful for the praise. I needed it after the trials from the road. It felt as though everyone had found me lacking, from Gillius, to Rowyn, to the Lyons.

Shit. I shouldn't be thinking about that. I tried to rein in my thoughts, but Lady Vianne's eyes had already narrowed. "Tell us what you know of the girl," she said.

Gillius frowned, glancing at Lady Vianne before looking back at me. Alexander was watching his wife. I was pretty sure Lord Obi was asleep. "Rowyn's range is pretty big," I said, belatedly trying to school my thoughts. Being around mind readers meant you always had to keep guard of yourself. "She lived behind the Shroud of Espiria her entire life, but I don't know if the magic of the shroud enhanced hers or if she enhanced the magic of the shroud." I frowned. "I don't know much about her, honestly, just that she's a Morganite and she really doesn't like nobility." I might've said that last part a bit bitterly.

"What of her family?" Lady Vianne asked. Damn it. She'd seen something. I focused on a memory, letting it fill my mind.

"I don't know much about them," I said. "I've seen her father, years ago."

"Did you notice if he had any magical ability?" Master Haris asked.

I shook my head. "No, he wasn't a sorcerer. He was

152

just a Morganite chieftain."

Lady Vianne was watching me far too closely, but I tried not to look guilty. It was impossible to tell how much she'd seen. I used my magic to ward my mind a bit, just to kick Vianne out of it. I was under no obligation to let her read my thoughts. If she was able to push her way in, then it was fair game.

Lady Vianne wrinkled her nose, the glimpse of whatever she'd seen, gone. After a bit more prodding, they let me return to the dining hall for breakfast.

Rowyn was already sitting at one of the ladies' tables next to Fin. I nodded to her as I came in. She looked well. The lines of anger were smoothed from her face, and she glanced curiously around the room while talking to Fin and Galena. The fact that it was sunny outside spoke volumes about her mood.

"How was it?" Marc asked as I took my seat across from him and Idris.

"Well enough," I said, accepting the roll Idris offered. "They were more interested in what I could tell them about the Morganite girl than hearing about the quest. I guess Lord Alexander had already filled them in."

Idris looked over his shoulder at the ladies' table. "She's pretty," he said with interest. "Are there markings all over her body, I wonder?"

I tried to ignore the stab of jealousy and anger. "I wouldn't know," I said perhaps a bit too sharply.

"Barbaric custom," Marc muttered under his breath. "Marking women like that."

I glared at them both. Idris didn't mind dandling with girls' affections. Not noble ladies, of course, though he'd welcome the challenge. Usually, it was the lower born ones who forgot their sense of propriety in the face of his abilities and noble status. He was an heir, after all, though Juno was quite small. Idris always grew bored with them over time. My skin seemed to tighten at the thought of her . . . and him. "She doesn't like nobles," I said, breaking off a piece of bread. "Besides, she's had a hard enough time as it is. Do me a friend's favor—stay away from her."

Idris and Marc glanced at each other, then back at me, Idris chewing slowly. "You want to tell us something?"

They wouldn't drop it without me giving them a reason for my concern. The gods knew I wasn't going to tell them how she seemed to invade my thoughts.

"She didn't grow up with much of an education and she'll have a terrible enough time trying to get a handle on things without us making it hard on her. She's already earned the Lyons' ire. She doesn't need ours as well."

"I hate those prats," Idris muttered, stirring his mug of tea. I nodded in agreement, then watched as Rowyn stood and went out the door with Fin. I resisted the urge to follow her, very aware that Marc and Idris were watching me. The conversation about Rowyn left a sour taste in my mouth. I wanted to steer clear of it, not out of indifference but because I felt conflicted. I couldn't imagine what they'd say if they saw me struggle with my feelings. My thoughts about Rowyn were an intricate web, a blend of respect, irritation, and an odd sense of intrigue. And so, I retreated into silence, letting the morning's chatter wash over me as I chewed thoughtfully on a piece of bread.

Fingertips brushed my shoulder, and I looked up. Ingrid smiled down at me after sparing Idris and Marc a glance. "Will we see you later?" she asked. "Some of us ladies thought to take a ride on the beach now that the weather is warmer. Though, I know you probably don't miss the heat."

I mustered a return smile. "Of course, after dinner?"

Ingrid nodded, her eyes dancing. "I want to hear all about your trip to Yliria." She turned and followed her sister, Lisbet, out of the room and toward her healing class. I turned back and saw Marc and Idris watching me.

155

"What?" I asked. They shook their heads and rose. I followed them out to the gardens where the sorcerers met before their lessons.

AFTER CHECKING IN with Lord Alexander, I stepped into the forge that I had taken over when I'd come to Solridge four years before. It was just as I left it, the stone oven cool, the anvil covered in a fine layer of dust. I breathed deep, the sanctuary of soot and steel offering solace. I lifted my apron from its hook and got to work cleaning, relieved to finally be alone with my thoughts. With each passing moment, I tried to banish the troublesome worries that lingered in the recesses of my mind—thoughts of the Lyons, Rowyn, and the tangled web of emotions that entwined them. With each stroke of the broom, I willed myself to focus solely on the task at hand, to let the physical exertion distract me from the emotional turmoil within.

But try as I might, questions surfaced, like stubborn embers refusing to be extinguished. How had Rowyn's meeting with the council gone? What did she and Fin speak of that put her in such a good mood? What did the sorcerers of Solridge plan for her while she was at the academy?

Before long, I surveyed the now-tidy forge, a sense of accomplishment relaxing me. The tumultuous thoughts that plagued me earlier seemed momentarily muted, overshadowed by a fleeting sense of peace. I checked Sol's position in the sky and realized I still had some time to work. There was an ancient blade of bitter steel in the armory that I'd been using for research, so I headed in that direction, wiping my hands on a rag before shoving it in my apron pocket.

The Solridge armory was a place of orderly chaos, filled with weapons of all sorts and the heavy scent of well-oiled steel. As I stepped inside, a cry of pain echoed through the room, followed by a heavy thud. Alarmed, I pushed the door wide.

Rowyn stood with her back to the door while the Lyon brothers—Elias and Seith—groaned on the ground at her feet.

I grabbed Rowyn's arm as she reared it back. She spun toward me, her fist cocked, then lowered it, looking me up and down as though the very sight of me surprised her. For a moment, she appeared unsure of how to react, her eyes flicking from my face to the groaning Lyon brothers on the floor.

I couldn't believe I was so worried about her with them. Clearly the girl could handle herself. She'd shown me as much in Helena, with Sir Alexo. Something akin to amusement bubbled up inside me, spilling out in a sudden burst of laughter.

"Go," I managed to get out, a grin still tugging at my lips. I stepped aside, watching as she left the armory. I looked down at the Lyons and saw a book on the floor. I'd known the brothers long enough to know that it wouldn't have been theirs. I scooped it up and hurried back out into the hall.

"Rowyn, wait," I said, having a sudden thought. I reached out and grabbed her arm, leaving a sooty handprint on her sleeve. She looked up at me, uncertainty in her gaze. "Don't tell anyone."

Gillius had done an abysmal job of handling the Lyons in Ayastaren. I had no wish to repeat that mistake now that we were at Solridge. Especially since they were away from the protection of their father.

"Why?" Her confusion was palpable. "Shouldn't everyone know what pigs the Lyons are?"

"Everyone already does. It's not like it's a secret," I said, my amusement fading. "It'll only make them behave worse toward you."

Rowyn snatched the book from my hands. "They'll try to best me again."

She wasn't wrong, but I was tired of handling things Gillius's way. He insisted she was my charge, so I would manage it . . . especially when it came to the nobility. "I'll take care of it. Just try not to catch yourself alone with them. And give me your word you won't say anything to Gillius."

Rowyn straightened and glared at me. "I don't need you to fight battles for me, Lord Destrian. I can handle the Lyons myself, thank you very much!" Her breath was coming faster, more agitated. "If they come at me again, I'll kill them."

I tried to exude calm. No sense in her losing control on her first day at school. It wouldn't do for the other students to see how little control she possessed. "I know, but give me your word, all the same."

I sensed her hesitation. Considering Rowyn balked at any perceived weakness against her, I could just imagine her reaction if I told her I intended to handle the Lyons on her behalf. It would probably involve a lot of yelling and flinging insults at me. After a moment, she nodded.

"Fine, I swear I won't say anything."

Finally, something with her had come easily. I could deal with the Lyon brothers on my own. I waited until Rowyn disappeared down the hall before reentering the armory. Elias and Seith had sat up, both looking murderous.

"Where is that little witch?" Elias snarled. "She

attacked us!"

I crouched against the door, relieved that the Lyons were away from the protection of Ayastaren, and I could finally deal with them as I liked. "I don't know if your father has put you up to making Rowyn's life more difficult here, but I'm warning you, Rowyn is Morganian. If any harm comes to her, I will take it as a personal attack against Helena."

Elias scoffed. "I didn't take you for one to lose your seat over a little slut."

I raised my brows. "I would remind you that Morgania is *still* the only region in the empire with steady harvests. What happens if our shipment to Ayastaren is *accidentally* waylaid by rogues? Lost at sea maybe? I'm not the only noble whose future seat is unassured. Can Ayastaren withstand another rebellion?"

"You dare threaten my family?" Elias hissed.

"I think *you* should rethink whether or not your father would appreciate you escalating tensions between Ayastaren and Morgania. I'm sure he already has a plan in place to win my seat away from me. Let me ask you, has he told you what he intends? Does he trust you enough to let you in on his little secrets? Or are you two just sabotaging his alliances and seeking forgiveness later?"

Elias's jaw flexed. I knew I had him there. The

Duke of Ayastaren would not approve of his sons making trouble without his express permission. "Do not touch the girl again, or I will personally thrash the both of you."

I rose and left, untying the apron and clutching it in my hand as I headed to lunch. I hadn't found the chance to work on any of my projects, but the morning had been productive nonetheless.

THERE WAS A FAMILIAR RHYTHM to my evenings in the dormitory at Solridge Academy. Marc would hunch over his desk, working on lesson work or buried in a book or a scroll.

I preferred the tactile comfort of my weapons. That night, I was meticulously cleaning my longsword, the familiar hiss of oil against steel filling the room with a satisfying sense of tranquility. My hands always felt at peace with a weapon in my hand, whether melding it, wielding it, or cleaning it. I cared not which.

"Destrian," Marc began, not lifting his eyes from the letter he was writing to his brother, "I need to talk to you about something."

"What?" I continued to move my cloth up and

down the gleaming length of my sword. My mind was finally off Rowyn and back where it should be. I was looking forward to my ride with Ingrid after dinner and was reminded why I entertained her company. Ingrid was charming and easy to be around . . . unlike others whom I'd recently met.

"Elias said something to me at dinner," he said, finally looking up, his eyes serious and a bit troubled. "What did you do?"

I paused in my motions, setting the sword down. "I caught them bothering Rowyn, so I was warning them away from her."

"Just as you warned Idris and me? Why do you put yourself in the way for that traitor?" Marc sighed, rubbing the bridge of his nose. "Don't take this the wrong way, Des, but I would keep my distance from her if I were you. Guilt by association is a real danger in our circles, and the Duke of Ayastaren would love to catch you in a slip."

I rolled my eyes and picked up my sword again, running my cloth over the blade in measured strokes. Marc meant well, but his family wasn't as versed in sorcery as mine since magic so rarely arose in his bloodline. I'd never spoken to any of the others about how the cycles worked, and I'd never heard them speak of it either. I doubted Marc could see the bigger picture, at least not yet, and I was loath to tell him or anyone else, for that matter. Rowyn would be instrumental in changing the course of the empire, and the less people knew, the better.

"She's just a girl who happens to have been born into a clan. That's not her fault."

"You said yourself she'd been involved in raids . . . against *your* soldiers. I understand your sentiments, Destrian," Marc replied patiently. "But you know in our world, perception often outweighs reality. Being seen as friendly with a rebel faction could cause unwanted attention and potential trouble."

I stared at the polished blade in front of me, the sharp edge reflecting my troubled face. "She has a right to be here, just like us. Besides, it was about time someone stood up to the Lyons. Their behavior has gotten worse, not better, and the masters can't take it in hand because most of them aren't nobility . . . even though we defer to them as lords and ladies."

Marc glared at me. "So now you're taking on the Lyons?"

I didn't say anything. I just gritted my teeth, wishing Marc would mind his own business. He'd never sought to intrude on my affairs before, so why now? What made Rowyn different?

"Of course, the Everetts have always done as they

pleased. My father was right, you lot are stubborn asses," Marc grumbled. "But it's not always about what you want. Sometimes, it's about what's best for everyone."

I shrugged, running the cloth down the length of my blade one last time before sheathing it. "And who's to say what's best for everyone, Marc? The empire? You know as well as I do that they're not always right. So, who then . . . the Lyons? They've only ever thought about themselves."

"Don't instigate with the Lyons," Marc snapped. "If you think you can start a war with Ayastaren, and that my father will come to your aid, you have completely misplaced your faith in him. He would never use our soldiers to fight another noble of Lyrica. They would only be used if they come to *our* door."

"It baffles me that you all fall in line so nicely behind them." Tension wound through my shoulders. Marc had never spoken so forcefully with me before. We'd had disagreements, sure, but nothing a rousing match on the practice fields didn't solve. This was something more. I didn't like the way he kept calling Rowyn a traitor, as though he'd already judged her as an enemy. I'd take Rowyn's side over the Lyons' any day.

"It is the order of the system." Marc's voice

hardened. "The same system that protects *you*."

I sat back in my chair, arms crossed. "Rowyn is Morganian. She's a citizen of *my* territory, an asset to *my* seat, and it is my duty to protect her. If you really can't understand that, then this conversation is over."

"Oh? What happened with the two of you in Helena?"

He'd gone too far. Marc, Idris, and I knew about each other's romances, but we never pressed about them. Not that there had been much for *me* to tell, given the fact that unlike Idris and Marc, I refused to flirt with the girls at the inns and raise their hopes. I liked to think it was my honor that kept me out of girls' beds, but there was the—not insignificant—issue of Ingrid, who had made her intentions quite clear early on. There was no way I would do anything to earn the ire of that family. Not for something as fleeting as a dalliance. "I promised Ingrid a ride after dinner," I said, rising from my seat. "I have to go."

"I'm curious, what does Ingrid think about the girl?" Marc continued pointedly.

I refused to take the bait. "I'll see you later." I shut the door behind me, glad to be away from him, and took a deep breath. Marc and I hadn't ever really argued before. Then again, we'd never had reason to.

Marc wasn't wrong. I was playing fast and loose

with the Lyon brothers, but I was tired of them being allowed to walk all over the rest of us unhindered. Rowyn was right. We couldn't just stand by and do nothing.

Chapter 13

"LORD DESTRIAN HERE HAS BEEN TESTING different mixtures of metal to strengthen weapons," Lady Madeline announced with a sense of pride. "He supplies many of the lords to the west and has even gained commissions from nobles on the eastern shore as well."

I held back a grin, appreciating Lady Madeline's words but not wanting to seem too smug. After all, my skills in the forge were as much a result of my sorcery as my training. But still, Rowyn was there, wandering around the perimeter of the blaze, her eyes on the weapons hanging on the wall.

I tried not to notice her too much. What was it she'd called me, "a spoiled consul's son"? She'd not really warmed to me on the road either. But in the hall, when I'd come upon her in the armory with the Lyons, she'd been different. She hadn't yelled at me . . . she hadn't called me names . . . Maybe she *was* starting to change her mind about me. I tried not to read too much into it, but the surging in my chest would not go away as I let myself hope. Even that thought was foolish. I was letting myself hope for . . . what? If Rowyn didn't know about her legacy, which I strongly suspected was the case, then when she eventually found out, she would be after my seat along with all the other nobles vying for more power.

No. I squashed the little ball of hope in my chest. I just liked to look at her, was all. I indulged myself, watching Rowyn out of the corner of my eye as her gaze continued to drift around the room, lingering on the forge and the equipment scattered around.

"Where are your bellows?" she asked, her tone full of genuine curiosity.

"I don't need them," I replied, picking up my hammer and iron tongs. I rolled up my sleeves, revealing my forearms covered in the telltale smears and scorch marks of a blacksmith. "I can regulate the temperature of the fire myself. It's what makes me so skilled at forging in the first place."

Conscious of her eyes on me, I reached for a hunk of raw iron, thrusting it into the heart of the forge. The fire flared up in response as my gem pulsed with a warm glow. The fire's intensity increased, radiating an almost unbearable heat that flooded the small hut. Was I showing off?

Maybe.

Then again, it was best that she go back to her clan saying that I was someone who was skilled at his many crafts then someone who was a complete imbecile. It would do well to give the Morganites pause.

The clang of metal hitting metal rang out as I used the hammer, the monotonous sound a sort of music echoing against the walls. I was conscious of Rowyn's eyes as I worked. I'd never seen her look at me in that way before. Studying . . . calculating. I wondered what was going through her mind. She turned, closely observing the blades that hung on the wall. What did she think of my work?

Rowyn's time in the forge was short-lived. Lady Madeline soon escorted her out and left me alone. I returned to my task, the memory of her presence a distracting undercurrent as I worked.

I looked out the window as Rowyn began to ascend the hill overlooking the sea and hills beyond Solridge. I cooled the forge and stepped out, just as curious as all the other sorcery students who stopped what they were doing to watch the test. Everyone had to do it at some point.

A tense hush fell over the landscape as Rowyn raised her arms toward the sky.

Nothing happened.

I squinted, trying to see her expression in the distance. I shifted.

Rowyn looked nervous . . . frustrated . . . even

169

scared.

I stepped forward.

Shit. She was pushing her emotions back down.

A sharp gust of wind swept over the hill, strong enough to make the onlookers sway. I felt the rush of cold air whip past me, carrying a hint of what was to come.

I began to run. Rowyn still hadn't figured out that to funnel the magic, you had to give in to your emotions, not run away from them, not act as though they didn't exist.

The rain came, not in delicate droplets but in a torrential downpour, the likes of which Solridge hadn't seen in years. I scrambled up the hill as the storm raged around Rowyn. Lightning punctuated the heavy drumming of the rain, while thunder reverberated across the hill, making the ground under me vibrate.

Rowyn crumpled just as I reached her. I fell to my knees at her side as something inside me jolted.

Master Gillius and Lady Madeline hurried over, their faces filled with concern and surprise. Master Gillius kneeled next to me, his hand on Rowyn's brow. He glanced at me and nodded, waving his hand.

I let out a sigh of relief as I scooped Rowyn into my arms, her body limp and alarmingly light. Her wet hair clung to my arm, and her face was cold and white against my chest.

"Are you all right, dear?" Lady Madeline asked, reaching out to touch Rowyn's cheek. Her eyes had fluttered open, unfocused and blinking away the rain. She looked frail and ethereal, her skin now flushed from exertion.

"I think so," Rowyn replied, her voice weak. I could feel the power of Gillius's magic washing over her, searching, mending, healing.

"That's a lot of excitement for our first go-around," Lady Madeline commented. "You're quite the conductor, my dear."

Rowyn looked up at me, her expression inscrutable. I tightened my hold as I tried to step carefully down the slick hill.

"Where are the others?" Rowyn asked, her voice steadier.

"After they were satisfied with your skill, they went inside to be out of the rain. Don't worry, though, you did well for your first time. Very well indeed," Lady Madeline assured her.

"Take her to the infirmary," Gillius murmured to me before walking away with Lady Madeline. Whatever had happened, it wasn't life-threatening. Rowyn probably just needed some rest.

"Were you always this much trouble in Espiria?" I

teased, hoping to ease the tension.

Rowyn stiffened in my arms. I looked down and saw her glowering at me. "Let me down, please," she demanded. I was trying to lower her carefully when she just jumped out of my hold, landing with a wobble.

"Whoa!" I reached out to steady her, but she shoved my arms away. "I'm just trying to help."

"Stop thinking I need help from you!" Rowyn exclaimed, her voice sharp.

Her words struck me, but I bit back my response. She was yelling at me again. I knew what was coming next.

"You shouldn't judge all of us nobles as evil," I said. "There are still some good men left in the realm." My chest tightened with my disappointment. I'd thought things were different now. I thought she could see that I wasn't who she thought I was. Who she was raised to believe me to be. I'd had her in my arms again. I was holding her close, and in an instant, it felt as though I was back where we started.

"And you presume that you and your father are some of them? No, Lord Destrian, you all are not good men." There it was again, the name-calling, the insults. The hate in her voice was palpable.

I wanted to say something, anything, but the words were stuck in my throat. Instead, I turned and left her there, feeling a strange emptiness. Her words echoed in my mind, a bitter reminder of the chasm that existed between us. A chasm that, try as I might, I couldn't bridge.

THE SUN WAS NESTLING behind the ridgeline, painting the eastern sky with strokes of dusky pink and fading orange, when my friends and I approached the beach. The echo of hooves clattering on the stony path was mellowed by the rhythmic whispers of the approaching tide. A sea breeze carrying the scent of brine and kelp permeated the summer air. We rode along the beach, our horses' hooves skimming the waves, the steely blue waters undulating under the evening glow.

Marc rode with an air of easy confidence. His gaze was locked on the horizon, but I could see the sidelong glances he kept stealing at Araceli. Despite her chestnut curls getting tossed in the wind, she managed to look both regal and aloof, her gaze constantly evading Marc's. I felt bad for him sometimes. Araceli was clearly not interested, though I'd often wondered why. I *usually* enjoyed having Marc as a roommate. He was nice, though his family was far more conservative than those from the East. If he would just shut his mouth with his opinions, then maybe he would get somewhere with her. After all, no lady liked being lectured.

I thought back to my encounters with Rowyn in Helena.

Those weren't lectures though. I was simply informing the uninformed.

Behind us Idris attempted to charm Lisbet and Ellora with his witty banter, though it would never go very far with Ellora and we all knew it. Marc was far more protective of a brother than I'd ever been, probably because I was the youngest. Marc knew Idris entirely too well to agree to any form of romance with his sibling. Still, Idris was fun. His laughter was infectious and easily spread among the ladies. They liked being flirted with, even if it never went anywhere.

Ingrid, as always, rode next to me, her dark eyes gleaming in the fading light. Every time I stole a glance at her, her cheeks would bloom a delicate shade of pink, her smile never failing to evoke one of my own. She was at her playful best around me. Her spirit unrestrained. She had an innate talent for saying just the right thing at the right moment.

Ladies of Caldeaon were among the most talented of the West, and probably the East too. Though it was Ingrid's father who held the noble title, there was a matriarchy within the Byrnes that had been active for several generations, and it emphasized a lady's education. Ingrid and her sister, Lisbet, were extremely learned. They could speak multiple languages, drew extremely well, played instruments, and had a myriad of other hobbies and skills that would be desirous in a noble wife. Any man would be lucky to be with them. *I* was lucky to have caught Ingrid's attention.

Marc was right. I shouldn't mess it up.

As we rode along, Ingrid turned to me. "Destrian, you must accompany me to the SeaPort market. Lisbet and I discovered a sweet stall while you were off questing that you absolutely must try. Their almond cakes are a treat straight from the gods."

I felt my lips curl into a half-hearted smile. "A market visit? I don't have much available time on free days. I have to keep up correspondence with Helena." I tried to keep my friends from knowing how bad it was at home with my father's governing. It wouldn't do for them to run home and tell their parents that Helena was weak. Marc suspected though.

Ingrid shot me a pouting look, her brows furrowing in playful disapproval. "Destrian, I understand your obligations, but it's just a sweet stall, not a conquest."

I chuckled at her reply. It was true. My duties often clouded my judgment, and she always reminded me to seek comfort, to taste the sweetness of life. Yet, it wasn't the allure of the sweet stall that made me hesitate, but rather the swarm of correspondence waiting for me back in Helena. There was just far too much to do and far too little free time.

As Ingrid continued to tell me about the sweet stall, my thoughts drifted to someone else.

Rowyn.

She lingered in my thoughts, the echoes of my past mistakes haunting my mind. I couldn't seem to get away from her, as she seemed to follow me from class to class, her presence beckoning me toward her. While the company of friends provided a welcome distraction, it was in solitude that the storm of my thoughts roared loudest.

My gaze turned to Ingrid, her profile highlighted by the dying rays of the setting sun. Her charm was undeniable, her spirit a beacon in the tempest.

But Rowyn . . . Rowyn was the storm.

Ingrid, as though reading my thoughts, turned to Ellora. "How is your new roommate settling in?" she asked. An innocent enough question if you disregarded her sneer.

Ellora shook her head under Marc's questioning glare. "I hid my gold and jewelry during lunchtime," she admitted. "I honestly can't fathom why the masters would allow a common thief to attend school at Solridge. Don't they think about the dangers to the rest of us?"

"I can't fathom why they allow their women to mark their skin so," Marc muttered with a shake of his head.

"Isn't that the Morganite way?" Araceli asked with a glare at Marc. "We haven't even given her a chance to settle in."

Like I said, the man should know when to shut his mouth.

Ingrid leaned forward in her saddle as though she were about to bestow a secret. "I heard that Morganite women are complete harlots. They save nothing for the marriage bed."

"Who told you that?" Araceli's eyes narrowed.

"Our maid," Lisbet said, nodding in assent. "She has a brother who lives in Morgania."

My mind flashed back to the Morganite clansmen and their vile accusation on the southern road. "That's not true," I snapped, gripping my reins. "I'm from Morgania and I've never heard that."

There was a long, uneasy silence.

It was Marc who finally broke it. "What do you make of her powers?"

I considered my words carefully, taking a moment

to gaze out at the darkening sea. "Think about it." I glanced at each of them in turn. "If she is trained, if her powers are honed and directed . . . what then?"

Marc furrowed his brow, obviously not liking where my thoughts were heading. I pressed on. "So far, she has been an asset to Morgania, despite how she was raised."

There was a pause, the sound of the tide and our horses' breaths the only punctuations in the silence. The others seemed to wrestle with their thoughts, discomfort clear on their faces. Eventually, however, there were nods of begrudging agreement. As much as they disliked the idea of Rowyn in Solridge, the prospect of what her abilities could mean for the empire was not something they could easily dismiss.

As we rode further onto the beach, two figures came into view. I recognized Fin and Rowyn, though I worried for a moment when I saw Rowyn with a bow and arrow in her hands. Did something happen?

"Should you two be riding alone?" Marc asked from beside me, likely thinking the same thing.

I looked at Rowyn, hoping that our chance meeting wouldn't devolve into further insults, especially in front of my friends. Here I'd been defending her, and she couldn't even spare me a kind word.

"Gillius said that I could leave as long as I was

accompanied by someone else," Rowyn retorted, securing her weapons on the saddle.

"Bandits roam the southern road from time to time," Araceli remarked, though her voice held its usual kindness. "It's better to go out in a large group."

I snorted. Among other things, advice was something Rowyn despised. "Rowyn can take care of herself," I said, nodding to her bow. "She's the only rogue here."

"Come." Lady Ingrid sniffed. "I don't want to be watching my purse all evening."

I bit back any defense I had for Rowyn in the face of Ingrid and all my other friends. Ingrid wasn't wrong, after all. Rowyn and her entire clan were thieves . . . but she certainly wasn't being nice about it.

We rode back in silence, the beach steadily retreating behind us.

The familiar, comforting presence of my friends did little to quell the restless thoughts that dwelled in the recesses of my mind. As the evening drew to a close, I was left with the disquieting realization that the tranquil life of Solridge was starting to lose its charm, overshadowed by Rowyn's volatile presence.

Chapter 14

THE TRAINING YARD WAS FILLED with the usual sounds of clanging metal, grunts of exertion, and the occasional thud of a man falling. It was an orchestra of combat, a melody I was well-acquainted with. Among the young men of Solridge, weapons training was a fundamental routine, one that even the Lyons could not evade, despite their preferences for less physical pastimes.

Rowyn's presence was like a stone thrown into a calm pond, disrupting the rhythm of the morning ritual. Her attire was practical, the soft fabric of her dresses replaced with form-fitting breeches and a simple shirt. A ripple of discomfort spread through the men as they registered her arrival. Their eyes studied her curves. I found my grip on my weapon tightening involuntarily.

The words of doubt and scorn filled the air around us, but she seemed unaffected. Her eyes were alive with the spark I'd seen on the road. With that spark came a feeling of relief. Her back was rigid as she eyed the young men around me with the ferocity that I'd missed since Ayastaren.

Her eyes met mine, then slid away. Color blossomed in her cheeks. I gritted my teeth, remembering her words from the day before, then turned back to Tudor who stood across from me.

"I don't know what the masters are thinking," Tudor muttered under his breath. "Letting her join us in the mornings. As though we need that kind of distraction."

"She defeated one of Helena's best knights in a duel," I remarked.

Marc and Idris had stepped back to their spots beside us and were looking at me. "Could she win against you?" Idris asked, his dark eyes going back to her slight figure.

"Probably not," I said, following his gaze as Rowyn moved into an empty training area with Lord Alexander. "But she'd keep me on my toes. It wouldn't be an easy fight."

Rowyn began demonstrating her skills. Every move she made was fluid, calculated. There was an undeniable grace in the way she handled the weapons, a skill that was usually honed over years of practice. Even among the ridicule and the jests, she held her own with skill and focus.

I could see the other men watching her, their expressions a mix of confusion and admiration. Even the

Lyons seemed taken aback by her skill, their crude jokes replaced with surprised silence.

Eventually, Tudor was ready to finish our practice match. I tried to ignore the girl shooting arrows across the yard, but when it was time to wrap up, I allowed myself to steal another glance at her.

She looked angry. Hurt.

A part of me wanted to see what was wrong. But I knew better. I had learned the hard way that Rowyn was not one to welcome assistance. Each time I had tried to help, to offer guidance or simply be there for her, she had pushed me away with fiery words and scathing remarks. It left a bitter taste in my mouth, to be met with such resistance despite my genuine intentions.

I exhaled a long breath, my gaze locked on Rowyn as she disappeared into the school. I tore my eyes away and turned to leave the training ground, feeling a pang of longing.

I SAT IN THE BACK of the lecture room, my attention wandering from my assigned work. My gaze drifted to the front, where Rowyn was seated next to Fin in a spot that I'd occupied not long ago. I still remembered the feeling of relief the moment I'd realized that Fin's notes were superior to Sir Walter's lectures. I'd sat next to her from that day on, sneaking peeks at her parchment and copying her scrawl.

Now, Rowyn sat at Fin's side, her jaw set in determination. She was struggling.

Sir Walter, the aged professor of mathematics, hobbled over to Rowyn's desk, a sour expression on his face. He was notoriously impatient. He peered over her shoulder at the parchment, his frown deepening.

Sir Walter's condescending tone cut through the air like a blade. His words were laced with disdain.

"It is utterly astonishing that the people who supposedly educated you failed to teach you even the basics of numbers." Sir Walter sneered, his brows furrowed with displeasure. "Mathematics is an essential skill, a language of logic and precision that every educated individual should possess. Yet, here you are, stumbling through the most elementary concepts."

Rowyn glared up at him with stormy eyes. There was no fear in her gaze, no embarrassment or shame. She met his frustration with her own, refusing to be cowed. Sir Walter huffed in irritation and stamped off, leaving her to struggle with the problem alone.

Quietly, Fin slid a notebook toward Rowyn,

catching her eye briefly. Her gesture was subtle, a silent show of support. Rowyn's lips twitched with a hint of gratitude before her gaze dropped back down to the parchment. She crossed something off with a swift, angry stroke of her quill and then paused, her eyes narrowing as she stared at the equation. After a moment, she started the problem again, her quill scratching against the parchment in determined strokes.

I found myself smiling. Rowyn wasn't the type to give up easily. She didn't back down when faced with challenges, didn't let others' disapproval sway her. It was admirable, that resilience of hers.

"Lord Destrian, are you paying attention?" Sir Walter's voice brought me back to reality. I quickly returned my gaze to my own parchment.

Chapter 15

I FELT THE MAGIC BUILDING in the air from the forge. I wondered if Idris was practicing his blasting—the concentration was so strong—but when the sunlight dimmed outside the forge windows, I calmed my fires and stepped out.

A dark cloud hung over Solridge, black as night.

"Do you feel that?" I asked, seeing Marc and Idris walking toward the stable. Marc's tracking was pretty sensitive to magical workings.

"Yeah, it's the Morganite," Marc said, his eyes going to the hill where Rowyn and Gillius were standing, the cloud practically boiling above them. "She's going to lose it."

The blast of air swept us against the side of the stable. I cursed, getting back up and helping Idris to his feet. Lord Alexander was already at the door to the school, looking out to the hills beyond.

Lord Alexander's eyes met mine. "Check on the farmers and make sure it didn't reach them," he said, always wary of how Solridge's magic was viewed by the villagers and common people around SeaPort. Not all of us were like the Lyons, who never cared about their actions affecting others.

Idris, Marc, and I ran to the stables and led our horses out before mounting. I galloped up the hill, unable to stop myself from checking on Rowyn first.

"What was that? The whole of Solridge is in an uproar!" I shouted, reining in my horse to come to a halt.

"Rowyn couldn't keep herself under control!" Master Gillius yelled back, his usual calm demeanor in tatters. His voice filled with a mixture of frustration and disappointment. He stormed away, leaving Rowyn looking up at me with watery eyes.

Sympathy bubbled within me. We all made mistakes in the beginning, trying to get control of ourselves. It wasn't her fault that her mistakes were so catastrophic.

Marc broke through my thoughts. "We must go. Lord Alexander asked us to check on the families that farm down the way and inspect the damage."

"Let me go with you," Rowyn said, turning those watery eyes back to me as though she could see how weak she made me feel.

"Lord Alexander didn't mention you," Idris said, obviously irritated that his morning plans had been sent asunder.

"Please," Rowyn said.

I shook my head, gritting my teeth. "Idris is right. The masters don't want you off the grounds."

Rowyn grabbed my stirrup, her eyes full . . . so hopeful. I refused to believe she had no idea how she made me feel when she looked at me like that. She had to know I'd be unable to resist. "I'm sorry for what I said before, but I'm asking for your help now."

I sighed, extending my hand towards her, my fingers tingling with anticipation, as though they longed to touch her again.

"Fine, but you'll have to face them when you return," I murmured. As she took my offered hand and gracefully swung her legs over Valor's back, exhilaration began to pump through me. The warmth of her body sent shivers down my spine. I inhaled sharply, hoping she couldn't feel the wild thumping of my heart against her chest.

I tried to focus on catching up to Idris and Marc and found them at the base of a nearby hillside. A home had once been there, its quaint appearance now marred by the devastating impact of Rowyn's magic. The sight of the distraught farmer digging through the debris for his wife was heart-wrenching.

Idris was quick to react, and soon we were all wading through the rubble. Relief washed over us when the farmer's wife was found alive, coughing but miraculously unharmed. Idris wasted no time in getting her to Master Gillius.

The farmer, surprisingly, was not angry but thankful that his wife was alive. He had handled it far better than any of us expected.

"I'm so sorry," Rowyn said, her eyes on the ruined home. "I'll help you rebuild."

I stepped forward, but Willim was already shaking his head. "No, a lady of Solridge doesn't belong out here, toiling in the dirt."

Rowyn, the stubborn girl that she was, would not be dissuaded. "I give you my word. As soon as we check on the others, I'll be back."

"Nay, you won't be," Willim grunted. "You've much to do, and you've saved us all from a worse fate."

Marc glared at me, and I dutifully leaped onto Valor's back and hauled Rowyn up in front of me to check on the remaining farms. Rowyn was lucky. Though everyone was startled, their homes didn't suffer damage, and no one else was injured. Relieved, I turned Valor toward Solridge.

"I said I was going to help him!" Rowyn said suddenly as we passed the damaged home.

I took a deep breath, trying to calm my irritation. Did she not forget the assassin? Did she still not understand how precious she was? "No, Gillius told you he doesn't want you off the grounds without others present. We'd best return to Solridge."

"I gave him my word!" Her voice echoed in the quiet meadow.

"He said himself he doesn't expect you to keep it, and besides, I'm hungry," I reasoned, trying to persuade her. But before I could finish, she was off the horse, her determination as clear as day.

"Rowyn! Blast you!" I called out. As I watched her determined figure storm away, I reluctantly followed, trying to keep my rising apprehension at bay.

"Come back! You could get hurt. Besides, you don't even know how to help him!" Her headstrong nature was both her biggest strength and her greatest weakness. But Rowyn, as always, was unfazed.

"Yes, I do. I helped at home when it was time to create new quarters. I've built before," she shot back.

"You have?" The spark in her eyes had returned. I both feared and admired it.

"I did this, Destrian. It's up to me to help right it. It's only fair."

With that, she continued toward the rubble, leaving me there like some lovestruck idiot.

I looked at the devastation one last time before following her. "Blast you, Rowyn," I murmured under my breath. My horse's hooves thudded rhythmically against the ground.

Willim was already on the task of rebuilding his

home when we approached. I could see a flicker of surprise in his eyes as they landed on me. "I'd not dared to believe you'd be back."

"Well I'm here now. What can I do?" Rowyn offered, stepping forward with a sense of purpose that I couldn't help but admire.

"What can we do?" I echoed, trying to ignore the subtle undertone of discomfort that crept into my voice as I dismounted and tied my horse to a nearby post.

Willim guided us through the process of cutting the sod brick, and when he was satisfied with our efforts, he turned his attention to salvaging what was left of the wreckage.

"They'll worry about us," I pointed out after a while, sitting back and wiping the sweat from my brow. I was really going to hear an earful when I returned to Solridge, though I was sure that the masters would know who was to blame.

Still, I couldn't pass up the chance to be closer to her. I told myself it was in order to ingratiate myself towards her. Afterall, I was her overlord.

"No, they won't. Marc knows we're here. He'll tell the others," she reassured me as though she and Marc were friends. Marc and Idris had kept their word to me and stayed away from her. I made sure that the Lyons stayed away, too, though it was less about them fearing me and more about the fact that they were unsure of her.

"They'll be gossiping by nightfall," I added, wondering why I was concerned about rumors. I supposed I didn't want Ingrid to feel slighted. I *did* enjoy her company, and I *did* think she was very bright and pretty, but I wasn't entirely sure how much she actually liked me, or if she was more interested in becoming the wife to the wealthiest consulship in the Western Empire. As much time as we spent together, I had a really hard time knowing whether she was genuine.

"You're free to leave whenever you wish. I'm staying. Besides, I don't need to be watched over. I can take care of myself," she responded curtly, her focus on the work at hand.

I let out a slow breath.

Every. Time.

Rowyn had to snark at me every time I tried to speak with her. Why was she so against me helping her? Did she really think that my giving her assistance was a weakness? Everyone needed help from time to time. That was the first thing Lord Alexander had taught us in governance. You couldn't handle everything yourself, and if you tried, you would fail at everything.

"You're good at self-preservation—I'll give you that. But even you can be overwhelmed." I tried not to let my irritation show. Perhaps if I stayed calm, she wouldn't move past the yelling and onto the insults.

My show of serenity only incensed her more.

"Look," I said quickly, "you're Fin's friend. You may not believe me when I say this, but it means a lot that Fin has found someone she could be friends with at Solridge. Ellora, Ingrid, and the other ladies aren't especially nice to her. The circumstances of her birth can be a thorn in some high-borns' sides. She was lonely before you came."

"You mean . . . you and Fin?"

Oh, for the love of the gods. "No, we're just friends," I said, hoping to cut off the misunderstanding before it could take root. "Just take care of yourself, for her sake."

"I've never put myself in harm's way on purpose, my lord."

I couldn't help but snort. Did she really have so little understanding of herself? "Do you so quickly forget Ayastaren?"

That seemed to shake her, and I instantly regretted the harsh reminder. "I think about those children every day . . . How dare you!" Her voice trembled with emotion.

"I wasn't trying to accuse you," I tried to apologize. But it was too late. I had unwittingly struck a raw nerve. She was quick to her feet and stormed off, her hands clenched at her sides.

I shouldn't have let my thoughts and mouth get away from me. Rowyn always seemed to trigger something in me. I couldn't seem to think rationally when she was around.

"Rowyn, wait." I tried to call her back. She was deaf to my pleas. I got up and raced after her. "Rowyn!" I reached out, grabbed her arm, and spun her around to face me. We were close now, and I could see that the spark had turned into flames of anger, burning bright in her eyes.

"Why are you so quick to push me away?" I blurted out, frustration seeping into my voice. What did she see that was so wrong with me? Why did I keep making these mistakes? Why couldn't I stop myself from feeling this way?

I glanced down at her lips. What would happen if…

Shit. I needed to stop thinking that way.

Rowyn glared at me as though she loathed every fiber of my being. I had to stop myself from grabbing her shoulders and shaking her. Why couldn't she see who I actually was?

"I've fought against your kind my entire life," she

snarled. "How can you expect me to welcome your attention?"

Was she serious? Did she not understand that I was her overlord? Couldn't she see that the best way for her to get what she and her clan wanted was through me?

"I tried to understand you—remember? You never even gave me a chance to show you that you could trust me. Can you not see that it's in your clan's best interest?" Her words had left a sting, her accusations a painful reminder of the divisions between our worlds. We were two casualties caught in the crossfire of a war both of us had been born into and neither of us could help.

Rowyn balled her fists at her sides, trembling in anger. "You don't have the right to ask for friendship. After what your father did to my family? No, what you ask could never be!"

"You lie," I growled, my pride flaring. How could she lump me in with the sins of my forefathers? I wanted her to see me for who I truly was, not what hid in the shadows of my family's past.

"I saw it with my own eyes. I saw the devastation your father wrought with his fervor to end us. How can you stand here and say that none of that matters to you?"

194

I threw up my hands, exasperated. "I'm not my father, Rowyn. Even if what you say is true, I didn't do those things. I wasn't even there!"

"And if you were? Would that have changed anything! I've watched you stand idly by and let every manner of evilness happen without so much as a word. What of how your father spoke to me when I first came to Helena? Did you admonish him then? What about the poor beaten woman in Ayastaren? Did you say anything, do anything?"

Rowyn's words sliced through the very heart of me. Lashing me as though in punishment. "How about when the duke put his hands on me? Or when the family was hanged? Or when the Lyon brothers spread their wicked lies among you? You stood by and did nothing. So maybe you weren't there when your father made the order, but had you been, I know you wouldn't have stopped it, for you are the worst kind of coward, Destrian. You may well be skilled and brave in battle, but when it comes to stopping true evilness and speaking up for what is right, you choose the easy way every time—complete and utter silence."

I stood there, rooted in place, unable to defend myself against her accusations. She was right. I had stood by, a silent witness to the injustices that unfolded before my eyes. I had failed to speak up, to take action when it mattered most. The weight of my silence pressed heavily upon my conscience, reminding me of my shortcomings. She thought me a coward. A *coward*.

I wanted to explain, to tell her that I had my reasons, that I had struggled with the burden of my name and the expectations that came with it. I wanted to tell her that I *had* confronted the Lyons for her sake. But her words, delivered with such passion and conviction, rendered me speechless. The truth in her accusations stirred a mix of guilt, regret, and self-doubt.

The thought that Rowyn thought me so low...so vile... seemed to still my heart.

"Is that really what you think of me?" My voice was barely a whisper.

"Yes," she said with a defiant scowl.

I tried to formulate a response, to defend myself, but the words caught in my throat. Instead, I turned my gaze to the sprawling landscape stretching out before us, seeking solace in the vastness of the moor.

Why was Rowyn capable of cutting through to the very depths of me? "You're right," I admitted, the bitterness of truth tainting my words. "Let's just finish this and get back."

I had expected her to yell, to argue, but instead, she just sat next to me and resumed her work, her anger seemingly spent. The silence between us was deafening, and I could feel the resentment radiating off her. Or maybe it was my own.

WHEN THE SUN DIPPED LOW in the sky, Rowyn finally agreed to leave. Willim looked grateful, his gaze lingering over the large stack of bricks we'd prepared. I walked over to Valor and untied him from the post. Rowyn looked so exhausted that she could hardly hoist herself onto the horse.

"Here," I said, my hands on her waist.

I was surprised when she allowed me to lift her into the saddle. Once she was secure, I swung myself up behind her. With my arms around her waist, we began our journey back to the academy.

"They're going to be furious with you," I warned as the scent of her hair filled my nose. My heart seemed to stutter. Rowyn seemed to fit so well in my arms. Yet, she found my company so bothersome. She likely wished me dead.

"I had to right the wrongs I caused, my lord."

I sighed. "Please call me Destrian. This 'my lord' stuff is for the birds."

Her snort caught me by surprise. "Do you think the

197

sorcerers will let me come back tomorrow?"

"No, you've already missed your lessons for today. They'll be absolutely livid . . . with you and me, come to think of it. Lean back. I can't see."

Awkwardly, she did as I asked, her body conforming to mine. My mind seemed to go mad for a moment. My heart sang in my chest. I prayed she couldn't feel my desperation.

"You didn't have to stay," Rowyn mumbled after a while. I couldn't deny the pang of guilt her words caused. It distracted me from the feel of her. "But thank you. I'm glad you did."

"I was happy to," I barely got out. I never wanted this ride to end.

A moment of silence passed between us, broken by her soft voice. "What I said . . ."

"Don't speak of it," I interrupted, my heart still aching from her earlier accusations. "You were right. I can be a coward sometimes."

With her body pressed so close against mine, I was able to relish the scent of rain on her—a smell unique to Rowyn and something I found unexpectedly soothing. It brought a comfort even though her words from earlier still pricked at me.

We fell into a comfortable silence after that, the tension between us easing slightly. Despite our rocky relationship, there were moments like this—just the two of us under the vast sky—when everything else seemed to fade.

Chapter 16

THE MOST POPULAR ACTIVITY at Solridge, among the nobles, was to take evening walks in the gardens around the castle. We would chat, build early alliances, play stones in the path, and otherwise relax in each other's company, away from the common students who found refuge elsewhere.

During one of those evenings, I found myself strolling next to Ingrid and listening to her talk about the Parade of Arts that occurred every three years in Caldeaon.

"People come from all around," Ingrid was saying. "The inns are filled a month before the parade begins. It brings a lot of coin to the city, as you might imagine. Our tradesmen and artisans spend a full two years preparing for that weeklong festival. My mother is in charge of the planning, but my sisters and I help. I'm sure Ilisa is helping with the one coming up this summer."

"I always wanted to attend," I admitted, smiling down at her. It was easy to enjoy myself in Ingrid's company.

But Ingrid could also be cruel. Not in any overt way,

nothing that could be arguably seen as unladylike. Her meanness tended to lie beneath the surface. She preferred only to speak and interact with ladies who came from the "right" families. Everyone else was ignored and excluded. Fin and Galena had gotten it the worst, seeing how they were the lowest born at the school. Galena, being mute and a slave, at that, warranted barely a notice from Ingrid and Lisbet. Fin had come to Solridge a couple of years before, excited to make new friends. That excitement faded when she realized that she was distantly related to Lord Alexander and the Byrnes, and Ingrid took the same approach as Fin's father, General Ivar, and simply pretended she didn't exist.

"You should make an effort to come," Ingrid was saying, her eyes lightening as the eye of Sol sank over the stone towers of the school. "Bring your father. I was even thinking you could throw something like that in Helena. We see few northern consulships at the parade, but there must be artisans who would enjoy the competition, and there's loads of gold to be made with all the travelers who come into town . . . not that you need it," she said, her cheeks tinged a lovely shade of pink.

"It's a possibility," I said offhand. There were so many more important things for me to worry about with my seat: trying to dodge an uprising by the Mor-ganites, bolstering the guard, and countless other tasks that I had to get done while away from home.

As we continued walking, we passed the library win-dow, golden candlelight illuminating the tables and bookcases within. That's when I noticed Rowyn giving Pedr Tore her rapt attention while he strummed his lute.

I stopped in my tracks…stunned. Rowyn didn't like nobles. That was the entire reason she loathed my very existence. Yet there she was, leaning forward and smil-ing, her chin in her hand, all for Pedr Tore. He was nice, I supposed, though I thought him whiny at times. He was pitiful at weapons work but brilliant at govern-ance and history. He wasn't even handsome. His ears stuck out, not helped by whoever he hired to cut his hair, and he abhorred most forms of exercise.

But there she sat . . . with him . . . smiling.

Pedr Tore.

Fucking Pedr Tore.

The bane of my existence.

"Now that's a fitting couple," Ingrid said next to me, her eyes having followed mine.

I fought the burn that had started at my fingertips. "What do you mean?" I asked through clenched teeth.

Ingrid snorted. "Queer ducks flock together, do

they not?" she asked before turning and continuing on the path.

I flexed my fingers and took a deep breath, my eyes still on the window.

"Are you coming, my lord?" Ingrid asked. "The others wanted to compare notes on history."

"Yes," I said, ripping my eyes away from the tender scene. When I reached Ingrid, she wrapped her arm through mine and smiled up at me. I tried to return it, but my mind was still lurking in the library, wondering what Rowyn saw in Pedr that she didn't see in me.

"DESTRIAN!" MARC SAID, striding into our room with Idris in tow. "We need to talk."

I'd taken lunch in my room and was writing some directions for my father's steward, Til, who was beginning to balk at my orders. I would have to switch my correspondence to someone else at the castle that I trusted, quickly and at a distance. I hadn't made up my mind on who it would be yet.

Marc's usually stoic demeanor was replaced with a look of worry and anger, an unusual combination that immediately had me on alert. I rose. "What's going on?"

"It's about Rowyn," Marc began, his brows furrowed. "Apparently some *creature* attacked her and Galena while they were harvesting in a nearby meadow."

A chill ran down my spine at the mention of the assassin.

"Is everyone all right?" I asked quickly, my chest tightening. How many times could we count on Rowyn getting lucky?

"They're okay for now," Idris said, "but the masters seem to know about it, and nobody is giving us any information."

Whoever it was must still be targeting Rowyn. Even after all this time. Seeing her that day in the rain, broken, as the world she'd known was drifting away. I just . . . I kept going back to that moment. What was it she'd said? She was so used to everyone wanting to kill her? And there I was, whining and pouting that she shouldn't be my problem. Rowyn was right. I was a spoiled, entitled coward.

Marc's nostrils flared. "Did you know about this?"

"What do you mean?" I asked, the hackles on the back of my neck rising.

Marc's voice was measured, carefully enunciating each word. "Someone mentioned that she had been attacked before . . . Did you know about that?" Marc's eyes were bright and he was being far too careful with his words. He was upset about something.

"Whoever it was didn't show their face again on the road, nor in Solridge until now," I retorted. "I didn't even think to mention it. I was more worried about the Lyons."

"My *sister* shares a room with her!" Marc yelled. "My fucking family, Des! My blood!" Marc clenched his fist and thumped it against his chest. "You're telling me that you knew there's some murderous creature after Rowyn? You all have put Ellora in danger! What if he gets past the wards?"

Shit. He was right. I felt a surge of anger, not at Rowyn, but at the situation. Rowyn didn't ask for any of this, but she was stuck in the middle of it, a target for a creature we knew nothing about.

"I'm sorry I didn't tell you," I admitted, holding my hands open and out. Idris was obviously taking Marc's side, his arms crossed, eyes narrowed. "I honestly thought we were past it."

"So, you really just meet this odd girl from the woods and warn all of us away so you can baby her through Solridge? You put the rest of our lives at stake so she won't get her feelings hurt?" Marc asked.

"Are you serious?" I snarled. "How do *you* not see

how important she is?"

"Oh, I see that she's *very* important . . . to you," Marc drawled. "Far more important than the rest of us. You've made that abundantly clear."

"Knock it off," I growled. "You have no idea what's at stake for me!" How could Marc understand what it felt like to have Gryse, and Ayastaren, and every other noble in the empire out to get you and what you have?

"But clearly it's our friendship that isn't," Marc finished before turning and striding out of the door.

Idris was glaring at me.

"What, are you here to tell me there's something wrong with me too?" I asked, turning my back on him.

"Maybe Elias is right," Idris said, his voice calm but patronizing. "You think you can just collect all the pretty girls and pop them in your back pocket? First, we can't talk to Fin because you're afraid we'll be mean to her. Ingrid is off-limits because she's so obviously fawning all over you, and now Rowyn. Are you going to pick one?"

White flames licked up in the fireplace. I froze, my fists clenched at my sides. Idris was, quite literally, playing with fire. "I'm just trying to offer them some form of protection. It's not like anyone else is bothering to take their safety into hand."

"Seriously? No one is trying to take care of *Rowyn*?

All of the masters are taking her studies and welfare seriously. She doesn't need you."

"I just . . . I know how we nobles can be sometimes, especially to the ladies, and—"

"Why are you even friends with us if you think we're such terrible people?" Idris asked, cutting me off.

"I don't think you're a terrible person." I glared at him as I went to open a window. The flames in the fireplace faded to orange. "I'm sorry that you see it that way. That was not what I intended. You can talk to Fin . . . or Rowyn . . . or Ingrid, whoever you like. I don't have a claim to any of them."

I was beginning to hate myself. Every instinct was failing me. I'd fucked everything up and was doing everything wrong, and my entire world was crumbling. I was about to lose everything.

"None of us want to talk to Rowyn. She scowls too much," Idris snapped. "Why can't you just admit you like her?"

"Who?" I asked, my throat closing. It was obvious who he meant. Yet, I had trouble admitting it to myself.

"Exactly," Idris said, shaking his head and leaving me.

I stood at the fireplace, watching the wood burn, feeling as though my life was crumbling into ashes.

Chapter 17

THE NEXT EVENING, I walked through the garden again, this time alone so I could freely watch Rowyn and Pedr talk over a pile of books. Rowyn was frowning but not in the angry way she seemed to reserve just for me. No, her lips were quivering.

My heart stuttered to a halt.

Tears collected at the corner of her eyes, before spilling over, running down her cheeks.

The burn seared through my chest. I moved, striding to the first door I saw, and hurtled toward the library.

As I approached the doors, I slowed, taking a deep breath, my head bowed as I pushed the door open.

Rowyn's eyes widened when she saw me. Pedr looked over his shoulder.

"I was just coming for a book," I said, hoping neither would see through the lie. "I didn't mean to interrupt."

"It's no matter," Pedr said quickly, sweeping his books into his arms. "I must be getting back to my room anyway . . . Rowyn?"

Rowyn wiped her cheeks as she followed Pedr.

No.

I grabbed her arm and held her back.

"Are you all right?" I asked, studying her. "Pedr, he didn't . . . ." Because if he did, he would be ashes on the floor.

"What? No, of course not!" Rowyn exclaimed, wiping her eyes. "It's nothing, Destrian, just dusty in there."

"You must think me a fool," I said, my heart sinking in disappointment. Rowyn didn't trust me. She would never let me see her so vulnerable. Yet she trusted Pedr. Pedr Tore, who she'd only just met.

I watched them hurry down the hall together, Rowyn glancing back at me over her shoulder.

Why? Why did the gods make a mockery of my life?

I couldn't return to my room. Marc was there, and it was awkward as he kept his distance.

I went to blow off some magic in the forge. If I didn't, I would lose my ever-loving mind.

Pedr. Fucking. Tore.

Why did Rowyn go to him? Why did she go to *him*? I chided myself. There wasn't anything wrong with Pedr. We had none of the same interests and pretty much nothing in common since he wasn't a sorcerer, nor an heir, nor interested in weapons, which in theory would be fine. Yet I found myself hating that pitiable boy. And I shouldn't hate him. I was just . . . literally fucking up my entire life for Rowyn, and she didn't even care to notice.

WITHIN THE CONFINES of Solridge Academy, a myriad of activities filled each day. However, none seemed to command my attention more than the sight of Rowyn. Despite the hum of activities around me, her presence was as undeniable as the pull of the moon on the tides.

I found my eyes drawn to her as she trained with Fin and Araceli, her expression serious as she walked through different motions with them. I felt my heart echo to the rhythm of her blades, every swing resonating within me.

Later, as I leaned against the wall outside class, talking to Marc, I noticed Rowyn, Fin, and Pedr hurrying toward us. Gods, the others were already talking about her . . . and him. I wondered if that was why Marc had been friendlier the past couple of days. I listened as Rowyn and Pedr made plans to join each other in the library *again* that night. She could meet with him *every night*, yet couldn't spare me a kind word or a moment's notice?

We took our seats and began, the discussion soon turning to the ongoing troubles in Lyrica, the drought and plague, the economic decline, and rising discontent. The subjects were heavy, but the tension became palpable when the topic shifted to the empire's exploitation of Morgania.

I glanced back at Rowyn, knowing she had strong opinions on the issues. I wondered what was going through her mind. Thankfully, I didn't have to wonder long.

"What's wrong with these people?" Idris asked from Marc's other side. "Lyrica built schools and expanded trade throughout the entire empire. They loved us when we were wealthy; they took all the advantages we afforded them. Now when it's time to save the empire from ruin, they swing the blade. Ungrateful is what they are. Treason is anyone who would seek to rise against the empire." Idris looked around as though the rest of us couldn't help but agree with him.

"That's an interesting perspective. Would anyone else care to share?" Lord Alexander asked, looking around calmly.

"How can we put the burden of feeding the empire onto the shoulders of so small a territory?" I asked, knowing that it would lower me in the standings of my friends, yet possibly raise me in Rowyn's esteem. It wasn't that I was doing it for her though. I really did believe it. I just hadn't had the courage to say anything before. "Is it fair to strip the farmers of Morgania the fruits of their labors?"

Idris's eyes were wide as he stared at me. "Have you ever seen the starving? Their bodies are sunk in. They look like walking skeletons. You wouldn't be so quick to dismiss their suffering if you had. While your and Rowyn's people remain fat and nourished from your land, the rest of us are wasting away."

"You're certainly not wasting away," a clear voice said behind me.

Marc twisted in his seat, glaring at Rowyn. "Surely, everyone knows that rising will only lead to more destruction, more death. The empire will always have a vast army. You'd be foolish thinking you could overcome it."

"Marc brings up a fair point, but I, for one, would like to hear what Rowyn has to say since she comes from a different background. She may add perspective to the discussion," Lord Alexander said, his eyes on Marc and Idris fuming beside me.

Everyone turned to stare at Rowyn, which gave me the opportunity to look at her without feeling self-conscious.

212

Her eyes were on Pedr.

"Well, we Morganites feel differently on the matter. We were never welcome in the empire in the first place. The Lyricans drove us west, then crossed the sea and retook our lands again. You all did your damnedest to wipe us off the very earth during The Cleansing. So, I suppose I don't see why you feel we should be grateful to the empire for anything, Idris."

"The Cleansing was a long time ago. You can't fault us now for something our forefathers did," Idris challenged.

"Maybe so, but Morganites are still persecuted today. Where have our temples gone? Our traditions? Many outside our clan refuse to work with us. The Lyricans spread lies that we are thieves and murderers while stealing the bread from our tables!"

That comment was directed at me. I could feel the weight of her gaze as I turned forward. Maybe if I played her a little song on the lute, she would lighten up. Perhaps she and I were just too alike.

"Maybe we're hoping you vile heathens will die off," Elias said from the other side of the room.

Rowyn stood, her hands slamming against her desk. "Do you see what I mean? Right there! That's why we don't conform to your beloved empire. That's why we'll never follow any of you. Living under the empire has only brought us death and destruction. So if that's what comes from rebelling, then so be it. We know no other way."

I WATCHED ROWYN all through dinner. The conflicting emotions within me battled for dominance—the desire to reach out and the wariness of being rebuffed once again. It was a maddening cycle, one that left me feeling torn and uncertain. Dare I risk feeling like a fool again? I wasn't entirely sure I could take another refusal.

The memories of our initial encounters played out in my mind like a montage of missteps and missed opportunities. The arguments with Gillius, the jabs and taunts directed at Rowyn about her heritage—it all came rushing back with a surge of remorse.

How could I have been so blind? So callous? I'd let my pride and ignorance guide my actions, failing to see the impact they would have on Rowyn, not realizing how vulnerable she was. And when she needed protection the most, when danger loomed over her like a dark cloud, I had faltered. The weight of that failure pressed heavily upon me, weighing down my conscience.

I gritted my teeth, frustration and self-loathing intertwining in a tangled knot. I wished I didn't care so deeply, didn't think about her incessantly. But the truth was undeniable—Rowyn occupied my thoughts in a way that no one else ever had. Her presence had become an unrelenting force that seemed to pull me in, despite either of our wishes.

Yet, despite my desire to show her my remorse, my sincere efforts to change, I couldn't shake the fear that she would never forgive me. It pained me to think that she might forever view me as an adversary, a reminder of the pain I had caused.

Rowyn possessed a strength that surpassed anyone I had ever encountered, an unyielding spirit that refused to be broken. And yes, there was no denying that she was beautiful. Her features held a fierce grace. But it was her strength, her tenacity, that truly captivated me. In a world where power and cunning often reigned, Rowyn stood as a beacon of unyielding resolve.

I couldn't give up. I couldn't let my regrets and doubts consume me entirely. I had to continue trying, continue showing her through my actions that I was sincere in my remorse and my desire to make amends. I longed for her to see the efforts I was making, to understand that I had learned from my mistakes.

I rose when Rowyn did and followed her. I grabbed her arm as she entered the hall and she turned, her brows raised when she saw it was me.

"I apologize for the others in class," I said. I smiled, hoping she would accept my peace offering but steeling myself if she didn't. "Not all of us nobles have the same mind in terms of governance."

"That's all right," Rowyn replied, continuing on her path toward the library with me beside her. "You were gallant in your views."

"It's what I honestly believe." I wished she would walk slower. "I try not to go against what seems right in my head."

Rowyn nodded. "I hadn't realized that you and your father were against Morgania's harvests being carted away."

"When the people are happy, the rulers will be happy." I shrugged. "I understand they're doing what they feel is right. The needs of the many outweigh the needs of the few. But in Morgania, our people are joining the rest of the empire's unrest because of it. So now there are even more unhappy people, not to mention the war. Of course, it will all change now."

"How do you figure?" Rowyn asked, stopping outside the library doors. This was our most pleasant interaction yet, and I didn't want it to end. I leaned against the doors, blocking her from going in. I hoped she didn't notice.

"The war is winding down," I said with more relief than she knew. "People are starting to return home and, well . . ." I almost didn't finish.

I'd watched Rowyn closely in the past weeks. Ever since we'd met in Helena, if I was honest with myself. I was astounded to conclude that Rowyn had absolutely no idea how important she was. She was exactly what the empire needed. A girl from the wilds with a rigid moral code for what was right and what was wrong. And she had the power to save us all.

This was a sorceress who held the upper hand in every negotiation she'd be in. By mastery, this girl would have all the bargaining power. There wasn't anything she wouldn't be able to get. It was unreal, a gods-beloved princess, and she was ignorant of it all.

So why was I finding it so hard to tell her that?

"We have you," I said simply, resisting the eloquent speech on the tip of my tongue about what she meant to me. What she could mean to the empire.

"Don't say that," Rowyn said softly with a shake of her head.

It shouldn't be this hard to convince her of how much good she was bringing to the world. "It's true, though. The drought has already ended here at

Solridge. The harvest will be plentiful and the market full. Since we're right by the port, that food is making its way east to the others who are starving, and the people here are making quite a profit from it. Lady Madeline said even the bog is returning. The region's changed in a short time, and you're the reason for it."

Rowyn was looking at me as though she were trying to piece me together in her mind. I hoped that this time, she would see me for who I wanted to be, and not who I'd been to her before.

"Well," Rowyn said, "you've given me plenty to think about."

I nodded. Rowyn shifted her feet, her eyes on the door. She was ready to get back to Pedr and grace him with her pretty smiles. It was I who wasn't ready to give her up.

"So, how are you enjoying Solridge so far?" I asked.

"It's all right, I suppose. It's far from home."

I nodded, wishing she would give me more. I wanted her to tell me what she thought of Fin, and Solridge, and anything else that would keep her standing in front of me.

"What about you?" Rowyn asked. "Fin says there are more powerful friends to be made at the capital. Why didn't your father send you there?"

So, Rowyn was curious about me. She'd thought

enough about me to wonder, then ask. Hope swelled in my chest, warming it. "She's right, but my father has never liked the capital. He's only been a handful of times and prefers me closer to home."

"Have you ever been there before?"

"I have. Actually, I was just at the capital this spring with Lord Alexander and a couple of others. I left from there to visit my father in Morgania when you came to our halls."

Rowyn looked suspicious. "What were you doing there?"

Memories flashed behind my eyes. "I'd just finished questing for my gem. Lord Alexander had gone with me to Yliria as my companion, so we decided to visit the capital on our way back and met Gillius there. It was quite a grand place. Everything that people have gushed about is true: gold plating in the great hall, delicious food every night, all sorts of entertainment throughout the city. The people there, though." Gods, the nobles of the east made the nobles of the west look like amateurs. It was a cutthroat bid for power within every hall. "Honestly, it was kind of frightening in a way."

"I hope never to set foot there," Rowyn said vehemently.

I'd heard her say it so much. I thought back to the

book in the library back home. My eyes went down to her rose marking. The intricately inked petals emanated a wild beauty. Yet, beneath the fragile allure of the petals, there lay a subtle menace—an arrangement of thorns, sharp and formidable.

"I know," I said, hearing a light step prepare to turn the corner. I knew who it was before she spoke.

"Destrian!" Ingrid called, her smile false as she waved to me. She shot a glare at Rowyn that set me on edge. "You promised to throw stones with the rest of us in the garden, remember?" Ingrid turned back to me, her expression softening. I recognized the act immediately. "Lord Marc is boasting that he'll best you, but I know how prideful you are."

"Of course, Lady Ingrid, how could I forget," I said since there wasn't anything else I could say with Rowyn standing right there. But I turned to her, the hope refusing to retreat. "You should join us. You could probably beat Marc yourself if you put your mind to it."

"We already have even teams," Ingrid said, her hand clenched at her side. She gave Rowyn her false smile. "But you could watch if you'd like. There'd be no harm in that."

Rowyn rolled her eyes and turned to me. "Thank you, but no. I was meeting Lord Pedr to talk about a book. But I hope you enjoy yourself."

"Well, we would hate to keep Lord Pedr waiting, wouldn't we, Destrian?" Lady Ingrid said pointedly.

I gritted my teeth but took Ingrid's hand. It wouldn't do to throw everything away and anger one of the more prominent families of the Fens.

But as I walked out into the garden, I felt lighter, my burdens momentarily lifted by the hope that Rowyn had finally chosen to see me, if only for a fleeting moment.

And I did beat Marc at stones.

Chapter 18

I SHOULDN'T HAVE BEEN SURPRISED that Rowyn would be terrible with a shield. Lord Alexander had started Rowyn on sword work and insisted she manage how to incorporate a shield. Rowyn actively struggled. Lord Alexander didn't understand that Morganites used the terrain as a shield in most cases. They made fighting in forests and mountains an art form, one that we had yet to learn.

Rowyn fought, her defiance and strength more evident than ever. I couldn't keep my eyes off her sweat-drenched skin that seemed to glow in the morning sun, her stormy eyes alight with a challenge. The crease above her nose grew deeper as practice continued.

My father had told me about falling in love. He said it felt awful and scary and was the most wonderful feeling, sometimes all at once. That was how I felt around Rowyn. An ache had been building in my chest, and now it was a pulsing heat. Her presence seemed to invade every part of me until I even began to dream of her.

But shadows of words unsaid lurked within those dreams. I needed to tell her what I knew about her legacy.

Then where would I be? She would have the world at her feet, and who was I? A consul's son from the mountain wilderness. I wasn't enough.

Not for her.

"Can you focus?" Marc snapped when I tripped a second time.

"Sorry," I mumbled, turning my focus back to him.

We went through the motions again, this time with me in step with Marc and hitting the stance. Marc nodded and walked with me to put our blades up.

"Listen," he said, his eyes on Rowyn as she trudged into breakfast. "What is your deal with Rowyn and Ingrid?"

There was no agreement between Ingrid and me. Apparently, if a noble were not completely deranged, ladies fawned all over them. Ingrid had staked her claim to me, and I'd let her to a point, but I'd never sent a formal request to her house.

Ingrid would make an excellent nobleman's wife. But she would hate Morgania. I knew she viewed my wealth as something she could help me spend, but I already had an immense list in my head, and most of what she was passionate about wasn't on it.

My father had not stopped spending money out of sheer neglect; he just didn't trust himself to be the one to spend it. He was saving it for me, as my right, and I refused to be distracted by Ingrid trying to turn Helena into a northern Caldeaon. It would never be that. Morgania was cold and brutal. It was magnificent, but with the mountains and magic steeped into the forests, it was the most dangerous area of the west.

Ingrid would wither away there when she realized I couldn't give her what she wanted. Not from myself, nor Helena. She deserved better for herself.

I often wondered if she was using me to protect her from Elias. If that was the case, then I was content just letting myself be used because I enjoyed her friendship. I just knew her limitations.

"They both care quite a bit about my title, though their feelings are opposite," I said.

"It's Rowyn who has you all tied up, isn't it?" Marc asked with a frown.

"Don't tell anyone," I said with a sigh. I'd barely just admitted it to myself. There was no reason to spread my feelings to everyone else. Especially since Rowyn didn't return them.

"Have you told her? How you feel?" Marc asked.

I shook my head. We'd only managed a single conversation without bickering.

"You never know what she will say if you don't tell her," Marc commented, walking next to me in the building.

"Thanks," I said, bumping his elbow with mine. "I'm sorry—about before. I shouldn't have been such an idiot. Of course, you were upset. I would've been too."

Marc nodded. "It happened; it's done with. Have you found anything out about the creature yet?"

I shook my head. I didn't have time with my obligations to Helena weighing me down.

"Are you coming to the gardens tonight?" Marc went on.

I shook my head again. "I'm going to work tonight. I need to think."

Marc clapped me on the back, and I felt relieved that we were back to as we were.

THAT EVENING, I WENT to the forge, the familiar smell of heated metal and ash bringing me comfort. The rhythm of the hammer on the anvil served as a distraction from my thoughts, something tangible I could control.

As the heat of the forge mirrored my anger, the

weight of the hammer in my hands became an extension of my frustration. Each hit was a word unsaid, a feeling suppressed, a beat to the symphony of my internal turmoil. The way my heart seemed to skip a beat every time I saw her, how my mind lingered on every word she said. Slowly but surely, the rhythm of the forge began to replace the chaos of my thoughts, each blow of the hammer a step toward regaining my control.

I couldn't just let her go. I'd tried and failed. I would try and fail again. Sometimes, I wished I'd not let myself get so entangled in this web of feelings.

My grip tightened around the hammer, my knuckles white with the effort. With every hit, I tried to carve out my frustration, my jealousy. But the metal, much like my feelings for Rowyn, remained stubborn and resilient, refusing to bend to my will.

As I left the forge, I recognized a figure down in the practice yards, shield in hand as they danced around a practice dummy.

Marc was right.

I had to tell Rowyn how I felt.

I walked down to the pen and leaned against the fence, enjoying being able to watch her without the fear of what anyone else would say. A mix of longing and admiration washed over me. She was more than just a girl I was infatuated with. Rowyn was special, not only to me but to the empire. She would undoubtedly achieve great things, far greater than anything I could ever hope for. And yet, I couldn't bear the thought of her choosing anyone else but me.

I tried to gain the courage to tell her the things that dwelled on my mind about her. How deeply I cared for her, how my heart leaped every time she entered a room. What I learned about her past. The fact that her future would outshine mine, yet I couldn't bring myself to think of a future without her.

But how could I express all of this to her? How could I make her understand the depth of my feelings? I wanted to tell her that she had captured my heart like no one else ever had. That she had ruined me, that no other woman could ever compare to her. But the words remained trapped within, aching to be set free. The fear of rejection, of her pushing me away again and returning to the way we were before, held me back.

"How can someone so talented with the sword never have mastered the shield?" I said instead, settling for something safe. Easy. It wasn't hard to see that fighting felt safe to Rowyn. It was what she knew.

"Father said that hands were meant for weapons," Rowyn grumbled, walking toward me. There was a smudge of dirt on her cheek. Her blue eyes seemed bright in the darkness and the cool night air seemed to kiss her dewy skin. The sudden urge to taste it flitted into my thoughts.

"A shield is a weapon." I couldn't help but interject, rerouting my thoughts. I climbed the fence and leaped down. I reached out to take the shield from her. Demonstrating its usage, I said, "You can use it to strike . . . like this." I jabbed the edge of the shield. "Plus it gives you cover from archers. There's no reason not to use one."

Rowyn's sigh echoed her exasperation. "I know . . . it's just . . . I'm tired of feeling so ignorant here. I still can't wrap my head around numbers, my courtesy is abysmal, and Lord Alexander makes me feel foolish at weapons work." My heart leaped at her words. She was opening up to me. She was letting me peer into her world, just as she'd let the others.

"I thought Fin was helping you with mathematics," I said, willing her to give me more. "She's the best in class!"

"I know, but I'm so behind . . . it just feels hopeless."

Rowyn's vulnerability was showing. I had to hold myself back from reaching out and drawing her to me. "I wouldn't worry about it if I were you. Sure, your mathematics is poor, but you bring the rain. For the love of the gods, that has to be worth something and . . . I'll help you with the shield."

Her bewilderment was apparent, and she asked, "Why this kindness?"

I shifted, scuffing his toe in the dirt. "I guess I feel honor-bound to it. I mean, you're Morganian as well. And I know the others have been . . . somewhat ruthless to you."

"So, you pity me, is that it?" Rowyn asked, turning to go back to the dummy, but I grabbed her free arm.

"No . . . wait . . ."

Rowyn looked down at my hand and the stain my sooty fingers left on her sleeve. "I don't need your pity."

But I only strengthened my grip, turning the sleeve black. "That's not what I mean. Stop twisting my words."

Rowyn stopped fighting and studied me with a narrow gaze. "What do you mean then?"

Now was my chance. "I . . . I don't know . . ." I sighed. "I suppose I sort of . . . admire you."

"Really?"

I couldn't believe her surprise. How had she not seen what she meant to me. Could she really be blind to it all? "I know it seems odd, but I fully expected you to come here and try to manipulate the others to your cause, or flirt with the men in the hopes of getting a rich husband to help raise your clan." I laughed at the absurdity of what I was saying.

"I would appreciate your help with the shield, but I have nothing to offer you," Rowyn replied as though that would matter to me. Just being next to her was enough.

But I knew her. She would want to pay me back. "That's not necessarily true, now is it?"

Rowyn shook her head. "I'll not betray my clan's secrets to you if that's what you mean."

"Of course, that's not what I meant," I said, rallying. "You were right back in Morgania. I don't know enough about the people I'll be ruling. You could teach me your clan's ways."

Rowyn studied me, her gaze piercing. "Won't the others gossip? I wouldn't want to step on Lady Ingrid's toes, or upset your standing with Marc and Idris."

"You're not afraid of wagging tongues with Pedr Tore," I replied, jealousy darkening my thoughts.

"That's different."

I furrowed my brows, frustration mingling with my jealousy. Could she really not see? "How is that different? If you think no one whispers about you two, then you're sorely mistaken. There's been much said at your expense."

Rowyn's glower deepened, her eyes flashing with defiance. "I'm his friend, Destrian, nothing more."

I took a step toward her, holding the shield out as a peace offering. "That's all I'm asking for. Can we not be friends?" The words rang hollow in my ears, for I knew deep down that my feelings for her were far beyond friendship. But I dared not confess them, fearing that it would push her away.

As Rowyn reached out and took the shield from me, her touch sending a jolt of electricity through my veins, she muttered, "My ancestors are turning over in their graves right now."

"Let them turn," I said with a grin, my insides leaping with exultation that she was finally letting me close to her. For now, I would cherish these stolen moments.

Rowyn laughed. "Fine, here, show me how to hold it again."

As we practiced shield work, the clashing of metal and the sound of our heavy breaths filled the air. I seized a moment to divert the conversation to something less strenuous. "So, what can you tell me about the Morganites?"

"What do you want to know?" she asked, readjusting the shield that kept slipping down her arm.

"What do you all celebrate? I know you all celebrate

the equinox and solstices, but is there anything else?"

Rowyn's face softened as she caught her breath, the sheen of sweat on her brow glistening in the light of the setting sun. "There is the Revelry. It's every full moon. The Imorati announces Imor's words for the coming month, and then we dance and drink a lot."

"What kind of words does the Imorati give?" I asked, curiosity getting the better of me. I'd heard that the Morganites danced by the light of the full moon but didn't know why.

"Well, Imor speaks to different issues depending on what month it is," Rowyn said. "In the spring, he speaks about what we need to do to prepare for the upcoming raiding season, or what crop will have the greatest harvest. In the fall, he might say we need to gather morwood pine to smoke out the spirits of the dead. You know, little tips here and there that give us an edge for the trials coming up."

That's why she smelled like pine. They burned it.

"What else?" I asked, desperate for a deeper understanding. More knowledge of her, more knowledge of the Morganites, who had long been viewed as adversaries. But now, as I stood with Rowyn, I began to see a glimmer of a different path, a path that could lead to unity and strength rather than conflict and division. My heart thudded with the weight of realization.

What if Lyrica's approach had been misguided all along? What if the key to securing Helena's greatness and preserving our hold on the region wasn't in defeating the Morganites but in forming an alliance, in honoring their customs and traditions?

Rowyn was a bridge that could connect our worlds. If I wanted any hope for a brighter future, for a prosperous and unified Helena, I needed to let go of old prejudices and preconceived notions. I needed to open my heart and mind to the possibility of forging a different kind of relationship with the Morganites.

Rowyn, with her fierce spirit and unwavering determination, became the catalyst for change. She was the embodiment of the Morganite people, their hopes and dreams entwined with her own. And as I looked into her eyes, I knew that if I wanted to make a difference, if I truly wanted to lead Helena into a new era, I had to start by honoring her, by forging a bond based on trust and respect.

I walked through the moves Lord Alexander had shown Rowyn as she blocked. While we worked, she told me more about Morganite rituals, what they did on festival days, and the old ruling houses of Morgania. When it got dark, I called a ball of fire that burned brightly above us, lighting the practice yard. I didn't want our time together to end. I would've stayed in that training yard all night if Rowyn would let me.

"Here, let's try it free-form," I said, holding my practice sword up.

Rowyn agreed and took my stance.

I wanted to impress her. I wanted to show her that despite everything, we did have some things in common. I swept toward her quickly, moving through the drills Lord Alexander used.

Our practice intensified, each of us moving through Lord Alexander's drills at a brisk pace and then, in a twist of fate, we collided. Rowyn tried to bring the shield up a half second too late and ended up tripping on her feet and barreling into me. I grabbed her as we went tumbling back into the dirt, Rowyn landing on top of me.

Rowyn lifted herself, her hands on either side of my shoulders. Her closeness, the scent of her hair, the deep blue of her eyes, the ocean of stars that blanketed the sky above us. It was like a drug speeding through my veins, gathering at my fingertips until the only thing I could focus on was her lips, slightly parted, a soft pink that was just inches from me. I wondered again what she tasted like, how it would feel to kiss her. Would they be as soft as they appeared? I wanted to kiss her and then have her tell me all her thoughts and secrets until she was laid bare before me, and even then

I didn't think it would be enough.

"I can't do this," Rowyn said, her weight disappearing as she pushed herself off me. A sudden emptiness replaced the warmth of her body.

I quickly got to my feet, my body mourning the loss of her warmth. I followed, unwilling to let the moment go with everything left unsaid.

My words were a desperate plea. By all the gods...don't go.

Don't. Go.

"Wait, what's the matter? I didn't mean—"

Rowyn ignored it, ignored me, as she gathered her shield and sword, her cheeks red, her hands trembling.

"I'm sorry!" Rowyn shouted, her voice breaking with emotion, as though being close to me was physically painful. "I know I said it was all right, but I just . . . I can't."

No . . . she wasn't just talking about the moment . . . she was talking about everything. Our friendship, our alliance, every future that I imagined with her. She was saying no to it all.

What had I done? Did she read the thoughts on my face? Was the feeling of being close to me so abhorrent to her?

"Rowyn!" I called desperately, the rain beating down, drumming over my skin like little barbs, cutting down the hope I'd allowed myself to feel and soaking me to the bone. But she didn't hear me, or perhaps she chose not to. I watched as she disappeared into the distance, my chance of getting closer to her fading with each step she took.

I lifted my face to the sky, letting the rain wash the soot and sweat from my brow, frustration and anger causing an inexplicable warmth that spread through me like wildfire.

It infuriated me.

It infuriated me because no matter how much I watched, no matter how much I yearned, she remained as distant as the stars above. Every smile, every shared glance seemed to pass me by like a ghost, leaving me with a hollow ache that gnawed at me.

I hated myself for it. Hated the way my heart seemed to betray me—the way my mind conjured images of her when I least expected. I was caught in a maelstrom of emotions I didn't want, ensnared by a wild flame that refused to be quenched. And the worst part? She wouldn't have anything to do with me.

Every stolen glance, every muted conversation was a poignant reminder of the chasm that lay between us. And so, I was left in my torment, caught in a storm of desire and despair, left watching a girl who was as captivating as she was untouchable.

Thunder rumbled overhead. I strode back to the school, not caring that I was dripping, soaked through from the deluge of Rowyn's rejection. When I got back to my room Marc rose, his eyes filled with concern.

"Des?" he asked, stepping forward as I pulled off my soaked shirt.

His eyes went to the window where the rain beat down against the crystal panes. "Did you tell her?"

I flung the soaked shirt on the floor and called a fire to the fireplace, the flames blue and vibrant as they licked the air with their tongues.

"She doesn't want anything to do with me," I choked out.

"She doesn't know you," Marc insisted. "Once she gets to know you, she'll see."

I shook my head. "You weren't there in Helena. The things I said, the words I used against her—her clan." I leaned against the chair. It was useless. "She will never change her mind about me."

Marc let out a sigh, his tone tinged with indifference. "Destrian, sometimes it's best to accept that someone isn't meant for you. Maybe Rowyn just isn't the right fit."

His words struck a chord within me, fueling the doubts that had already taken root. I'd be a fool to hold onto a fantasy that would never exist. But the sinking in my gut betrayed the truth. I was my father's son. There would only be one for me . . . and it was her.

I angrily shoved the chair into the table. "I wish you were right," I said. "But I can't get her out of my thoughts."

Marc raised an eyebrow, his skepticism evident. "You've known her for such a short time. Are you sure it's not just infatuation?"

I shook my head, a mixture of frustration and sadness welling up within me. "No, it's more than that. I can't just let go."

Marc sighed, his patience wearing thin. "Well, Destrian, sometimes we have to accept that our feelings aren't reciprocated, but there is always Ingrid. You know, someone who actually cares about you." His words stung. I had been clinging to a hope that was slowly slipping away. "Don't waste your time pining over someone who doesn't see your worth."

I wished it were so simple. I didn't have the courage to tell Marc how much I'd tried to spurn my feelings already. How many times I'd willed my eyes to look away. How many times I'd forced my thoughts into some distraction to keep her voice, her eyes, and the memory of her skin against mine at bay.

I didn't correct Marc. I didn't want him to worry about me.

The truth was that I'd become resigned to my fate. I would keep trying, keep hoping, and keep finding ways to break down the barriers that Rowyn forced in front of me. Because the truth was that I'd found the one thing in the world worth fighting for.

It was her.

It would only ever be her.

The End

WIND AND WINGS

Tempest Rising 2.5

Fin's Story

Elliott VanDruff

Belle Rose Press

Dedication

This book is dedicated to the original Fin fans:
Patrick Wolfgang, Galen Gould, and
Cayce Berryman.

Map of Lyrica

Chapter 1

BREEZE PULLED AT HER REINS. "*Not happy.*"
I nodded, brushing the dust off my worn-out cloak. I knew how much she didn't want to interact with anyone with a whiff of "otherness," but we couldn't get into Horan without a guide unless we wanted to be killed on sight. There were only a couple of gatekeepers to choose from, and only one was the best.

Master Haris and I traveled through the dry, barren desert of Narne for days before we finally reached the ramshackle cabin of Thorn Beyond-the-Border. I studied the house, somewhat taken aback by the loose boards clinging to the side and the cracked windows that were sure to blow away during the next storm. Knowing this was home to someone who guided souls between realms, I had expected something . . . more.

With a glance at my reflection in a nearby water barrel, I attempted to comb through my ash-blonde hair and hide the exhaustion from my eyes. After all, Thorn wasn't just anyone. He was a half-breed, part fae, part human—a connection between two worlds. A rarity since the King of Horan had outlawed the creation of half-breeds to discourage human poaching.

Master Haris broke the silence, his face shadowed by the impossibly large brim on the straw hat he'd worn to give him relief from the sun in the desert. Even though it was effective, it made him look ridiculous. "Remember, Fin, be respectful. Thorn's help is indispensable to your quest."

I calmed my annoyance. When I'd heard Master Haris was to accompany me as my mentor, I'd groaned internally for an entire night. I hated how patronizing he was—as though I couldn't understand how much was at stake. I wished the other masters at Solridge would stop putting me in his way like I was Haris's personal fountain of inspiration.

The entire time I researched, I worried he would nag me for information about the animals around us so he could write another volume that I didn't care to help him with. I held good humor about it for a time, but a pilgrim's quest was supposed to be about the sorcerer gaining their gem, not their companion's scholarly pursuits.

Master Haris just sighed, looking as though he found me wanting. Most people did, if I was being honest with myself, but they were all judging something I had no control over nor could change. I didn't think I was so bad. I wasn't snotty, not like Ingrid who was distantly related to Lord Alexander and the emperor, evidenced by their tanner skin and blonde hair. I was related to them, too, but if I ever mentioned it to anyone, there would probably be a price to pay.

Other nobles thought me fun. That I was a little bastard-almost-lady who could talk to animals . . . How cute! I knew I was thought of as pretty and people considered me quiet—and overall nice.

I wasn't all that nice, truth be told. I learned all I could about the lords and ladies who frequented the academy. I learned what I could about the sorcerers who taught classes. Once animals realized they could speak to me, they talked about absolutely *everything*. I drank it up, absorbing every little detail I could about their lives just in case it would be useful later.

Honestly, one of my finest and most useful traits— but also the one I was most ashamed of—was how calculating I could be. How deviously I considered my actions sometimes. I wished Rowyn were more like that. I think I would open up to her more about my thoughts if she was. She always seemed as if she were barely surviving, holding on so tightly to anything so as not to sink and disappear into the depths of the empire. I had to admit, she did have a lot going on. My life dramatically improved when I came to Solridge nearly five years ago, but Rowyn's was just different, and she'd lost so much already. I couldn't burden her with my problems.

I was excited to see what she'd become when she returned. I was excited to see how my quest changed me. I wanted to be more like Rowyn, if I was being honest with myself. I'd relied on others for my entire life, and I wouldn't say I was better off for it. I wanted to learn to fight back, to survive on my own.

With the life of a sorcerer, that was possible.

That's why I didn't need Master Haris to remind me how much was at stake. I'd come from nothing. I knew what that felt like. I was going to Horan to be someone. To find out what my life could look like without the stifling atmosphere of Solridge Academy. The students there were so conservative, so . . . discouraging. Apart from Rowyn and Destrian, I would've run away if I had anywhere else to go. The problem was that I didn't and I was well provided for at the school. I knew what it was like to go hungry, and I wasn't going to throw away my comfort so easily. I was simply waiting, biding my time, until something better came along.

The "something better" wasn't going to come at the capital, though. I already knew that. The man who fathered me would've never let me go to Somme and Maryse where *he* frequented. There was an entire empire to hide me away with some task to do. The sorcerers would be happy to arrange it.

But I was not that little, sweet bastard girl. I planned to be somebody. The empire was huge, and if Lyrica didn't work out, then other empires would happily step in and accept a sorcerer like me.

Empires hoarded them for a reason.

Rowyn was important for a reason.

A single sorcerer could change the fortune of a realm if used correctly. It had happened time and again through the ages. A single sorcerer tipped the balance of the Lyrican crossing a hundred years ago. A single sorcerer on the Ylirian side was the reason Lyrica struggled to conquer in the war.

They tried to take out the ambivalent Farid Vesper, an illusionist, and instead incited him to join the war. When he tapped a natural projectionist, he took out half of Lyrica's forces. He was eventually killed but only after the treaty was signed in blood. By then, Lyrica wasn't interested in continuing a war that everyone in the kingdom viewed as folly and drove the people to revolution.

Horan might even welcome sorcerers. If I liked it there, who said I had to leave? What was my father going to do? Break into Horan to get me? Not likely. Life with the Others seemed interesting, and I was looking for a home that wouldn't put limits on who I could be.

Because the nobles at Solridge were wrong about me. My father, General Ivar, and stepfather were wrong. I would become someone they couldn't ignore. I wanted to make them beg for forgiveness for the way they ignored me and whispered behind my back and refused to offer friendship. I would become greater than all of them. My magic was a gift, and I planned to use it.

The door creaked open before we could knock. A man stepped out and I looked up and then up some more. Ram horns seemed to sprout from his dark, tousled hair, which spiraled over the sides of his head. A tail flicked behind him, a testament to his Woltari heritage. His face was ageless, with not a wrinkle in sight. A tunic covered his broad shoulders. Weathered from the desert's unforgiving sun, the fabric hung loosely over his well-muscled arms. His skin was ruddy behind a well-maintained beard, his eyes gold like the desert sun. His smile was devilishly handsome, and I felt a flutter in my chest as he took another step closer.

"Welcome, Fin, Master Haris," he greeted, his voice deep and soothing.

I smiled, ready to put my plan in motion. From now on the key was to ask lots of questions. The Others could not tell a lie.

"Good afternoon," I said, speaking for myself and Master Haris who had all but shrunk beside me under the great height of the man. "Might we be at the home of Thorn Beyond-the-Border?"

It was an easy question. The Others used surnames to denote where they were from, caring less about familial ties and more about location, since their magic was essentially a number of enchantments derived from the elements around them. So, Thorn Beyond-the-Border was named as such because he was born and lived beyond the border of Horan.

"Indeed, welcome to my home," Thorn replied, a teasing smile playing on his lips. His eyes seemed to sparkle with hidden mirth, turning his seemingly daunting presence into one of playful intrigue. He slapped his hand against the wooden doorframe. "It's not much, but it does well for a charming bachelor like myself."

Master Haris seemed taken aback for a moment, as if not expecting the lightheartedness. There was a comforting warmth that radiated from him and eased my nerves.

"Your journey must've been exhausting," Thorn continued, his eyes meeting mine. "You can stable the horses in the barn and then buy me a drink and dinner." He pointed to an outbuilding that barely stood beyond his cabin. The roof had a big, glaring hole in it. "We'll discuss the next leg of your journey at the tavern. Fargus, my neighbor, will look after your horses while we're away. He's got a knack for it."

I stabled Breeze and Haris's mount, brushing them down and assuring them that they would be taken care of and that, no, they did not wish to go to Horan. Finally, I joined the men back at the cabin door. Master Haris had taken our packs inside and now stood in awkward silence next to Thorn who appeared to be silently laughing at him. I liked him immediately.

"Shall we?" he asked.

The tavern was a little ways off, nestled within a small desert hamlet. As we walked down the dusty road, the setting sun bathed the landscape in a golden hue. Thorn had his hands tucked in his pockets, and his horns cast grotesque shadows on the road. Master Haris and I walked side by side, our cloaks rustling in the breeze.

"Tell me, Master Haris, where do you call home?" Thorn asked, the crunch of our footsteps accompanying his question.

"Solridge," Master Haris replied without a moment's hesitation.

I watched Thorn nod out of the corner of my eye. "A school—that is a fitting place for a well-known scholar such as you." His voice was light and playful, dancing on the breeze.

Thorn had done his research on us. I bit my lip, wondering what he'd learned of me.

"So, to the fae, you'll be Haris Of-Solridge," Thorn turned to me. "And you, Fin, where would you call home?"

Thorn's question pricked a sore. Where did I call home? I could see Lark Harbor in my mind's eye, where Mother lived. But could I call it home when it had been years since I'd last been there? And Solridge, where I lived now . . . it wasn't home either. It was a place of learning but also a place of loneliness and exclusion.

I opened my mouth, then closed it, feeling a lump form in my throat. I looked at the desert road, the dust swirling in the breeze.

"Cheapside," I said for want of a better place.

Thorn looked surprised, his eyebrows lifting. "Cheapside?" he echoed. Every major city had one. Cheapside was a nicer word for the slums, where those who had no roof over their heads or food in their bellies dwelled.

"It's where I grew up. On the streets, before my mother got married. It's far from perfect, but . . ." I trailed off, not knowing how to explain the complicated feelings he'd triggered with his question. There was something in me that refused to be ashamed of who I was and where I'd come from. No matter if the nobles judged me for it. We couldn't all be born with a silver spoon.

Thorn nodded. "Very well. To the fae, you'll be Fin Of-Cheapside. It's not always about where you are currently, but where you feel your truest self."

As we neared the tavern, Thorn's face broke into a broad grin. The sounds of jovial laughter, clinking glasses, and lively conversation spilled from the open doorway, warming the cool desert night. A wooden sign hanging above the door creaked slightly in the breeze, proudly proclaiming the establishment's name—The Chalice.

As soon as Thorn pushed the door open and we stepped inside, the chatter paused. All eyes were on us, or more accurately, on Thorn. He was a known figure in this place, a spot of color amid the desert's golden palette. The fact that he wasn't entirely human didn't seem to dampen their spirits.

The patrons went back to their conversations quickly enough, some nodding in Thorn's direction, others raising their mugs in silent salute. Thorn navigated through the crowd with ease, his tail flicking behind him. He greeted a few patrons by name, sharing a quick joke here and there. His larger-than-life persona ballooned, filling the room with his warm air and inviting smile.

A barmaid with rosy cheeks and a flirty made her way to us. "Evening, scoundrel," she greeted Thorn, a playful sparkle in her eyes. "What can I get you and your guests?"

Thorn leaned back in his chair, greeting her with a smile of his own. "Three of your finest ale, please," he ordered, "and dinner if it's good."

The barmaid smacked Thorn behind the head. "You want Vince to hear you say that? He'll not let you come back if you don't keep a civil tongue about his cooking." Thorn chuckled as she walked away. When she returned with the frothy mugs, she held out her hand expectantly. Thorn gestured to Master Haris and me. "The lady will pay tonight, I think."

I blinked, then reached into my pouch. My fingers brushed against the cool coins, and I carefully counted out the right amount. The barmaid seemed surprised that I, a woman, was paying, but she took the coins without comment. She gave Thorn another flirtatious smile before moving on to the next table.

Settling into the worn wooden bench, I took a cautious sip. The ale was stronger than I was used to but not unpleasant. The barmaid returned and placed a plate of food for each of us on the table. It smelled different but good.

Thorn watched me with amusement. The nervous flutter returned as I admired the golden flecks in his eyes. "So," Thorn said, waving his fork between Haris and me. "What do you two know about Horan?"

Master Haris cleared his throat, looking as if he were about to launch into a lecture. "The Others have—"

"Not *others*," Thorn said with a scoff. "They prefer to be called fae."

"We know the fae cannot lie," I volunteered, interrupting Master Haris, my back stiff. "I know that you all age remarkably slow and that you're able to funnel your magic from the elements. Fae are very rule-oriented."

Thorn's smile widened, a spark of interest in his eyes. "Go on."

I hesitated for a moment, my mind buzzing. "Despite their aversion to lying, fae love to play tricks. They adore a good, honest deal—a fair trade."

At this, Thorn laughed, a deep, hearty sound that seemed to make the whole tavern vibrate. "Yes, we do love our games," he conceded.

"There are various types of fae," I went on, taking a bite of smoked lizard and roasted cactus. "Some are nocturnal; others thrive in the daylight. They vary in size, from small pixies to large trolls. Some are carnivores, some herbivores, and some omnivores."

Thorn raised his mug in salute. "A comprehensive answer. I'm impressed."

A faint blush crept up my cheeks. I shrugged, trying to brush off his praise. "I studied everything we had before I came, though the library at Solridge only has Lyrican texts, and we honestly don't know all that much."

He chuckled. It was a soft, warm sound. "Ah, yes. Books can tell you a great deal, but experiencing it firsthand . . . That's a whole other story." His eyes fixated on me. "So, you're the sorceress in need of a fae gem?"

I nodded solemnly. "We are aware of what that entails."

Thorn's smile wavered. "That may be so, but I will go over the guidelines so there is no *confusion* or *misunderstanding* about what you feel my job is. You see, everyone's first lesson is always that fae prefer truth to come to light. So, I will outline my intentions ahead of time, that way no surprises are lurking in the shadows. They *abhor* being surprised . . . They *love* watching other people get surprised. It's one of the funnier things about them."

"Are you not fae?" I asked, nodding to the horns.

"As you can see, I'm a half-breed," Thorn replied.

I took a bite, trying to hide the flinch. It sounded like a slur when he said it.

Thorn's gaze pinned me with an intensity that sent tiny shocks down my spine. "True to the essence of who I am, I straddle two worlds. As a half-breed, I belong neither wholly to the realm of the fae nor the world of man. I tread the bridge that connects them, gleaning the best of both."

"And yet, you serve under King Valon Of-the-Castle instead of Lyrica," I observed, the curiosity in my voice barely concealing my underlying fascination.

"Indeed," Thorn acknowledged. "His Majesty entrusts me with the task of overseeing his visitors. It's my job to prevent them from inadvertently stirring up trouble on fae land. However, if they decide to stir the pot themselves, well . . ." He trailed off, his eyes glinting with an irresistible mischief. "I'm not liable."

I raised an eyebrow. "So, King Valon doesn't hold you accountable for any unsavory actions taken by the guests?"

Thorn shook his head, the faintest shadow of a grin tugging at the corners of his lips. "Man can be stupid, and the king has the wisdom of many years. He knows this."

I giggled despite myself. Thorn's smile widened, re-vealing a dimple that sent my heart racing. His allure was undeniable; his otherness only served to heighten his charm. He was disconcertingly handsome, and it was increasingly hard to ignore the strange warmth that spread within me.

"In Horan, it is imperative you stick by my side." Thorn leaned forward. "Humans have a knack for dis-appearing there if they're not cautious. Certain fae have developed quite a penchant for the hunt."

"To be sure," Master Haris said, taking a drink. "I'd read that several races of fae considered humans part of their diet when they were cohabitating in Morgania. I was curious how they fared in the Canyonlands . . ." Master Haris trailed off when he noticed Thorn study-ing him with furrowed brows.

"Perhaps you can ask them when we go through the gate," Thorn said, his voice deceptively light.

I glared at Haris. It was already starting. He was go-ing to turn this trip into his own, personal fact-finding expedition instead of focusing on me . . . the person he'd been assigned to help and protect. I turned back to Thorn. "Do you know King Valon Of-the-Castle personally?"

Thorn's eyes flicked down and he brushed some-thing off the table. "He's my adoptive father," he said with a note of caution. "Valon has no wife nor children. So, over the years he has adopted various orphans and outcasts who have needed help in some way. He's been a father many times over in that respect."

"What happened to your . . . actual father?" I asked. The questions were going to be my only lifeline in Horan, so it was best to practice now. Keep asking, keep getting information. Fae were extremely clever. If I didn't ask the right questions, I left myself open to be fooled, swindled, or killed.

Thorn ran his fingers through his hair, leaving the dark curls looking tousled and lovely against his tan skin. "Valon executed him. My father, he . . . crossed the border to prey on humans. Valon had already outlawed that by then."

"Was he a good father?" I asked, intrigued. Valon had actually been included in the information Solridge had of the fae since he'd been alive for over a hundred years.

Thorn raised his mug for another gulp of ale. "I spent six months in Narne with my mother and six months in Horan at the castle every year of my life until I reached adulthood. Valon didn't feel as though I needed to choose one world or the other. He wanted to ensure I could navigate both. Now I go back and forth as gatekeeper and serve him well."

"You are still close?" I pressed before taking another bite. I didn't realize that background about Thorn, and it was starting to make sense why he was seen as the best. If we wanted good access, Thorn was the man to go to.

"Close enough to know that the king wasn't at all surprised that I'd received your letter," he said, waving to the barmaid for a round.

I pulled another coin out of my purse to be ready. "What do you mean?"

"He does not tell me everything," Thorn said, scraping his plate. "I am a gatekeeper, but I'm to treat you as a royal guest and that's not common. We get merchants wanting fae goods to sell for exorbitant prices in the human lands, the odd adventurer desiring to rub shoulders with danger, and even the naturalist every once in a while. But, to be a guest of the king is quite something. It has set you apart, Fin Of-Cheapside, and I'm curious what the king has seen of you."

That made two of us. I appreciated Thorn's forthrightness. While he was incapable of lying, he could have easily shrouded the truth behind half-truths and omissions.

Thorn straightened, his gaze focused on me and me alone. "I'll get you into Horan and back out, but I require half the payment up front."

I didn't hesitate, reaching into my pocket for the small bag of coins. I placed it on the table, pushing it toward Thorn. He opened the bag and rifled through the contents, before nodding, seemingly satisfied. We were going to the land of the fae. The reality of it all was finally sinking in.

Thorn leaned back, the worn wood of his chair groaning slightly under his weight. A pointed finger punctuated his next words. "But I am not a babysitter, nor your knight in shining armor. If you come to Horan looking to stir up trouble, or if you make a bad deal with one of the fae because you can't keep your wits about you, then you are on your own. My duty is to guide you safely in and out of Horan, not to save you from your own folly."

Master Haris nodded solemnly, clearly taking in Thorn's conditions. "Thorn, I assure you, neither of us intends to create unnecessary trouble or make rash deals."

Meanwhile, I found myself swallowing down a knot in my throat, nodding along with Master Haris's statement. Thorn's intensity was contagious and provoked an exhilarating mix of fear and anticipation. This was real, we were really going to step foot in the mystical land of the fae, the place of legends, of cautionary tales.

"Understood," I managed to say, finally. The words tasted bitter but necessary on my tongue. His point was well taken.

Thorn's eyes dwelled on me for a moment, before he slapped the table with his hands and stood. " Very well, tonight you will stay with me in my home. We should rest now. Dawn breaks early, and so do we." Thorn lifted his ale and gulped the rest of it down before setting the mug on the table and moving toward the door of the tavern where he waited for Master Haris and me to follow.

For a moment, I was envious as I watched Thorn interact with the patrons. Not because he was well-liked or because he was flirtatious, but because he seemed to have found a home among these people. Even though he was different, he wasn't an outsider. He was comfortable, he belonged, and I wondered if I would ever find a place where I felt the same.

STEPPING INTO THORN'S HOME was like walking into another world entirely. Its exterior, a simple hut nestled amid the desert landscape, did little to hint at the lavishness that lay within. Surprise washed over me as

I took in the expansive space, its one room filled to the brim with an array of beautiful objects. I remembered reading that fae loved gifts and trinkets. Looking around, it wasn't hard to believe.

Thorn gestured to a plush-looking sofa. "Master Haris, you may rest here." His gaze then landed on me, and he pointed to a cozy trundle bed against the wall. "And for you, Fin."

With a nod, I moved toward the little bed, arranging my things while trying to stifle a yawn. I found my attention snagged by a swift motion in the periphery of my vision. Thorn was there, effortlessly disrobing, his movements natural and unapologetic. The breath in my lungs hitched. The sculpted lines of his physique, his sun-kissed skin—they tugged at something deep inside me, sending ripples of unanticipated interest and intrigue through me. It was as if my body was acknowledging something my mind was struggling to keep at bay.

There was no denying it. Thorn was incredibly attractive, and his current state of undress was doing nothing to diminish his appeal. In fact, it only seemed to amplify it. Then, his hands at his waist, he brought down his breeches. I choked, my eyes wide, before spinning toward the wall as heat surged to my cheeks.

He'd seen me watching.

His laughter filled the room, deep and warm, sparking my curiosity. I couldn't help it; I stole another peek from the corner of my eyes and realized he was posing for me.

"Lesson number two for those journeying to Horan," Thorn said, amusement clear in his voice. "The fae hold no reservations about their bodies."

I quickly focused my attention back on my belongings, my heart pounding against my chest. "I'll . . . bear that in mind," I managed to respond, trying to sound nonchalant. But this was only the beginning, I knew.

Taking a deep breath, I sat on the edge of the trundle bed, my back to Thorn, and began to undress. Even in my awareness of Thorn's presence, a spark of daring had me slipping out of my clothes without hesitation.

The faint rustling behind me paused, and I sensed his eyes on me. Even though my back was to him, I could feel his gaze, almost like a physical touch, warm and heavy. I suppressed a shiver.

"Is there someone waiting for you back at Solridge?" Thorn asked, startling me a little.

I resisted the urge to turn toward him and tugged a nightgown over my head. "No, there isn't." Ensuring that the gown hung properly, I turned and met his golden eyes.

His lips curled into a slow, satisfied smile. "The fae

will enjoy your company, Fin," he said, his voice low, almost a purr. It was meant to be reassuring, but I felt warmth pool within. What had I gotten myself into?

"Well, we'll see about that," I retorted, trying to keep the trepidation out of my voice. I moved toward my bed, pulling the covers over me and sinking into the comfortable mattress.

It took a while for sleep to come. First, I was thinking about how lovely Thorn looked without his shirt on . . . and I allowed myself a full minute and a half to remember him without pants, too, until my mind meandered to more unpleasant topics. Thorn's earlier question had needled me. Where *did* I call home? It was hard growing up the bastard child of an alley wench. My mother instilled in me that a child on the streets was a burden and when I went to Solridge, everyone there was so conservative . . . so proper.

Yet, I'd found my solace among animals. With them, there was a brutal simplicity to existence. They didn't judge based on who my parents were or how I dressed. With them, everything was about the here and now. You had to prove your worth in every moment, and they lived in the present so intensely that their joys and sorrows were all the more vivid, all the more genuine.

I turned to my side, trying to silence the incessant

267

whirring of my thoughts. As my mind wandered over the events of the day, an image of Thorn seeped back in—the curve of his muscles, the intent gaze of his golden eyes. It felt strangely soothing, the thought of his presence. Maybe, just maybe, this strange journey could bring about something more than what I had initially bargained for.

Chapter 2

THE EARLY MORNING LIGHT spilled into Thorn's cabin, rousing me from my sleep. Thorn was already up and, thankfully, dressed, stuffing his belongings into a large pack. His movements were swift and practiced, a clear sign of his experience with travel. I noticed the intricate beadwork on his pack. The craftsmanship was exquisite and mesmerizing. I wondered if it was fae-made. He was wearing earrings, too, an entire row of them down one ear. I could feel the enchantments on them and wondered what they did. Knives were holstered on various parts of his body, the wooden handles worn but the blades razor-sharp. Along his belt hung several leather pouches, also decorated with glimmering beads and gems.

I rose into a sitting position and rubbed the sleep from my eyes. Master Haris was awake, too, scratching the top of his head and shuffling to the outhouse behind the cabin.

Thorn had waited until Haris left to address me with a smile. "Have an egg." He tossed me one that had been boiled. "I like to keep breakfast light. We'll be in Horan by nightfall, and there will be some good food where we'll be stopping."

I carefully peeled it, depositing the shell into a bowl that had been placed on my table. I watched Thorn as he inspected each item he placed in his sack, very aware that I was admi—looking at him. He held up a dagger, running his finger along the edge that had runes scratched in it, before sheathing it on his belt. He did the same to an identical one on the other side.

"You did research on us, didn't you?" I asked, figuring that in order to build the habit of asking questions, I had to practice. I was sure that Thorn couldn't lie, just like the fae . . . at least . . . pretty sure. "What did you find out?"

Thorn smirked. "The fae have spoken of others in your family line. You are the daughter of General Ivar of Maryse, which means you also share blood with the emperor, yet you are not considered nobility."

I appreciated the fact that Thorn seemed to be good at his job. He'd certainly found me out. Nobody had ever blatantly said that to my face before. I smiled, for want of a better thing to do. "So, what did the king say about us? Why was he expecting me?"

Thorn shrugged. "The king, he told me nothing. He only said he was expecting a girl and asked to read your letter. After he was done, he looked . . . thoughtful.

Like it wasn't what he expected. Or who he expected. I don't know. Valon's been preoccupied with the seer and fortunes lately. There is a scent in the air, the perfume of coming change, and it's making all fae restless."

"Will I meet him?" I asked, seeking whatever answers I could get out of Haris's earshot. They'd given him to me as my companion because he'd asked to go, not because it would benefit *me* in any way, but it would benefit *him*. I held no qualms about keeping any information I'd gained from him.

"King Valon has requested that we stay at Alden-Ester. It is an honor that he should want you underfoot. The palace is crowded, just like everywhere else," Thorn said, holding up another egg in offering. I shook my head and began to dress, conscious that Thorn's eyes were resting on me.

I reached for my breeches. They were a pair of well-oiled leather pants, worn from many a training session with Rowyn and Araceli back in Solridge. Pulling a sandy-colored tunic over my head, the lightweight fabric was a welcome choice for the sweltering heat I knew was to come. It was a sleeveless design, loose enough to allow a cool breeze to tickle my skin, yet fitted enough not to interfere with movement.

I donned boots next. They were built to withstand

rough terrains. The laces were worn but held strong when I pulled them tight, the leather molding comfortably to my feet.

Once I was dressed, I turned my attention to my weapons. I'd picked up a bow from a merchant during one of SeaPort's bustling market days. The yew wood had been beautifully crafted, the curve of the bow smooth and the string tightly strung. I'd haggled for a good price, and the merchant had thrown in a quiverful of arrows to sweeten the deal. Nestled next to the quiver that hung from my belt was a dagger with a delicate rose design etched into the hilt and a boundless waterskin filled to the brim with a mix of water and silphium, the lady's herb, a gift from Galena.

Finally, were my pair of pearl earrings, a thoughtful present from Lady Vianne. They'd been charmed to protect the wearer from minor fae enchantments and illusions. I touched them lightly, the cool magic reassuring beneath my fingertips. Over my head, I wrapped a blue scarf to cover my mouth as it was quite dusty, and to help shield me from the sun.

When Master Haris returned, he dressed in what he normally wore, a plain, brown, homespun robe. He added his wide-brimmed straw hat and held a wooden walking stick. Before we set off, Thorn gave us some time to bid our horses goodbye.

"Hey girl," I whispered to Breeze, running my hands along her soft neck. Her velvety muzzle nuzzled into my palm in response, her warm breath a familiar comfort. Saying goodbye, even if temporarily, stung more than I expected.

"*I wait now?*" Breeze asked, her voice tinged with fear. "*I should come with you.*"

"I know, Breeze," I said, trying to keep my voice steady. "I wish you could come with us too." She nudged me gently, a silent comfort. "But it's not safe for you. We'll be back before you know it, okay?" Breeze would lose her mind in Horan. The terrain was rough for horses, and many fae enjoyed eating large pack animals.

"Take care of them, Fargus," Thorn said, walking toward us.

The neighbor, a burly, friendly man, tipped his hat. "Don't you worry. Horses are no matter. Keeping these two out of trouble in the fae lands . . . well . . . best of luck to ya."

Thorn led the way down the road, with Master Haris and I following. I kept looking over my shoulder as the last remains of the human realm faded into the distance behind me.

The desert sun was high in the sky as we trudged across the sea of dust, heat waves distorting the air before us. As we walked, Master Haris peppered Thorn with questions about the fae for his upcoming book, while Thorn would occasionally look over his shoulder as though to make sure I was still following them. As though I would run away from the adventure of a lifetime.

Thorn was patient, answering with a jovial nature. I listened, pinpointing the times when I heard Thorn choose his words a little too carefully as he probably hid some piece of information from us. It was to be expected, of course. Humans were not actually allied with fae, especially Lyricans.

The Others were shoved back to the border of Horan when Morgania was conquered in the final conquest. Since then, they'd left us alone, sealing off their world from ours so as not to invite Lyrica's wrath. One would think the fae wouldn't fear us as much as we feared them, but fae were very protective of their long life. They resisted war at all costs.

The sun was high and hot overhead, baking the desert beneath our feet like an oven. Thorn called for a break, guiding us to the shade of a lone, gnarled tree that somehow seemed to flourish amid the harsh conditions. We gratefully shed our packs and sat on the relatively cooler rocks.

As Thorn unwrapped some of the food he'd packed—dried fruits, cheese, hard bread, and cured meats—I found myself drawn to the tiny movements in the sparse underbrush. A pair of bright-eyed lizards emerged from a crack in the tree trunk, their scales glimmering in the dappled sunlight. In the sky, an eagle circled, its sharp gaze keenly observing us from the endless blue.

"There are several gates to Horan, each guarded by a gatekeeper like myself. There's one in Rudin and another in Korballis," Thorn was explaining to Master Haris, gesturing vaguely in different directions as if we could see those distant cities.

One of the curious lizards with brilliant blue scales scurried across the hot desert floor, then stopped before me. I leaned down, extending a hand toward it. In its own way, the creature communicated to me about the harshness of the desert, the scarcity of water, and the beauty of the vast sky above.

Thorn chuckled, watching me. "What does it say?" His golden eyes sparkled with amusement.

"He says there hasn't been rain for many turns of the moon," I said, dusting off my hands as I stood up. "They usually know the land better than we do. Their advice has been helpful before."

Thorn inspected a large growth of cacti that had taken up one side of the road, then added, "Just remember, even the animals that dwell beyond the border are unlike anything you've encountered before. They're as beautiful and deadly as the desert we're crossing. Intriguing, but dangerous if you don't respect them. Be cautious, and never forget that."

My eyes brightened. "The Lyrican texts said that there were dragons in Morgania back before the Morganites crossed the sea. Are they still around?" I would dearly love to visit with a dragon.

Thorn's eyes shadowed. "The larger predators began dying off relatively quickly, about forty years back. The fae have been holed up too long behind the border, and there just isn't enough room. Some have even started moving north to the Nightlands. The dragons were the first to go."

A prickle of fear moved up my spine. Rowyn had read that there might be fae in the Nightlands, but I hoped she didn't meet any. I would imagine that any creature trying to survive in the land of darkness would be ferocious and terrifying indeed.

"Some of the elves breed unicorns though. They are useful to ride through the canyons and have medicinal properties if you have the space to house them. Several chimera live in the cliffs on the western border of Horan, and wyvern roam the northern mountains."

"And none of them can leave the border?" Master Haris asked from his place beside Thorn. "King Valon has contained them all?"

Thorn chewed thoughtfully. I wondered if he was trying to find an honest way to shield the truth. "Some have been known to escape. The sea is the hardest to contain since Valon's magic is tied to the earth. It's usually the sea fae who've been able to sneak out. A group of merpeople and sirens discovered a hole in the border a few years back. The king is *still* trying to round up everyone who went missing in that debacle."

Thorn had only mentioned species of less dangerous fae. I wondered what other creatures had escaped that he hadn't mentioned. A pod of dolphins around Solridge had told me that there was a shadow in one of the underwater fissures that would drag sea creatures into the depths. They weren't talking about small fish either. The dolphins had known of a herd of toothed whales that were trapped and decimated as they swam over the cavern.

I wondered where else fae might be lurking in our world that we didn't know about.

"How often do you get asked to cross the bridge?" I asked.

Thorn rested his hands on the back of his head and leaned against the tree, his legs splayed out in front of him. The muscles in his arms flexed, and my heart skipped a beat in excitement. He had no right to be so gorgeous. "Quite often, actually. You'd be surprised how many people need to journey into Horan."

"Who are they?" Haris asked, joining the conversation.

"Oh, all sorts. Besides your merchants, scholars, you've got those seeking remedies. Fae medicine is renowned for its effectiveness, you know. Some ailments that baffle human healers are mere child's play for the fae," he added with a hint of pride.

"Doesn't it get dangerous?" I asked, glancing at the daggers belted to his side. "Not everyone would have good intentions . . ." Rowyn taught me the basics of dagger handling back in Solridge, but our training had been cut short by our respective quests.

Thorn tilted his head as he studied me, and I began to squirm under his gaze. "True, not everyone comes with peaceful intentions. Humans like to poach fae just as much as fae like to poach humans. But that's why we gatekeepers exist. To maintain balance, ensure peace . . . and deal with those who disturb it." His hand went to one of the blades. "We don't often get women, though, and even fewer have as fair a face as you."

Heat seared through me at the compliment.

Master Haris leaned forward, tension emanating from his jittery knee. "The girl is not to be trifled with." A touch of warning colored his tone.

Thorn's eyes moved from me to Haris, a glint of amusement flashing within their golden depths. "The woman, you mean," he corrected. "There's a reason that most men from Lyrica leave their women behind when they go to Horan. When we cross the border, Fin will be regarded as her own person, with her own voice. She doesn't have to defer to the wishes or rules of anyone if she has no wish to."

I didn't get a chance to respond. The eagle that had been circling above descended onto my shoulder. I bit back a shudder as its talons, sharp and cold, grazed my skin.

"*Danger lies ahead,*" it cautioned, its voice grave.

The eagle's words sent a shiver down my spine, and I glanced at Thorn and Haris, who were going back and forth about what to expect when we crossed the border. For a moment, I considered warning them. Yet, the eagle's forewarning felt vague. I decided to press for more details.

"Danger?" I asked barely above a whisper. "What do you mean?"

The eagle's gaze turned toward the horizon. "*There's*

a wall of illusion ahead. A barrier created by magic. Even we, the sky roamers, dare not approach."

My pulse quickened. "Why?"

Its amber eyes flicked back to me, piercing and solemn. "*It's a place you do not venture if you value your life.*"

I turned to Thorn. "Are animals not able to cross into Horan?" I asked, sure that the eagle was speaking of the border. The eagle, Noble One, continued to sit on my shoulder, studying Thorn as though he knew Thorn wasn't of his world.

Thorn nodded. "The magic has to remain strong to keep things orderly. Some get through during crossings—small rabbits and lizards and such—but Horan has an entire ecosystem to itself. That's how King Valon is able to ensure order."

I looked back at the eagle. "We'll be all right," I assured it.

The eagle gave me an appraising look and ruffled its feathers. "*Many fools have said that before you. Many will say it after.*"

The eagle took off as though it refused to bother with me since I was a lost cause. I hoped I could prove him wrong. Everything would be fine, surely.

Chapter 3

"HERE WE ARE, the gate of Horan," Thorn announced as we made our way toward the distant shimmering mirage. As we approached, it morphed into a massive, swirling cloud suspended in the sky, reaching from the ground to the heavens.

Thorn unshouldered his pack and pulled out a small, ornate flute. He lifted it to his lips and played a lilting melody that resonated with the desert air. It was as though the land itself were listening.

As the last note faded, there was a moment of anticipation, a hush in the desert. And then, the cloud began to change. It started to swirl and churn, parting slowly, revealing a portal filled with a soft, warm light.

"Remember, stay close," Thorn said, stowing his flute and stepping into the chasm.

I took a breath, about to step through, thrilled with all the life choices that led up to that moment. The excitement of marching into unknown waters and going on a journey that promised to change my life forever was extremely appealing to me.

Master Haris grabbed my arm before I could make

my way through, his voice just above a whisper. "Fin," he started, his tone heavy with a seriousness I hadn't often heard from him. "I need you to listen carefully to what I'm about to say."

I noted the worry creases on his forehead. A slight unease began to creep over me. "What is it, Master Haris?"

He exhaled slowly, his gaze moving to where Thorn had disappeared. "This is a strange land, and we're about to meet strange beings. I want you to remember that no matter how friendly they seem, or how much they may help us, you can only trust me."

"Even Thorn?" I whispered. "He's our guide. He's supposed to help us."

Master Haris's lips twisted into a grim smile. "Especially Thorn, Fin. Remember, he belongs to both worlds. He is not our friend. He is our guide. There is a difference."

His words hung in the air between us, a sobering reminder of our position. I nodded, swallowing the lump in my throat.

Passing through the gate was like stepping through the looking glass—we crossed an invisible threshold, and suddenly everything changed. As the last wisps of the portal's magic receded, my senses were engulfed by a spectacle of raw beauty. I blinked rapidly, struggling to comprehend the fantastical landscape before me.

The edge of the Canyonlands stretched before us, an infinite canvas of burnt orange and crimson. Massive stone pillars rose from the earth, weathered columns that reached toward the heavens like stalwart sentinels keeping watch over their ancient kingdom. The rich hues of red, orange, and white created a stunning natural tapestry for those brave enough to see it.

Treading cautiously, we began our descent into the endless expanse of red canyons etched with time's relentless chisel. Their jagged edges cut silhouettes against the sky, the red stone blazing as if caught aflame. The air even felt older, heavy with magic and history. We were no longer in the familiar territory of Lyrica; this was the realm of the fae, the otherworldly creatures of lore and legend. We descended on carved steps. Smoothed over time, they led us deep into the heart of a bustling city.

"Stay close," Thorn said over his shoulder, his eyes on the myriad of fae pushing and shoving around us. There were small, sprightly fairies with gossamer wings that flitted through the air, chattering in high-pitched voices. Two elves appeared out of nowhere, their skin the color of the canyon wall. Taller fae with delicate horns spiraling from their heads moved with a certain grace and nobility, their robes rich with the colors of nature. On the ground, smaller creatures scurried about, their bright eyes gleaming with curiosity at our arrival.

Master Haris was captivated. He stopped to inspect some markings staining the walls. It was obvious he was thrilled at the opportunity to learn more about fae culture firsthand. As much as I grumbled about Master Haris, I did like the man. He was a respectable scholar and he was kind.

But, he did have his annoyances, like how most of his pack was comprised of parchment and spare quills, and his fingers were forever stained with the black ink that Solridge made with soot and berries. Still, I supposed if the man wanted to survive with two measly robes for the entire expedition, then that was his business. I just hoped he remembered to wash them.

As we walked deeper into the city dug into the sides of the canyon walls, the noise amplified. Homes, shops, and public spaces formed a network of rooms and passages. Everywhere I looked, there were signs of life—fae artisans showing their wares, performers showcasing their talents, youth chasing each other around the winding streets.

As we navigated the streets, I couldn't help but be on high alert. Thorn was right; I felt numerous sets of eyes on us, watching curiously, some with a hint of hunger. The carnivorous fae were particularly unsettling with their razor-sharp teeth.

I barely had time to gasp when a hand as pale as moonlight darted out from a shadowed alley, its long fingers clamping around my wrist. But Thorn was quicker. In the blink of an eye, he was at the vampire's side, a sharp, silver blade glinting at the creature's pale throat.

"Easy there," Thorn murmured into the vampire's ear, his golden eyes now dangerous slits. "I know you remember who I am. We're here under the protection of the king."

The vampire grumbled, his red eyes narrowing at me. "The king gets fresh humans to toy with while the rest of us starve. It's not fair," he hissed, his grip on me slackening as Thorn pressed the knife closer.

"Life rarely is," Thorn replied. "Now, I suggest you find your meals elsewhere before I lose my patience."

With one last venomous glare, the vampire withdrew, vanishing into the shadows from whence he came. Thorn returned the knife to its sheath, then turned to me, a playful glint in his eyes.

"Always an adventure with you humans around." He chuckled, then placed his hand on my lower back, and I felt a shiver of excitement at his touch as he guided me back to the street where Master Haris was nervously looking around. "Shall we continue?"

As we delved deeper into the city, we eventually found ourselves standing before a whimsical abode. Fairy lights danced over a leaf-shaped door, casting playful shadows on the ground. Thorn turned to us with a grin. "Here we are. Home for the night."

With a knock, the door swung open, revealing a stout female fairy with bright teal wings shimmering in the interior light. A warm smile danced upon her lips as she fluttered over. "Thorn, it's good to see you! And you brought friends?"

Thorn nodded and introduced us. "Fin Of-Cheapside, Master Haris Of-Solridge, meet Nettle Above-the-Crimson-Gorge. She runs this lovely bed and breakfast and makes the best jollypot stew in all of Horan."

"Oh, please," Nettle said with a blush. "If Tansy heard that, she'd curse your horns off."

Thorn grinned mischievously. "Tansy's brickle-berry pie is better than yours."

"To the dungeons with ye," Nettle said, smacking Thorn on the back of his head with a wooden spoon.

Pleasantries exchanged, Nettle ushered us inside. The dwelling was cozy and filled with quaint fae furniture, the walls glowing with what looked like some sort of luminous moss. In the center was a low table, upon which an enticing array of dishes was spread out.

Thorn sat at the head, Master Haris—his usually furrowed brows relaxed in the comfortable environment—sat to Thorn's right, and I on the left. Nettle settled across from Thorn on a stool, allowing her wings to fold down behind her.

"What do you think of Horan so far?" Nettle asked, handing each of us a plate decorated with fae runes.

"We are very thankful for being allowed in," Master Haris said, adjusting his spectacles. "We understand it's an honor to be granted entrance, and we appreciate you hosting us on this worthy endeavor."

Nettle blinked. "I'm not the king or anything. You don't need to wax poetically with me."

I tried to hide my smile.

Thorn made no such effort. "We have a scholar here, Nettle. Master Haris seeks to learn everything he can about the fae so he can write a book and educate the Lyricans on our ways."

Nettle wrinkled her nose in distaste. "I'll never understand how they gathered enough power to take over both shores. I felt for the poor Morganites when they crossed over . . . I really did."

The conversation naturally flowed from topic to topic as we passed dishes around the table until Nettle brought up the subject of my gem, right as I was sneaking a cracker to a waiting mouse under my seat.

"Thorn tells me you have a fascinating ability, dear," Nettle said, her eyes shimmering in the low light. "You converse with animals, do you?"

It wasn't often that my abilities were spoken of with such curiosity and respect. Thorn glanced at me, a smirk playing at the corner of his mouth. I could tell he was amused by my discomfort, but he didn't say anything.

"Yes, most of them anyway."

Nettle's eyes widened in interest. "How does it work? Can you understand them all? Do they speak the same language?"

Master Haris, who had been quietly eating, now chimed in, his scholarly interest piqued. "I believe each animal has its own unique way of communicating. Isn't that right, Fin?"

Nodding, I added, "Yes, it's more about understanding their emotions and intentions. The exact words aren't as important. It's like . . . learning to interpret a different kind of language. We usually speak through our minds, if they feel up to it, and have something specific they want to say."

Nettle let out a low whistle. "I must admit, I'm impressed. It's a rare ability, even among the fae. Oh, what a precious gift you have, dear!"

"I wondered why you were here so soon after your last expedition," Nettle went on, filling Thorn's glass with a glowing nectar-like beverage. The windows of the cavern home were open, looking out over the canyon city and revealing a sprinkling of stars in the night sky, now that dusk was ending.

"Don't get me started," Thorn harrumphed. He turned to me. "Some people don't give me much notice when they want to cross the bridge, and they act like I should share their emergency."

"What if someone shows up and you're already on a mission?" I asked before spooning some of the jolly-pot stew into my bowl.

"Then they learn the beautiful art of patience—and waiting," Thorn said with a shrug. Turning his golden eyes to Master Haris, he asked, "And you, Haris. How are you finding our cuisine? Can it compete with your human dishes?"

Master Haris paused, adjusting his spectacles. "Indeed, it's an entirely new range of flavors and, I must say, quite enjoyable." He gestured to the plate before him laden with glistening fruits, sparkling jellies, and steaming meat from some fae creature. "I've been noting down the tastes and textures. Fascinating."

Thorn burst into laughter, making the silverware on the table tremble. "Can't you enjoy a meal without studying it?"

Before Haris could respond, Thorn turned to me, his eyes still twinkling with mirth. "And what about you, Fin? How do you feel after your first day in Horan?"

I chewed thoughtfully on a piece of the strange, yet delicious meat, my mind wandering back to the day's events. "It's so beautiful here," I said, looking at Nettle. "I've not been to very many places, if I'm being honest, so I don't have much to compare it to except two ports and a school."

Nettle's eyes softened. "You're from Cheapside? When I lived farther east, there were a few Cheapsides in the bigger cities of Morgania and Adair. Which were you from?"

"I'm not from the West at all," I said with an embarrassed smile. "I'm from Lark Harbor, in Lyrica."

"Ah," Nettle said, glancing at Thorn. "A tried-and-true Lyrican then. We don't often get your kind around here."

I shrugged. "I don't claim much kinship to anyone, if I'm to be honest with you. I've not had much cause for loyalty."

"To be sure," Master Haris cut in with a frown. "Solridge has taken you in and nurtured your gifts. You are well cared for and want for nothing."

290

I met Master Haris's eyes. "Yes, only because of my 'gift.' Nothing was provided to me until you all discovered I had power. My father probably knew I was his but didn't care. I know you feel I should be grateful, but everything my father has since provided for me was already long past due."

Actually, the greatest gift my father had ever given me was the fact that he didn't care to know me. I was so relieved when I'd found out. After my stepfather, I didn't have it in me to battle another man fighting for control of me.

When my gaze caught Thorn's, an unspoken understanding passed between us. A wisp of a smile played on his lips. He raised his glass to me in a silent toast, and I couldn't help but smile back.

Chapter 4

I STOOD AT THE BALCONY entrance to Nettle's home, admiring the fae city of Crimson Gorge. Looking down, the city was like a network of glowing embers embedded into the earthen fabric of the canyon, giving the impression of a grand beehive in the heart of the wilderness.

Balconies and verandas, hewn from stone, hung over the sheer drops, offering dizzying views of the stunningly blue river that serpentined its way through the heart of Horan. Fairy lights swirled around in a delightful display of radiant colors, casting long, flickering shadows that danced along the hoodoo walls.

Despite the unfamiliar environment, the foreign tastes, the alien conversations, there was a surprising familiarity to it all. I'd shared a meal with new friends in a far-off land. What started as an exciting adventure during the day was turning into a beautiful memory by night.

"Are you always so quiet, Fin Of-Cheapside?" Thorn stepped to the other side of the arched opening, leaning against it and following my gaze out to the city. "You let Master Haris question me nearly to death on our hike here and then again at dinner. Do you just not care to speak? Is my presence so bothersome?"

"No," I said, trying not to admire him out of the corner of my eye. "I've just had a lot on my mind."

"With your quest?" Thorn asked, his brows raised.

I shrugged. "Among other things."

"You come here for more than a gem, I think." Thorn took a sip of the glowing nectar wine.

The parlor was silent, so I figured Nettle and Haris had retired for the evening. It was a late dinner. Sleep tugged at my eyelids, but I was enjoying the peaceful night away from Haris's snores.

"Did you have trouble fitting in growing up?" I asked, looking back at the fairy lights to avoid Thorn's eye as he studied me. "Did the humans or fae ever act like you didn't belong?"

Thorn's eyes narrowed. "Such a personal question. If you would like me to answer, you must tell me why you ask."

I shrugged again, resting my head on the cool stone arch. "I've never fit in," I admitted. "Not at home, not at school. I know others have it much worse than I do, and I'm not trying to complain, but they all speak of home so fondly, and I've never felt as though I've had one."

Thorn tilted his head to the side. "Why did you say

you were from Cheapside? It's been many years since you've lived on the streets. At least, that's how I understood it to be."

I continued to avoid his eye and, instead, gazed at the stars. "It was the only place that felt like home, and we didn't even have a roof over our heads. When we lived on the streets, we had so many nice moments that I remember and then when Mother married, they all began to dwindle until there was nothing left."

Why was Thorn so easy to talk to? Perhaps I was deluding myself into thinking that I was simply doing it to get him to trust me. It was another step in ensuring my quest succeeded. But that wasn't only it. I was telling him things I'd never told anybody. Not even Rowyn.

Was it a compulsion? Did he have a spelled token that made him irresistible to secrets? Could he drip honey into people's ears like the sirens? As much as I wanted to attribute it to some magic and be done with it, my instincts told me it was something more. I wanted to be him. He could've been painted as an outcast. Yet, he was clearly at home in both the world of the fae and the world of humans.

Thorn sank to the floor with his leg draped over the edge of the balcony. I joined him. He handed me a glass of wine and I took a sip.

"My mother loved me very much growing up," Thorn said. "At first the villagers were wary. It took about twenty years for everyone to lighten up, but when they did, it felt like home. Still feels like it, honestly. Growing up with the fae was the same. Valon was a gracious and caring father. He told me what he could give and followed through. Fae can be very straightforward about expectations. They don't dance around issues like humans do."

"So, you've had a happy life so far," I said, more jealous than surprised.

"Mostly, yes," Thorn said, taking another sip of wine. "Did your animals keep you safe when you lived on the streets?"

I frowned, thinking back. "I don't really remember it then. My first memory of understanding the animals started after my mother married my stepfather."

"Really?" Thorn rested his arm on his knee. "Your gift didn't crop up until later?"

I nodded.

"Tell me about your mother," Thorn said, swirling the wine in his glass. "Does she not miss you when you're away?"

"I don't think so," I admitted. "Mother hadn't minded me when she thought I was normal." I had some good memories of her sneaking me sweets from a stall while the shopkeeper's head was turned. Giggling as we watched the noble ladies ride through the city, admiring their pretty dresses.Mother thought to be one. She'd held out hope that my father would come back. She'd contacted him countless times about me, but he never responded. She'd sent letters to Maryse, to the capital, to Bruin, only to be ignored.

I went on. "When Mother married and settled into a normal life, it was then that she started to notice that I was strange. Her husband did not like me. He thought I was a huge liability and wanted me gone as soon as possible. Then again, he doesn't particularly like her, either, nor his own children. He is an unhappy man, but he makes a good living, and Mother and my siblings are taken care of."

When I wasn't angry at Mother, I pitied her. She'd scratched and fought and clawed her way to a normal life, and there I was, about to destroy it. When Mother finally wrote to General Ivar about my powers, the response was immediate. She was to take me to Solridge and he would send money to me there. Lord Alexander was to direct any and all necessities if there was something I was not able to problem-solve myself. So, I went to live a new life at Solridge.

"I'd always wanted to be taken away," I admitted. "I feel bad because I can't bring myself to go back, but it feels better this way."

"What did he do to you?" Thorn asked, his voice lowering.

"Who?" I asked, feeling a sinking in my gut.

"Your stepfather."

There were some things I didn't talk about.

With ANYONE.

There was no point in revisiting that part of my life. It was in the past, and I refused to let it dictate my future. He didn't get to be any part of who I would become.

"Nothing," I said simply, hoping that Thorn would understand the cue.

He leaned forward, his eyes a burnished gold in the dim light. "You are *lying*."

I breathed deeply. "You ask too much," I said, this time my voice clear. "You don't need to know this to help me get my gem, so we can either move on or call it a night." It was a miracle my voice didn't waver, but it didn't.

"I've made you angry." Thorn leaned back once more. "You are right. You do not owe me an answer if you do not wish to."

I nodded, then looked back out to the city. I'd probably just ruined my chances of getting any special treatment from Thorn. Oh well. I never spoke about my past. I certainly wasn't going to speak about it now.

"Ask me a question," Thorn said, his hands out-stretched in a peace offering.

"What does the king expect of me?"

"We aren't beating around the bush, are we?" Thorn frowned. "Very well. He will ask a favor of you in exchange for assisting you in obtaining your gem."

I nodded. "Do you know what the favor is?"

Thorn smirked. "Basic respect among fae is that you communicate those things clearly yourself. Even if I knew, it is not my place to tell you. You must hear his words alone."

"So, there's nothing else?"

"Not that he has shared with me. I will know more when we arrive and you meet with the king. That is how it should be," Thorn said, his voice brooking no argument. "Now, I have a question for you."

"Go ahead."

"Have you met your real father?" Thorn asked, his brows raised.

"No," I admitted. "We send letters every once in a while, but it's really just him gathering information and giving directions. We are not family."

"I imagine it was painful for them to let your skill slip away."

A part of me—though, admittedly, not a big one—

was secretly tickled that Maryse lost out on a generation of my power. It was one of their stronger lines and extremely well-regarded and useful to the empire.

My father had only promised to take care of me *after* they noticed my powers. Even then, they left me to take care of everything on my own. I traveled to Sea-Port alone, hired a maid, picked out some clothes, and came to school feeling as though a new leaf was turning.

I shifted, daring to dangle my foot off the ledge too. "They've made their feelings clear on the matter. Honestly, I'm better off for it. Most sorcerers can make their own way and live a good life. I aim to be one of them."

"And your school? What do you think of your education?" Thorn prodded.

"The masters at school think well of me. I have some friends, Rowyn and Galena and Araceli, so I'm doing all right."

"You say that with hesitation. You are not telling the entire truth," Thorn said, motioning with his hand for me to go on.

I stopped myself from sighing. "The other students, the nobles, barely acknowledge my existence."

One would think that I would've grown up to be moody and angry, but it's actually quite the opposite.

It's not because of some weird inner fortitude. It was just because there was an exception.

Animals loved me.

They clamored to speak to me, and tell me I looked pretty, and what a lovely person I was, and it absolutely fed my ego. Animals thought I was pretty wonderful, so I'd decided that if people were going to judge me for something I had no control over, nor could change, then I just had to move right along. I didn't hate my life, honestly.

I secretly loved it.

Being ignored was a lovely thing when it came to doing whatever you wanted without consequence. I didn't abuse the privilege, but I did exercise it.

"I see why you struggle to find a home with the choices in front of you. Have you entertained the idea of Horan?"

Thorn wasn't being accusatory or anything. More like he was curious. I wondered what the king would say if I did ask to stay. "I've thought about it," I replied. "It's certainly something I would consider, if the time was right and the opportunity was there."

"And what opportunities are you looking for?" Thorn pressed.

"Ways to enjoy life," I said, and it was the truth. I was ready to be somebody, to show my worth, and to hopefully find happiness on that journey.

"Very well," Thorn said. "I think that's enough for tonight. We have a very busy day tomorrow and will need to be at our peak if we want to get to Alden-Ester without you two getting eaten."

I bit my lip, disliking the joke.

Thorn led me to Nettle's only guest room. Thankfully it was large, and Haris was already snoring on one of the beds. His spectacles were neatly placed on the nightstand beside it and his robe hung on a hook. Thorn went to his bed and began to undress. I knew it was coming, so I was able to keep my eyes trained away and my breathing calm.

Though I wanted to look.

I wanted badly to look.

I began to undress as well, but instead of facing away, like I'd done the night before, I stayed facing him, not paying any attention to whether or not he was looking as I pulled off my tunic and slipped out of my breeches. Grabbing my nightgown, I pulled it on—but not too hastily, lest Thorn think me too nervous and timid for fae ways. He was nice to look at but cocky. He didn't need my admiration.

I wondered what Thorn thought of me as I lay on the fairy mattress. In some ways he reminded me of Destrian. Prideful but kind. My heart tugged at the thought of the heir and Rowyn, together in the Night-lands.

My memory swept back to two years before. I'd grown content not having human friends when Lord Destrian peeked over my shoulder to copy my notes in mathematics one day. I raised my brows and smiled, glancing at Sir Walter whose back was turned.

From then on, Destrian always copied my notes. He'd sit between Marc and me and ask about what his horse, Valor, said about him. I loved him for it. My heart would skip a beat when he sidled in, his hands in the pockets of his breeches. Sometimes he'd whistle a tune.

I always hid my admiration. There was no telling what Ingrid would do if she heard about any feelings I might have. I didn't even tell Galena for fear that she would say something to Lady Madeline. I was happy with things as they were. Lady Ingrid wasn't outright mean or hateful. She just ignored me, and most of the others followed suit.

Except Destrian. He was never overly friendly or anything. We never spoke outside of class, though he would acknowledge me in the halls. He never gave me any indication that he harbored the same feelings for me as I did for him. I wouldn't have, either, because Ingrid had obviously staked a claim to him, and I wasn't about to invite an apocalypse on the school.

Still, Destrian was my first love, and I imagined all sorts of scenarios where I would leap into his arms and he would spin me around and confess his love for me and I would become the richest woman in the West and have a handsome, nice husband who adored me and had magic to boot.

Then Gillius and Destrian returned to Solridge alongside a little Morganite girl who looked as though she could force the world to bow to her will with just one glare. I thought I could see he was in love with Rowyn even then. I just deluded myself into thinking he wasn't.

Probably because I was in love with her too.

It hurt to move on, but I was used to hurt.

Besides, look where I was now.

Chapter 5

THE MORNING WAS HURRIED as we tried to gather our things and say goodbye to Nettle. Thorn promised her we would visit again on our way out of Horan, and we left, taking a series of steps that wound throughout the city and down toward the river.

As we ventured deeper into the canyon, our senses were filled with an array of sounds, sights, and scents. The fae revealed themselves in forms as diverse as the myriad hues of the Canyonlands themselves. Sprites flitted around glowing flowers, their laughter akin to the tinkling of tiny bells. Nymphs lounged by a clear, sparkling river, their songs intertwining with the gurgling of water.

We stepped down to a platform where a series of canoes were tied. Thorn waved oddly over a modest vessel carved from what appeared to be a single, enormous tree trunk. Its interior was smooth and polished, the dark wood gleaming in the sun that filtered down through the canyon walls.

Thorn deftly untied the rope tethering the canoe, his muscles flexing beneath his tan skin. He gestured for Master Haris and me to board, and I hesitated at the edge of the water. Though I'd crossed many bodies of water in my lifetime, this one felt different—as if the river itself was sentient. I glanced at Thorn, who smiled encouragingly.

"Don't worry, Fin," he assured me, pushing off from the bank once we'd settled. "The rivers of Horan are kind to those they deem friends."

As we swept through the water, the rhythmic dipping and lifting of the oars lulled me into a peaceful trance. Thorn sat at the bow, his powerful strokes guiding our canoe smoothly through the river, while Master Haris sat in the middle, his gaze fixated on the grandeur of the landscape. The towering canyon walls rose high above us, their red and ocher tones glowing in the warm sunlight.

Suddenly, Thorn's oar stilled, and he pointed skyward. I followed his gaze, squinting against the piercing brightness of the sun. There, soaring high above the ragged tops of the canyon, was a sight that took my breath away.

A griffon.

It was massive, with the body, tail, and back legs of a lion and the head, wings, and talons of an eagle. Its golden plumage shimmered in the sunlight while its tawny feline body was a blurred motion of power and grace. Its wings, spread wide, carried it on the wind with an ease that spoke of its mastery of the skies.

Its keen eyes, the color of molten gold, surveyed the world below with an air of majesty and arrogance. I felt a shiver run through me when those eyes locked onto mine for a moment. It pulled up, flapping its great wings as it perched on a dead tree that had made its way downriver.

The griffon gave a loud, echoing cry, a sound that vibrated through the air and echoed off the canyon walls, filling the expansive landscape with its resonant call. "*Be wary,*" it called to me. "*Danger lurks ahead.*"

"What does it mean?" I asked, looking at Thorn.

"What did it say?" Thorn asked calmly.

"Danger lurks ahead," I repeated, waving at the griffon as it took off once more and disappeared over the cliff's edge.

"Could be any number of things," Thorn said, continuing with his rowing. "It's probably talking about the rapids that lie around the bend, though."

"Rapids?" I asked, my eyes wide and frightened.

Thorn smirked. "Don't worry, you're with me, an expert. Just make sure to listen carefully to directions and hold onto this." He handed me an oar.

The peaceful rhythm of our journey was shattered as we turned a bend and were confronted by a churning froth.

"Fin, we've got a wild ride ahead!" Thorn called out, his voice steady over the roar of the water. He gripped the oar tighter, his knuckles white with the strain.

A lump of anxiety formed in my stomach, but I swallowed it down. I nodded, gripping my own oar, ready.

"Listen to my commands, Fin!" Thorn ordered, his voice echoing in the narrow canyon walls. "And stay calm. We're going to ride this together."

I felt the canoe dip as we were sucked into the first wave. It crashed over the bow, soaking me to the bone. The icy water took my breath away, but I shook the shock off and tightened my grip on the oar.

"Left! Hard left!" Thorn's command cut through the cacophony. I dug my oar into the raging waters, throwing my weight behind it. The canoe tilted alarmingly, but it avoided a sharp rock jutting out from the frothy waters.

The world turned into a blur of adrenaline, water, and Thorn's sharp commands. "Right! Back paddle! Hard right!" My muscles burned, my heart pounded in my chest, and every instinct screamed at me to flee. But I couldn't. I had to trust Thorn—trust his experience and his steady voice guiding us through the treacherous current.

Time seemed to stretch and compress, moments of terror merging into a wild, exhilarating ride. Eventually, we shot out of the rapids into a calm pool. We both let out relieved breaths, the adrenaline still buzzing in our veins. The canoe bobbed gently in the still waters as the canyon widened, the water growing deeper.

The echo of rushing water faded into the distance, replaced by the gentle splashing of a calm river against the canoe and the beat of my heart slowly returning to its normal rhythm.

"There aren't many more of those, are there?" Master Haris asked, clutching his pack to himself as he tried to protect his precious parchments from the water.

Thorn shrugged. "There's a fair few on the way to the palace."

"How many days until we reach Alden-Ester?" Haris adjusted his spectacles that had gone askew, along with his large hat.

"By river, about four, if we don't hit any traps."

I let my fingertips skim the cool water. "Traps?" I sensed fish darting around in the shadows below us. I didn't have much luck talking with fish. Either they weren't very smart, or my magic just wasn't attuned to them as well as it was to mammals, reptiles, and birds.

Amphibians gave me a hard time too.

I looked up to realize that Thorn was smiling at me. "Have you ridden rapids before?"

"No," I admitted. "But I grew up in Lark Harbor. I know how to paddle a boat. I know how to swim."

His eyes moved to the canyon wall. "You did well. I'm impressed."

I was beaming. I let out a breath, the adrenaline finally gone. It felt as though I'd passed a test. I looked around at the beauty of the canyons, the sun high overhead, and the hum of magic in the air. It was such a beautiful moment, I knew I would remember it for the rest of my days.

I wished I had someone I loved with me to share it with. Rowyn would've been an excellent partner. Destrian's face even flitted through my mind.

I looked over at my companions. Even though Master Haris was wet and haggard, he was gazing around, enjoying the moment. I knew with his magic he would certainly remember it, and I realized that maybe he'd wanted to come with me for that same feeling I did, to make good memories, to have an experience, and to be part of something good and fun and exciting.

The gods had tested me with the river and I had passed. I looked at Thorn. He was grinning—that smirk was starting to make me weak in the knees. I realized I didn't mind sharing the moment with them. We were people who desperately needed it.

I sat back and enjoyed the sway of the boat, my fingertips skimming the water's surface as the world of the fae passed before me.

THE DAY WAS ALREADY WANING when Thorn suddenly sat upright in the canoe, his face stern and alert. I could see him scanning the ripples on the river, and his hand instinctively moved toward the dagger at his belt.

"What is it?" Master Haris asked, his voice reflecting the same alertness. The scholar had grown accustomed to Thorn's instincts and knew better than to dismiss them.

Thorn didn't reply at first, still focused on the water. Then, the river began to churn beneath us, turning from a tranquil flow into a roiling mess of white water.

"Sprites," Thorn growled, reaching for his oar.

The creatures launched themselves at our canoe, their scaled bodies hitting with enough force to rock us violently. The impact jostled Haris, and he dropped his oar with a yelp. I grabbed the sides of the canoe, my knuckles turning white with the strain.

"Fin, help me steady it!" Thorn ordered, using his oar to push against the oncoming waves and the circling fae.

I grasped the oar, thrusting it into the water and pulling against the current. Despite our efforts, one of the scaled creatures slammed into the boat, throwing Haris to the side and dangerously tilting the canoe.

"Haris!" I cried out. He clung to the rim, his face pale and eyes wide with panic.

Before we could attempt to pull Haris back in, a powerful blow flipped us over entirely. The world seemed to spin as I hit the river, my breath stolen by the shock. Water rushed into my ears, muffling the chaos above.

I struggled against the current, trying to surface. The world blurred as I broke through, gasping for air. Thorn and Haris bobbed nearby, both looking as drenched and disoriented as I felt.

One by one, we managed to grab the overturned canoe, gasping for breath. We were all okay, but our supplies and gear were floating down the river, quickly swept away by the current.

And as I caught my breath, the sprites circled us,

their dark eyes glinting in the last light of the day.

"Who is your friend, Thorn?" one sprite asked in a voice that seemed to bubble up from the depths of the river itself. It was a strange, unearthly sound, but unmistakably a voice.

Thorn's annoyance was clear. "She's Fin." He shot a pointed look at the sprite. "And she's off-limits."

The creature seemed to take in this information with interest, its gaze shifting to me. "Fin," it mused, rolling my name around as if it were an interesting new taste. "Your human smells like magic. Fun magic."

"I'm a sorcerer," I shouted before Thorn could respond, meeting the sprite's curious gaze with my own.

The sprite seemed to consider this for a moment. As it was considering, another popped out. "Want to play?" it called, its voice like the lull of a lullaby.

Thorn's response was immediate and firm. "No, she doesn't wish to."

I looked at him, surprised by his certainty. How did he know I didn't want to play with the sprites?

But then I remembered the terror of being pulled underwater, of feeling the powerful currents around me, and I understood. This was a game I didn't want any part of.

The sprite blinked at Thorn's refusal, seeming genuinely surprised. "She doesn't want to play?" it asked, tilting its head at me.

"She's a guest of King Valon," Thorn snapped, his voice leaving no room for argument. "She's not here to play games."

The sprite studied Thorn for a moment, then let out a short bark of laughter. "Fine, fine," it said. "No games, then."

With that, it dipped back beneath the surface, leaving us in the quiet of the canyon. It was only then that the weight of what happened truly hit me—the danger we'd been in, the vulnerability we now faced. But alongside it was the thrill of the adventure, the excitement of being in this magical world.

"I guess we should get to shore," Thorn finally said, breaking the silence. "We might as well camp for the night."

As the sun began to dip behind the canyon wall, painting the sky in brilliant hues of orange and pink, we swam our canoe to the nearest shoreline. The sandy bank was firm underfoot, lined with a sprinkling of rugged trees. An ideal spot for setting up camp, and much welcomed after the earlier aquatic encounter.

Thorn effortlessly pulled the canoe onto dry land. Master Haris followed suit, although with significantly less grace, clutching a sack of parchments to his chest as if they were made of gold.

I stumbled out after them, still unnerved by the unexpected incident with the sprites. The solid ground was a relief beneath my sodden boots. My clothes clung to my skin, the fabric cold and heavy. Thorn must've noticed my discomfort because he quickly grabbed a soaked blanket that had been tied inside the canoe and draped it over my shoulders.

"We'll start a fire," he said, his eyes soft but determined. "You'll dry off in no time."

I thanked him with a nod, moving toward a flat rock nearby to sit. While Thorn busied himself with gathering what little firewood there was available, Master Haris rummaged through his sack.

Suddenly, a pack was tossed onto the shoreline from the river. Then a water pack. Then a belt of knives. Thorn collected each one.
"Thank you!" he shouted to the river but shook his head when he returned to us, dropping the supplies. "Fucking sprites," he grumbled.

AS THE EVENING CHILL DESCENDED, Thorn had a fire blazing, illuminating our small camp with a warm, comforting glow. The smell of wood smoke filled the air as Thorn then set about preparing a simple meal of dried meat and roots.

Haris pulled out paper and a little piece of coal before turning to me, his gray eyes hopeful. "Do you want to help me draw the griffon?"

When I declined, the look on his face sent a pang of guilt through my chest. Not enough guilt to change my mind, but enough to make me frown and tell him I was sorry for hurting his feelings. Haris was a good artist, but he preferred my drawings of animals to his.

I just wanted to rest and relax. The serene beauty of the Canyonlands as dusk gave way to night was calming, the stars twinkling brightly above us, unfettered by any city lights. The eerie calls of nocturnal creatures echoed in the distance, adding to the enchantment of the moment.

"Are your journeys often disrupted by others?" I asked, lying back on the stone and gazing up at the stars.

"Sprites are notorious tricksters, but they mostly mean no harm. They can be . . . persuasive, especially when they want something." Thorn smiled at me. "Some act like it's their duty to make my job harder. It keeps me in a job though.

"The important thing is not to let their antics get under your skin," Thorn continued. "Don't let them pull you into their games. It's mostly harmless fun for them, but it can turn . . . complicated . . . very quickly."

"Sounds like a good rule for dealing with the entire fae court," Master Haris remarked from where he was scratching with his charcoal, his voice heavy with sarcasm.

"Very observant, Master Haris," Thorn agreed with a smirk. "That's exactly right."

With the warmth of the fire seeping into my bones and the rhythmic lullaby of the river in the background, the day's tensions began to fade.

As I watched the flames dance and flicker, I found myself stealing glances at Thorn. He sat across from me, his golden eyes reflecting the firelight.

I didn't say anything, not with Haris there. It seemed that the unspoken words between Thorn and me were building up in Haris's presence, and they always came spilling out when we got a mere moment alone. I wondered what the rest of the trip would be like. What about the palace? What about the king?

Later, as I lay on the cool stone, I felt oddly at peace. The day had been long and eventful, and the night was promising a well-earned respite. The wild chorus of nocturnal creatures lulled me into a sense of tranquility. Our conversations dwindled, replaced by the sounds of the wilderness. As my eyelids grew heavy, I felt sleep creeping in, ready to wrap me in its comforting embrace.

Chapter 6

AFTER FOUR DAYS OF NAVIGATING the winding river and encountering a variety of fae—with mixed results—Alden-Ester emerged in the distance. The city was built into the canyons where several rivers met. It rose above the water, a colossal vertical city that reminded me of how Rowyn described Espiria. She'd even said that Espiria used to be a fae stronghold, and when the Others fled the Lyrican invasion, they'd left it to the Morganites to use. But Alden-Ester seemed to be something else entirely. I'd never seen anything like it in my life. It wasn't like the hoodoos in the first city we were in, where everything was red stone. No, Alden-Ester's canyons had different colors streaked through the surface of granite, and they were colossal, with rows of trees growing up the sides. I could see why this place was the crown jewel of the fae world.

It was truly magical.

"Here we are," Thorn announced, his eyes bright with anticipation, his usual nonchalant demeanor replaced by an eager restlessness.

Master Haris was also alert, his quills and

parchments forgotten for the moment, replaced by wide-eyed wonder. His gaze moved rapidly as he tried to absorb as much of the city as possible. I could see the scholar in him relishing the opportunity to document everything he saw firsthand.

As we neared, the beauty of Alden-Ester further unfurled. Buildings carved from massive tree trunks towered over us, their moss-covered rooftops glimmering with dew in the morning light. Canopies of luminescent flowers floated above the waterways, casting vibrant reflections that danced on the surface. Gossamer-winged fairies zipped through the air, their laughter ringing out in the fresh air.

Thorn maneuvered the canoe toward a wide dock populated by a diverse range of fae creatures. As our canoe nudged the dock, a fae with bark-like skin and leaves for hair approached us with a piece of birch where something was written in a spiky scrawl. He exchanged foreign words with Thorn before moving on to the next approaching boat.

We disembarked and started our way through the city. The streets were lined with market stalls displaying an array of colorful fruits, sparkling gemstones, and items of exquisite craftsmanship. A group of pixie children chased each other, their screechy laughter mingling with the chirping of birds and the soft whispers of the wind.

Thorn led the way, his confident strides revealing his familiarity with the place, though he gripped one of his blades as he maneuvered through the variety of fae that was passing through the streets. Master Haris was caught between trying to keep up and pausing every few steps to whisper hurried notes about everything he saw. I found myself torn between soaking in the unique sights and sounds of Alden-Ester, and keeping an eye on the fae who occasionally looked our way with curious gazes.

Thorn pointed out important landmarks—a temple dedicated to Imor, a grand art house towering several stories high, a shop filled with enchanted trinkets, luscious fruit, and a wide variety of produce. But nothing prepared me for the spectacle that was the Royal Palace.

Nestled at the city's center, climbing up the side of the canyon wall, was a colossal structure, its towers dug out of striated stone in an intricate fusion of wood and rock, with elegant archways and soaring spires that rose to brush the sky.

"Welcome to the heart of Alden-Ester, the Royal Palace," Thorn announced, barely masking his pride. Master Haris let out a breath of awe. I felt a rush of excitement, the palpable energy of the palace stirring

320

something within me.

The entrance to the cavern yawned before us, swallowing the remnants of daylight as we ventured into the fae court. Crystals hung from the ceiling like stars in a twilight sky, casting an ethereal glow that played upon the magnificent stalagmites jutting from the cavern floor. The air hummed with ancient magic, a symphony of power that sent shivers down my spine.

Fae of all sorts went about their duties, moving with purpose and reverence. Some nodded as Thorn passed, acknowledging his presence with respect. It was a far cry from the wary gazes we'd attracted during our journey. Others studied Master Haris and me with luminous eyes, their heads tilted, nostrils flaring. Uncertainty crept up my spine when a few stepped closer. I felt a lock of hair being lifted and turned. Something snarled behind me.

A reptilian fae was leaning toward me, its amber eyes gleaming in the torchlight. It had my lock of hair caught between its claws. With a swift, almost elegant motion, it severed the lock with a menacing smile.

"Hey!" Thorn said, grabbing my arm and pulling me behind him.

The creature withdrew, its scales shimmering a myriad of colors as it retreated into the shadows. The hiss it emitted was a chilling sound, echoing faintly as it disappeared. My heart pounded in my chest, the sound unsettling, to say the least.

"Stinking garodiles," Thorn grumbled, looking over his shoulder as he pushed me ahead of him. He leaned toward my ear. "Don't worry, many fae use human hair for weaving enchantments, but they won't affect the bearer."

I nodded and tried to calm my racing heart.

Thorn stopped at a large, arched entrance that led deeper into the caverns. A Woltari with spiral horns and a long coat decorated with scales of some sort stood to the side, looking bored. "Welcome," he said, his voice sharp and authoritative. He turned to Thorn and began speaking in an alien tongue. I glanced at Master Haris.

Thorn, however, responded fluently in the same cryptic language. The exchange carried on for a few moments before the Woltari finally addressed us. "Fin Of-Cheapside, Master Haris Of-Solridge, welcome to Alden-Ester. I am Yew Of-the-Castle, your liaison at court."

"I was under the impression that Thorn Beyond-the-Border was our gatekeeper and guide," I said, straightening. I didn't like not knowing what they said upon our arrival. If Yew Of-the-Castle could speak in the shared tongue, then why hadn't he used it? What were they hiding? I felt a jolt of anger at Thorn. Was he keeping something from me? The nagging feeling of deception, an all-too-familiar enemy from my time on the streets, gnawed at the edges of my mind. I was no stranger to the undercurrents of dishonesty, and I wasn't about to let my guard down now.

"This is common," Thorn assured me, "when you are guests of the king."

"Very well," Master Haris said, glancing at me with questioning brows. "We thank you for your generous hospitality. Lyrica sends its regards and appreciates your assistance in helping our young pilgrim here."

Yew rolled his eyes. "Well, Lyrica is welcome, I suppose. Come, let's get you to your quarters. Food will be sent up, and we'll let you get some rest for the night. Tomorrow morning, King Valon will wish to see you."

"We can be ready first thing," Master Haris said, stepping forward with his pack in his arms.

"Actually, he wishes to meet with the young sorceress—alone."

"Why?" Master Haris adjusted his spectacles. "I can assure you this is most irregular."

Yew drew himself up. "You are not in the position to know what is regular or irregular in the court of Alden-Ester, Master Haris. King Valon has ordered a private meeting, and a private meeting it will be so there is no point in an argument. He does not intend to harm the girl. We have offered you safe passage through our realm entirely out of goodwill. Would you deny your esteemed host this simple request?"

"Of course not," Master Haris stammered. "I'm just trying to take care of the girl."

Yew studied Haris a moment longer before turning back to me. "This way," he said, leading us down a crystal-lit corridor. "I'm sure Thorn has informed you already, we are quite crowded here at the castle. You will be sharing a guest room, as I'm sure you've had to do on the passage here."

I nodded. It *had* been expected. I glanced up at Thorn, wondering what he was thinking about that odd interaction. His face was impassive, his eyes on Yew's back.

As Yew navigated us through a labyrinth of canyon tunnels, each illuminated by the gentle glow of crystal lights, I found my gaze continually drawn to the assorted fae we passed. From bickering gnomes clutching their hats to a squadron of fairies zipping above us, their high-pitched voices echoing off the stone walls, the variety of fae life was breathtaking. My heart pounded in my chest, anxiety and excitement battling for dominance.

Finally, we stopped at a door. I was glad Thorn was

with us because I had no idea where I was or how to get out. Yew opened the door and motioned us in. I gritted my teeth as he said something to Thorn in their language again, then shut the door and left us to unpack and catch our breaths.

I turned on Thorn, a frown pulling at my lips. "What was he saying to you? Why did he conceal it?"

Thorn's shrug was nonchalant, his expression betraying nothing. "He concealed it because he didn't want you to hear. We were shifting your itinerary, and Yew was keeping me abreast of the king's wishes. I also gave him a few updates so that our visit could go smoother."

I was taken aback. "What updates?" I couldn't shake off the niggling sense in my gut that I'd learned to pay heed to at Lark Harbor.

Thorn raised his brows. "There are many fae who welcome the opportunity to meet with human guests. So, I keep a running list of who shares interests with humans, and when someone comes who meets their desires, I invite them to meet you."

"You're selling access to us?" I asked, my brows wrinkled as I crossed my arms.

Something in Thorn's expression changed and his tail began to snap back and forth. "I'm the guide," Thorn said, his voice measured and low. "It's my job to make sure you have a good time. If there is someone who I think will improve your stay, then I will introduce you."

"And vice versa?" I asked. "What if they want something from me that I don't want to give?"

Thorn stiffened, his nostrils flaring. "That's not how this works." Master Haris, watching the exchange with worry behind his spectacles, went completely ignored. "The fae way of life revolves around consent. I'm making sure your stay is comfortable—that is all. Why are you so suspicious?"

I didn't know, truth be told. Maybe Rowyn was starting to rub off on me. She was always suspicious someone was out to get her. Who would want me? I was nobody. At least, I was nobody at the moment, though I was determined to change that.

But his anger was startling, raw, and unexpected. I found myself stumbling over my words, trying to articulate my confused feelings. "I just don't like feeling like you're keeping something from me," I managed, giving my bag a sound smack when it tried to nip at my fingers. I cursed the fairy dust that still lingered in its folds from an earlier altercation.

"You asked, and I've told you," Thorn said, angrily ripping open his own pack and pulling clothes out.

"Who did you plan to meet with me?" I asked as I

took my clothes to the wardrobe and began hanging them. I wished I hadn't angered Thorn.

"I told Yew to prepare a person who works with the fae creatures, like griffons and unicorns. I thought you'd be interested in speaking about his work and meeting one or two of the animals he's worked with. I asked for Lullaby Beside-the-Pine for Master Haris. They sing ballads full of fae history that Master Haris could use for his work."

I clenched my teeth. That sounded perfect actually. "I'm sorry I doubted you," I said softly.

Thorn nodded as he came up beside me and hung some clothes next to mine. His voice dropped lower. "If you have any complaints about my ability to take care of you, just let me know."

"I don't have complaints," I said hurriedly. Master Haris was frowning at Thorn, and I didn't want more of a confrontation than I'd just created. "You've done a wonderful job."

And he had. We hadn't just encountered sprites on our trek to Alden-Ester, but a troupe of ogres had come upon us on the road and threatened to eat Haris until Thorn showed them a sigil and badge that the king had gifted him. Then our packs and belongings had been stolen by curious pixies. By the time we'd found our stuff, it was strung all over the western bank of a ledge covered with fairy dust. I wrestled with my bag as it tried to bite my hand for a full twenty minutes before I was able to brush off enough dust to slow the enchantment. It still tried to snap my fingers every once in a while, though it wasn't as quick as it was in the beginning.

Thorn had taken charge of it all. He negotiated with the ogres, his hand on a pair of wicked blades that he had strapped to his waist. On his belt also hung pouches of enchanted fairy dust. One lit fires that burned for an hour before he had to sprinkle more. Another healed minor cuts and wounds, of which we earned plenty on our trip down the river.

The fae were leagues ahead of the sorcerers when it came to mobile enchantments that could be placed by non-magic users. Their magic came from the earth, and they were pros at putting enchantments on objects that traveled well too. Honestly, it was a shame Lyrica feared the fae to the extent that they did, because they had a lot to offer in trade.

We fell into a heavy and uncomfortable silence. As Thorn busied himself with unpacking, I found myself regretting the confrontation, second-guessing my own paranoia. He'd thought of everything.

"I'm sorry I doubted you," I added, swallowing my pride. His curt nod was the only acknowledgment I received.

I thought back to the people who Thorn was setting me up to meet. The few times we were alone, he made a point to ask more candid questions in that flirty way of his that I'd come to enjoy. It felt nice to be flirted with, but I couldn't help but worry that I was a mark he was trying to fool. After all, fae loved to play tricks, and I didn't want to be painted as a gullible human. Still, Thorn hadn't given me any reason to think he would make me look ridiculous. It just took a lot for me to trust someone, I guessed. I wasn't someone who received a lot of attention from humans. There was always someone far more talented, or pretty, or noble next to me.

"What are we to expect in the next few days?" I asked.

Thorn arranged the couch a certain way, then tossed his shoes off and lay back. "King Valon will see you in a personal meeting, but we will dine in his court, and you all can mingle then. We want you to enjoy yourselves, but take only drinks and food that I've permitted. Some of the fae like to cause problems with guests when it suits them."

"I appreciate your precautions," I told him, trying to sound sincere. He merely nodded in response, not even looking at me. My heart fell. I should've realized my suspicions would hurt his feelings. He must be more prideful than I initially thought.

Thorn faced the fire. "Try to get some rest. It's been a long journey, and the king's court can be overwhelming, especially on your first visit."

I glanced at Master Haris, who seemed to be on the verge of nodding off in a plush armchair. Weariness was settling into my own bones, the adrenaline from our arrival finally beginning to fade. "I will, thank you."

As I prepared for bed, I couldn't help but cast a few glances at Thorn, who was seemingly lost in thought on the couch. The firelight cast his features in sharp relief, adding a certain intensity to his profile that was both unsettling and intriguing.

Shaking off these thoughts, I slipped into bed, pulling the blankets close around me. As I drifted off to sleep, I couldn't help but wonder what the following day would bring.

Chapter 7

THE FIRST GOLDEN RAYS of dawn streamed through a gap in the cavern, casting long, flickering shadows on the rock walls. I had barely slept, my mind spinning with anxious thoughts and curiosity. I was meeting King Valon, ruler of the fae and one of the most powerful beings in existence.

When I rose, I didn't see Thorn.

"He awoke early to meet with the king," Master Haris said, sounding slightly put out.

I tried to hide my disappointment at his absence and began readying for my own audience with the monarch.

"Now that we're finally alone," Master Haris said, pulling a fresh robe over his head, "we will need to go over a few things."

I sighed, knowing the conversation had been coming. Master Haris was going to lay ground rules. He had to do it.

"What are you planning to tell the king?" Haris asked as I splashed water on my face.

"The truth is easy enough," I said. "I'm here for my gem."

"You must not speak about how Lyrica is run, nor how we are in a bad way with the drought. The Consul of Korballis sent a letter warning that he feels the fae have been testing the border. It could be that he will try to find out about our western defenses and press you for information. You cannot give him anything vital about the state of Lyrica's governance."

"Why did we push them into Horan?" I asked, brushing through the snarls in my hair. "There's a lot we could learn from the fae." I thought about weaving a braid but reconsidered. Unlike the humans, most fae left their hair down . . . wild and untamed. I decided to let the pale strands fall behind me instead of bothering with a style.

"The Morganites and fae are children of Imor. It suited them to ally. Make no mistake, when the Lyricans crossed over, the Morganite sorcerers used a bevy of fae enchantments that almost lost us the war. It wasn't until Jude Masqari took out the Morganite court that we actually had a chance to win."

I quieted. Rowyn was right. The Lyricans should never have crossed over. But, what's done was done. "I will say nothing, but I must try not to lie. If King Valon deems me untrustworthy, then he won't help us, and I can't afford to let that happen."

"I know it's a fine line," Master Haris said. "But you

are a very smart girl. You will be able to find a way to earn his trust while also maintaining your loyalty."

I mused over Master Haris's words as I walked to the wardrobe. My loyalty? Really? I'd never thought to question it, not in the way that Rowyn had, but now that I was thrust into this position, I was starting to reconsider. Did I really hold loyalty to the Lyrican nobles when I was an outcast among them? The nobles of the West were just a taste of how people would treat me on the eastern shore if I was ever allowed to go, which was a slim possibility because of my father and his family's wishes. I didn't think I was wrong in thinking that he would actively hold me back if he thought me a threat to his family.

"It's different, isn't it?" Master Haris asked, his gaze drifting over the organic curves and hollows that made up our accommodations.

"Different doesn't quite cover it," I replied. I'd never considered where I stood in regard to loyalty to the crown. I'd never had to. I'd spent my life focusing on survival. Anything else just wasn't deemed important enough for me to think about.

I wondered what the king wanted to discuss with me as I pulled out the nicest dress I owned, a gown that I'd fallen in love with when I'd gone to SeaPort. I'd venture into the city with Breeze every other weekend and browse the stalls and send letters, as well as visit with the animals I'd made friends with there. There was an old nag, Priscilla, who lived at the community stable and always enjoyed a chat. I made sure to bring my oils to clean out her ear mites, and she would tell me who she saw stabling horses in the inn. Humans didn't think much of animals when they were around them, but it was my experience that the domesticated beasts were extremely knowledgeable about their human keeper's routines.

On my way through the market, I would walk by the tailor's shop and admire the dress, its bodice wrapped in silk, the shimmer of the greens and blues flowing down the train like water.

I'd scrimped and saved for that dress, counting my coins greedily as the purchase date grew closer. I'd even bartered with the shop owner and gotten him to cut the price in half, leaving me a tidy sum left over.

Luckily, my father, General Ivar, sent an allowance every month. Being from Maryse and a military commander, he was well-off enough for me to enjoy that benefit. It was a stark difference from what I was used to. Some said you never knew what you had until you lost it. I'd grown up with absolutely nothing to lose, and now that I finally had something, an actual chance at a life of my own, I felt the urge to protect it at all costs. I wanted to make sure that I never needed saving again.

I began pulling the dress on. After adjusting the arms and bodice, I asked Master Haris to help me tie the back. I then pulled out a few paints that Galena had helped me make—so I wouldn't have to spend any of my precious gold—and began brushing some on my cheeks and eyelids.

"How do you feel about meeting the king?" Master Haris asked. "If you're uncomfortable with going alone, just let me know and I will ensure that I accompany you."

I almost laughed. "I'm fine with it," I said, dabbing a tinted rose ointment on my lips.

"Very well." Master Haris rubbed the bald spot on his head. "Just be careful about your bargain. Fae are tricky. They will always come out ahead in a deal or gamble."

"We can't expect them to help me gain my gem for nothing," I reminded him.

"We need to be careful when making agreements, Fin. Remember, every deal has a price. I cannot stress this enough. I'm trying to protect you."

"I will try my best." It was as noncommittal of an answer as I could manage as I turned around in the mirror and studied my reflection. I liked my hair, at least. It went well with the dress, though I'd not done much to it other than ensure there were no knots. Satisfied with my appearance, I began to pace as Master Haris set out his bottles of ink and quills on the only desk in the room. Before he could ask for my assistance with anything, I opened our door, wondering if Thorn was coming to get me or if I would have to find the fae king alone.

An elven guard was waiting outside. "Are you ready for your audience?" he asked, his nostrils flaring. "I'm to escort you there."

I nodded, shutting the door behind me and turning shyly around. "Will this look all right for His Majesty?" I asked, gently lifting the skirt and letting it fall.

"You look good enough to eat," the elf said, shooting me a sharp-toothed smile as his eyes roved over my body. I smiled and blushed, then froze as he licked his lips.

I frowned. "Wait, you mean actually eat, don't you."

The elf's grin grew wider. "I'm betting you would taste divine roasted over a fire of cedar and heartwood." His eyes trailed over my body a second time as if not noticing the horror that crept across my face. "Topped with an elderberry compote and accompanied with prickle pear wine."

I tried to figure out if that was a compliment as he

began leading me down the hall. I allowed him a wide berth. His figure was long and lean, his hair a black sheaf divided by two pointed ears that seemed to twitch at the sounds that echoed in the cavern hall.

We stopped in front of a wooden door with some kind of growth curling around the outside of the arch and glowing a bright iridescent mix of green and yellow. Standing on either side were two formidable figures whose hulking silhouettes resembled tales of trolls from the stories I'd heard as a child. On their backs were strapped enormous axes, the blade nearly the size of my torso. They went back and forth with my elven guard, speaking in an alien tongue that echoed down the halls.

Annoyance clawed at me like a hungry cat. I shifted my feet, not knowing what they were saying and hating the feeling of losing control.

The elf turned to me with a razor-sharp smile. "He is with someone else right now. He will be ready for you shortly."

I sighed. Having to stand outside and stew about it wasn't doing my nerves any favors. My mind was a whirlpool of what-ifs. What if I said something wrong? What if I agreed to a life of servitude? King Valon was spoken of with reverence, as though he was a just and fair leader, but he was still fae.

I felt a twinge of regret for my earlier brashness, Master Haris's cautionary words echoing in my head. Why was I to meet the king alone? What was Thorn discussing with him? The thoughts were gnawing at the edges of my composure.

As if my will had conjured him, the wooden door creaked open, revealing Thorn. His golden eyes flashed as they swept over me, the warmth in his gaze flaring brighter.

My nerves were momentarily forgotten. The new dress was a good decision, a small victory amid the chaotic spiral of my thoughts.

"Fin," Thorn said, stepping forward. I adored the way he said my name. It fell from his mouth like a petal from a day-old flower, drifting out of his lips and landing a little too close to my heart. "You'll be fine. Be truthful."

I took a deep breath, nodded, and managed a tiny, hopefully confident, step toward the imposing door. I looked over my shoulder, catching Thorn's supportive gaze. "Will you wait for me?" I asked, inadvertently glancing at the smirking elf.

Thorn followed my gaze and nodded. "I'll be right here." His smile soothed my lingering anxieties.

With that assurance, I mustered the courage to face what lay beyond the door. At least I had Thorn waiting outside. The last thing I wanted was to offend King Valon and end up a feast for the overzealous elf. Fae were unpredictable, after all.

Taking deep, steadying breaths, I pushed the door further open, lifted my head with as much confidence as I could muster, and stepped into the unknown.

The room beyond was a small, stone-like grotto. Stalagmites and stalactites adorned with crystals stretched toward each other, with shimmering veins crisscrossing over them, casting the room in iridescent light. A trickle of water could be heard making its way through the cracks in the wall and pooling in a wide, shallow pond.

Two grand chairs made of crystals and gemstones awaited, one already occupied by who I could only assume was King Valon. Woltari, like Thorn and the king, appeared stronger, with broad, square faces and shoulders sculpted with muscle. The elves and fairies, in comparison, held a more delicate air about them, their features appearing more chiseled and elegant.

The king's silver-white hair reached past his shoulders with half braided along the top of his head between a crown of large and imposing horns that curled over his temple and spiraled back down. His eyes, like Thorn's, were gold.

"Fin Of-Cheapside," the king greeted me, his voice

deep and resonant. "I've been looking forward to this meeting."

I took a deep breath, curtsying as I'd been taught. I was definitely second-guessing my choice of surname. It didn't sound right falling from the king's lips. "Your Highness, it's an honor to be here," I said, hoping that my voice didn't betray my nervousness.

King Valon waved his hand to the chair at his side. "Please have a seat. There's no need to be afraid."

Gathering my courage, I approached, feeling the king's eyes on me every step of the way. I ran my hands down my back, smoothing the gown as I sat, then adjusted the folds so that they fell just so. Sitting up straight, shoulders down, I met the king's eyes.

"You've journeyed far to be here, Fin," the king said, his gaze more studious than anything else. "Few humans have braved the path to Alden-Ester." I didn't feel anger from him, nor greed. It was as though he were merely curious.

"How could I refuse the invitation?"

King Valon's brows rose. "Indeed, though I think you will find our court to be most welcoming. Most humans who visit as guests give glowing reports."

"Do you often entertain sorcerers?" I asked. "I would think they would be clamoring to see how you all use magic."

"I understand that Lyrica keeps its sorcerers rather busy." King Valon rested his chin on his fist as his eyes trailed down my body. "We've had very few over the years, and even fewer that we actually cared to meet, if I'm to be completely honest."

Hmph. He didn't like Lyrican sorcerers? So why did he invite me to his palace?

"We were excited to read your letter," he went on. "I'd met one of your grandsires and enjoyed his company when he came questing for his gem."

I smiled. "We are long-awaited friends then?" The king's mouth crooked, but that was all he gave me. My cheeks warmed, and I hoped I hadn't sounded coy. Honestly, I'd wondered if anyone would recognize my skill and family. Fae lived extremely long lives, their bodies imbued with magic as they were. It felt like the only real connection I had to my father's side. He would be green with jealousy if he ever heard about it.

King Valon was watching me with those sharp eyes of his. "You look absolutely mouthwatering when you blush," he said, his nostrils flaring. I thought back to the elf. "Would you join me for a drink?"

A fairy flew into view and placed a crystal goblet in my hand. King Valon drew up the most extravagant decanter I'd ever seen and pulled the stopper out of the top. "You need to blow in the glass," King Valon said, motioning toward the goblet.

I blew, and a sparkling cloud curled away. "Fairy dust?"

King Valon nodded as he poured. "Always blow out a glass before you use it," he said in a tone that hinted he'd said it many times before. "Fairy dust and poisons only have effect if the correct quantity is used for the size of the person or object being enchanted."

I noted that tidbit to tell Master Haris later. I raised the glass to my lips and was about to take a drink when I remembered Thorn warning against eating or drinking anything that he did not provide. I hesitated.

King Valon noticed. "I promise that the wine I poured is safe to drink," he said as though that statement would suffice.

"It will have no effect on me whatsoever?" Just because something was safe didn't mean it wouldn't do anything.

King Valon tilted his head, his expression inscrutable. "It is juneberry wine. The fae enjoy strong alcohol, so too much will inebriate you, but it holds no other enchantments."

I sipped. It was sweet and tasted like a mix of blueberries and apples. I waited a moment, fearful of what King Valon determined was "strong." The alcohol swam lazily to my head, but it was altogether pleasant.

I took one more sip, so as not to make myself look ungrateful, then placed the crystal goblet on the small side table that sat between the chairs.

"Are you always so gracious to travelers?" I asked, scooting forward in the seat. It wasn't the most comfortable chair. The gems made for an uneven back and seemed to hit my bones all wrong.

King Valon took a sip of his own glass, then pointed at me. "I see why Thorn likes you."

He hadn't answered my question, just diverted from the topic. I wondered what he wasn't sharing. Yet, he could only speak the truth.

Thorn liked me? I hadn't messed it up last night with my suspicions? I tried to calm my giddy heart. Though Thorn had features similar to the king, I thought him altogether more handsome. Thorn's skin was more swarthy, his hair a dark, deep brown. Thorn's facial hair made him appear more human, which didn't seem to be a fae trait at all. "He is a credit to you," I acknowledged, hoping that the king couldn't guess how I was feeling.

"He is," the king agreed, his eyes unwavering. It was odd. Few people looked very closely at me. "He is one of my adopted children that turned out well. I've lived a long time, and others did not grow to be so . . . worldly as Thorn. I made fewer mistakes with him, and the boy had a good mother."

"What happened to the others?" It seemed strange that a king would take it upon himself to adopt children, but the fae were different from us in many respects.

"Some are still alive, of course, busy with various tasks. Others have died. It's the way of the wheel." The king leaned forward. "But enough pleasantries. Let's delve into the marrow of it. You need a gem, yes?"

I nodded.

"The tourmaline you mentioned, the same type of gem your grandsire used, is found in a cave that can only be accessed on the full moon, in two weeks' time."

"How will I get it?" I asked.

"Thorn mentioned that you can swim?"

My heart sank. I could swim, but I was also very aware of the dangers water posed. I'd hoped to avoid having to dive for my gem, but a sorcerer chose very little when it came to how we would be tested on our quest.

"Is it far from here? Who will accompany me?" The questions began to bubble out of me. "Will I be able to bring any equipment?"

King Valon held up a hand. "Thorn will guide you to where the caves are, accompanied by Master Haris if you desire. I have already spoken to the Merchief of the Ng'Baoba tribe. She's arranged for two of her own to accompany you. It is a difficult task, as all ways to obtain gems are, but its risks are minimal with the correct precautions."

His words lessened some of my fears. He'd clearly planned for my arrival and was trying to make my journey as easy as possible. But why? What was the catch? How did he benefit? Why would the king of all fae care about me?

"You seem to have thought of everything," I said, absentmindedly running my fingers over the bumpy gems on the side of the throne. "How do you require payment for your assistance and hospitality?"

King Valon sat back in his chair. Clearly his was more comfortable than mine. Of course, he was king. "For a hundred years, Horan has been a haven for fae, but times are changing. The fae grow restless. Our hearts yearn for the thrill of adventure, the beauty of discovery, the connection to the world beyond our borders."

His gaze met mine. "I want to make a deal to open the borders that have kept us hidden away for so long, and I need a mediator."

I blinked, trying to process his words. Help the fae open the borders? It was far worse than what Master Haris had mentioned. The idea seemed colossal, beyond my capabilities, and I knew that if the consuls were against it, the emperor would be too.

"And what . . . what would you want me to do as . . . mediator?" I asked, apprehension seeping into my voice. It was better than "Who the hell do you think I am?" How in the world did he expect me to help him achieve such a task? No consul on the western shore would agree to it.

King Valon tilted his head to the side. "You have influence—connections. You are a sorceress from Solridge, one of the esteemed schools of magic in the empire. And you are soon to be a gem-bearer. You can sway the minds of others—convince them that we mean no harm."

I almost laughed at King Valon using the words "others" to describe Lyricans. But what he asked for was no laughing matter. "I don't think you understand who I am. I have absolutely no sway over anybody. The nobles at Solridge wouldn't give me the time of day even if I asked, and my father has made it very clear that he expects me to stay away from the eastern shore."

King Valon's eyes narrowed. "I was given to understand that Lyrica placed a high value on their sorcerers."

"They do," I agreed. "But that's about as far as it

goes in Lyrica. It's a lot of what can you do for the empire and less of what the empire can do for you, type thing."

"You speak to animals," King Valon said. "Your forefather could shapeshift into animals. I would think that the empire would have great use for you and heap rewards upon you. Is this not the case?"

I opened my mouth to speak, then shut it. I didn't really know how to explain it to King Valon because he was right—that's probably how it *should* be—but that wasn't how it was, at least in my case. Then, my mind went back to his words.

"Wait, did you say my forefather could shapeshift?"

King Valon's lips twitched. "Yes, he could shift into animals that he was knowledgeable of, at will. I believe his favorite was a wolf."

I shouldn't have asked him. I betrayed the fact that I held less knowledge of my skills than he did. It wasn't like it was my fault though. My father certainly didn't take the time to go over the history of my gift within his family, and the library at Solridge, though adequate for studying history, was not as complete as the one in Somme when it came to sorcerers.

"He trained with one of the fae shapeshifters," King Valon went on. "I have already sent notice that you were coming to Claw, but I can request that she train you if that is your wish."

"And what price would this Claw ask in return?" I was already weary with the number of favors I supposedly owed the court of the fae. The king was really heaping on gifts, and I was starting to feel as though he was getting ready to take advantage of me. Then again, his request was astoundingly out of the realm of possibility for someone like me.

"Claw already owes me a favor," King Valon said simply.

Hmph. "So, I would owe *you* more?"

King Valon shrugged offhand, but his eyes betrayed his increased interest. Misgivings pooled in my gut. There was something he was keeping from me. A truth he was hiding.

"I don't see a way I can achieve what you're asking," I admitted. "Honestly, my father wants me nowhere near the eastern shore, to protect his family, and the emperor would never agree to open borders to Horan. The Marendeslys have never, and will never, trust fae."

"You underestimate your own abilities," King Valon said. "I want you to spend the day thinking on the possibilities. Thorn will bring you to the feast tonight, and I will have your answer then."

That was as clear a dismissal as any. I rose, my heart hammering in my chest as I tried to wrap my head around King Valon's request.

Chapter 8

EMERGING FROM THE KING'S meeting room, I felt as though I was stepping out of a surreal dream. The weight of the conversation within those walls seemed to hang heavily on my shoulders. As the door closed behind me, I blinked back reality and found Thorn waiting, as he promised, leaning against the wall with muscled arms crossed, looking like a steadfast anchor in the sea of my tumultuous thoughts.

"How was it?" Thorn asked, a single brow raised.

"Not great," I admitted. "What he wants is an impossibility."

The echo of our footsteps bounced off the cold stone walls of Alden-Ester's intricate hallways as Thorn walked at my side, his golden eyes pensive.

"Trying to convince Lyrica to open the borders to Horan . . . it's an impossible task, even for a seasoned diplomat," I explained, breaking the silence that had stretched between us.

A bitter laugh escaped me. "And I am hardly that. I'm not noble. No one in the empire would listen to a word I have to say." My voice was thick with frustration, my hands balling into fists at my side. The king's request was not just a tall order; it was a mountainous one.

But I wanted his help badly.

I could learn to shapeshift.

I could have more help to reach my gem.

King Valon had certainly gone out of his way to make the decision difficult for me.

Thorn's gaze was sympathetic and understanding. "Fin," he began, reaching out to lightly grasp my arm, causing a shiver to travel up my spine. His touch was surprisingly gentle. "King Valon wouldn't have asked if he didn't see potential in you."

I shook my head. "Potential or not, I am not sure I can fulfill his request. It feels like being handed a mountain to move."

We reached our door, and it opened to reveal Master Haris waiting, his face a mask of worry and anticipation.

"Well?" Haris said before I could so much as set foot inside. "What did he say?"

I sighed, pressing my fingers to my temples. "He . . . he wants something," I began, deliberately being vague as I strode to a chair and sank down. "A voice that he can use in the human lands . . . in Lyrica."

Haris's face contorted into a frown. "He wishes that

person to be you?"

"Yes," I replied, my mind racing as I tried to avoid divulging too much. Haris would lose his ever-loving mind if he found out that the king's intention was to open the border entirely. He'd probably make me leave, with or without my gem. Why did anyone care whether or not I came into my full powers? Especially when the price would be to unleash the fae back into the world.

I cared though. I would do it, too, if it was possible. I was absolutely selfish enough to sacrifice the border and peace we've had from the fae for my gem.

"What message does he wish you to give?" he pressed, his words clipped. "Did he mention terms? Conditions?"

"He . . . didn't mention any," I lied, crossing my arms over my chest. "He just . . . he wants an ally to change the thinking around the fae."

Haris frowned, clearly not buying my story. But he seemed willing to drop the topic. "Very well. We'll figure it out later. For now, let's focus on getting your gem."

"All right," I said, rising from my chair. "What is on the itinerary for today?"

It turned out that Thorn, as our official guide, had a full day planned to show us around the beautiful palace of Alden-Ester.

A sense of awe descended upon us as Thorn guided us into the vast archives. High, towering shelves filled with numerous ancient tomes and scrolls stretched as far as the eye could see. The air was thick with dust and the faint, musty scent of old parchment, but an undeniable magic permeated the place.

"Welcome to the mind of Alden-Ester," Thorn declared, his voice echoing slightly off the stone walls.

Master Haris looked as though he had just been presented with the greatest gift in the world. His eyes lit up with joy, a sharp intake of breath his only response. He scanned the room with an almost reverent expression, his fingers lightly brushing the embossed spine of a weathered leather-bound book. "Incredible," he murmured, his voice barely above a whisper, almost drowned by the silence of the vast chamber.

Thorn smiled at Haris's reaction, his eyes sparkling with amusement. "And this . . ." He gestured to a figure hunched over a desk laden with scrolls and texts. "Is the head archivist, Winnow."

Haris all but sprinted to the desk, bowing reverently to the elder fae, who looked up in surprise. Haris gushed, expressing his admiration and gratitude for being allowed to see the sprawling labyrinth of knowledge. As Master Haris eagerly began to pore over the texts and with the enthusiasm of a child discovering a hidden treasure, I found myself pulled in a different direction.

Thorn was beside me, his magnetic presence impossible to ignore. A teasing smile danced on his lips as he picked up a timeworn book, its pages faintly glowing with otherworldly script. "This one," he said, his voice a low rumble, "spins tales of star-crossed lovers bound by the cosmos. Intriguing, isn't it?"

His words held an air of nonchalance, but his gaze was anything but casual. A silent dare flickered in his eyes, a challenge that set my heart racing. Struggling to keep my emotions under wraps, I forced a lighthearted retort. "Only if they can read the stars."

As I reached for the same book, our fingers brushed. The contact ignited a spark, a current of electricity that pulsed through me, making me withdraw my hand abruptly. The hint of a triumphant grin flashed across Thorn's face, but it was gone before I could fully register it.

"Master Haris, you are more than welcome to stay

here and explore the archives." Thorn's voice echoed in the enormous hall. He turned to face me, a concealed glint of playfulness twinkling in his eyes. "Fin, if you'd like, I can show you the gardens while Master Haris indulges his curiosity."

Master Haris straightened, looking between us, a touch of conflict visible in his eyes as he rubbed the bald spot on top of his head. "I . . . I should accompany you. It wouldn't be wise to leave Fin unattended . . ." He glanced longingly at the towering shelves surrounding us, then back at me, clearly torn.

"Isn't this the reason that you came?" I didn't fancy being stuck in the archives all day, as interesting as it might be, but Master Haris would be kicking himself the entire journey home if he didn't take this opportunity.

Master Haris waffled, his hands fluttering down at his sides.

"This is a once-in-a-lifetime opportunity," I reasoned. "Think of the knowledge here you can use for your book."

His eyes gleamed at the mention of his dream project, a comprehensive manuscript about the fae. But still, his mentor instincts were annoyingly hard to shake off. "But Fin, I promised . . ."

I cut him off with a wave of my hand. "I'll be safe.

Thorn will be with me." I shot a glance at Thorn who nodded in silent agreement.

"But what if . . ."

Thorn smoothly intervened. "Master Haris, trust in my experience. We'll explore the gardens, nothing more. I've promised to keep her safe."

Haris seemed to mull over Thorn's words, the lure of the archives battling against his protective instincts. After a long pause, his face softened into a reluctant smile.

"All right," he conceded. He turned to me, his eyes serious but warm. "I'll see you this afternoon, to prepare for the feast."

With a final nod, Master Haris retreated into the maze of books, leaving me and Thorn alone. A rush of anticipation spread through my chest, and I couldn't conceal the smile that tugged at the corners of my lips as I glanced up at him. "So, those gardens . . . ?"

Thorn's smile was enough to set my heart aflutter. As he began leading the way, I took one last look at Haris, now lost in the world of ancient scrolls, before giving my full attention to Thorn. For the first time since our journey began, I felt a surge of pure, undiluted excitement.

Thorn leaned closer to me, his voice dropping to a whisper. "You know, seeing the archives, the very essence of fae history, is quite an honor for a human. Not many are granted access."

"Was this the itinerary change you were talking about?"

A warm smile tugged at the corners of his lips. "Yes, though I admit my motives weren't entirely honest."

"What do you mean?" I laughed. "It's a great kindness! He's over the moon about it."

Thorn chuckled. "Honestly? I was trying to get you alone."

I blinked in surprise. "What?"

"I've been . . . curious about you," Thorn admitted.

My heart pounded at the unexpected thrill of his words. Before he had a chance to say more, the path led us toward a span of canyon-carved bridges that connected two parts of the castle. The wind whistled through the natural hollows, creating a melodic hum that resonated in the air.

Thorn's gaze held a measure of pride as he watched me. "This," he began, sweeping an arm over the bridges, "is also a rare sight few humans have seen."

The whispering bridge deposited us into a verdant haven that couldn't have been more different from the grandeur of the castle and the austerity of the archives. The gardens sprawled all around us. The lush greenery and vibrant blooms climbed the steep cliffs, creating a tapestry of living artistry. But, despite the view, my attention was focused on the person beside me.

A sudden fluttering caught my attention, and I saw a flock of small birds approaching, their orange bodies contrasting starkly against the blue feathers of their breasts. They circled us, their chittering echoing off the stone walls. One bravely alighted on my outstretched finger, its tiny claws digging into my skin. It looked into my eyes, its beady gaze almost human in its intensity.

I concentrated on their chitters and tried to translate. It was a language of chirps, trills, and pauses. My eyes widened as I deciphered their frantic message.

"He says there's a thunderbird," I translated for Thorn.

Thorn frowned before his eyes rose along the side of the canyon. I turned, following his gaze.

A gargantuan creature was perched on the edge of the canyon. The underside of the thunderbird was white, and it studied us over a curved beak. Its gaze bore down on us with unblinking scrutiny that made the air thicken with unease. It leaned forward, as though to inspect us closer, and a shadow fell over the canyon as it blocked out the sun.

My breath hitched in my throat. I'd never been this close to such a massive creature before. It was terrifying and humbling all at once.

A warm hand enveloped mine, startling me. Thorn's firm grip anchored me, his thumb tracing soothing circles over the back of my hand.

"Don't worry," Thorn whispered. "A thunderbird is too large to fly into the canyon. We're safe here."

Emboldened by his words, I turned my attention back to the creature. I used my mind to ask where it roosted. The thunderbird's response was a deafening squawk that echoed off the canyon walls. I flinched, hastily covering my ears. Then, the colossal creature unfurled its wings and launched itself into the sky. A gust of wind roared into the canyon, sending us tumbling backward.

Before I knew it, Thorn pulled me into his arms with a swift, protective movement. The world tilted and swayed, but his grip was secure, unyielding. My heart galloped against my rib cage, which seemed to echo in the silence left by the departing bird. I clung to Thorn, my fingers curling into the fabric of his shirt, my breath coming out in shaky exhales.

As the shadow of the magnificent thunderbird receded and the world regained its equilibrium, my pulse began to steady. A thrilling warmth rushed through me in a sense of awe and exhilaration. Thorn's hold on me gradually loosened, and I stepped away, craning to see the shadow over the horizon.

"Are you all right?" Thorn asked, his voice surprisingly calm, but I could hear the slight quiver betraying his adrenaline rush.

I nodded, my gaze still transfixed on the now-clear sky. "That was beyond incredible." My voice rippled with excitement. "It's as if I've just lived a lifetime's worth of wonder."

As I turned my attention back to Thorn, I found a curious glint in his eyes. "Can I kiss you?" Thorn asked suddenly.

My smile froze in place. "What?"

"I just . . ." Thorn stuttered, his eyes on my lips. "I really want to kiss you right now."

It felt like someone had sucked all the air out of the gardens. My pulse was pounding in my ears.

Thorn took a step forward, his hand coming up to gently brush a strand of hair from my face. "May I?" he asked again, the intensity of his gaze making my heart pound in my chest.

I swallowed hard, my mouth suddenly dry. I'd never been kissed before. The thought was both thrilling and terrifying. But looking at Thorn, seeing the desire in his eyes, I knew I wanted this.

"Yes," I said, the word almost a sigh.

Thorn's eyes sparkled with something like relief or victory, or maybe both. He closed the distance between us, his hand sliding around to cradle the back of my head. He leaned in.

"Thorn Beyond-the-Border, as I live and breathe!" someone shouted before pounding feet began making their way toward us.

Thorn groaned as I spun, finding a hulking man behind us.

"Mack, this is Fin. Fin, Mack," Thorn said, gesturing to each of us in turn.

The giant of a man leaned down, his hands on his knees. "Pleasure to meet you, Fin," he said, shooting me a gap-toothed grin. "I hope this young ne'er-do-well has been keeping out of trouble."

Thorn shook his head with an exasperated sigh. "Don't listen to him. I take my job very seriously."

"You do *now*." Mack slammed his hand down on Thorn's shoulder, causing his knees to buckle. "But not at first. Need I remind you about the fiasco with the governor of Brickelsby?"

"Don't," Thorn growled.

"What happened with the governor of Brickelsby?" I asked, a smile creeping across my cheeks when Thorn glared at me.

"This young pup was on his second ever guiding tour when the governor mentioned he'd had a grandfather who communed with demons."

"Oh?" I glanced at Thorn who was growing redder by the minute. His tail thrashed behind him.

The giant chuckled heartily, a mischievous twinkle in his eyes. "Aye, and our good Thorn here thought it would be a brilliant idea to call his bluff, he did. 'I can find your granpa's demons,' he said. And do you know what happened?"

Thorn's glare could have melted steel, but I couldn't help but lean in, eager to hear more about Thorn's past misadventures.

"Please, do tell," I coaxed, grinning widely.

"Well . . ." Mack rubbed his hands together glee-fully. "The minute our good man, Thorn, mentioned the name of the grandfather, the demons went wild. Seems that the grandfather had stolen something of value from them before the border went up. So, they grabbed the governor and ran off with him, refusing to give him up. Thorn had to commission the king, with his tail between his legs, to finally get the governor back. By then o' course, the damage had been done."

I couldn't help myself. "What kind of damage?"

Thorn scowled. "The governor refused to be res-cued. Demonic past-time is an acquired taste, but for them it seemed to run in the family."

Mack slapped Thorn on the shoulder again, bellow-ing laughter echoing over the bridges as we left the gardens and made our way down to the city by the river. "I still remember the look on your face when we found the man. Literally fit to be tied, he was."

Laughter bubbled up in my chest and escaped before I could stop it. I looked at Thorn, who was seething but also seemed to be struggling to keep a grin off his face. "You did that?" I managed to ask through my laughter.

"Yes, all right?" Thorn said, rolling his eyes. "I was young, and Mack likes to exaggerate the story."

"Anything to humble our Thorn," Mack cut in, his laugh echoing around us.

"So he had a good time . . . with the demons . . ." I asked.

"Presumably," Thorn muttered.

"The poor man's probably still there," Mack insisted. "I'd not heard of him escaping. Have you?"

Thorn shook his head. "He's probably dead by now for all we know. But he wouldn't budge, despite his wife pleading with him to return home to his duties and responsibilities."

I smiled despite Thorn's glowering. We followed Mack away from the gardens and back into the castle. Thorn hesitated, then took my hand, leading me through the tunnels until we were dumped into the city streets.

"You can't see Alden-Ester like that!" With a smirk and a hearty laugh, Mack hoisted me onto one of his shoulders, promising a better view of Alden-Ester. My heart fluttered with a mix of surprise and exhilaration. I was high above the crowds, taking in the vibrancy of the city in a whole new light.

"Be careful with her," Thorn warned, dancing around Mack as though he would throw me off at any minute.

From my elevated perch, I could see the city unfurling in front of me. The ornate stone buildings, their roofs covered in a patina of age, and narrow cobblestone streets bustling with people of every stripe. Street vendors hawked their wares, musicians played lively tunes, and children ran about, their laughter mingling with the cacophony of the city.

When we reached a tavern nestled in a crevice lined with flowers, Mack lifted me off his shoulders and set me beside Thorn. We went in, Thorn and Mack ordering us drinks while I looked over the other clientele. An elf was tearing into a meal of meat and flowers, while two sprites sat in the corner, their scales catching the light from the windows and sending it around the room in a rainbow of color. Thorn handed me a drink before turning back to Mack and bantering with some of the local patrons.

Despite my attempts to focus on the conversations around me, my thoughts were becoming frequently diverted to the request King Valon had made. Could I really persuade people to open their borders to the fae? And why did the thought of refusing the fae king send a pang of disappointment through me? Was it because it could mean distancing myself from Thorn?

Convincing Horan to open borders with Lyrica was a task of colossal proportions, one I was uncertain I could fulfill. If I accepted and failed, the consequences could be catastrophic. The uncertainty of it all settled like a stone in my gut.

My heart clenched at the thought of leaving Alden-Ester, the alien beauty of this place having grown on me more than I'd realized. But if it came to it, I was ready to find my gem on my own rather than risk angering the fae king when I couldn't fulfill my side of the bargain.

I cast a glance at Thorn. Would he still guide us even if I rejected the king's proposal?

Thorn leaned toward me. "Are you all right?"

"Thorn," I began, carefully choosing my words, "what if I decline King Valon's offer?"

Thorn frowned and faced me, my hand still clasped in his. "I would do as you have hired me to," he replied, his gaze never leaving mine. "I'd guide you to the cave and help you as much as I'm able. It was you who hired me, not King Valon."

I sighed, considering the king's proposal. It demanded too much and offered little certainty of success. Thorn's commitment to our agreement brought a strange sense of comfort.

In that moment, I made my decision. I would decline the king's offer. It was a risk I was not willing to take, a task I doubted my ability to fulfill. I didn't say anything to Thorn. The king would hear it from me first. Instead, I was determined to enjoy the rest of the day until our impending departure. I'd never had someone go out of their way to try to impress me before, and Thorn was a welcome distraction.

Chapter 9

T HE GRAND HALL OF THE PALACE was teeming with fae throwing themselves into the enchantments of the evening with abandon.

Thorn and I had scarcely parted since arriving in Alden-Ester, a secret smile playing on our lips that served as an invisible tether between us. Every time our eyes met, a thrill shot through me. Our silent exchanges went unnoticed by most, but Master Haris, with his sharp, observant gaze, was clearly sensing the subtle shift in our dynamics.

Recognizing this, Thorn, ever the tactful diplomat, quickly ushered Haris toward a fae who stood a head above the crowd, their lithe form moving with an otherworldly fluidity that was as hypnotizing as it was enchanting. Skin the color of moonlight was adorned with shimmering silver tattoos that snaked across their body like flowing rivers of stardust.

"Master Haris, may I present Lullaby Beyond-the-Pine," Thorn began, artfully diverting Haris's attention. "Their stories breathe life into our histories, and their songs weave tales of our lands as vivid and enchanting as the landscapes themselves."

Caught by the tantalizing prospect of unexplored lore, Master Haris's eyes lit up like stars, his earlier suspicion momentarily forgotten.

"After this many encounters, Master Haris is bound to start noticing your uncanny talent for diversion," I teased Thorn as Haris engrossed himself in conversation with Lullaby. I watched his eyes twinkle with mischief. "He might just start suspecting something."

With a hearty chuckle, Thorn retorted, "Better to be under scrutiny for our cunning than any other shared interests we may acquire." His words hung in the air, charged with unspoken sentiment. He leaned closer, his breath a gentle caress against my ear. "Remember, don't eat or drink anything unless I've given the clear."

I nodded, suddenly feeling the weight of many eyes upon me. I cast a glance around the hall and realized that numerous fae were staring, their gazes curious, cautious, and intrigued. The gravity of being the center of their attention, of existing in this magical yet alien world, suddenly hit me with an overwhelming force.

Thorn took my hand and escorted me through the bustling gathering, beneath a circle of fairies in flight as they danced above us. A collection of sirens lounged in the corner, their voices filling the hall with an ethereal melody. As I listened to the song, my mind began to grow fuzzy.

Thorn pulled me to his side. "Tune your ears away from their words or you will fall under their enchantment."

I blocked out the words to the melody and felt my mind clear. Thorn handed me a glass of water and I took a drink.

He guided me past a row of tables laden with exotic fruits, roasted meats, and an array of dishes that looked and smelled both strange and alluring. With a mischievous grin, Thorn grabbed a small, radiant fruit from one of the platters. "Try this," he encouraged, holding it out to me. Uncertain but trusting, I took a bite. The taste was sweet, tangy, and something else I couldn't quite name. A burst of flavors I had never experienced before.

As we walked farther, we passed a group of dwarves, their voices thunderous as they exchanged bawdy jokes and laughed heartily, the clinking of their drink mugs echoing in the hall. A gaggle of pixies fluttered around a fountain, splashing and playing in the water.

The energy in the hall was infectious. Despite the inherent strangeness of the setting, a sense of delight coursed through me, amplified by Thorn's presence at my side. His laughter rang in my ears as he watched me try another strange fruit, his enjoyment of my reactions adding to my own.

I took a sip of the fairy wine he handed me, relishing the tart berry flavor that exploded over my tongue. Those around us were openly staring. Unease crept up my spine and I self-consciously tugged at my gown. "I wonder what they're thinking," I whispered to Thorn, my eyes on the crowd.

Thorn leaned forward, his lips brushing my ear. "We are all wondering what you taste like," Thorn said, his mouth crooked in that mischievous smile of his.

Throbbing heat flooded my core and I inhaled sharply.

"Stunning," Thorn murmured, his gaze sweeping over me. "You look so lovely when you blush." His tone was unapologetically admiring.

All breath escaped my body. "Stop talking like that," I hissed. "That's what the king said."

Thorn tilted his head back and laughed. "That's honestly what we're all thinking."

I pointed to the sharp-toothed elven guard who was watching me from the corner. "*He* said he wanted to roast me over a fire of cedar and heartwood, then enjoy me with his favorite cactus wine and elderberries."

Thorn followed my gaze and nodded. "Yes, the fae have missed human flesh in a variety of ways."

As I swallowed the last morsel of a particularly

delightful dish that reminded me vaguely of honeyed almonds and ripe peaches, an elf made her way toward us. Her eyes sparkled with a mix of curiosity and mischief, her form wreathed in a shimmering gown that changed hues with her movements.

"Fin Of-Cheapside," she purred, her hair a flowing vermilion, the color of stone at Crimson Gorge. "Would you grace me with a dance?"

Before I could answer, Thorn's hand tightened around mine. Leaning in, he whispered, "Dancing to fae music can be perilous, Fin. The rhythm, the melody . . . they can bewitch your feet so they refuse to stop."

Looking into his earnest eyes, I knew he was cautioning me for my safety. Gratitude warmed my heart as I turned to the waiting fae. "I am honored by your offer," I replied, offering her a small smile, "but I fear my human feet might not do justice to your beautiful music."

There was a momentary pause, then laughter bubbled up out of her mouth. The lady bowed graciously. "Perhaps another time then, Fin Of-Cheapside. Until then, enjoy the evening."

In the midst of the lavish feast, the hall teeming with abandon, Thorn's fingers danced lightly up my arm, causing a delightful shiver to course through me.

He leaned in, his breath ghosting over the sensitive skin of my neck. An involuntary gasp escaped my lips as his mouth met my skin, the tingling sensation amplifying into a thrilling current that traveled down my spine.

"Thorn," I murmured, my voice barely audible above the fae music and laughter. His response was a soft hum, his lips still pressed against my neck as he breathed deep, as though to drink me in. The closeness, the charged atmosphere, it was intoxicating, mesmerizing . . . until I caught sight of a figure observing us from a distance.

Seated in a secluded alcove, adorned in his black and silver robe, was King Valon. His regal bearing was unmistakable, even from afar, with his strong, horn-crowned silhouette. His countenance was solemn and piercing. His golden eyes locked with mine.

A chill passed over me, Thorn's warmth momentarily forgotten. The king raised a hand, crooking a finger toward me. An unspoken command hung in the air, his piercing gaze unwavering. In that moment, the revelry of the feast seemed to fade into the background, my attention riveted on the king.

As though in a trance, I pulled away from Thorn. "He's calling for me," I murmured, my voice sounding distant even to my ears. A tight knot formed in my stomach, the anticipatory fear of facing the king's wrath pricking at my senses. I still planned to decline his offer. Though I was apprehensive about engaging in my quest without the king's assistance, the greater fear was for the king's reaction when he realized I would be little use to him in his bid to open the borders to Lyrica.

Thorn followed my gaze to where King Valon still sat, his form commanding even amid the merriment of the court. An understanding seemed to pass between Thorn and the king. Thorn's hand rested on my lower back, guiding me through the whirl of dancing fae.

I could feel the eyes of countless others as we made our way toward the king. When we reached the secluded alcove, the king had risen from his seat. His tall, formidable figure was even more impressive up close, his golden eyes reflecting the torchlight ominously.

He nodded at a young fae page nearby, who promptly scurried toward a previously unnoticed door, pushing it open to reveal an antechamber. It was dimly lit compared to the vibrant hues of the main hall. With a gesture of his hand, Valon indicated for me to enter.

"Go," Thorn whispered, his voice steady but his grip on my arm betraying his concern. "I'll be right here."

Summoning every ounce of courage I had, I

stepped into the antechamber. The door closed behind me with a soft click, leaving me alone with the king.

Chapter 10

THE ANTECHAMBER WAS A SIMPLE ROOM, the walls adorned with tapestries depicting fae legends. King Valon stood at the door, his hands clasped behind his back as he scrutinized me with ageless eyes.

"I trust you have considered my offer, Fin Of-Cheapside," he began, impatience lacing his words.

I took a deep breath, bracing myself for the possible backlash. "Your Majesty, I appreciate the trust you have placed in me, but I'm afraid I must decline your offer." I tried to keep my voice steady.

For a moment, the king's face remained impassive. But then, a muscle twitched in his jaw, the only indication of his disappointment and, perhaps, irritation.

"I can't let that be your answer." King Valon's nostrils flared.

I frowned, confused. He offered me a deal and I declined. It should be as simple as that for the fae. The idea of consent was what their entire society was built upon.

King Valon regarded me with narrowed eyes, his austere features thoughtful. "What do you desire,

375

Fin?" he asked, his voice betraying none of the tension that seemed to lurk beneath his calm demeanor. "What is it you aspire to in life?"

The question caught me off guard. I hadn't been expecting such a personal inquiry, especially not from the fae king. Yet, as I stared into his penetrating gaze, I found the words rising within.

"I wish to prove myself," I confessed, my voice echoing in the quiet room. "I want to become someone . . . greater. Greater than the people who ever doubted me or looked down upon me because of my status."

Images of the past flashed through my mind. The haughty, dismissive looks of the young nobility at Solridge. My father's indifference. My stepfather's cruel sneer. Even my mother's resigned acceptance of what she thought was my fate. I wanted to show them all that I wasn't just some hopeless waif picked up off the streets. But that I was capable, determined, and worthy.

"And what if I told you, Fin, that I could provide you with the means to achieve that?" King Valon's voice broke through my reverie, startling me out of my thoughts.

His statement hung in the air between us, offering a tantalizing promise of the opportunity to rise above my past and become something more . . . if I accepted his proposition.

I straightened. "Even if you offered more, I still don't feel I can accept because what you're asking for is impossible. Lyrica will never open its borders to you."

King Valon shifted, his eyes on the tapestry at his side, and I followed his gaze. A variety of fae had been embroidered in the work of art. The detail was astounding. But hidden among the fae, I noticed humans with tiny imorets stitched by their eyes. "I wondered, when she said a girl would come, if she meant you. For the longest time I've been expecting a Morganite."

"A Morganite?" I repeated, my brows furrowed. I knew the fae and Morganites had been allied before, but that was over a hundred years ago. Suddenly, my heart sank. "You mean Rowyn."

A ghost of a smile appeared at the corner of the king's pale mouth. "You know Rowyn the Morganite?"

"She's my greatest friend," I said without thinking.

The king's gaze returned to the tapestry. "I felt when she left the shroud. I'd dared hope that she'd find her way here, but alas, the gatekeeper from Rudin told me that she was rumored to have gone south and had an unfortunate encounter with Lyrican nobility."

The hackles on the back of my neck rose. "What do you want with Rowyn?"

King Valon studied me thoughtfully. "If you want my truth, you have to give me yours. What do you know about that young woman?"

I met his stare, refusing to give despite his royal status. "What do you mean?"

King Valon studied me, his nostrils flaring as though he could smell my unease. "You seem protective of your friend. She must have done *something* to inspire your loyalty. Is she kind? Is she just? Does she have warts on her nose? What is her favorite color? I will take anything at this point."

"But why—"

"You first," King Valon interrupted firmly.

I clenched my teeth, thinking for a moment. I could give him some information. Nothing that would endanger her, surely. It would help me get to the bottom of what the king wanted with Rowyn. She had enough people scrambling in the shadows to reach her—to bend her to their will.

"Rowyn has black hair. Her eyes are blue, like mine. Her favorite color is blue," I said, "like me."

King Valon's ghostly smile reappeared. After a moment, he waved his hand for me to continue.

"She fights better than many of the young men at

the academy. She's the one who taught me the bow and knives. Her parents died around two years ago, so she's been on her own."

King Valon was nodding. "I'd known the mother and grandmother had been lifted to the stars," he said, "but I'd not heard about her father."

"You know she brings rain?" I asked.

King Valon nodded again. "That is known all over the West. Morius was before my time, but I'd heard his story."

"What do you want with Rowyn?"

Valon narrowed his gaze, his voice a low growl. "I need more."

I should've been fearful, but I was merely annoyed. "She's kind," I snapped. "She believes in fairness, but she can also be entirely too headstrong and makes enemies far too easily. She's terrible at courtesy but is pretty good with history and governance. Her power will probably change the course of Lyrica. Everyone is quite excited about it."

There, I'd given him everything.

Everything except Destrian. I didn't like the way King Valon leaned closer when I spoke of my friend, and I didn't think he would have kind intentions when it came to Destrian in Rowyn's life . . . especially since Destrian's father, the consul, would be advocating against Lyrica opening the borders to Horan and the region of Morgania.

King Valon's expression shifted to a predatory glare. "Is she well? Is she safe?"

"She's gone to the Nightlands to gain her gem," I said, surprised he didn't already know this. He seemed to have learned so much already, I wondered why he even needed me. Was he seeking to gain control of Rowyn's power too?

"So, tell me, what do you want with Rowyn?" I asked, brooking no argument—with no thought at all that I was addressing a king. Fear for my friend seemed to be driving my folly.

"There was a pact," King Valon began, his voice a tempered whisper that echoed off the walls of the chamber. "Sealed a century ago between the Morganite king, Theramon, and myself." He paused, as if reliving the moment. A deep-seated tension pulsated beneath his words. "A blood bond to stem the tide of Lyricans drifting northward from Adair."

"Oh?" I asked, feeling a sinking in my gut. What would a blood alliance between the old Morganite king have to do with Rowyn?

"Then, a shadow of tragedy. Nearly the entire royal family was assassinated shortly after the pact was made. My intended was killed as her father watched."

There was a hardened edge in King Valon's voice, a ripple in his calm demeanor. "The youngest princess, I never had the fortune to meet. She was reared in a distant castle by an aunt when the massacre ensued. But they aided her flight to Espiria."

I frowned. That couldn't be right. The entire Morganite royal line had been wiped out. It was one of the more successful strategies of the Lyrican invasions. "How do you know this but Lyrica does not?" I asked.

"Because she went behind the shroud, and anyone who helped imbibe the shroud with magic can feel its presence," Valon countered, a sly grin tugging at the corners of his lips. His gaze held mine with a charged intensity. "In good faith, I strengthened it during the pact, using Theramon's blood as an anchor. I sensed the familiar tie when one of his lineage crossed through." An underlying layer of smug satisfaction seeped into his tone.

"Rowyn is descended from this Theramon?" I asked, piecing the rest of the story together. "But how does that help you now? Even if Rowyn were descended from the old king, how does that release the land from Lyrica's control? And I still don't see what any of this has to do with me and the bargain you are trying to make!"

King Valon took a patient breath as he stepped

closer. "The tides are changing, along with the world as we know it."

"You think Rowyn could reclaim Morgania?" I asked, the skepticism plain in my voice. Rowyn was haunted by her past and apprehensive of the present. She had little capacity to consider the future. But perhaps, given time and safety, that might change.

"If she had the right allies. Blood magic creates the most profound bonds." King Valon's voice dropped to a near growl, an undercurrent of barely restrained fervor pulsating in his words. "Every fiber of my being compels me to uphold my end of the alliance, to shield the last of Theramon's lineage until the pact is satisfied."

The question escaped my lips, fueled by a simmering anger. "Why did you not protect her after the loss of her parents?" It was a bitter echo of my past, of my father's neglect. Rowyn was grappling with her parents' loss and a deluge of trauma, and this king—bound to safeguard her—did nothing? Perhaps now that she was honing her powers, becoming Lyrica's formidable sorceress, she had become of use to him.

"When Rowyn hid behind the veil, a magical shroud I strengthened, it subdued the blood pact's urge," King Valon admitted. "She was secure, shielded by a ward I'd reinforced. It satisfied the gods. When she emerged beyond the shroud, I'd hoped she'd be drawn to Horan, beckoned by the blood bond, but she wasn't. And I'm in the dark as to why. Ever since her departure, my strength has waned, my focus fractured, the blood magic's call dominating my thoughts. I need to safeguard her, else I risk losing myself."

By all the gods, this changed everything. "There is something I've neglected to share," I began, glancing uneasily toward the door. The last thing I needed was Master Haris eavesdropping on this conversation. "Someone within the empire already has a hold on Rowyn."

King Valon stepped even closer, his gaze cutting into mine, sharp as a dagger's edge. "Who?"

"Well," I said, looking up, my hands twining together nervously. "I mean, she has the power to summon rain, and there's a drought at hand." I mentally apologized to Master Haris. According to his measure of being a good, loyal little Lyrican, I was failing on every count. "There's someone in the capital who sees potential in her abilities. She's well taken care of. Her allowance equals mine, suggesting a wealthy patron. A high-ranking noble, probably. At first, I thought it was the emperor, but something Gillius mentioned led me to believe he doesn't meddle in the political aspects of sorcery. He's only interested in what they can do for him. It's undoubtedly someone on the Council of Five."

"Do you not know who it is?" King Valon's tone was laced with both curiosity and concern. I found myself pondering if he had his own covert operatives who could cross the border on his command. It wouldn't be out of character for him.

"I don't know who it is, but what I do know is that it's not just Morgania you'll need to wrestle from Lyrica's grasp, but Rowyn herself."

King Valon drew back, absorbing my words. His golden eyes were deep pools of thought, reflecting the flickering lights from the torches. After a tense moment, he finally spoke, his voice resonating within the confines of the chamber. "The task becomes more challenging, yet it is not insurmountable. I knew there would be difficulties. But it is not just about Rowyn or Morgania. It is about maintaining a balance that has been disrupted, about fulfilling oaths and keeping the fabric of our world intact."

"Perhaps, but I doubt I'm the right person for this mission." I sighed, my shoulders sagging under the weight of his proposition. "Not that I lack the will, but she's more skilled in these matters. How could I assist her effectively?"

A wry glimmer appeared in the king's golden eyes.

"Unforeseen power often lies in the most unexpected places. You might not see yourself as the ideal choice for this mission, and therein lies our upper hand. We will ensure you're prepared. Thorn is one of the more adept fighters within my realm. Given that you seem to . . ." The king's eyes slid down my body. ". . . appreciate his company, he can train you to fight effectively. Claw has already agreed to mentor you with shapeshifting. My goal is to give you everything you need to thrive."

"But wouldn't one of your kind fare better as a protector?"

King Valon's head shook, a grave firmness in his expression. "They would draw too much attention. I've decreed that no fae is permitted to cross the border. Wouldn't it be hypocritical of me to grant an exception for myself or someone on my directive?"

"Still . . . why me?" I retorted, my frustration simmering. "Surely there are others . . ."

"Do you suggest Lady Rowyn has a multitude of close friends? Or perhaps a legion of other sorcerers willing to traverse the perilous path to Alden-Ester to parley with the king? No, you are the envoy Imor sent, and you're the one I must employ. My choices are limited."

"And so, I have no choice either?" I shot back, my

tone venomous. "So, your grand design to restore the open passage to the human lands is for me to serve as Rowyn's shield and assist her in securing the Morganian throne. You must take me for a fool. Are you sincerely suggesting your sole interest in Rowyn is to guard her? Are you asking me to conceal this from her? Because I abhor secrets."

King Valon's gaze bore into me, a fierce determination glowing in his golden eyes. "In Horan, I have been patient, keeping vigilant watch over the shroud for a signal. When I sensed the girl leave, I knew the moment had come. The resurgence of the Morganites is nigh."

I met his glare with one of my own. "What you're suggesting is high treason. My father is a general. He is my sole protection in this perilous world. Committing treason against the empire would leave me defenseless."

"Your father's protection would be irrelevant if you were under mine."

I took a deep breath, pressing my palms to my temples. There was a tremor in my hands, a fear of what I was considering, of the path that lay before me. But underneath that fear, there was also a strange thrill, a sense of an impending adventure that tugged at the deepest parts of me.

"Your protection," I started, my voice quieter than I would have liked. "What would it entail?"

King Valon held out a hand, walking beside me to the window that looked out over the river below. Fairy lights reflected on the water and the jubilation from the hall could be heard. He stood quite close to me, enough for me to smell the lingering, wild scent of earth that all the fae shared.

"Intrigued, are we, Fin Of-Cheapside?" he teased.

I felt a blush creep up my cheeks, but I didn't move away. If this was a game of courage and wills, I wasn't about to back down.

"Only curious, Your Majesty," I replied, a defiant edge in my tone. He chuckled. But the seriousness returned as quickly as it had faded. "I need to understand what I'm agreeing to if I decide to . . . help."

There was a moment of silence. Then, King Valon nodded slowly. "Fair enough," he said solemnly. "I can promise you this—under my protection, you'll have the strength of the fae behind you. We'll train you, equip you, support you in every way possible to ensure Rowyn's and Morgania's liberation from Lyrica. Let my home be yours. Go to any gatekeeper on the border, and they will bring you both straight to me. I *will* shield you if you feel unsafe."

As he laid out his promises, the weight of his words

settled around me. A daunting task, an incredible challenge, yes. But also, an opportunity to make a difference, to protect someone I cared about, to be more
than just "Fin Of-Cheapside." King Valon's offer was
tempting, his words weaving a web of possibilities I'd
only ever dreamed of. But the question remained—
was I brave enough to take the leap?

King Valon's gaze did not waver from mine as he
took in my expression, likely reading the swirl of emotions that I was sure was mirrored in my eyes. His eyes
softened a bit, the earlier harshness transforming into
something more gentle, more understanding.

"I do not wish for you to feel as though you've lost
agency. That is not our way. When I ask you to guard
her, I wish you to do it as you see fit. I will give no
orders other than requests for information and keeping
her alive and well. When you feel the opportunity presents itself, when you see a sign, as I did, you will tell
her your truth and implore her to come hear mine."

"You ask for so much," I said, unsure how I felt
about the wealth of information King Valon had just
given me. He aimed for Rowyn to take back Morgania
and petition *her* to open the border. By Sol above, what
was I getting myself into?

"I've been waiting a long time to reignite the alliance with the Morganites, and I can't stress enough

how important your presence in Horan is for me." King Valon stared down at me. "Until the contract is fulfilled, I fear I'll be bound to it, forever restless. So, do we have a deal?" he asked finally.

"It still doesn't feel like I've been given much of a choice," I admitted, a frown creasing my forehead.

"Remember, Fin, you came to Horan seeking my aid," King Valon reminded me, his voice dropping to a murmur. "Imor has chosen you to carry my message."

Despite the fear that lingered on the edges of my mind, King Valon's proposition held an undeniable allure. It was an opportunity I couldn't ignore, a path to the life I'd always desired—to rise beyond those who had once belittled me.

Undeniably, it felt rash, risky, and dangerously secretive. There was no way I could share any of this with a single person at Solridge. But my gut was practically echoing with a vehement yes. "All right," I agreed, my gaze locking with the king's. "I accept."

A subtle change crossed King Valon's face, his stern countenance softening into something almost warm. He extended his hand toward me, and without a moment's hesitation, I placed mine in his. He raised my hand to his lips, placing a delicate kiss that sent a flutter through my heart.

"Then we have a deal, Fin," King Valon said, bowing slightly with a hint of chivalry that felt oddly comforting.

The page reentered and motioned me to the door. I cast one last glance over my shoulder at King Valon, who had turned back to the window, his hands clasped behind his back as he admired his city.

I didn't have time to dwell on the question of what I was getting myself into, because pure excitement was pumping through my veins. He would train me to fight as well as Rowyn. I might be able to turn into animals. I would be able to go anywhere, do anything that I wanted. But he offered me more than that. He'd offered protection too. A home offered was not something I could ever afford to take lightly, and the draw of the fae was strong. It was exciting being among them.

As soon as the page left me alone, the whirlwind of the feast disarmed me. Two fae approached. Both tall, one had blonde hair and wings that shimmered with the purest white feathers, his eyes a striking shade of sea blue. The other was a contrast to him, with his dark skin, leathery, bat-like wings, jet-black hair, and eyes as black as the starless sky.

"Well, isn't she positively exquisite?" The blonde one leaned in, taking a deep breath near my hair. His voice was like velvet and honey, but it made me squirm uncomfortably.

A flash of annoyance flickered through me. "I'm not something to be eaten."

"Oh, but darling, you misunderstand," the dark-haired one replied, his voice low and sultry. "We simply meant that you are delightful to the senses."

Before I could respond, a familiar presence materialized beside me. Thorn, his eyes hardened, subtly positioned himself between me and the flirtatious fae.

"Do you wish to be entertained by the twins?" Thorn's tone was frosty as he glanced from me to the brothers.

"Not especially," I admitted, stepping closer to Thorn.

The dark-haired one sneered at Thorn, recognition lighting up his black eyes. "Gatekeeper," he said.

Thorn merely nodded in response, his gaze never leaving the fae. His entire demeanor was protective, and I felt a strange warmth bloom within me at the sight.

The dark-haired one turned his attention back to me, a smirk on his face. "When you're ready to handle a full blood, do let me know." His eyes twinkled with mischief. With a laugh that echoed in the wind, he and his brother dissolved back into the crowd, leaving me with Thorn.

Without wasting a moment, Thorn scanned the room, his gaze finally landing on the page who had left me unattended. He signaled him over with a wave of his hand, his eyes not leaving the young fae until he stood before us.

"You were supposed to bring her to me." Thorn's voice was stern, an underlying note of irritation threading his words. "Not abandon her in the middle of the feast."

The page faltered, his dark face paling under Thorn's intense gaze. "I, I apologize. I thought she'd be fine, given the king's instructions . . . She is a guest of honor . . ."

"A guest, yes," Thorn interjected, his voice a low growl. "But one unfamiliar with our ways and customs. This is her first feast, is it not?"

"Yes, Gatekeeper," the page stuttered, shooting me an apologetic glance.

"Then remember, the hospitality of the fae extends beyond just merriment. It is our duty to ensure that our guests feel comfortable and safe, especially when they are in a realm not their own."

Thorn's voice echoed with authority, and the page bowed in understanding before murmuring a quick "Yes, Thorn."

The page scurried away, leaving me alone once again with the gatekeeper. His stern demeanor softened as he turned to me. "Are you all right?" he asked, his eyes reflecting genuine concern.

"May we return to our room?" I asked, feeling an immense surge of exhaustion and a desperate need for solitude to process everything.

"Certainly," Thorn agreed, his brows furrowing in concern. "Let's first see to Master Haris and then I would be more than happy to accompany you back." Thorn extended his hand toward me, an offer of comfort amid the overwhelming wave of uncertainty. I inhaled a deep, steadying breath and gratefully accepted his offered hand.

Chapter 11

O NCE INSIDE OUR ROOM, Thorn released my hand, allowing me to retreat to the privacy of my thoughts. I fell into the plush chair by the fire and watched the flicker of shadows on the wall. Shadows and secrets.

Thorn moved to sit opposite me on the couch, a measured distance that gave me room to breathe but kept him within reach. He studied me for a moment, his dark eyes probing for unspoken answers. "Fin," he began, his voice holding a warmth that felt oddly comforting. "You seem . . . troubled."

I glanced at him. Trusting Thorn felt like a precarious balancing act, but the words tumbled out, nonetheless. "Did you know what he was going to ask of me?"

He blinked, clearly taken aback. "I had some idea, but the specifics? No, I didn't know." His voice was firm, yet doubt gnawed at the edges of my trust.

I frowned, grappling with the enormity of what was expected of me. It felt like I was teetering on the edge of a precipice with nothing but the promise of failure waiting below. "I can't tell Master Haris. This . . . this is treason we're discussing. This could get us all killed."

Thorn didn't say anything. He just waited, giving me space to think. The room, bathed in the gentle glow of the twilight seeping through the windows, suddenly felt too intimate, too close. Thorn's gaze hadn't wavered from mine since we started talking. He finally broke the silence.

"And what, precisely, did you agree to?" His voice, usually so steady, held a note of uncertainty that mirrored my own.

"He wishes for me to act as a protector . . . a guardian of sorts to my friend, Rowyn."

I hesitated, my gaze dropping to my lap where my hands were restlessly fiddling with a loose thread on my dress. "He . . . he said you'd be training me. In combat." I glanced up through my lashes, my heart pounding at the surprised but intrigued look that crossed his face.

In the ensuing silence, the air between us seemed to crackle with unspoken promises and the whisper of possibility. My mind went skipping back to the almost kiss. I'd wanted it so badly. I'd never been kissed before and Thorn was . . . well . . . Thorn. Handsome and rugged and absolutely, mouthwateringly wild.

Thorn's gaze became intense, his eyes filled with an emotion I couldn't quite decipher. "I see." He paused, his gaze dropping to my mouth for an electrifying moment before he leaned back, creating a breath of much-needed distance between us. The corners of his mouth twitched upward into a small smile that held a hint of something darker. "Well then, it would be my pleasure."

My heart fluttered at the way his voice dipped, the raw, unvarnished truth in his eyes. The warmth in the room intensified, a heat that had nothing to do with the fire in the hearth.

But then, I shifted uneasily, the chemistry we'd been dancing around suddenly taking on a sinister hue. "Thorn . . . am I just a target to you?" I asked, the words tumbling from my lips before I could consider them. "A mark to be hunted? Did the king ask you to 'keep me happy' or something?"

The minute Thorn's smile faltered, I knew I was stupid for giving a voice to my fears. His playful demeanor evaporated, and a cloud of regret passed over his features, the hurt flashing in his eyes as though I'd physically struck him. "Is that truly what you think of me, Fin?" His voice was low, the edge of his normally jovial tone replaced by a somber echo.

"I'm just asking," I said softly. "Nobody . . . has ever acted toward me the way you do. I find myself wondering why you would."

He sighed heavily and reached to gently take my hand. "I find you incredibly appealing. My interest in you is genuine. And it saddens me that you would think otherwise."

I sighed, running a hand through my hair. "I just . . . I don't know. There is so much happening . . ."

Thorn shifted closer, and I felt the warmth of his body radiating against my own. The atmosphere was charged, yet beneath the simmering tension, there was genuine concern etched on his face.

"Fin, you can trust me," Thorn said, his voice barely above a whisper. The sound thrummed through me, the words coiling around my racing heart. He reached to brush a loose lock of hair from my face, the touch sparking a jolt of something potent.

"I don't know if I can do this," I admitted. "Protect her, I mean. She's lethal. She defeated a golgeman. I almost feel as though the king is getting the worst end of this bargain because Rowyn is perfectly capable of taking care of herself."

"It takes more than strength to protect someone. I do not feel as though I'm wrong in thinking that you are cunning. Use your mind, your magic, to aid you."

I thought for a moment. "Spies," I blurted out.

"Spies?" he echoed, raising an eyebrow in intrigue.

"Yes, the animals. I've used them before . . . to

gather information. I . . . I could use them to keep an eye on what's going on. To watch over her. King Valon already said he wanted information. I can give him that."

A flash of approval flickered in Thorn's eyes, and his lips curled up slightly in a smile. "Clever," he commended, his grip on my arm tightening in encouragement. "You said that you will be working with Claw as well? With the right training, you could be a formidable force. We'll start with the basics, a short blade perhaps. Then we could progress to unarmed combat. The key would be to utilize your quick thinking and agility."

The murmur of our conversation was abruptly shattered by the sound of the door swinging open. Lullaby Beside-the-Pine filled the entrance, cradling the limp form of Master Haris.

Thorn swiftly untangled himself from me, rising to his full height, an eyebrow raised in surprise. "What happened?"

"A bit too much wine," Lullaby said, laying Master Haris on the couch with surprising gentleness. "I forgot how delicate you humans can be with your liquor."

Master Haris groaned, his face pallid. Suddenly, he lurched forward, and the room filled with the unmistakable sound of retching. I winced as a splatter of fae wine marred the immaculate floor.

"Oh, dear," Lullaby sighed, stepping back and wiping their hands on their trousers.

Thorn shot me an amused glance as he turned back to Lullaby. "Ensure this doesn't happen again."

"Of course, Thorn. My apologies." Lullaby gave a respectful nod before they sauntered out of the room.

With the door shut, my eyes wandered to Master Haris's slumbering form, and an exasperated sigh slipped past my lips. His role as my mentor was proving to be a paradoxical blend of a boon and a bane. His assistance on our journey thus far had been negligible, and his presence in the palace had been more about serving his own interests than aiding my quest.

Strangely, I found no anger bubbling within me for his selfish approach. I doubted I could have agreed to the king's terms under Haris's watchful gaze. Yet, guilt washed over me when I contemplated the fallout that would ensue once the other sorcerers at Solridge discovered my treason, while my mentor's attention was elsewhere.

I shrugged it off, hardening my resolve. That would be his burden to bear, not mine.

Chapter 12

THE CHILL OF MORNING ROUSED me from sleep, the tendrils of my dream clinging to my waking mind. I sat up, groggily, wiping the sleep from my eyes as I looked for the others. Thorn was shirtless and in the process of maneuvering into his breeches. Bare-chested Thorn was quite a sight to behold. His bronzed skin, kissed by the desert sun, gleamed subtly under the morning light, highlighting a chiseled torso. His tail—which I was beginning to think was quite cute—threaded its way through a carefully designed opening in the back of his pants.

"By Sol above," Master Haris groaned from the other bed, wrenching me from my lustful thoughts. "Never again!"

"How are you feeling?" I asked, running a brush through my hair. I hastily braided it and tied it off with a leather cord before rising and donning my own clothes, breeches, and a tunic.

"Like there is a little man with a hammer pounding inside my head," Master Haris said. "I'm afraid I'm not up to much adventuring today."

I glanced at Thorn who winked at me. So, we would

be alone again? My heart skipped a beat at the thought.

"Thorn offered to train me in combat." I tried to sound offhand, completely disregarding the fact that the king had ordered it as part of his bargain. Master Haris hadn't asked more about my deal with the king, and I hoped it would stay that way.

Master Haris nodded, his eyes remaining shut. "That all seems well enough. The others at Solridge deemed it appropriate when you trained with Rowyn, so I don't see how this would be any different. I trust you'll manage without me?"

Thorn's gaze flitted to me, lingering just a moment longer than necessary before he nodded at Haris. "We'll manage." His voice held a teasing note that made the corner of his mouth curl up slightly. The words were simple, but they carried a promise that fluttered in my stomach, settling my nerves.

We set off together, descending through the twisting stairways of the castle and out into the sunshine. The morning was fresh, the dew still clinging to the bushes and flowers that battled their way through the cracks and crevices of the canyon wall.

"We'll start with the basics," Thorn began, leading me to an open balcony that overlooked the valley. "You said that you trained with a dagger already. Show me what you're made of."

I pulled the dagger that Rowyn had gifted me from the belt on my waist and crouched.

"What have you got, little human?" Thorn taunted silkily. He drew his own dagger, mirroring my stance.

Our eyes locked. Tension hummed in the air, not only from the impending clash but from an underlying current, a stirring of something more personal, more intimate.

With a swift step, Thorn advanced. His movements were a ballet of precision and power, every lunge and swing carefully calibrated. I parried, my smaller blade clashing against his, the impact jarring the bones in my hand and wrist.

Despite my best efforts, Thorn was undeniably the better combatant. Each strike I landed was effortlessly countered, his strength outmatching my own. Our dance of blades became increasingly intense, our breaths hitching as we moved in sync, the boundaries between a fight and a dance blurring.

With a swift twist and flick of his wrist, he disarmed me. My dagger skittered across the rocky floor. But even in his victory, his gaze held no triumph, only a smoldering intensity that sent my heart racing.

As I bent to retrieve my dagger, I could feel his eyes on me, burning with an intensity that left me breathless.

Thorn paused, studying me for a moment. The intensity of his gaze was unnerving, but I met it head-on. "Good," he finally said, his voice carrying a note of approval. "That fire, that determination, is what will keep you standing when others fall. But, there are a few moves that will help you gain the upper hand over a stronger opponent. Let me show you," Thorn offered, his voice a murmur in the morning air. "May I?"

He extended his hand. At my nod, he stepped forward, closing the distance between us until I could feel the warmth radiating off his body.

His hands, strong yet gentle, moved over mine, adjusting my grip on the hilt of my dagger. I bit my lip, a wave of unexpected heat flooding through me. His touch was deliberate, professional, but it sent an unexpected shiver down my spine.

He guided me through the motions, his body pressed close to mine. He showed me the proper way to angle my blade, how to pivot and turn. He whispered instructions into my ear, each word amplifying my awareness of him, of us.

I tried to concentrate, to focus on the movements he was teaching me. But my heart betrayed me, thudding loudly in my chest in response to the proximity. I tried to mask the effect he was having on me—the flush on my cheeks, the quickened breath, the nervous fluttering in my stomach—but when his hands moved to my waist, correcting my posture, I held my breath, my body quivering slightly under his touch. His gaze met mine, a question lurking in the depths of his golden eyes. I nodded and swallowed hard. His eyes softened, an understanding passing between us that made my heart stutter.

"Like this," he murmured, guiding me through the sequence once more. The tension was still there, a thin veil barely concealing the longing and desire swirling beneath the surface. It was in the way his fingers lingered just a little longer than necessary, in the way our eyes locked, in the unspoken promise that hung in the air between us.

As we continued the rhythm of training, I caught a glimpse of a small squirrel perched at the corner of the balcony, busily munching on a nut. Its small, beady eyes flicked between its meal and our dance, a silent spectator to our efforts. I felt a sudden desire to reach out to it, to engage it in conversation, as I had done countless times before with animals in the human lands.

As Thorn guided me through a spin, I tried to stretch my mind toward the little creature, sending it a mental greeting. It paused, nut halfway to its mouth, and turned its head toward me. For a moment, our gazes locked.

Yet, there was no response to my greeting. The squirrel simply tilted its head, as if curious, then returned to its nut.

I frowned. Back in the human lands, the animals had always responded, their thoughts clear and direct, full of simple emotions and desires.

Here, in the fae lands, I'd noticed a difference. The animals were . . . quieter, their thoughts not as easily accessible. Could it be that their thought patterns were indeed different here?

I pondered the thought as Thorn guided me through another series of moves. My mind was split between the training and the lingering sensation of Thorn's touch. I chided myself, needing to focus, to learn, to prepare for what was to come. I needed to be ready for what King Valon had asked of me.

The sun climbed higher in the sky. Thorn's instruction had moved to a more complex move that involved a considerable amount of close contact. He stood behind me, one arm under my shoulder to support my weight, while his other hand slid up my inner thigh, guiding my leg for a sweeping kick. My breath hitched in my throat. He must have heard it, because the next second he was looking down at me, at my lips.

"Do you like that?" he murmured, his voice low and

dripping with lust.

"Yes," I breathed as his fingers dared to journey higher. He gripped my chin and drew my face toward him, the promise of a kiss lingering between us like an exquisite torture. A shiver of anticipation ran down my spine.

Suddenly, the sound of a throat clearing cut through the haze of romance. Startled, Thorn released my face and lowered my leg, an apologetic look in his eyes. I turned to find a naked fae woman lounging on the edge of the balcony, exactly where the squirrel had been. She was grinning at us, seemingly unabashed by her lack of clothing.

I looked down, felt my cheeks heat, and I tried to keep my gaze trained on her face. She was pretty for a goblin, I supposed, with auburn hair shorn till it fell just around her ears. Her skin bore the tint of green that was common in their kind, and pierced through her elongated ears were rows of golden hoops.

"Fin," Thorn began, his voice steady despite our interrupted moment, "allow me to introduce you to Claw. She's the shapeshifter that King Valon spoke of."

I greeted her, my voice slightly hesitant. Claw grinned. "Please, no need to stop on my account. I was enjoying the view."

What was it about the fae that just made me lose all sense of loyalty and inhibitions? Who was I in danger of becoming?

Thorn, after a final heated glance at me, addressed Claw with a pointed look. "I trust the king's guest of honor will be safe in your charge. I need to check on Master Haris, as he was feeling unwell this morning."

I looked over my shoulder, my eyes pleading with Thorn to stay. He shot me an apologetic look but slipped off the balcony all the same. As Thorn disappeared into the castle, I found myself left alone with Claw, my skin still flushed from the recent encounter. Seemingly unconcerned about her nudity, Claw sauntered over to me, her bare feet padding lightly on the stone floor.

With a disconcerting interest, she circled me, taking in my form from head to toe. I shifted uneasily under her unabashed scrutiny.

"Are you . . . going to put some clothes on?" I asked, my voice sounding small in the expanse of the balcony as I tried to ignore the sway of her breasts.

A soft chuckle slipped from her lips as she shrugged, her muscular shoulders moving in a languid motion. "Rarely. I spend so much time in animal form that I've gotten quite accustomed to the feeling of air on my skin."

Her openness did nothing to ease my discomfort, but I forced myself to nod. Claw paused in her inspection, her gaze resting on my face. Her eyes traveled from my hair to my eyes, a knowing smile playing on her lips.

"You look nothing like Gregorio," she mused. "Have you ever tried to shift before?"

I blinked at the abrupt question, taken aback. "No, I . . . I didn't know I could."

A speculative look passed over Claw's face, and she crossed her arms over her chest, drawing my attention momentarily to the stark lines of her muscular form. "Call a nearby creature to you. Start there."

With a shaky breath, I nodded, closing my eyes to focus.

The balcony became a stage of silence and waiting, the world around me fading as I delved into my mind, reaching out for a connection.

Focusing inward, I sought out the minds of the animals nearby, my consciousness brushing against the smaller and simpler thoughts of creatures who called the castle home. Then, I felt it—a tiny flicker, quick and alert. A lizard basking in the sun on the castle wall.

I reached with my mind, calling to it. There was a hesitation, a brief pause before I felt the acceptance of my invitation, a small mental nudge as it began to make its way to me.

"Good," Claw murmured, a note of satisfaction in her voice. "Now, try to see what it sees. Feel what it feels. Connect more deeply."

Taking a slow, steadying breath, I tentatively extended my awareness toward the lizard. In an instant, I was flooded with a wave of sensations that were utterly alien, yet curiously familiar. The grainy roughness of stone beneath its belly, the glorious warmth of the sun soaking into its scales, the tiny vibrations of life all around it . . .

"Imagine all these little details—the physicality, the senses, the instincts—like a package," Claw advised, her voice a distant echo against the backdrop of the lizard's perceptions. "Absorb that package. Pull it into yourself. That's the first step toward understanding the essence of the creature, the key to transformation."

I focused on the bundle of sensations that were not my own. I tried to internalize them, to let them permeate my being, to make them mine. The lizard's world— its sharp vision, the heat beneath its belly, the minute tremors of the ground beneath its feet—I attempted to embrace it all, willing myself to transform.

Yet, nothing happened.

I repeated the process again and again, squeezing my eyes shut, channeling all my energy into the pursuit.

Each attempt left me more drained, more frustrated. The lizard sat there, placid, its slitted eyes observing me with an inscrutable gaze.

And Claw, patient and persistent, kept offering suggestions, tweaks, small adjustments in my approach, yet none seemed to make any difference.

Finally, when my mental exhaustion reached its peak, I opened my eyes, blinking away the fatigue. That's when I noticed Thorn standing in the entrance to the balcony, his gaze fixed on me. His lips were set in a firm line, his arms crossed over his chest.

"Claw." Thorn's voice cut through the lingering silence, his tone authoritative yet calm. "I need to take Fin. It's time for her to get ready for dinner."

The naked goblin glanced at Thorn and then back at me, her smile undeterred. "Very well," she said, stepping back and letting her gaze wander over me one last time. "We'll try again tomorrow, Fin. Perhaps with a different creature."

I nodded, managing to summon a weak smile in response. I was grateful for her patience, even if I felt a stab of disappointment in my own failure.

"All right, Claw. Thank you," I said, the words holding more weight than simple courtesy. The goblin merely inclined her head, her gaze still harboring a spark of playful mischief.

Chapter 13

AYS FLOWED INTO EACH OTHER seamlessly as I settled into the rhythm of the palace. I spent my mornings training with Thorn, our exercises taking on a grueling intensity that I found exhilarating. I made strides in my combat skills, a feat I attributed largely to Rowyn's teachings at Solridge.

Despite our close proximity during these intense sessions, a barrier seemed to have descended between us. It was almost as if Thorn was consciously holding himself back. The lack of further intimacy frustrated me, as his hands would trace my form during training, correcting and adjusting, yet never straying beyond the professional after that first morning.

In the afternoons, I continued my sessions with Claw. Over several days I began to relax in her company, her unflinching professionalism coaxing me out of my shell. Her candid approach to nudity grew to be less unsettling with each passing day.

Master Haris continued his seclusion, engrossed in the archives and meetings with Lullaby Beside-the-Pine. His visits were sporadic, albeit well-intentioned, his concern barely veiling his preoccupation with his own pursuits. His lack of constant supervision both freed and unnerved me, with the realization of my purpose in the palace looming larger with each passing day.

Evenings were a whirlwind of social engagements. Dinner with Thorn consisted of introductions to various fae associated with mythical beasts. One night I found myself chatting with a unicorn herdmistress and exchanging recipes for ear mite oils. Another evening, I met a pair of griffon riders who invited me to meet their steeds bearing names that twisted my tongue in knots.

Despite the flurry of activities and ceaseless interactions, Thorn maintained a certain detachment, a distance that did nothing to quell my growing frustration. We were perpetually busy, a calculated move on Thorn's part, perhaps, that made the time until I obtained my gem pass by much faster than I anticipated.

THE DAWN OF OUR DEPARTURE DAY, Thorn was wrapped in his usual charisma, teasing the boundaries but never fully crossing them. Sharing a room was both a blessing and a curse. I loved seeing him barely dressed as I daydreamed about running my fingers over his broad back. It didn't help that the court of the fae was so open when it came to affection. It turned my thoughts, far too often, to what it would feel like if Thorn actually *made a move*. By Sol above, the frustration was going to be the death of me.

Once dressed and packed, Thorn led us out of the castle and back to the river where his canoe waited. As I stepped in, the boat rocked. Thorn gripped my arm, a current passing briefly between us. A roguish smirk lit Thorn's face at my reaction, but it quickly vanished as he withdrew his hand, maintaining the growing distance that had progressively etched itself between us. The frustration inside me burgeoned with each touch, each playful comment that was not acted upon. It was as if an unseen wall had risen, putting into question the kiss and every smoldering glance.

I settled myself, trying not to look at Thorn, and instead lifted the oar, waiting for him to finish helping Master Haris clamber in.

"We should reach the sea by evening," Thorn said, using his oar to ease us out of the dock and into the current. "The mertribe will be waiting for us there."

We moved swiftly. Alden-Ester disappeared behind a bend in the river as Thorn maneuvered the boat into the western fork.

413

As the river led us back into the depths of the Canyonlands, the scenery shifted. The verdant forest greenery was gradually replaced by rugged, towering cliffs, the walls worn down over countless millennia by the ceaseless current, forming intricate, twisted sculptures of stone. Some of the more artistic fae had carved into them. Massive friezes were depicting different stories from fae history. I recognized one as the fae prince, Shadow Within-the-Abyss, as his father tossed his infant body over the edge of a cavern. Another depicted Shadow's rise a hundred years later. He held the severed head of his father while his mother looked on.

Shadows passed beneath the boat, a myriad of shapes and colors flitting through the water below us in a world unseen. I closed my eyes and reached, listening with all my senses and using my magic to amplify it. A serpent had just swam under us with a trout in its jaws. Beyond, in a little underwater cove, was a clan of sprites, just being roused from their slumber by the dark cloud that shadowed their world from above—the canoe.

Deeper into the Canyonlands, the river widened and slowed, creating placid pools that mirrored the sky and the towering cliffs. Thorn guided the canoe to a rocky outcropping and after tying it to a gnarled tree that hung over the water, he helped us clamber up to a rocky platform that housed a shadowed cave.

Above, birds of all colors darted between the cliff faces, emitting a symphony of echoing calls. They sang of the midday sun and where a patch of plants had just dropped their seeds. Master Haris was catching his breath after the climb, fanning himself with his notes in the shade of his wide-brimmed hat. Thorn was rummaging through his rucksack, pulling out a bottle and some wrapped food.

I tried to enjoy the view of the river, but my attention kept getting caught on the dark maw of the cave behind us. I walked toward it, squinting to see inside. Uneasy, I sent my senses out and slid over something old, and grumpy, and fae-like.

"Something's there," I whispered as I felt a disturbance, a growl reverberating through the stone. My skin prickled with the echo of unfamiliar magic, the call of a creature I hadn't encountered before.

I was frozen for a half second, gripped by terror. My breath stopped on my lips.

No.

I would not face my first challenge like a fearful imbecile. I'd never once seen Rowyn freeze in a fight. Rowyn was absolutely fearless.

I forced myself to move, to remember my training. I gripped the rose handle of my dagger and drew it.

"Thorn," I called, my eyes fixed on the dark cavern, "there's something in the cave."

"What?" Thorn looked up from the food he was unpacking, a confused furrow forming on his brows. But then he heard it, a low and guttural growl rumbling from the shadows.

"Chimera," Thorn murmured, dropping the food back into his pack and shouldering the bag. "They usually don't live this close to water. Master Haris, get down to the canoe as fast as possible. It's steep, so we'll need to go one at a time." Thorn stood quickly and moved toward me.

The sound of crunching gravel echoed across the area as Master Haris hastened down the slope.

The chilling growl echoed through the cave mouth once more and a monstrous creature stepped into the light. The chimera was a fusion of several beasts—a lion's body with a serpentine tail whipping behind it, barbed like a scorpion's, the scales catching the sunlight. Its breath was a venomous green, shuddering through the air, while the twin goat horns that crowned its mane gave it an air of strange nobility.

I reached with my senses, attempting to placate the beast. "*We mean no harm.*" I sent the thought out. "*We will leave.*"

But a sensation flooded back to me. Hunger. Raw,

416

primal hunger.

"Just back up," Thorn said beside me, his eyes on the beast. "You'll follow Haris next. I can handle this."

"Are you sure?" I whispered, clenching the dagger.

But then, another sound.

A yelp.

A splash.

I spun around, my heart hammering in my chest. Master Haris was gone from the cliffside path, and in his place was a rapidly disappearing splash in the river. The current had him and was pulling him away with terrifying speed.

"Master Haris!" I screamed, but the roar of the chimera and the river drowned out my voice. I turned back to face the creature.

The chimera lunged. I dodged the attack, my dagger slicing along its side as Thorn and I separated. The animal bellowed in pain, its angry roar bouncing off the canyon walls as it swiped a paw at Thorn.

Shit. Now I was by the cave entrance, while Thorn was near the cliff's edge. "Get Haris!" I shouted as I crouched, the dagger still in my hand. "Quick, before we lose him!"

"I'm not leaving you!" Thorn shouted back, feinting toward the chimera with his blade. The creature turned, prowling toward me. The serpent tail lashed in

Thorn's direction.

With a swift slash, Thorn's blade cut through the air, catching the tail just beneath the barb. The creature yowled in pain, lurching to the side.

But Thorn's attention wasn't on the beast. His gaze was locked on me. I could see the conflict within him, the need to stay and fight battling with the urgency of rescuing Master Haris. But he was closest to the cliff face, and I was trapped by the cave entrance.

"Go!" I screamed again, the creature rearing back, preparing for another attack. "Go! Now!" We were out of time.

For a moment, he hesitated, looking from me to the swiftly moving river, then back again. His grip tightened on his dagger, his knuckles white.

The injured tail lashed out again, sending Thorn over the cliff's edge and into the rushing waters below. The chimera had decided for him.

I sent a quick prayer to the gods that they would protect Thorn. Alone, with my heart pounding in my chest, I tightened my grip on the dagger, focusing all my energy on the beast before me. The chimera snarled, a terrifying sound that echoed on the walls of the canyon around us. Its gaze locked onto me, its next target.

Taking a deep breath, I centered myself. Raising my

weapon, I prepared for the next attack.

With the seething fury of the wounded, the chimera lunged. Its golden eyes narrowed, its jaws snapping, revealing razor-sharp teeth. I planted my feet and plunged my dagger forward.

A roar of agony echoed, so loud I could feel it vibrating in my bones. Its blood was hot and slick on my hand, but my grip on the hilt didn't falter. What I hadn't anticipated, however, was the sudden pull as the chimera twisted away, the blade caught between its ribs. I gasped, my hand empty, and then screamed as the chimera's jaws clamped down on my leg.

White-hot pain flared, and I was being dragged toward the cave. Desperation clawed at my insides, and I clawed back at the earth, my nails digging into the dirt, searching for anything to anchor me.

The hilt of my dagger jutted out from the beast's side. With a final surge of energy, I lurched toward it, my fingers wrapping around the blood-slicked handle. With a triumphant yell, I yanked it free and plunged it with all my strength into the creature's throat.

The chimera's roar cut off abruptly. Its body convulsed and then it was collapsing, its weight bearing down on me. I gasped as I was pinned beneath the creature, my chest tightening with the sheer weight of it. The world was spinning, the pain in my leg blinding, but finally, the creature's body was still, and its breath ceased.

The river and the distant calling of birds tempted me to close my eyes and sink into unconsciousness, but I shook my head awake. There was no time to rest. I still needed to find Haris and Thorn. I shoved the creature's body up, trying to drag myself from underneath it.

With one last surge of strength, I managed to push the body off, and it rolled to the side. Its heavy form thudded onto the rocky ground, revealing my bloodied and mangled leg. I fought back a whimper, biting down on my lip. Every movement sent sharp waves of pain through my body, but I couldn't afford to pass out. Not yet.

Slowly, painstakingly, I began to crawl, dragging myself toward the cliff's edge. My breath hitched with every pull of my arms, every drag of my injured leg. Sweat was dripping down my face, staining the rock beneath me, but the sight of the river and the canoe tied to the rocky outcropping spurred me on.

I reached the cliff's edge, peering down at the empty canoe bobbing in the gentle sway of the river. Gritting my teeth, I swung my legs over the edge, using what little strength remained in me to slide down the cliff face with a tumble of rocks and dirt.

My landing was anything but graceful as I descended into a cloud of dirt. The canoe rocked dangerously as I wrenched my worthless leg into it. My wound throbbed, but I pushed the pain to the back of my mind, settling into the canoe before reaching out to untie it from the gnarled tree.

Once the canoe was free, I grabbed one of the oars, the wood rough under my sweaty palms. I was exhausted, my body screaming for rest, but I pushed through it. I had to find Haris and Thorn.

As I paddled away from the shore, the wind swept over me, drying the sweat on my face, but the smell of blood lingered, a grim reminder of the battle I'd just fought. And as I disappeared around the bend, the cliff and the cave and the lifeless chimera were swallowed by the towering canyon walls, vanishing from sight.

With a renewed sense of determination, I grasped the oar firmly, pushing the canoe forward. Each stroke was a test of my resilience, the pain in my leg threatening to overtake me. But the thought of Thorn and Haris needing help drove me forward. They had come on this journey to help *me*. I would not let them down.

Amid the exhaustion and pain, I found a thread of my magic, a thread that I followed upward toward the birds that flew overhead. I reached out to them, my mental call a desperate plea for their assistance. I showed them the images of Haris and Thorn, as clearly as I could muster, despite my waning strength.

And they responded.

I shielded my eyes and looked up as several flocks of birds spread out across the canyon, their eyes becoming mine, their flight a beacon of hope. The high vantage point gave me a sweeping view of the river and its winding course through the canyon.

Soon enough, I caught sight of a lone figure. It was Haris, his body plastered against a rock tree, arms wrapped around it like it was his lifeline. Relief washed over me, but it was short-lived. I could see his hold on the tree was weakening, his strength waning.

My heart pounded harder in my chest, and I pulled on the oar with all the strength I had left. But the current was swift, and the wind was against me. As I fought against the river, the birds alerted me to another sighting. Thorn was farther ahead, in even more peril. His body was bobbing in the water, the river's current dragging him relentlessly.

A surge of fear clenched my heart, but I knew I couldn't afford to panic. I had to reach them, and fast.

With a newfound burst of energy, I paddled harder. I knew I would have to make some hard decisions soon, but for now, I followed where the birds guided me, hoping against hope that I would be fast enough.

Finally, I saw Haris in the distance, his hands lodged in a crevice in the stone. I paddled quickly, easing the canoe to the other side of the canyon wall. I knew I wouldn't make it to Thorn in time. If he couldn't get out of the water soon, who knew what would happen to him. I hoped to all the gods that he was all right.

Biting back a groan of pain, I reached with my magic again. As my senses spread, brushing against the scales of fish and the slippery bodies of water creatures, I mentally urged them to aid me.

I sent a visual image of Thorn's predicament.

The river was alive with activity, the animals within it responding to my call. I focused on the image of Thorn, his head bobbing above the water with the horns and tail that marked him as part Woltari. "*Help him stay afloat*," I urged them. "*Get him to land.*"

With every ounce of strength left in my battered body, I pulled the canoe through the water, toward Master Haris who hadn't even noticed me yet.

Just when I thought I wouldn't make it in time, green scales surged around the canoe, wedging me between the large boulder and the canyon wall. Haris yelped in surprise, losing his grip. I grabbed his robe before he could be swept away. Leveraging my bad leg, I wrenched Master Haris's upper body into the canoe with a scream as pain tore through my entire being. I

423

blinked away the tears and pulled again, this time on Haris's shoulders, and dragged him the rest of the way into the safety of the boat.

Master Haris groaned, his breath labored. "Oh, my dear," he managed, his voice quivering like a frail leaf. His eyes, half closed and shimmering with fear, met mine. "Oh, I was so afraid it was the end."

I felt a lump in my throat. The sight of his helplessness, his vulnerability, tugged at my heart. But there was no time for sentimentality. "We need to find Thorn," I shouted over the sounds of the rushing water, my voice choked with worry and pain. With a grimace, I pushed us back out into the current.

"I saw him . . ." Haris began, his words coming out in jagged, tired breaths. "I tried to . . . to reach out . . . but he was . . . too far." His eyes fluttered shut, his body slumping against the bottom of the canoe.

My leg throbbed mercilessly, the wound a hot, searing mark of the chimera's final attempt to win. Despite my injuries, I was fighting. With every stroke of the paddle, the world swirled around me, the pain making my head spin. I took a shaky breath to stay focused. Once more, I reached, my mind brushing against the consciousness of the birds.

My heart thudded violently in my chest as I saw that Thorn was crouched on the shore, his face etched with

424

frustration. An odd, unfamiliar creature blocked his path, its form shimmering with scales.

Each time Thorn tried to make a move—either toward the water or toward the sheer cliff face—the creature advanced, pulling him back with an eerily gentle but firm grip. It didn't harm him but made it clear that he was not allowed to leave. I watched as Thorn balled his fists, his anger visible even from the bird's high vantage point. But despite his evident frustration, he didn't attack the creature.

"We're almost there," I whispered into the wind.

Chapter 14

WE TURNED A BEND, and the rocky strip of land where Thorn waited finally came into view. The strange creature turned its attention to us. Its body was reminiscent of a fish, its lower half shimmering in the shallows of the river, scaled and elegant, glistening with a grayish-green sheen under the dappled sunlight. Its head was that of a horse, with large, soulful eyes, a regal snout, and long ears that twitched in our direction. Its mane was thick, not with horsehair but with what looked like strands of kelp flowing down its neck and framing its face, swaying gently as if moved by unseen currents.

As we approached, Thorn took a step back, relief washing over his face when he saw us. The creature, which I now recognized as a kelpie, turned to me. Its large eyes watched us, wary and vigilant.

"*You called,*" it accused.

I let my mind fill with thoughts of relief and thankfulness. "*Thank you for saving him,*" I sent. "*He is dear to me.*"

"*He smells bad,*" the kelpie replied, its eyes back on Thorn. "*He smells of earth and heat and fire.*"

426

I laughed despite the fact that nothing at all was funny. "*I'm sorry he assaulted your sensibilities.*"

Thorn didn't waste a moment. He splashed through the shallows to meet us, grabbing the end of the canoe and hauling it to shore. His eyes took in my bloody leg, the paleness of my face, and the exhaustion clear in my eyes. His relief was quickly replaced with concern.

"Fin, you're hurt," he said, his voice tight. He grabbed my arms and steadied me as I tried to get out of the canoe. Finally, he just picked me up and carried me to dry land.

"I'm sorry I had to kill it," I admitted. I was going into shock. Master Gillius had described shock to us, and I couldn't really feel my leg despite the gaping wound. My mind was disjointed from the world, not quite registering the danger I was in. Instead, I dwelled on the life I'd been forced to take.

The chimera was only hungry, and we were possible food. It was primal. It didn't make it hurt any less, though, to kill a creature as noble as that.

My vision began to blur. Adrenaline was beginning to ebb. I looked down. My arm was vibrating. My breath ragged.

"Hey," Thorn said, lowering me gently to the ground. "I've got you. I can take care of this."

Tears pooled at the corners of my eyes before

flooding my cheeks. I sniffed, lifting my arm to wipe my nose. "I'm sorry," I gasped. "I feel so stupid." Rowyn would never have burst into tears like that.

Thorn cupped my cheek, tilting my head up. "You are not stupid," Thorn scolded. "You are fearless is what you are. I don't know how you're supposed to react after you defeat a chimera because most people haven't done it. What you did is not nothing. And it is most certainly something you can cry over. Just let the tears fall." He smirked, that damned half-grin that melted my heart every time.

"My dear girl," Master Haris said, rising from the canoe to look at me as though Thorn's words spurred to remind him that it was he, in fact, who was supposed to be taking care of *me* on this trip. "I didn't realize you were so badly injured."

Behind us, the kelpie stomped its hoof, the ground trembling slightly. Its large eyes watched us closely, as if daring us to make a wrong move. Trying not to show my pain, I reached my hand out to it. The kelpie walked toward my outstretched fingers, then nudged them with its muzzle. I stroked its head, my fingers sliding through the kelp-like mane. It felt cool to the touch, like the river it guarded. The kelpie let out a soft neigh, the tension in its stance easing slightly.

"What's your name?" I whispered, my voice raspy.

"*River-Dancer,*" the kelpie said, letting the words filter into my mind.

"*Thank you again, River-Dancer,*" I replied. I hoped the creature understood my gratitude. With a final pat, I pulled back as the kelpie turned and sank back into the river with barely a splash.

Behind us, Master Haris had rolled himself out of the canoe and was lying flat on the shore, his chest heaving with exhaustion.

THE AFTERNOON SUN WAS HIGH in the sky, its heat drying our clothes and belongings as we lay under the golden rays. Master Haris was fast asleep, snoring in the shade of a large rock.

Thorn was beside me, a mixture of worry and awe etched on his features. He was tending to my injuries, his eyes focused, yet distant, as if he was lost in thought while his hands automatically performed the task of sprinkling fairy dust over the gouges from the chimera's teeth, then wrapping my leg with a roll of linen cloth torn from one of his shirts. There was a hesitance in his touch, a certain restraint, like he was holding back.

I watched him, a pang of longing surging within me.

"Thorn?" I finally broke the silence, my voice barely more than a whisper. His dark eyes met mine, but his gaze was guarded. "Why . . . Did I do something . . . to upset you?" I finished. I was about to ask him why he hadn't asked to kiss me again but thought better of it. Perhaps he just didn't feel like kissing me. I would probably be bad at it, having never kissed anyone before.

I saw his hesitation, his gaze flickering away before returning to mine. He seemed torn, wrestling with words that he was struggling to find. The silence stretched. When his gaze met mine, a war of emotions played in his eyes.

"The king has made it clear that you are not just important to *him* but that you will play a pivotal role in the future of the fae. I didn't want my . . . feelings . . . to cloud your judgment."

Anger and frustration flared, mixed with a peculiar sense of hurt. Did he view me as some naïve, sheltered girl incapable of understanding my own emotions or making sound decisions? I had proven myself time and again, faced and conquered challenges far greater than any ordinary girl my age.

Was he insinuating that I was incapable of separating personal feelings from duty? That any affection I felt for him would somehow impair my ability to make sound decisions? No, I was made of sterner stuff. Why couldn't he see that?

"You think romance would cause me to lose my ability to reason?" I asked.

Thorn's eyes fell away from mine, instead focusing on the river. "I'm fifty years old, and you . . . you're just starting out on your journey. The last thing I want is for you to feel like I'm leading you on or . . . or taking advantage of your inexperience."

What Thorn failed to realize was that he wasn't leading me on or taking advantage. My heart fluttered every time he was near. My mind was filled with thoughts of him. I relished the delicious feeling of being near him.

"You know, Thorn," I began, amazed with how steady my voice was despite the fact that my leg was screaming with pain, and I couldn't get my head to keep up with the conversation that *I* had started. "I may be young, but that doesn't mean I can't make decisions for myself. You have no idea how much I've had to hold my own. How much I've had to grow up just to survive."

I reached and brushed his hand, my voice lowering. "You aren't leading me on, and you aren't taking advantage of me." I paused, drawing in a deep breath before adding, "And if it's not clear enough, I want to give us a chance. I don't have feelings like these for just anyone."

His gaze softened, his stern exterior cracking slightly.

"I'm not saying this is anything more than it is," I said, my voice dropping to a whisper. "I just like you. It's . . . different. It feels . . . real. And I want to know if it's real."

The silence following my confession was deafening, punctuated only by the gurgle of the river. I could almost hear Thorn's internal debate waging within him.

"But I am not like the humans when it comes to relationships," he admitted. "For many of us fae, being tied to just one person through marriage . . . it's not the norm."

A thick silence lingered for a moment, filled only by the gurgle of the river and Haris's soft snores. It was as if Thorn was allowing his words to sink in. He glanced up, his eyes troubled, his tail swaying behind him.

"You're saying that, even if we did work, we don't have any sort of future?" I asked softly.

A muscle in Thorn's jaw tensed. "No, I'm saying that if we want there to be a future, it's not going to look like the relationships you're used to seeing. I've always embraced an open approach when it comes to love and companionship—taking each day as it arrives. That's simply who I am," he admitted, his gaze never wavering from mine. "I don't want to mislead you, or let you believe that I could be someone I'm not. If you need someone who adheres strictly to the Lyrican way . . . unwavering fidelity, marriage, and the like . . . I'm afraid I'm not that person."

I didn't know what he saw on my face, but his voice grew heavier. "My first allegiance will always be my duty as a gatekeeper. It's an oath I've taken, a responsibility that's become a part of who I am. I don't foresee a future where I settle down with a wife and child in the traditional human sense. I . . . I relish the ability to seize life as it presents itself. To love who I am with in the moment."

With an earnest look that seemed to burrow into my heart, he continued, "This doesn't imply that I'm incapable of commitment. It just means my form of commitment may not align with your expectations. And even though I can't lie to you, I desperately don't want to disappoint you, either." The sincerity of his words hung between us, their weight something tangible.

Thorn swallowed hard, his jaw clenching. "I've wanted to kiss you, Fin," he confessed, his voice barely audible over the crackling of the fire. "Every day since we've met. But I've been waiting for you to . . . to give your consent, to make a move. Because I want this to be your choice, not something you feel pressured into. And I wanted you to know everything before you made it."

His confession felt like a heavy weight hanging in the air between us. A small part of me felt a sting of disappointment. But it was short-lived, drowned out by a bigger part of me that respected his honesty. Thorn had chosen to bare his truth. He was laying out his boundaries. It was up to me to accept him for who he was or . . . not.

"I appreciate your honesty," I finally managed to say. "Whatever comes next . . . we'll figure it out."

His face eased, a smile of relief making its way to his lips. "Thank you for understanding."

My lips curved into a teasing grin, despite the ache that consumed me. "And," I added, just to be clear, "if you ever feel like kissing me, you have my permission to do so."

Thorn let out a short burst of laughter, his eyes sparkling with amusement as his curved horns cast shadows over my eyes.

"Not right now though," I quickly amended, leaning back against the rock that served as my temporary resting place. "I'm in too much pain to enjoy it, and I desperately want to enjoy it."

His laughter deepened, the warm sound echoing across the canyon. "Fair enough," he agreed, his voice brimming with mirth.

The laughter faded and silence settled in once more, broken only by the occasional rush of the river and Haris's steady breathing. It was in this silence, under the comfort of the afternoon sun, that I found my own confession spilling out.

"I'm not looking for commitment, either, you know."

A lopsided grin spread across Thorn's face. "That makes things easier." His eyes gleamed with a strange mixture of relief, amusement, and something that looked suspiciously like admiration. He leaned back on his hands, his gaze lingering on my face, making the pit of my stomach flutter with a wild, unfamiliar warmth. "Most of the human women I've met, especially the young ones, they want marriage."

I chuckled softly, the sound more bitter than I intended. "Well, Thorn, most of the human girls you've met have been raised to believe that their salvation lies in finding a man who will provide them with safety and security." I paused, my laughter fading away. "That's not me. I've never found comfort in the idea of someone having that much control over my life. It feels like the only way I'll be safe is if I rely on myself . . . you know?"

A silence followed, not uncomfortable, but rather thoughtful. "It seems we are more alike than I realized." He stared at me for a few heartbeats, his gaze probing, and then slowly, his lips curled.

"Isn't that what you like about me?"

"I like plenty about you," Thorn said, nudging me with his elbow. "You're smart and kind, and your *hips* . . . By the king's seat, if you took one look at me when you've undressed, you would've seen a man at the end of his rope."

"You like my . . . hips," I repeated, just to be clear. I'd never heard of that before.

Thorn smiled ruefully. "Fae don't have hips like human ladies . . . It gets me every time. And yours . . ." Thorn bit his lip. "I just want to bite them and kiss them and bury my face in them."

I burst into laughter. "Seriously?"

Thorn's cheeks reddened. It may have been the only time I'd ever seen him embarrassed.

He sighed. "I've said too much. I see that now. I've ruined the moment, and you will never look at me the same again, will you."

My laughter continued.

436

Thorn was still shaking his head at himself. "I'm sorry. Get some rest, Fin. You've earned it."

Chapter 15

I T TOOK MOST OF THE AFTERNOON, but as the river dumped us into the sea, Thorn announced, "We've arrived," a hint of reverence in his voice at the endless expanse of blue stretching out as far as the eye could see.

We followed the coastline for a bit before we came upon a beach. We paddled toward shore where Thorn hopped out into the shallows and pulled us the rest of the way.

We unloaded, then Thorn rewrapped my wound. Just as he was about to begin the task of preparing dinner, he heard something and turned.

Amid the waves, the Ng'Baoba tribe surfaced. Their fins reflected the brilliance of the sunset behind them. There were about twenty who emerged to greet us, many of whom carried weapons. I assumed . . . or rather hoped . . . that they were guards.

One of them swam forward, a female wearing a grand headpiece. Ivory pearls of varying sizes glistened like the moon's mirrored reflections, nestled among the delicate spirals of dried coral lined with clam shells. In the center of the headpiece was a bone-white skull.

438

Thorn raised his hand to the lady with the head-piece. "Chief Vin-Briony Of-the-Coral-Cove, the king wishes to thank you for agreeing to aid his guest into the Tourmaline Cave."

The merchief's strange, round eyes settled on me, her voice a curious lilt. "So, this is the human King Of-the-Castle wastes a favor on?" Her eyes skimmed over me, assessing, appraising. "Pretty," she conceded with a casual shrug, her indifference apparent. "For a human, but I see nothing special."

I shifted my feet, resting my weight on my other leg, hoping they didn't notice. My dagger was right by my hand.

Thorn met the merchief's gaze unflinchingly, his tone steady. "It's no secret the king seeks to rebuild alliances with the humans."

Her scoff echoed in the still air, disdain apparent in the curl of her lip and the flicker in her sea-green eyes. "Humans." She spat the word out, her nose wrinkling in distaste. "An alliance insinuates that we are equals"—the merchief's eyes slid to mine—"and we are most certainly not that."

"They have their strengths," Thorn countered, remaining calm despite the mounting tension. "Their resourcefulness, their tenacity . . . these are traits to be valued."

The merchief's gaze turned icy, her scorn evident. "And what of their wars? The way they slaughter their own kind without a second thought?" Her lips curled in a snarl, her voice turning vicious. "They don't value their own lives. Why should we?"

"There are many who still remember how much happier fae were when they dwelled among us," Thorn said, his arms outstretched.

The chief's eyes roved from Thorn's head to his feet, then back up. "You claim kinship with humans, yet they would only deem you fae."

"That is true for some, but not all," Thorn replied.

"They are a threat nonetheless," the merchief retorted, her voice dripping with finality. "I want to go back to the open sea. Why should the humans claim that they can keep us here?"

Thorn's gaze hardened, but his response was measured. "The king's mandate is clear, as was his request."

The merchief sneered but gestured to two others who swam forward. "These are two of my most trusted kin. Mor-Kale and Al-May will be your guides into the depths. They will assist your little human in obtaining her gem."

Mor-Kale was a striking figure, his blue-green skin shimmering in the moonlight. He had a roguish grin that suggested he was amused by all this. A spark in his eyes hinted at mischief as he looked at me, his gaze lingering a little longer than necessary.

Heat rose to my cheeks. I needed their help to get my gem, that much was sure, but I couldn't help but feel a tingle of unease.

Al-May was the opposite of her companion. Her eyes were cold and distant, her expression a perfectly painted picture of indifference. She looked me over with thinly veiled disdain that had me standing straighter.

"I appreciate you taking the time to assist me," I said, speaking as loud as I dared without my voice wavering. "The full moon is tomorrow night, so I understand we must dive then."

The chieftain didn't spare me a glance. She turned to Thorn. "They will return tomorrow morning to help prepare her, then assist in the dive."

"The king thanks you for your help," Thorn said, though he didn't seem happy about it. He and Mor-Kale were looking at each other like they were about to throw punches. What was the deal with that?

"I would also like to thank you," I said, this time directing my attention to Mor-Kale and Al-May. If the chieftain wasn't going to acknowledge me, then I wouldn't acknowledge her.

Thorn's gaze bounced between the merfolk and

me, his eyes filled with a clear worry that he was trying to mask. I couldn't shake off the unease. I was to be entrusted to creatures who were openly disdainful of my kind. Yet, I smiled, trying to convey a sense of confidence I was far from feeling.

It was Thorn who broke the silence first after the merpeople sank back into the depths. "Fin," he said, his voice strained. "I don't like this. I think we should wait until the next full moon so I can talk with the king. This doesn't feel right."

I placed my hand on his forearm. His muscles were taut, vibrating with tension. "I can't wait another month. Besides, I thought she was granting a favor to the king. Why would they endanger themselves by hurting me?"

Master Haris shuffled beside us. "It is up to Fin whether or not we wait," he said, his eyes on me. "But more journeys back and forth could just as easily kill us."

That was a rousing endorsement.

My anger at Master Haris was beginning to rise. He hadn't been particularly helpful the entire trip. Sure, he remembered lots of nice facts, but our time at the palace was brief, and now it felt like I only had Thorn to guard my back.

And Thorn was telling me that something was

wrong.

I clenched my teeth.

I needed my gem.

I felt its call at night while I lay awake, the back of my hand resting on my forehead, where the gem would eventually lie. Once a sorcerer found their gem, anything could happen. Sure, going for Mastery was preferred, but they already had their power. The gem was their safeguard. Everything after could be learned or figured out over time, with or without help.

"I will dive tomorrow night, as planned," I said, my voice brooking no argument. "I need my gem, and if they throw something at me, I'm just going to have to figure out how to take it."

Thorn's eyes were dark with worry. He drew a heavy breath, his gaze meeting mine. "Promise me you'll be careful," he said, his voice barely a whisper. "I thought that a favor to the king would be enough to keep them in line, but the merfolk are crafty. If they really are angry, if they truly mean you harm, it would be easy for them to kill you."

I squeezed his arm gently, offering him a comforting smile. "I will come back, with a gem, and everything will be fine." I tried not to let my doubts show on my face. "I'm not without my own powers, you know."

Even as I spoke the words, I couldn't ignore the seed of worry planted in my mind. The unknown was terrifying, but I couldn't let fear hold me back. Not now. I was stronger than that.

I had to be.

THAT NIGHT, WE LAY UNDER THE STARS, their glow softly illuminating our makeshift camp. Haris's rhythmic snores resonated through the stillness. He was oblivious to the anxiety hanging heavily between Thorn and me.

"Fin," Thorn whispered in the darkness, his fingers tracing circles on my arm. The touch was soft, gentle, and oddly comforting. "I'm powerless when it comes to the sea."

I turned to face him, studying his silhouette in the dim light, his horns a shadowed crown. His brows were creased with worry, his usual confidence replaced with a quiet helplessness that stung my heart. "Thorn," I said, reaching out to place my hand on his. "It's okay. I have trained for this, remember? I can handle myself."

Fingers lightly brushed my cheek. "The thought of

you alone in the depths . . ." Thorn whispered. "It terrifies me."

His admission was raw and unguarded, revealing a vulnerability he rarely showed.

"I'll be all right," I reassured him, my hand moving to rest on his chest, feeling the steady rhythm of his heart. "I promise."

There was no other choice.

It was what a Trial by Stone was.

His gaze searched mine for a moment. I saw hesitation, yearning, fear, but above all, I saw desire. My heart pounded against my ribs as he leaned in, the space between us dwindling to nothing. The anticipation sent a ripple of excitement coursing through my veins.

His lips met mine, warm and soft. The world dissolved around us, leaving only the sensation of Thorn's fervor. My heart hammered in my chest as our breaths mingled. I was addicted to the way he smelled. I was addicted to that half-cocked grin whenever he was flirting with me. Thorn was adventurous, and fun, and his positivity was so infectious. I adored being around him.

His hands were firm on my hips as he pulled me into him. My fingers explored the broad expanse of his back, the muscular planes of his shoulders, and the rough stubble of his jaw. His every touch, every graze of his fingertips ignited sparks under my skin, leaving me aching for more.

Thorn pulled away, breathless, his dark eyes almost wild in the moonlight. His hands moved up to cup my cheeks. "Can I make you feel good?" he murmured, kissing me on each cheek before meeting my eyes once again.

"Why just me?" I asked, running my hand down his lower back and over his firm buttocks.

Thorn lifted a loose strand of my blonde hair and brushed it behind my ear. "Tonight's about you," Thorn said. "Just you."

"All right," I breathed, having no idea what to expect.

His touch was gentle but filled with an intensity that left my skin tingling. His hands slid over my hips to the small of my back, his thumb brushing the skin under my breeches.

Thorn propped himself on his arm, gently easing me onto my back, his body hovering over me. He cupped my cheek once more, his thumb tracing my bottom lip. "You are one of the most beautiful beings I've ever met," he whispered, his voice husky. "Never doubt that."

He was killing me with those words. I ached to hear

them again. To feel his hands, hot on my skin. I tangled my fingers in his hair as I pulled him down to me. Our lips met in a heated kiss, a clash of tongues and teeth, a promise of what was to come.

Chapter 16

OR-KALE AND AL-MAY were waiting for me in the surf when I woke up the next morning cradled in Thorn's arms where I'd melted into a puddle during the heat of the night before. Master Haris was still sound asleep, the exertion of trouble from the day before proving to be overwhelming for him. We rose, hurriedly getting dressed and inhaling a quick breakfast before I approached my two merguides.

The sight of the vast expanse of water triggered a shiver of trepidation that I fought to suppress. I inhaled deeply, the briny air filling my lungs, and cast a fleeting glance at Thorn who watched from a distance, arms crossed over his chest.

Rowyn wouldn't have flinched in my place.

I took another deep breath, forcing myself to calm. With an impish grin, Mor-Kale broke the tension. His teal eyes gleamed with mischief as he walked up the sand with his webbed hands and arms thick with muscle. "So, you think you're a good swimmer?" His voice was light, infused with playful curiosity.

Al-May merely glared.

The day's first task was to show off my water skills. As I plunged into the ocean under Mor-Kale's watchful eyes and Al-May's terse instructions, the sea's cool embrace enveloped me, jolting my senses into heightened alertness. I propelled myself through the water with strong, determined strokes, the seabed falling away beneath me. As I surfaced, I shook the water from my hair.

Al-May looked bored as she leaned on her hands and lazily flicked her large tail in the water.

Mor-Kale was deeper in the surf, where he'd been waiting for me to surface. "Are you not worried that your clothes will catch on something? What is the purpose of wearing them in the water? How do they help you?" His tone was curious, but his smile was a clear dare.

I treaded water while I considered Mor-Kale's point. It was valid, but the thought of undressing . . . I cast a look toward Thorn, finding his gaze locked on me. A blush crept up my cheeks as I said, "I . . . well, they don't help per se, but . . ."

Mor-Kale cut me off, his grin widening. "Then they should go. We don't need unnecessary hindrances on your little quest, do we?"

I frowned, my cheeks warming further. But I knew he was right. Reluctantly, I nodded, swimming toward

449

a more secluded part of the seabed. Unhooking my tunic, I slipped it over my head and pulled down my breeches and undershorts. Clad only in my skin and belt of tools at my waist, I felt the full embrace of the cool sea and the sun above. It was a new kind of freedom, liberating and nerve-racking at the same time.

Back in the water, I avoided Thorn's gaze, not sure how he would react. Mor-Kale seemed to find my discomfort amusing. His eyes sparkled as he swam toward me. "Now, let me show you some strokes that could strengthen your swim," he offered sincerely despite the playful glint in his eyes.

For the next few minutes, Mor-Kale demonstrated how to move my arms more effectively. When it was my turn to try, I startled as his hands slid along the side of my body and over the crests of my breasts before moving behind my shoulders. I tried to focus on my form. But when I looked up, Mor-Kale's gaze was on Thorn, his smirk widening just a touch. Across the water, Thorn's attention was firmly fixed on me, his fists clenched at his sides, his tail angrily whipping behind him.

I felt a hot rush of indignation surge through me, pricking at my skin like tiny flames. I had assumed that Mor-Kale's intrusive touch was simply a part of his fae nature. But the sly glance he threw Thorn's way was revealing. He was deliberately provoking him. A wave of embarrassment crashed over me. I had been made a fool, and I loathed it.

"Enough with the antics," I snapped, whirling around to face Mor-Kale. I swatted his wandering hand away from my waist, my gaze hardening. "I agreed to train, not to be fondled."

His teal eyes widened a fraction, taken aback by my outburst, though his usual cockiness slid back into place soon enough.

My gaze shifted to Thorn. I couldn't decipher the emotion in his eyes, but his stance was resolute.

Al-May, on the other hand, looked thoroughly disinterested. She was a mere observer, contributing nothing more than her cold gaze. The difference in attitude between my two merfolk guides couldn't have been starker.

After my stroke was determined to be passable, we practiced sharing breath, a crucial skill for my upcoming dive. Al-May was brisk and efficient in her demonstration, her cool demeanor never faltering. I followed her lead, trying to mirror her calm precision as she placed her lips onto mine and breathed into my mouth. We practiced it above water first before she pulled me under and did the same, this time allowing me to sink further into the depths before giving me air to extend my time. It was bizarre having a strange person's mouth on mine, the slightly fishy breath filling my lungs, but it worked.

Then it was Mor-Kale's turn. Unlike Al-May, Mor-Kale had a playful twinkle in his eyes as he neared me. His lips grazed mine, a brief contact that seemed more like a kiss than anything else. I could almost hear Thorn's teeth grinding from where I floated in the sea. When his lips pressed against mine once more, he breathed in, but he'd grasped my face in his hands, and his tongue went about exploring my mouth.

I lurched away and slapped him across the face. "What in the gods do you think you are doing?" This was about more than their petty rivalries. This was about my life, *my* future.

Mor-Kale studied me for a moment. Then, he inclined his head, his lips curling into a smirk. "Apologies. It's been a hundred years since I've had a taste of human," he replied. He didn't seem particularly disturbed by my outburst or by the sting of my slap.

We continued for a bit longer until Mor-Kale told me to rest until nightfall. As the afternoon sun blazed high at its peak, Thorn guided me away from the water's edge and toward a sequestered spot tucked beneath the shadow of towering stone. The beach was nearly silent, save for the distant crashing of waves and the faint rustling of leaves in the gentle sea breeze. My body ached from the morning's exertion, and a blanket of exhaustion had begun to settle over me.

There was a careful delicacy in Thorn's touch as he began to redress my injured leg. He worked with gentle precision, applying more of the fairy dust powder that had begun to significantly speed up the healing process. Each contact from his hands against my skin sent tiny jolts of electricity through me, dancing through the coolness of the dust. Memories of the night before heated my blood.

"Is it still hurting?" Thorn asked. His eyes were on me, filled with concern.

"A little," I admitted, "but it's getting better."

A smile tugged at his lips, small and fleeting. "You're stronger than you think, Fin," he murmured, his thumb tracing a comforting circle on my knee.

I reached to him then, my fingers threading through his. Our eyes locked, and in his gaze, I found the reassurance I didn't know I needed.

Leaning in, he captured my lips with his in a tender kiss. He pulled away all too soon.

"Rest, Fin," Thorn said softly, his voice soothing the fatigue. I didn't argue. Instead, I settled against him, my head finding a comfortable perch on his arm. He was a warm, sturdy presence, protecting me against the dangers of the world beyond. But he wouldn't be there for much longer. In the depths of the ocean, I would be alone.

UNDER THE SILVER GLOW OF THE MOON, I stepped into the inky sea. I was nude save for my leather belt that held my dagger and a small pickax. The call of my gem had morphed into a song, tugging at my heart and drawing me into the salty brine.

I turned. Master Haris was waving, his gaze somber, knowing what the quest could cost me. Just because a sorcerer went through a Trial by Stone didn't mean they survived. The history of sorcerers told many tales of young pilgrims who died on the way to obtain the keys to their power. I would be a fool to think that I was guaranteed to survive the journey, but if I dwelled too long on what could go wrong, I'd lose faith in myself.

Beside Master Haris's somber figure, Thorn paced. His dark, curly hair was mussed around the base of his horns from running his fingers through it. I'd tried to reassure him as the sun began to set and night began to fall, but Thorn only grew more agitated. There was no helping it. I was going, no matter what. I would face whatever the sea had in store and either survive or be lost to the otherworld.

That's not to say I didn't take precautions. For the last hour I'd been reaching out to the creatures of the sea, checking for merfolk and chatting with various animals. The wild sea creatures held no allegiance to the merpeople and were willing to divulge lots of information. Apparently, the Ng'Baoba lived in a series of underwater caves farther north on the coast.

As the cool water enveloped me, Mor-Kale and Al-May surfaced, already waiting. I looked one last time over my shoulder, to Master Haris whose eyes were large behind his spectacles as he watched. Thorn was crouched now beside him, his tail helping him balance on his haunches as his eyes remained glued to mine. I took a deep breath and dove.

My eyes adjusted to the darkness quickly as we began to descend into the ocean's depths. The merfolk's powerful tails provided a steady rhythm that I tried to mirror with my kicks. My heart pounded in my chest as I swam into the darkness.

I felt the faint mental signatures of various marine life around us, each unique and distinct. A curious school of fish darted around me, responding to my call. Others, like the group of passing stingrays, seemed indifferent, continuing their graceful dance undisturbed.

On the outskirts of my range, a stronger mental signature stood out. A creature had heard me and was slowly heading our way. Its energy felt familiar, though it was still too distant for a clear identification. I poured more energy into my magic, trying to draw it closer, to make a more solid connection.

Meanwhile, I used the nearby animals as my eyes and ears, scanning for any signs of other merfolk in the vicinity. The merchief's enmity from the day before had not been forgotten. All seemed quiet, for now.

As I felt my lungs contract, Al-May swam toward me. Her hands grasped mine as we stilled our descent, her cool lips meeting mine in a shared breath. It was a strange sensation, but one that was becoming more familiar. As oxygen filled my lungs again, a few moments of rest provided much-needed respite as we breathed back and forth into each other.

We did that several more times as we continued our descent, the ocean floor drawing closer.

As I reached the bottom of the rock chimney Mor-Kale was leading us to, my lungs felt on the verge of bursting. Panic surged, threatening to take over. I looked around desperately for Al-May, but she was nowhere in sight. Instead, I found Mor-Kale's eyes upon me.

His eyes glinted with a hint of amusement as he swam toward me, his hands on my hips to steady me. Our lips met in a rush of bubbles, the life-giving air from his breath seeping into my lungs. He pulled me closer, his lips lingering on mine, his tongue exploring my mouth.

I tried to pull away. Thorn wasn't there to see so I didn't understand why Mor-Kale was continuing his harassment, but he gripped the back of my hair with one hand while the other tightened around my hip and he ground into me, his intentions clear.

Shock turned into pure rage. I mustered all the force I could, ignoring the discomfort in my lungs as I struck out at Mor-Kale. My fist connected with his face, but it was slowed by the water, with little to no effect on him. His grip on me tightened, his fingers bruising as he tried to pull me down onto him. My heart pounded with fear and anger. Every instinct screamed at me to get away, despite my need for air.

There was no way I was going to let this happen. By the gods, I would kill him and die myself if need be. But not this. Never again would I let this happen.

I was more powerful than this.

I clawed at his face, the taste of seawater and desperation filling my mouth as I bit down on his lip. He grunted, momentarily slackening his grip on me, allowing me a brief respite from his pressing body.

For a fleeting moment, I dared to hope that my struggles had deterred him, but then his hands were on me again. His mouth crashed onto mine while he forced breath into my throat.

Struggling harder, I clawed at his face, each rake of my nails a silent scream for him to stop. But every rejection seemed only to fuel his desire. His grip tightened. The pressure against my entrance became more insistent, the cold realization of what was happening making my blood run cold.

"*No!*" The word was silent, lost in the bubbling sea, but loud and resonating within me.

I was running out of air and energy. But I was not ready to give up. Frantically, I sought out the minds of the creatures around me. My magic lashed out, gripping the creatures nearest me, desperate for assistance. My thoughts connected with a small, darting fish nearby, frightened by the thrashing, and my consciousness intermingled with its primitive senses. In an instant, I felt a strange sensation crawling up my neck— gills were growing, quick and painless but utterly alien to me.

My lungs expanded with fresh water, drawing oxygen from it as if I had done it all my life. But the transformation didn't stop there. My body was contracting, skin prickling as it sprouted shiny scales. My limbs reformed into fins as my worldview shifted, turning from human-size to something much smaller.

Suddenly, I was free, Mor-Kale's grip gone. I took half a second to float, stunned that I'd actually, finally, made a transformation. The leather belt that had been strapped snugly around my waist drifted to the seafloor as I, now a small, nimble fish, swam away from the puzzled merman.

With the rock chimney ahead, I swam for dear life, my tiny heart pounding in my chest. The relief of escaping from Mor-Kale was countered by the worry of completing my mission without my tools. Yet for now, the main thing was to reach the safety of the cave.

I nimbly swam through the rock chimney's entrance before gliding up. I dodged a larger fish that darted at me, then swam as fast as my little fins could carry me until suddenly, I broke free of the water and launched into the air before landing back in the sea with a sickening splash.

I'd arrived at a cavern, its entrance glowing with something slick and wet. The euphoria that I felt now that I'd actually made it to my destination was short-lived. I darted around, seeking a way to return to my human form. I thrashed in the water, willing myself to

459

grow limbs and fingers, but to no avail. I felt a pang of desperation—I was stuck.

In the cool depths, I tried again and again. Thoughts of my human form filled my mind, images of my fingers grasping, legs running. But no matter how hard I tried, I remained trapped as a small, insignificant fish.

Then, an idea struck me. I needed to stop trying to imagine myself as human—I needed to feel human. So, I began to recall sensations of warmth from a hearth, the rough texture of a book in my hands, the weight of a bow, the earthy smell of the forest . . .

As the thoughts washed over me, I began to feel a change. The water started to feel too encompassing, too vast. Suddenly, the world grew with me, or rather, I was growing within it. My sleek fins stretched and divided, forming fingers and toes. My scales receded, replaced by the familiar sensation of my human skin. My small, darting body expanded, my senses realigning themselves.

As soon as I felt the water between my fingers, I clambered out and onto the cave floor. Shivering, naked, and still dripping wet, I finally allowed myself a sigh of relief. I was back in my own form.

Water dripped down my skin as I took cautious steps into the cave, slipping on the luminous algae that caused the water and stone around me to glow. The cold seeped into my bones, but I barely noticed. My attention was focused on something else, a pull, a call that resonated deep within me. It was a hum that echoed in the very marrow of my bones, a siren song that was impossible to ignore. It was my gem. I could feel it. Close.

My fingers itched for my pickax and dagger. But I had no belt, my tools lost to the sea.

I pressed into the cavern, following the incessant call that tugged at my being. Around me, the cave stretched into darkness, its silence and grandeur both intimidating and awe-inspiring. It twisted and turned, the path unclear. With each step I took, the call grew stronger, the pull more irresistible.

And then, a clicking echoed in the cave.

A cold shiver ran down my spine as I froze in my tracks. My heart pounded in my chest.

I reached with my magic.

There was something else here.

Chapter 17

FEAR CLENCHED MY STOMACH, but I swallowed it down. I had faced my worst fear in the sea, and I had survived. This was just another challenge, another hurdle.

I clenched my fists at my sides, gathering my courage. I was weaponless, defenseless, but I was not helpless. I had my magic, my will, and my determination. I would find my gem, I would face this creature, and I would survive.

I just had to believe it.

The clicking sound grew louder, more ominous, reverberating off the cave walls. My eyes darted around, desperately trying to penetrate the flickering shadows cast by the luminous veins in the cave's walls. Then, emerging from the darkness, I saw it.

A monstrous figure scuttled into the dim light. It was a creature of immense proportions, its stature dwarfing my own. It was like a living, breathing incarnation of a nightmarish fable, a hulking beast from the deep. A colossal crab, unlike any species I had seen or heard of before.

Its dark, glistening shell was a patchwork of

armored plates, the surface rough and studded, reflecting the luminescent veins of the cave with an almost sinister shimmer. Each powerful segment of its body was crafted for survival. Its formidable pincers, serrated and sharp, moved in a rhythmic, almost hypnotic motion, promising pain.

A surge of fear seized me, its icy grip threatening to freeze me in place. My heart pounded like a drum in the tight confines of my chest, the echo of its relentless rhythm drowning out everything but the monstrous spectacle in front of me. My breath hitched and my blood ran cold, yet I refused to let fear consume me.

I pushed back the tendrils of terror, forcing myself to focus. The clamor of my heart softened, the dread receding to a corner of my mind, locked away for now. My gaze sharpened on the formidable creature and the terrain around me. The icy shivers running down my spine were replaced with a hot streak of determination. I was naked, unarmed, and up against a creature that could tear me apart, yet I refused to be defeated. I was a survivor, and I would find a way out. I needed a plan. A strategy. And I needed it now.

Ducking behind a stalagmite, I evaded the crab's initial lunge. Its large pincers snapped shut where I'd stood moments before.

Bracing for the next attack, my mind latched onto a

sudden idea. I picked up a loose pebble and, with a swift, calculated movement, tossed it to the farthest corner of the cave. The pebble collided with the jagged rock, the resulting noise echoing and amplifying in the cavernous space.

The crab, driven by instinct, swung its monstrous body toward the sound, its eyes shimmering in the low light as it sought out the source of the disturbance. The diversion bought me precious, fleeting moments to enact my hastily thought-out plan.

While the crab was distracted, I reached with my magic, feeling the pulsating life force of the gargantuan creature.

Its emotions were chaotic, its hostility toward me clear as day. I was an intruder. My mind danced on the edge of the crab's consciousness as I concentrated on projecting feelings of peace and tranquility.

With each pulsating rhythm of its life force, I pushed forth waves of soothing thoughts, whispering promises of calm into its mind. I was not here to harm or invade; I was merely a visitor, as lost as a pebble in the vast ocean. My magic, gentle and pacifying, wrapped around the crab like a warm current, aiming to ease its tension and mollify its defensive instinct.

While it turned away from me, I clambered onto the back of its shell. From this position, my magic flowed stronger, the connection more direct. I willed the crab to calm, my thoughts echoing in the undercurrents of its consciousness, a lullaby of serenity amid the tempest of its agitation. As I held on, I could feel the initial ripples of relaxation beginning to flow through its massive form.

The crab paused, its antennae twitching in confusion. Its clicking slowed, its movements less aggressive.

The colossal creature seemed to pause. It was as if my melody of calmness was finally reaching its core. Each soothing wave I sent was met with a growing stillness. Its chaotic emotions, once a stormy sea, now resembled the gentle undulations of a calm tide. I continued to soothe it with my magic, my hands gliding over the hard ridges of its shell.

The clicking noise that had initially filled the cave with dread began to dwindle, replaced by silence. The giant crab's movements gradually stilled, the tension in its body dissipating as if it was slowly giving in to a long-fought struggle against sleep.

The pincers that were once snapping aggressively in the air now lay open and relaxed on the cool cave floor, its numerous legs tucked underneath its body.

For a moment, I held my breath, fearing any slight movement might disturb this delicate tranquility. But as seconds stretched into minutes, it became evident that the giant crab was asleep, its fearsome guard finally lowered in the sanctuary of its own home. A sense of relief washed over me, the tension that had been tightly coiled in my body finally unraveled.

With the crab pacified, I slid carefully off its immense shell and onto the cool cave floor. I waited a moment, standing behind the slumbering beast to make sure it was really out before turning my attention back to the task at hand. The pull of my gem was stronger now, insistent. It echoed in my bones, a resonating hum that guided me through the darkness.

My bones were humming. I followed the call deeper into the cave, my way lit by the luminous blue veins in the stone that had begun to pulse.

I turned a corner, and the cavern wall blazed with a dazzling light, nearly blinding me. Embedded within the stone was my gem. It called out to me, pleading, screaming for me to take it.

Without my tools, extracting the gem would be no easy task. My fingers traced over the cold, smooth surface of the stone, the gem just out of reach. I felt a twinge of frustration but quickly squashed it down. I wouldn't let a small hurdle dampen my spirits. Not when I was this close.

My gaze swept across the cave floor, finally resting on a handful of small rocks scattered nearby. One of

466

them was sharp, somewhat pointed—not as precise as my pickax would have been, but it would have to do. I picked it up, weighing it in my hand.

With a newfound resolve, I moved back to the gem-infused wall. Holding the stone tightly, I started to chip away at the rock. Each hit echoed in the silent cave. Dust and small rock fragments fell away with each strike, creating a tiny cloud around me.

It was grueling work, my hands ached, and sweat dripped down my face. But with each strike, the gem loosened. The thought of that alone was enough to keep me going, to keep me chipping away at the rock wall, one piece at a time.

With each strike against the stubborn rock, I saw glimmers of a future I could call my own, a life untethered from the discontent I'd come to know, a life where my choices mattered. I imagined the possibilities unfurling before my eyes. The freedom to make my own destiny, to choose who I wanted to be. That's what the gem symbolized. It was hope—hope for something better, hope for change.

An hour passed. Then another.

And then, it happened. There was a sharper echo, a different sound from the repeated rhythm I had grown accustomed to. I watched, almost in slow motion, as a piece of the cave wall crumbled away and split as it crashed to the ground, sending pebbles and stones skittering onto the cave floor.

The glow faded until only a single stone cast the blue light.

A wave of elation swept over me, rendering me speechless. I had done it. Despite the odds, despite everything, I'd done it. Falling to my knees, I carefully reached down, cradling the gem in my hands. Triumph surged within and I felt a well of untapped power seeping into my fingers. In that moment, I knew everything had been worth it. The risks, the fear, the danger—it had all led to this moment of triumph.

The stone was unlike anything I had ever seen. It was large and perfectly formed, glowing in myriad shades of blue. I studied it in awe, captivated by its beauty. It was heavier than I'd expected. Its cool surface pulsed with a rhythmic hum, syncing with the beating of my heart.

Cradling my gem closely, I went back through the cave tunnel, each step echoing with the confidence of my triumph. The pathway that had seemed so menacing before now lay subdued as I skirted around the sleeping crab and came upon the opening in the cave floor that led back to the sea.

As I neared the opening, I felt a pang of unease. How was I going to get back with my gem? The journey was too far to make in one breath. I couldn't transform again, otherwise, how would I bring my gem back?

I reached the precipice, where the cave opened into the water. There, floating effortlessly below, was Mor-Kale. His pale skin shimmered in the blue light. His smirk was wide and threatening, as chilling as the water around him. And there, dangling from his fingers, was my belt, with my dagger and pickax attached.

As I stood there, the cool weight of my gem still in my palm, I felt a surge of defiance. I wouldn't let him steal my victory so easily.

Gathering my courage, I squared my shoulders, my gaze never leaving his. I had overcome so much to get this far, and I was not about to let Mor-Kale ruin it all. If it was time for another battle . . . another test of the stone . . . then I was ready to fight again.

"Get away from me," I hissed, the echo of my words bouncing off the cave walls. My voice was steady despite the adrenaline coursing through my veins.

In the ethereal glow of the cave, Mor-Kale was a specter, an inescapable nightmare made flesh. His smirk widened, eyes glittering with malicious delight as he used his powerful arms to hoist himself onto the cave floor.

"I just wanted a taste of human again," he said, his words echoing eerily around the cavern. "I didn't think you'd mind, especially since you seem so . . . cozy with the gatekeeper." A bitter laugh echoed in the cavern, each syllable a lash against my dignity.

"Don't you dare try to justify your actions," I retorted, my grip on the gem tightening.

His eyes flicked to the stone in my hand, the smirk on his face morphing into something much more dangerous. "It's just like Vin-Briony said. The merfolk agreed to help you gain your gem," he began, inching closer with every word. "But we made no promises about ensuring your safe return."

A wave of dread washed over me, but I stood my ground. His words, however chilling, would not deter me. I had been through too much, fought too hard to be dissuaded by his threats.

I felt something stir behind me. "Stay back, Mor-Kale," I warned, squaring my shoulders and lifting my chin in defiance. His smirk faltered for a moment, a brief flicker of uncertainty that I seized upon.

I backed away, luring him deeper into the cave. He glanced around, his eyes reflecting the glow of the tourmaline veins running along the cavern walls. Yet, the promise of a kill kept him advancing, my belt clasped tightly in his hand.

470

Behind me, the giant crab's massive form rose from the shadows. I flooded it with images and emotions, presenting Mor-Kale as a danger, an intruder. I tried to make it understand that the merman was evil, a threat to its territory, and that it must protect its home. In desperation, I channeled one final surge of magic. My will was clear and unwavering: Mor-Kale was the enemy.

The crab reacted. With a speed surprising for its size, it lunged out of the darkness and toward Mor-Kale. The merman's scream echoed through the cave as the crab's massive pincers snapped toward him.

The scream was cut off abruptly as the pincers found their target. Something warm sprayed, drenching me as I stood in shock. Mor-Kale lay in two pieces in front of me. I looked down. A river of blood was coursing down my naked flesh . . . my hair . . . everywhere.

The crab wasn't finished. It lifted Mor-Kale again, reducing him to several pieces in a matter of minutes.

Something hit me in the face. I looked down.

It was my belt, still clenched in Mor-Kale's severed hand.

Get out! I screamed to myself.

The crab turned its gaze back to me, the indifference gone. It seemed its patience was at its end. I didn't hesitate this time, the adrenaline coursing through my veins lending me the strength to move swiftly. Scooping up my fallen leather belt, I made a dash for the water, my heart pounding in my ears. The scuttling of the crab resounded on the stone around me as I tore through the cave, my belt clenched in one hand, my stone in the other.

With a swift motion, I slipped the precious gem into the pouch of my belt, securing it around my waist. The weight of the gem against my hip brought an odd sense of comfort. It was a token of victory, a sign that I had overcome my fears, that I had survived.

I was on the edge of the water when I felt it. The familiar call was faint but unmistakable. Relief washed over me. I didn't even check the water when I reached the opening to the sea. I dove.

The kelpie emerged. Its familiar form swooped between my legs, nudging me gently, a silent offer of escape. With a grateful nod, I wrapped my arms around its neck, holding on tightly.

In a flash, the kelpie bolted, its powerful muscles propelling us back down through the underwater chimney with surprising speed. The sea world blurred around me as we shot out into the vast expanse of the seabed. The dark abyss swallowed us, but the fear that once consumed me was absent.

I held on tightly to the kelpie, its glowing form cutting through the inky darkness, leading us toward the surface and the promise of a new day.

As we raced through the inky depths, a sudden surge of water jolted us to a halt. The kelpie whinnied in alarm, its body twisting violently as it tried to maintain its speed. A strong grip snaked around my waist, yanking me from the kelpie's back and into the icy depths.

In the faint light, I recognized the malicious glint in Al-May's eyes. Her tail whipped around, and she moved with a predator's grace, her intentions clear.

I fumbled for my dagger, my fingers wrapping around the cool hilt. It felt reassuringly solid in my grasp. Yet, the water around me seemed to thicken, making my movements slow and sluggish.

We clashed in the murk, her strength against my determination. Her arm slid around my throat, and she dragged me down. The kelpie kicked her in the ribs, its blows landing much harder than mine. Al-May released me, but she was relentless, her movements fluid and lethal as she smashed a sharp piece of coral into the kelpie's face.

I fought to swim higher, to reach the surface, but I was losing air. I wasn't going to make it. I fought with all my strength, the thinning supply of oxygen fueling my desperation.

Al-May grabbed my foot, dragging me back down. Each stroke of the dagger met only water, and with every second, the need for air grew more urgent. My vision started to blur, the pressure in my chest mounting. The water around us was a flurry of movement, a whirlpool of chaos as we struggled for dominance.

In the heat of the battle, I could feel the weight of my gem on my hip, a constant reminder of what I was fighting for. I would not let Al-May defeat me, not after everything I'd gone through. I had to survive. For my freedom, for my future.

My consciousness was slipping, the darkness creeping at the edge of my vision. But I couldn't give in, not yet. I had one more move to make, and I hoped against hope that it would be enough.

I clutched my gemstone tightly, hoping it might give me some sort of boost. My mind reeled back to the fish, remembering the feeling of breathing underwater, the lightness of its movements. My body responded, beginning the transformation. Scales pricked at my skin, webbing extended between my fingers and toes, and a strange tickle formed on my neck. The burning lessened, replaced by an unfamiliar but not unpleasant sensation. I was drawing breath from the water.

Just as I was on the cusp of fully transforming, a

harsh grip wrapped around my ankle, jerking me out of my focus. My transformation halted abruptly, leaving me somewhere between human and fish. It was a strange feeling, my body caught between two worlds.

Al-May's expression was a mask of fury and surprise as she stared at me, her grip on my ankle tightening. But I could breathe, the fluttering gills on my neck extracting oxygen from the surrounding water. Though I wasn't entirely the fish I'd intended to become, I felt an unexpected sense of power surge through me.

Al-May's eyes widened. Her mouth opened, a yawning chasm as she screeched at me. I didn't wait for her next move. Using my webbed feet, I propelled myself forward and thrust the dagger into her throat.

Blood clouded the water. I didn't wait for anything else. A single drop of blood in the water was a beacon to sea creatures, and I had no power left to dispel the coming horde. The kelpie swam at my side, nudging me along as we swam past a vast coral reef, their vibrant hues softened by the refracted sunlight that was now streaming through the water.

The shore finally came into view. My legs felt weak and wobbly as I stepped onto the solid ground, the sensation strange after the weightlessness of the sea.

With my gemstone clutched tightly against my

chest, I forced my mind toward human form, envisioning lungs filled with air, my body free from the aquatic adaptations of the transformation. Gradually, my gills began retracting, my lungs recalibrating to their original function.

Suddenly, strong arms encircled me and hauled me out of the water. It was Thorn, dragging me onto dry land. I coughed, body convulsing as I readjusted to my land form.

"Did you get your gem?" Thorn's voice trembled with worry, Haris hovering anxiously at his side.

I nodded, reaching into my pouch to reveal the unfinished gemstone. Relief washed over their faces.

"We need to leave," I croaked, my throat parched and raw. "We need to leave now . . . before they find what remains of Mor-Kale."

"He's dead?" Thorn said, his brows raised. "And Al-May?"

"She is also very much dead," I replied. As I swam to the surface, I had felt the presence of sharks investigating the cloud of blood in the water. I tried to ignore their feeding but . . . she was gone. I was sure of it.

At my words, Thorn's eyes darkened. "You're alive—that's all that matters," he murmured, his arms wrapping around my shoulders and pulling me into him, despite the fact that I was soaked. There would be a reckoning when the merfolk discovered the fate of their kin. We couldn't afford to be there when that happened.

Without another word, Thorn lifted me and carried me up the cliff and away from the shoreline. Exhausted, I collapsed onto the soft earth, the last vestiges of adrenaline ebbing away. I'd retrieved my gemstone. I had survived.

I looked back at the sea, the rising sun casting a warm glow over the rippling water, and couldn't help but smile. Despite the challenges, the fear, and the uncertainty, I had emerged victorious.

Chapter 18

THORN MADE SEVERAL TRIPS to the beach to relocate us farther from the seaside so no mer-folk could surprise us in our sleep, not that Thorn slept any. He was a vigilant watchman, his eyes on the waves that lapped at the shoreline.

The gem needed to be cleansed—to be prepared. Master Haris handed me my kit, and as I started the meticulous process, the others began to strategize our next move. Thorn frowned, tracing the map of our path, his mouth tight in a grim line of worry.

"We can't risk the river," he murmured. "The mer-folk have allies among the river fae."

"But over land . . ." Haris began, the worry lines deepening on his face. "It could take us days. I read that it's perfectly within the fae's rights to hunt for ret-ribution."

"We don't have a choice," Thorn replied, his tone final. "Do you suggest we take to the air instead?"

Haris sighed.

Thorn stood, his eyes on the surf. The sea was boil-ing, countless merfolk rising from the depths. Thorn placed his hand on my arm. "They can't reach us here."

I shook my head. "I'm not afraid of them." I slipped the stone back into its pouch on my belt and smoothed my shirt and breeches before making my way down to the beach. Thorn followed, albeit reluctantly.

It was the merchief who greeted us. "How dare you bring that cretin down to treat with me," the chieftain said, glaring at Thorn as she dragged herself around. "It's not bad enough that she took the lives of our kind, but now you seek to parade her in front of us? What a worthless gatekeeper, who has no allegiance to his own kind!"

"I'm here as emissary to the *king*," Thorn snarled, pulling me behind him. "I am on your king's orders, so you either adhere to them or don't, but as far as I'm concerned, the matter is over and dealt with. You went against your part of the bargain, and you know it. Your anger is not with me. Your anger isn't even with her. The only thing you're fuming about is that your little henchmen *failed*."

"We promised we would assist her in getting the gem," she snapped. "We never agreed to help her back with it."

"He tried to rape me," I said as loudly as I could. I looked at the merfolk to avoid seeing Thorn's face. I hadn't had a chance to share that . . . moment. Would he view me differently?

I was glad that Haris was up on the cliff watching and not down where he could hear.

Silence fell. I had read that consent was big among the fae, and so far it had proven to be true. In the situations where it differed, it was always an individual who never followed those rules when it came to humans. Who viewed us as lesser beasts.

Fae like Mor-Kale and the chieftain.

That didn't mean all their subjects felt that way though.

A few merpeople looked at each other uneasily. The chieftain glared at me as though she could strike me dead with just a look.

Finally, she addressed me.

"I know all about *you*, Fin Of-Cheapside. A little bastard slut trolling around the Western Empire so her lascivious father doesn't face disgrace in the East."

I didn't realize I'd taken a step forward, my hand on the hilt of my dagger.

How dare she.

How *dare* she.

"I am a sorceress who has found favor with the king of the fae," I said with all the confidence I could muster. "I appreciate your *offer* of help, but I actually managed quite well on my own, as it turned out." I smiled, only serving to turn many of the merfolk irate.

480

I didn't stay to listen to their ranting. I turned on my heel and limped right back up that cliff, ready to be done with it all. I had my gem now, and the king had confined them to the sea. I'd already shown I could defeat two of their warriors, even without my gem. I was thrilled to imagine what it would be like with it.

Wait till Claw heard what I'd done.

I turned, hearing the unmistakable sound of Thorn's footsteps behind me. His eyes were livid with barely contained rage. It was then that I faltered.

"I didn't mean to make your job harder back there," I said, grabbing his arm. "I'm sorry that you are now a target."

Thorn grabbed my shoulders. "What the fuck are you talking about?"

"The chieftain . . . Now we can't travel by river. I'm sorry if that inhibits any of your . . . future business."

Thorn's hands moved from my shoulders to my cheeks. "You really have no idea how I feel about you. I don't give a shit about any of that."

Thorn matched my sigh with one of his own. "If you are able, could you please tell me everything that happened when you went into the water?"

I nodded. "It was fine at first. I swam down and Al-May shared her breath, but when we reached the rock chimney, it was Mor-Kale's turn, I guess, so that's when he tried to . . . you know . . . and I really didn't want it to happen . . . so I imagined what it would be like to be a fish . . ."

"A fish?" Thorn asked, his brows knit in disbelief.

"Well . . . yeah," I said, now losing steam. "I was trying to breathe because—that's why I was so vulnerable. Then . . . suddenly I turned into a fish and found the cave and got my gem, but then Mor-Kale was waiting for me back in the water. So, I awoke this giant crab that had tried to attack me before, and he pinched him in half a couple of times."

Thorn was silent for a moment. He was just staring at me in a really odd way that I found disconcerting. Since he didn't speak, I foolishly went on. "Then the kelpie came, and he was helping me out and then Al-May tried to attack me so I stabbed her, and a bunch of sharks came to eat her and then there you were pulling me out of the water," I finished.

A silence fell upon us.

All of a sudden, Thorn's arms wrapped around me, pulling me to him. I buried my face in his chest, his warmth and smell calming my frazzled nerves until I just wanted to sink into him right then and there. Sadly, he pulled away after a moment.

"You are the most brilliant little thing I've ever laid eyes on," he murmured, running a hand through my hair. "That's the craziest shit I've ever heard, and I grew up in Horan."

His eyes went back to Haris, who was standing on the cliff face shouting, "Are they still mad?"

Thorn's eyes narrowed with determination. "Pack up. We need to move. Now."

Chapter 19

THE SETTING SUN cast long shadows across the floor of our palace room as I landed on the windowsill, my eagle talons scraping the wood as I hopped to the floor. It now only took a few moments, my human form coming back as easily as I'd don a shirt. Naked, and still glowing from my flight with Claw, I sauntered past Master Haris who was studying one of the ancient scrolls with a convex glass. Since hearing of me successfully transforming on my quest, Claw had worked with me on turning into a variety of different animals, her changing with me so we could frolic together, wild and free. My favorite were the birds. Feeling the air sweep over my feathers, seeing the world from a place few humans had explored . . . It was pure magic.

I got the nudity thing too. When I transformed, my clothes fell off and I spent the first couple minutes of my animal form trying to crawl out of them. When I transformed back, I then had to go find the damned things. I grew more comfortable being naked over time, especially when I realized what a nuisance clothes could be.

Besides, I was in the king's protection now ... something he'd made *very* clear when Thorn, Haris, and I arrived back with my gem several weeks before, dirty and bedraggled from trekking through the canyons by foot. Within a day I had the head of Merchief Vin-Briony presented to me by the elven guard who'd missed several crucial spots when he'd tried to tidy himself of her blood.

Haris looked up at me as I stopped at the wardrobe, naked as the day I was born. He was used to the sight now.

"I've been thinking ... about our stay here in Horan," Haris began as I pulled a dress over my head. "I ... I often wonder if it wouldn't be best if we extend our stay here once more."

"And what brings you to that conclusion?" I asked, reaching behind me to tighten the laces of the dress I'd picked. We'd had this conversation before, at my request. I liked to think that what happened in the ocean was behind me.

Even though I'd been literally bathed in the blood of my enemy, I still hadn't come out unscathed. I was struggling to move past it. Mor-Kale had taken Thorn from me, the relationship not going the way I'd wanted in the weeks we were together. I'd tried to burn the memory of Mor-Kale from my brain, but the minute his face swam into my mind when Thorn kissed me, or when his hand came to rest on my lower back, I stiffened and pulled away.

Thorn stepped back every time.

That was how I wanted it. I wasn't going to poison what I had with Thorn by forcing myself to see Mor-Kale in his place. We would move on when I was ready, and Thorn, so far, had been immeasurably patient. I just needed more time. What happened in the sea had shown me that I wasn't someone to discount. I could do it if I put my mind to it. I could do anything.

So, I wasn't going to fault Thorn for it. Given my deal with the king, I would see him often in the future. It was just for the moment, and there was absolutely no reason for me to hurry. Besides, sometimes the road there was the fun part.

But maybe Haris was right. Maybe we just needed more time.

"Have we heard anything from Solridge yet?" I asked, walking to the mirror. Gods, my hair was one big snarl. I grabbed the brush and began dragging it through while admiring the gem now affixed to my brow.

I adored how the stone's hue matched my eyes perfectly. The same deep blue. It made me look powerful, helped by the muscles I'd begun to develop in my shoulders. It was probably all the flying that did it.

The weeks in Horan had melted away as I threw myself into training. Every day, I worked under the watchful eyes of Thorn and Claw. Every blow I landed, every animal I studied, brought a change within me—not just physically but mentally. The fear that had once clouded my actions was retreating, replaced with a newfound confidence.

I had a bargain to fulfill, and if I'd learned anything from what happened in the sea, I learned that I could do damn near anything if I put my mind to it.

I was not someone to discount.

Not anymore.

I was exactly who I'd always wanted to be.

My thoughts often wandered to Rowyn, and each time they did, I felt an overpowering surge of determination. I had a purpose, a mission. And with each passing day, I was becoming who I'd been destined to be.

Master Haris laid the glass down and faced me. "I got a letter from Vianne the other day. There wasn't much news. Everyone is still off visiting home or questing."

I washed my face in the basin and toweled it off before dabbing some of my tinctures on. "I wouldn't mind staying a bit longer," I said. I was progressing well in training, helped by my newfound confidence.

Things were progressing with Thorn, too, just a bit more slowly. I was starting to push Mor-Kale out of my mind in Thorn's presence, helped by the passage of time and how physical I had to be during Thorn's combat training sessions. It wasn't training with Thorn that triggered the sensation of drowning. It was when we tried to do . . . other things.

But I wanted to get there.

Master Haris and I turned as the door opened. The look on our faces must've betrayed us because Thorn glanced from Haris to me with his brows raised.

"Something wrong?" he asked, shutting the door behind him and leaning against it.

I shook my head. "We were just discussing the possibility of putting off our return journey a little longer. Do you have any tours planned that you have to get back to?"

Thorn shook his head. "I'll stay as long as you like, but the king is asking to see you . . . and there's something up."

I frowned. "What do you mean? Not the merpeople . . ." My heart seemed to fall into my stomach at the thought.

Thorn tensed as he always did when I spoke of them. "No, it's something else. I'm to bring you immediately. Haris, stay here." Thorn propped the door open with his foot. I hurriedly finished applying the tinctures and joined him.

"I'll see you at the feast later," I told Haris.

He nodded weakly. Ever since we returned with my gem, Haris had completely changed how he addressed me. No longer did I hear a drop of condescension in his voice. I was treated with a new air of respect. Especially when he saw how important I was to the king. I assumed he was happier not knowing what I was up to. He was probably safer that way too.

Thorn held out his hand as he walked next to me down the corridor . . . an offering. I took it with a smile. I could do hand holding.

"What's going on?" I murmured as a hag passed.

"I don't know, but he's seen something," Thorn whispered back. "It's upset him."

I nodded. The king wanted to tell me himself. Fair enough.

As I approached the king's private meeting room, a sense of unease clung to me. Thorn squeezed my hand. I took a deep breath and pushed open the door.

King Valon was standing next to the window, his hands clasped behind his back. He was clearly waiting for us. "Shut the door," he ordered Thorn, who immediately obliged.

I frowned, caught off guard by the abrupt demand.

The air was heavy, thick with some unspoken tension.

"King Valon," I greeted. "What is going on?"

"It is Rowyn," King Valon replied, his nostrils flaring. "I felt a flicker of her at the shroud, right before it was attacked this morning."

My voice caught in my throat. "Espiria was attacked? Is she all right?" Was Destrian?

King Valon nodded. "She's alive. She was taken by a man. A sorcerer bearing a white crest with an eagle."

I thought back to history. "The flag of Solin," I told them. "It's Agramon the Divine."

I took a deep breath. This was going to be harder than I realized. I would have to be extremely careful. I would have to hide.

King Valon was glaring at me. "It is time for you to deliver your end of the deal."

I looked at Thorn. His eyes were cast down, refusing to meet mine. I'd wanted so desperately to stay.

I took a step toward the king. "I will need to go to Solridge first. I will deliver Master Haris and gather whatever information I can before I head to where Rowyn is."

"You leave him time to try to hide her?" King Valon asked.

"He can't hide her from me. Animals see everything."

490

King Valon raised his chin. "Do you feel I have fulfilled my end of the bargain?"

"For now," I replied. I'd resolved to be honest. "But I assure you that I'm invested. I'll find a way to get close to her. I have no intention of disappointing you."

King Valon nodded, his shoulders relaxing. "Send messages to Thorn when you can. Keep me abreast of any information that could be of use to me in helping Rowyn wrest the crown of Morgania from the Lyricans."

"Thank you for the aid, Your Majesty. If you wish, we can leave immediately."

King Valon's gaze was sympathetic but firm. "It is my wish. I need someone close to her."

I nodded, then finally met Thorn's eyes. They were resigned. His lips stretched into a tight smile. Tears bubbled up. I knew it would have to end sometime. I just hadn't wanted it to be so soon.

But it was happening. Just as Thorn couldn't escape his calling as a gatekeeper, I couldn't escape the future that awaited me.

For a moment, no one said anything. This time I didn't shift my feet under King Valon's studious gaze. This time, I met it. "We will leave tonight."

King Valon's head tilted, his golden eyes taking in

my changed form. One thing I found in my training was that being dangerous was exciting.

"She is lucky, I think, to have a friend in you," King Valon said, his voice gruff. "If only we could all be so."

"You have my loyalty," I offered. "For now."

I BREATHED DEEP, letting the magic skim over my skin in glowing tendrils as I passed through the gate of Horan. It was but a moment, yet an entire world seemed to break away from behind me. All my stories in Horan, all my experiences, were whisked away into something so small as the portal.

But not for long.

Not if I succeeded in what I set out to do.

I found myself disappointed in the human lands when it came to greet us. It was desolate. The road was dry, with sharp, angry cacti littering the landscape. I looked over my shoulder, wishing I could capture the world beyond one last time.

I would be back. Of that much I was sure.

"Fin," Thorn called softly, meeting my gaze with lingering sadness.

I fought the tears. This was what we'd agreed to. It

492

had to work in the moment.

And the moment was gone.

Yet, the words I'd rehearsed in my mind slipped away.

His fingers gently brushed against my hand. A simple touch. But in my world, it was everything.

A farewell to the time we almost had.

A vow that I would see him again.

A prayer to be safe.

"Your life is so long," I said, cupping his cheek with my hand. "We will meet again, I warrant."

"Exactly," Thorn interjected, his gaze intense. "Which makes every moment I share with you even more precious."

My heart quickened, leaving me breathless as he lifted a blonde strand of my hair and tucked it behind my ear. "Though your life may be shorter, it's a life I want to be a part of, however small my role might be. And if you ever need anything, you know where to find me."

I nodded and sniffed, wiping an errant tear from my cheek. "Don't get into too much trouble."

"I won't." Thorn chuckled with a grin. "Now you get out there and make some."

The End

Ember and Flames

EMBER AND FLAMES

Tempest Rising 3.5

Destrian's Story

Elliott VanDruff

Belle Rose Press

Dedication

This book is dedicated to my husband, Bryan.

ELLIOTT VANDRUFF

Map of Lyrica

Chapter 1

I SAT ALONE IN THE DIMLY LIT ROOM, my father's lifeless body stretched out before me on the cold stone table. The flickering candles cast eerie shadows across his face and on the ancient walls of the citadel. The pain was suffocating. I was mourning two losses—my father's death and Rowyn's departure.

The once-vibrant halls were deathly quiet, a still, suffocating silence. It had been mere days before that I'd thought every hope, every wish, was about to come true.

Now I was surrounded by the ghost of my father and the bitter echoes of shattered dreams. I was back, no longer as the heir but as the Consul of Helena.

Yet, I'd lost everything.

I leaned onto my knees, crushed between the burden of my guilt and weight of my decisions. I had failed the people I loved the most. Father's final years were spent alone spiraling into his own grief. I was meant to relieve him of the duties so he could have joy in the last years of his life. He was supposed to travel, to visit

Onora and Ilisa. His dreams, like so many others, were now lost.

Despite it all, nothing compared to losing *her*.

She'd said she loved me. The nights since I watched her ride away from me, casting one last, longing glance over her shoulder, I'd wake up clutching a pillow to my chest as though I could feel the weight of her in my arms once more. I'd spent months holding her. Despite the dangers lurking in the darkness, I'd rejoiced for every moment. I would face a thousand more dangers if I knew she would be by my side once more.

Rowyn, who had occupied my thoughts from the moment we first met, had left with Agramon the Divine for Somme. She *ordered me* to stay away.

Rowyn needed me. Why couldn't she see that? I'd watched her back the entire summer, guarding her from being swallowed by the shadows. We'd survived together. Why was she trying to survive on her own?

Without me . . .

Without us.

I'd deluded myself into thinking that I'd proven myself to her. That in some realm of reality, she needed me.

Who was I kidding?

It was I who needed her.

Now, all my resolve was spent on willing myself not

502

to follow her to Somme. In the end, it was the seer's words that stayed my hand. Arda had been unambiguous. The path to Rowyn's heart would always be through my ears—I needed only to listen.

Rowyn had flat-out told me to stay away. If it was merely about her protecting me, I would've gone to her side immediately. But that's not all I saw in her eyes.

"Take me home."

The words that Rowyn spoke the night I thought she would die in my arms—from an arrow I had shot— seemed to haunt me. That night, I was afraid I would lose her forever. It took everything in me to show her that she could love me. It took braving the Nightlands, battling terrors, and defeating the very darkness that lurked in our world. In the end, even that wasn't enough. She was ripped from me anyway. But her words would always stick with me. "Take me home."

That night, when Rowyn was bleeding out, I knew I would never love another. Not in the same way. Not with the same passion.

So, when Rowyn told me to stay, I saw the message for what it was. By protecting me, she was also trying to protect her people. We'd talked about a vision for Morgania on our journey to the Nightlands. We'd planned it together.

I would stay awake to guard her while she slept and take notes in the small journal that I hid in the breast pocket of my cloak. The journey to the Nightlands wasn't only about wooing Rowyn to fall as madly in love with me as I had with her, but it had given me time to sit and think and plan. I had no letters I could send to my father's steward. I had no messages from friends, or meetings with important dignitaries, or schoolwork to fill ten lifetimes. It was just Rowyn and me and weeks of wishing upon stars and hoping we would reach the sun again.

The more I thought of Rowyn, the angrier I became. The flames at the end of the candles burned brighter, throwing my father's gray pallor into sharp relief. I wasn't angry at her. No, my wrath was reserved for her kinsman, Conal. The image of his smug face as he killed my father was burned into my memory, an open wound that refused to heal. He was the embodiment of all I hated about the Morganites—their ruthlessness, their disregard for the laws of honor, and their misplaced pride.

But if I ever wanted her back, I would have to make Morgania a place where she could be at peace. I had to make Morgania a place she could call home.

So why did I sit, licking my wounds in solitude?

Because, despite what I knew I had to do to

convince her to come back, I wouldn't give up on revenge. My fist clenched tightly, my ruby gem warming on my brow. I was an Everett. We had gone to battle to protect *them*. Conal's treachery would not stand.

The sight of him in chains would bring some satisfaction, some semblance of justice, but it would not bring my father back. I would deal with that Imorati. The peace with the Morganites would be secured but at a great personal cost.

I brooded in silence, my thoughts a torment under the bitter weight of grief.

Did she still love me?

Had she ever?

No. Rowyn was honest. It took a quest into the darkness for her to see that she could love me, but in the end, she loved me, and I loved her, and then I completely, colossally fucked up.

Why didn't I tell her about her legacy sooner? Who the fuck was I protecting? Her? Myself? Our relationship? Because the minute Rowyn found out, she was gone, leaving with the second most powerful sorcerer in the realm next to her. Duke Agramon. Would she have reacted differently if she'd known sooner? Could we have been better prepared?

The sound of soft footfalls broke my self-imposed solitude. I looked up to see my sister Onora stepping into the room. Her fiery red hair had been tamed, braided, and woven into a tight plait over her head. She shared a slight resemblance to Rowyn—the same height, the same determined gaze. But that was where the similarities ended. Where Onora's face was drawn to smiles and laughter, Rowyn seemed perpetually somber.

My brow furrowed as I watched Onora's lips purse, a surefire sign something was amiss. "What is it?" I asked. Had she heard news of Rowyn? She would've almost made it to the capital by now.

"Ilisa is at the gates," Onora said, her hand coming to rest on my shoulder. Her gaze darted back to the door and I followed suit. "Lady Ingrid Byrne is with her."

I sighed, my heart sinking. My already gloomy mood darkened further. Bracing myself, I rose from my seat. Each step toward the door felt like a march to the gallows, but duty called, and I was bound to answer.

Chapter 2

TAKING A DEEP BREATH, I braced myself as I reached for the door handle, my sister following suit. The grand entrance of our home swung open, and there stood Ilisa, our older sister.

"How are you?" she asked Onora, reaching out and kissing her on each cheek.

"I am well enough," Onora murmured, glancing at me over Ilisa's slender shoulder.

Ilisa turned, her eyes hardening as they met mine. "Brother, what happened?"

"We can speak of it later," I said firmly, turning to the girl beside her.

Ingrid looked well enough. Her beauty was undeniable, but today it was subdued, her demeanor somber. Her eyes met mine, and for a moment, I saw a spark in them that was more than just sympathy. But she quickly averted her gaze, her cheeks coloring slightly.

"Destrian," she greeted, her voice softer than usual as she extended her hand. Duty demanded I take it, and I did, though the contact sent my mind racing with questions.

Did Ingrid truly care for my well-being? Or was she

merely using my father's death, and Rowyn's absence, as a means to further her own desires? In her eyes, did my father's death present an opportunity to ensnare my affections?

I wished I had the answers. For now, though, I could only speculate. A part of me couldn't help but dread what her presence might mean for the days to come.

Despite my internal turmoil, I offered a tight smile to Ingrid, my hand retracting from the brief contact. "Ingrid," I returned the greeting, my voice strained with the effort to keep my tone neutral. She nodded, a smile gracing her lips. Her eyes flickered between me and Onora, the silence lingering in the air like a thick fog.

"I'm sorry for your loss, Destrian," Ingrid finally said, her gaze softening. "Your father was a great man." Her words, though likely meant to console, did little to ease the growing knot in my stomach.

"Thank you, Ingrid," I replied automatically. I could tell from the slight drop in her smile that she had expected more from me, a sign that my suspicions might not be unfounded.

Onora quickly intervened as if noticing the tense atmosphere. "Shall we go inside?" she suggested, her arm looping through Ilisa's with a practiced smile.

"We're preparing rooms for you both. I'm sure you must be exhausted after your journey."

Ingrid glanced back at me as they moved farther away, her expression a mixture of puzzlement and concern. But I couldn't care less. My gaze was firmly on the door that Onora was leading her toward—the room that Rowyn had used when she'd stayed at the castle.

I couldn't bear to watch as Ingrid stepped inside, the door closing behind her. Turning on my heel, I strode away with an ache that I doubted would ever truly go away.

My heavy boots echoed off the stone walls as we made our way back to the family hall. Onora and Ilisa chatted quietly beside me. In the morning room, Ilisa pulled off her cloak and hung it on the rack beside the door. I tried to be grateful that she was there. After all, her father had died too. But I could feel her judgment from where I stood.

"So, tell me. What happened?" Ilisa asked, her tone haughty and firm now that the guest was out of the way.

"There was a battle," I replied, walking over to my desk and sitting down. Onora took a seat on the couch while Ilisa sank into her favorite spot next to the window.

"Yes, so I've heard." Ilisa tilted her head as she glared at me. "A battle over some little Morganite girl."

"No," I replied, my voice measured and patient. "Ayastaren overstepped into our borders and we pushed them back."

"How could you have been so foolish?" Ilisa snarled. "To rise against an overlord? Do you seek to bring the rest of us down with you, brother?"

"Ilisa," Onora interjected sharply. "Destrian's the consul now. You can't speak to him that way."

Ilisa turned her icy gaze on Onora. "I can speak to him however I damn well please, sister, and you'd do well to remember that. I am the wife of a man who will be consul someday, same as you."

I refused to put up with Ilisa's accusations. I'd done what I thought was best at the time. I'd been guided by my conscience. "We are glad you are here, Ilisa," I said, rising from my seat. "You will have to pardon me, though, as there is much for me to do."

"Destrian," Onora said cautiously.

I ignored her. "Now that you're all back, we will hold Father's service in the Temple of Sol tomorrow." I glanced at them both. "I don't have time for bickering and dwelling on what I probably should've done differently. All I can do is move on. I suggest you both do the same."

With that, I strode from the room, trying to push the rage away until I was out of their presence. Part of the reason Ilisa was so perpetually angry with me was because, out of both my sisters, she'd borne the brunt of my outbursts growing up. Though I'd never liked her behavior toward me, I couldn't deny that I understood it.

I stopped in the hall, about to go to my own room next door, when I found myself staring at the two doors across the way.

The decision to enter my mother's room was as sudden as it was unexpected. As the door creaked open, an almost tangible wall of silence and stale air greeted me. Everything was covered in a fine layer of dust—a silent testament to the years of neglect.

In one corner, an old rocking chair stood by the window, its faded upholstery bearing witness to countless nights of silent contemplation. A half-empty bottle sat next to it, the only glass in the room not covered in dust. A chill ran through me. This was where my father sought solace from his pain.

I stood there, taking in the sight. It was as if time had stopped. The scent of dust and moth-eaten linen filled my nose, but beneath it, I could barely detect a lingering hint of her perfume, a haunting ghost of the past.

Images of my father sitting alone in this room, night after night, flashed before my eyes. A part of him had never left. It was as though he was stuck in that moment, forever mourning the love he had lost. He never did get over her death. It had turned him bitter, sowing the seeds of resentment toward the Morganites he blamed for robbing him of his chance to say goodbye to his beloved.

And now, standing in the room that had been both a sanctuary and a prison to my father, I felt the weight of his sorrow and regret.

I stepped farther into the room, moving slowly, half expecting some ghostly presence to rise in protest. But it remained as silent as a grave, the only sound the scuff of stone beneath me.

I reached the window and pushed aside the ragged curtains. The light from the setting sun streamed in, illuminating the dust floating in the air. I could see the ward below, and for a moment, my mind filled with what it must have looked like when my mother was alive—filled with laughter and joy, not the quiet, mourning silence it bore now.

I picked up the bottle by the chair and rolled it in my hands. The glass was cold, the liquid inside lifeless. How many nights had my father sat here, seeking solace at the bottom of this bottle? Too many, I thought grimly.

Suddenly, the walls of the room seemed to close in on me, a shrine to my father's pain and my own beginnings. I felt a lump in my throat, the grief and regret built over the years threatening to spill over. But I swallowed it down. I was the consul now, and I had a duty to fulfill.

"Destrian," a familiar voice said from behind me.

I turned to find Aunt Maureen standing in the doorway. Her white-red hair glowed in the soft evening light that filtered into the room, the crow's feet around her eyes more pronounced than I had remembered. She was dressed in her usual attire—a dark gown that hung loosely over her tall frame. Though age had taken its toll, the strength in her eyes remained unchallenged.

"Aunt," I acknowledged, my voice a near whisper. Her presence in Helena would always be a comfort. She'd run my father's household when my sisters and I were growing up. She'd been like a mother to me in many ways. Now, she helped Onora with her young son, Galvin. I was sure that when Ilisa had her first child, she'd travel to the Fens to help her and back and forth as needed, because what Aunt Maureen adored most in all the world were babies and children.

Aunt Maureen's blue eyes scanned the worn surroundings with a tinge of sorrow. She stepped next to me, her gaze following mine to the bottle in my hand. "I'm sorry, Destrian," she said. "Ilisa was too harsh on you. She doesn't understand . . ."

I shrugged off her apology. "It doesn't matter what Ilisa thinks," I interrupted. My sister always had a mind of her own, and while it stung that she blamed me for our father's demise, I couldn't afford to let her thoughts consume me. Not when I had so much else to worry about.

Aunt Maureen's mouth formed a thin line, the corners downturned in concern. "You've always had to carry too great a burden. More than any man your age should have to." She reached out a hand to rest on my arm.

"I must," I said simply. I had no other choice. The citadel, the people, my father's memory . . . they all depended on me now. And though I felt a chasm of grief and anger threatening to swallow me whole, I knew I had to persevere. For their sake and for mine. No longer would I dwell on the ghosts of the past. I needed to make room for the future.

"Can you talk to the girls for me?" I asked, setting the bottle back on the table. "Have them go through this room and Father's. They can take what they want, then I want the rooms cleared."

Aunt Maureen's brows shot up. "This room?

But . . . it hasn't been touched since . . ."

"I know," I interjected, my voice steady. "Have it cleaned—aired out. Make it livable again."

She straightened, nodding slowly. "Very well, Destrian," she agreed, then hesitated. "But may I ask why? You will go to your father's room . . . naturally. But who are you preparing this one for?"

Her question hung in the air between us, heavy and loaded. She'd heard the tales and rumors about Rowyn and me, about our adventure in the Nightlands.

"I don't know yet," I admitted, and it was the truth. Mostly it was for myself.

Aunt Maureen regarded me for a moment longer before finally nodding. "All right. I'll see it done." Her gaze lingered on me, filled with a quiet understanding. "And Destrian . . . it's all right to move on."

Chapter 3

A T THE HEART OF THE TEMPLE, on an altar covered with late summer blooms and boughs of pine, lay the body of my father. Clasped in his hands was an Everett blade. A necklace of my mother's was wrapped around his wrists. His face was peaceful, as if in a deep slumber, only disturbed by the shimmer of protection spells that had been placed over his body by the preparer so that we could delay laying him to rest in the earth.

On one side of me stood Onora and Ilisa, both with somber expressions on their nearly identical faces. Aunt Maureen, steadfast and constant, stood at the end of the row. Her normally bright eyes bore a touch of melancholy, but she held her head high.

Ingrid had pushed her way to my other side. Though her demeanor was muted, her golden hair pinned back modestly, her presence was only a reminder of everything else I had lost. I had not wanted to think of Rowyn that day. But with Ingrid standing next to me, how could I not?

Ingrid stood like a demure little lady. Eyes cast down. Head low.

Rowyn stood like a queen. It was one of the things that had first taken me aback about her. She stood defiantly, her chin raised, making it seem like no matter your stature, it was she who looked down upon you.

I absolutely loved that about her.

As the somber strains of the mourning song began, the attendees, nobles and commoners alike, turned their gazes toward us. I felt their sympathetic eyes, their silent condolences. But there was more—an expectation. It was as though the entire city were holding its breath, waiting for Helena to move on from the years of discontent and grief.

The people had all been waiting for me. My breath hitched in my throat as I looked around the massive crowd.

There wasn't a Morganite in sight.

I turned back toward the Solston as he shuffled up to the lectern.

There was a lot of work to be done.

The longer I remained in Helena, the more that I became certain that Rowyn really would want it this way. She was going with Duke Agramon for now, sure, but it was only a matter of time before she would be powerful enough to break away. She needed practice with her magic, and where best to do that than in the farmlands plagued by drought.

Despite the fact that she went unwillingly.

Despite the fact that it was so far away.

Rowyn was still doing some good.

Easing the drought would soften the other consuls' bloodthirsty appetites and stop them from looking at Helena like an easy meal. It would also put Gryse, who had been breathing down my throat, in a bad position. Less need for imported food in the East meant less profits for them. Helena, as the largest consulship in Morgania, had made plenty of money over the years, but now, it *would* be politically beneficial if others had more too. It would turn their eyes away from me and back to each other, where they belonged.

The Solston's words resonated throughout the temple as he spoke of my father's faith, his wisdom, and his unwavering dedication to his family. He clearly hadn't known my father very well. Father abhorred going to temple service. He wasn't very wise, nor did he have courage beyond what was required of his station. Yet, he was who I'd had, and I loved him. I loved him because he fashioned his entire being into loving my sisters and me.

Ingrid, in her silent, respectful posture, offered me a comforting squeeze on my arm, a gesture that I acknowledged with a nod and fought the urge to completely pull back. I knew why Ingrid was there, but I also didn't want to anger Ilisa by sending her away. After all, she'd been the one who brought her.

As silence stretched, the Solston raised his staff, a solemn conclusion to the ceremony. A part of me wished I could stay suspended in the moment, ensconced in the collective sorrow that seemed to dull the reality of my father's departure. But another part of me was eager to escape the weight of the day.

We walked out of the Temple of Sol, and the grandeur of the sunlight streaming through the grand entryway blinded us as we stepped into the street. Down the way, the craggy shadow of the pillaged Temple of Imor seemed to cast an oppressive shade. The once grand sanctuary now stood as a grim skeleton of stones and rubble, another brutal reminder of the division between the Morganites and the Lyricans.

I thought back to Rowyn's words, her deep conviction echoing in my mind. She'd been insistent: "You should rebuild the Temple of Imor."

Looking at the ruins, I felt a pang of guilt. I'd already wasted too much time in mourning. There was so much to do to make things right.

Beside me, Onora seemed to sense my unease. She shot me a quizzical look, but I just shook my head. This was not the right time or place to discuss my internal conflicts. As we walked past the remnants of the temple, I imagined what it could look like, standing proud as it had before.

"HAVE BERNARD MEET ME in the morning room," I told the man who took my cloak as we entered the castle of Helena. I'd grown irritated with my father's steward over the years I'd been at Solridge and had begun sending correspondence and wishes to Sir Bernard, an old soldier who'd relocated to Helena. Despite his gruff exterior, he was excellent at following orders. I honestly chose him because of Rowyn. She had never taken trust lightly, and for whatever reason, she liked the old soldier. Apparently, that counted for quite a bit with me.

"Will you not join us for lunch?" Ingrid asked.

I looked up. Onora was watching Ingrid with her brows furrowed. Ilisa was glaring daggers at me from beside Aunt Maureen, as though daring me to refuse.

I met Ingrid's gaze. "I'm afraid I have obligations elsewhere today."

Ilisa scoffed. "What obligations could you possibly have to keep you away from your family on our father's mourning day?"

I clenched my fist, willing my power to stay within my hold. "I've been grieving all these weeks I've been waiting for the rest of you to arrive, but now that I'm consul, there is a mountain of work I have to do."

"Father always made time for the important things," Ilisa snarled. "How soon you forget yourself, brother."

I wished Ilisa would keep her thoughts to herself in the presence of others. Especially Ingrid. I didn't want the other families of the western shore to catch wind that there was infighting in the Everett family. Legacies had been torn apart and ended for less.

"Father neglected his rule," I snapped back. "I've been trying to pick up the pieces of Helena for years, and now that I'm back, I must ensure that we can withstand pressure from those who wish to do us harm."

"Is that why you're emptying Mother's and Father's rooms?" Ilisa asked. "Does that help you withstand the 'pressure'?"

"Ilisa," Aunt Maureen warned.

But my sister shrugged her off. "No, Aunt, he needs to hear this!" Her eyes flashed. "All these years, all your promises, Destrian . . . where has it brought us? What has it achieved?"

I stared at my sister, anger and guilt churning within me. She was right, in her own harsh way.

"I'm doing my best, Ilisa!" I shot back, filled with frustration and defiance. "I'm trying to make amends—to fix things."

"Well, your best isn't good enough, Destrian!" she spat out, her voice echoing around the grand hall.

I flung my arms out. "You think you could do better?"

"Let's just go eat," Onora offered, holding her hand out for Ilisa to take.

"Probably! If it weren't for you, we wouldn't even be in this situation," Ilisa retorted, completely ignoring Onora. "At the very least, I'd be able to keep my pants on around traitors." Her icy gaze hardened as she stepped forward, closing the distance between us.

A ball of fire burst above me. A servant screamed and ran down the hall. Onora had her hands out, her eyes wide and full of warning. Aunt Maureen was frowning at Ilisa beside her. Ingrid stepped back, perhaps a little scared.

"Do not speak of her in that way," I growled, my voice rising to match hers. The cool façade I'd been maintaining started to give way.

Ilisa eyed the fire before her gaze came back to rest on me. Her eyes narrowed, but her voice calmed.

"Our father is dead, our people are grieving, and you . . . you want to go and hide and pretend that *now* you care about duty?"

"That's enough," Aunt Maureen barked, stepping between us. Her face was lined with concern, her gaze flicking from me to Ilisa. "Ladies, you will join me for lunch in the great hall. We will have no more argument. Destrian, you must attend to your duties, but remember, mourning is a process, not a hindrance."

I turned my gaze to Aunt Maureen, grateful for her intervention. She had always been the voice of reason. But beneath her stern gaze, there was an undercurrent of worry. She knew the weight of my position, the challenges that lay ahead.

I nodded at Ingrid and Onora, deliberately avoiding Ilisa's heated gaze. "Please enjoy your meal. I'll join you later if I can."

Ilisa made a sound of disgust but obediently fell into step behind Aunt Maureen, shooting me one last, venomous glance before exiting the room. I watched them leave, the heavy door closing behind them with a resounding thud that seemed to echo my feelings of isolation and uncertainty.

I stood alone in the hall, my thoughts spiraling amid the bitter words and heated accusations. But I couldn't let guilt and doubt consume me. I had to focus.

With a final glance at the door, I turned on my heel, my mind already on the challenges that awaited me.

As I entered the morning room, the dim light of the afternoon sun filtered in through the windows. My father's desk sat untouched on the opposite side of the hearth.

Driven by an unconscious urge, I crossed the room, pulled open the bottom drawer of his desk, and pulled out the bottle of liquor I knew he hid there. I poured myself a drink, the amber liquid casting a long shadow across the old mahogany desk. I stared into the depths of the goblet.

I took a gulp, the burn in my throat doing little to numb the pain. With a heavy sigh, I left the silence of my father's desk and moved toward my own, a mound of parchment already beginning to pile up.

I sat. The soft hum of the evening outside was a stark contrast to the tempest of thoughts raging in my head. I lifted my goblet to my lips and took a long draw of the amber liquid within. Its warmth spread through me, a temporary reprieve from the cold anxiety pricking at the edges of my mind.

As I set the goblet back down, my eyes drifted over the piles of parchment scattered across my desk. Each was a declaration or request, an appeal or petition, all requiring my attention. Yet my mind stubbornly returned to Ayastaren's silence. Not a word, not a single missive. It wasn't like the duke to be quiet, not when there was power to be grasped or a rival to be ousted.

I leaned back in my chair, my gaze losing focus as I considered the man Duke Roland Lyon. Though he hungered for the wealth Helena had to offer, it would be short-lived under an oppressive rule like his. Even gaining the seat would prove difficult. After all, two of his sons were dead, victims of his relentless ambition and foolhardy ventures. His grand war machines, once the terror of the battlefield, were now little more than scraps of metal and wood. His once formidable army was now a shadow of its former self.

A bitter smile twisted my lips as I thought about the irony of it all. In his ruthless pursuit of my seat, Roland had secured it for me. In his quest for power, he had lost his strength.

But despite the satisfaction, I couldn't shake off a nagging feeling of unease. Silence from a cornered animal was never a good sign. It meant the beast was plotting, waiting for the perfect moment to strike.

The sound of the door opening broke my concentration. I glanced up to find Sir Bernard, his grizzled face stoic, entering the room.

"Bernard," I greeted, my stern tone echoing in the silent room. The aged knight nodded in acknowledgment, his gaze briefly drifting toward the goblet in my hand.

"Ye asked for me, Consul," Sir Bernard said gruffly.

"I did. I need an update on the Imorati," I said, my tone measured.

"Ah, Conal," Bernard grumbled, scratching at his stubble. "The men I've hired for information didn't see him move into the valley with the other Morganites. They figure he's still hiding out in the shroud."

"The man is an Imorati, Bernard, not a phantom," I snapped, my patience wearing thin. "I need him found. I need him to answer for what he did."

Bernard's gaze softened slightly. "We're doin' everything we can, my lord. But the shroud is as impenetrable as ever. There are still a few people there."

I slammed my fist down on the table, sending a handful of papers flying. "I'll not let him get away with what he did." The look on Rowyn's face when her uncle and the Imorati turned their backs on her. She was betrayed by her own family. Finding Conal wasn't just about Father. He and Baylin could've stopped Agramon from taking her. They could've protected her. Instead, they fed her to the wolves. They sent her to be used, knowing full well what might happen to her and not caring at all.

I took a deep breath. I really needed to get my shit together and calm down. Especially if I wanted to win the Morganites in the end. At least I had a way to show that. I pulled out a scroll I'd signed early that morning and handed it to Bernard.

He took the scroll and read it. His brows rose. "Ye wantin' to rebuild the Temple of Imor?"

"Find people who might be skilled at heading up the task. We'll need an Imorati to help and head the temple when it is finished. I figured we can ask for one when we go to Caymir's Rook." I then remembered to smile. "Thank you, Bernard."

He nodded again, then with one last glance at the goblet in my hand, he left. I took another sip of my drink and went to the window. Looking out over the city, I took a moment to organize my thoughts. Rebuilding the Temple of Imor was a risk—a bold move—but one that was needed if the rest of my plan were to work.

With renewed resolve, I turned back to the table and plucked the next piece of parchment, the next task, which sang for my attention.

Chapter 4

M Y SISTERS AND INGRID always waited for me in the morning room, the three of them perched on the furniture with embroidery in their laps. I smiled at Onora as I strode to my desk and the pile of work atop it. Finding my little notebook, I began looking over the list I'd made myself the day before.

Respond to at least five condolence letters a day.

Appoint a judge to the citadel.

Meet with the treasurer to outline compensation plans for new troops.

Find an Imorati.

Send a renegotiation for the port taxes in Gryse.

Choose a master builder for the temple.

Write letters to Rudin and Eslin requesting the advertisement for troops for the expansion of guard and army.

Reach out to Caymir's Rook requesting to visit.

Schedule a council meeting to outline projects.

Find someone willing to go into the shroud to look for Father's murderer.

Find suitable buildings in the city that might be utilized as schools.

Locate an insider in the capital you can trust.

I rubbed my hand over my face. I felt as though I'd worked sunup to sundown every day for a week, and it still didn't seem as though I'd made much of a dent in the list of tasks it would take to make Morgania even marginally safer than the present for Morganites.

"Good morning, Destrian." Ingrid's gaze lingered on me for a second too long.

I responded with a "Good morning" and a nod, trying to ignore Ilisa's glare over her stitching. My jaw tightened as I forced myself to focus on the documents in front of me.

Aunt Maureen came in, then, carrying a tray of tea and breakfast cakes. I grabbed one and accepted a steaming cup before settling down to go over my correspondence.

It had been a week of this repetitive dance. Each morning, the ladies would join me in the morning room, filling it with their murmurs of light conversation and laughter. I would sit at my desk, trying to ignore them while wading through a mountain of work. Ingrid or Ilisa would require me to accompany them somewhere almost daily.

The first day it was riding. Before lunch I obliged them with a three-hour tour of roads that circled Helena, meeting guards. I asked them what they thought would improve the defenses and had received quite a few different answers and one or two excellent ideas. Ilisa and Ingrid grew bored halfway through and rode back together. Onora stayed to get away from them.

The next day Ilisa suggested the "family" go to market together, to show solidarity. I spent the entire ride making notes in my notebook and chatting with different vendors about how market days were run. There were a few Morganite vendors, though not as many as I would've liked, who I got to have a conversation with while the ladies shopped. I found out that the Morganites were charged extra to run a stall on the official market street. That's why most set up in the aisles to the side. I gritted my teeth, not liking that response at all. Poor Bernard already had so much on his plate. I resolved to find out what I could do by myself and then find additional assistance as soon as possible. The list of things required to run and alter my consulship in a year's time was insurmountable.

The problem was that it was impossible to concentrate when I could feel the tension mounting from Ingrid as she smiled at me from across the room. She would pose, as though to catch my eye with her loveliness, and I, most laughably, had no time for that nonsense. Mostly, I tried to ignore the girls and celebrated the few days that they managed to leave the morning room without guilting me into coming with them.

So, each morning, I braced myself for Ingrid's advances and tried my best to maintain distance. Despite my clear discomfort and disinterest, Ingrid showed no signs of stopping. Each small rejection was met with a tighter smile, a more daring comment, a lingering touch that lasted a little too long. Her persistence was wearing me down, making me irritable and antsy.

Finally, I settled down to work, the ladies' conversation like an empty song in the background until I heard *her* name.

"The empress was attacked in the company of Rowyn the Morganite," Ingrid was murmuring to Onora who was nodding.

I glared at them, setting my quill down and stretching my fingers. "No need to hide your words. Speak louder."

Ingrid didn't seem to breathe for a moment. I worried her heart had stopped until she glanced at Ilisa and spoke louder. "I'd just heard that Rowyn had been around a bit of trouble at the capital," she said.

Ilisa tilted her head at me moodily. "*I* heard that the Duke of Ayastaren is now putting forth a suit instead of an army," Ilisa snarked. "Mellan Lyon is always at her side, and the Butcher of Bruin has been tripping over himself to ingratiate her to him."

The Butcher of Bruin? I was more surprised than anything else. I'd never met Baron Samael, commander of the Lyrican forces. During my time in Yliria, he'd been leading the main army elsewhere. Yet, the sight of what he left behind was still etched into my memory. The towns he passed through, the people's lives cruelly ripped apart, their homes turned into charred skeletons by his blood tactics. My hatred for war, for needless violence and destruction, was fueled by witnessing the aftermath of his ruthlessness.

A pang of anger and fear shot through me. I knew that Rowyn would draw the attention of others once she stepped foot in the capital. Yet, the thought that it might be a man as monstrous as the baron . . .

I ran my fingers through my hair, frustration bubbling up inside me. What could she possibly see in a man like that? Rowyn was compassionate, empathetic—everything that the Butcher of Bruin was not. A knot formed in my stomach, a terrible dread seeping into my thoughts. Could Rowyn really have forgotten me so quickly?

I took a sip of tea, trying to push the thought of Rowyn in the arms of another man out of my mind. Especially one as loathsome as the baron. My hand tightened around the cup.

I should've told her the truth sooner. No wonder

she doubted my love. Why did I think I could claim to love her while lying to her and keeping her legacy a secret?

Ilisa asked after Onora's son, Galvin.

Onora's eyes brightened as she spoke of him. "He's growing so quickly, almost able to walk now."

"Aww, I want to go see him," Ilisa said, her gaze filled with longing.

"Kendrew is asking for my return," Onora offered. Ingrid watched me, the little wrinkle above her nose the only sign of her apprehension.

Ilisa clapped her hands together. "We should visit. It's been forever since I've been to Eslin."

Onora smiled at the suggestion. "You would be most welcome. I know Galvin would love to see his aunt. You would be welcome, too, Ingrid."

Ingrid, who'd been quiet till now, looked at me with a hopeful gaze. "Would we all go?"

I looked up from my papers, glancing between their expectant faces. A small part of me was cautiously relieved by the prospect of them leaving. Their constant presence grated on my nerves. Yet, another part of me felt a pang at Ingrid's hopeful gaze.

"I would be unable to join you," I said, turning my attention back to my work, "as there is still too much to do here, but I bid you all go to Eslin and have a wonderful time."

Ingrid frowned, clearly disappointed that I could, in fact, live without her. My sisters immediately started discussing potential travel plans. I couldn't help but notice the way Ingrid's gaze kept drifting back to me, her longing clear. I took a deep breath to steady my nerves. I had a city to run, people to protect, and a future to build. I didn't have the time or energy for a romantic entanglement I wasn't interested in.

Onora and Ilisa left with Aunt Maureen, going over everything that would need to be done before they left. Ingrid waited behind, her eyes on the window as though in no hurry to begin her day. The tension in the morning room rose as she slowly approached my desk, a sense of unresolved conflict hanging in the air.

Her fingers grazed my shoulder. The gesture was intimate, almost possessive, and it made my skin crawl. "What are you working on?"

I stiffened, moving away from her touch, my tone cold. "I'm trying to choose a master builder for the Temple of Imor." I'd interviewed a few promising candidates with Sir Bernard the day before. Now all that was left was to go over their plans and figures to see which suited my needs best. The thing was, I didn't know which plan was best because I wasn't a Morganite . . . I wished Rowyn was with me. She'd know. I sighed. I was in desperate need of help. There was no way I could do it alone.

Ingrid leaned into me, her voice by my ear. "You don't need to be so proper. We don't have to abide by the school's restrictions any longer. We are not children."

I rose quickly, putting distance between us. "Ingrid, enough."

She looked at me, surprise flickering across her face before it was replaced with a veil of cold anger. "What do you mean?" she asked, her voice low and dangerous. "Why are you all of a sudden pushing me away?"

I gritted my teeth. "You know why."

Ingrid tilted her head. "Perhaps, but I want to hear you say it."

I studied Ingrid for a moment, wishing I'd never pursued anything with her in the first place. I'd enjoyed it at first. She was one of the most eligible women in the West, after all, and she'd seemed to have chosen me, of all people. It had given me a big head at first. Now it was merely a hindrance. Her family was powerful, and I already had enough enemies as it was.

But I couldn't lead her to believe there was a future where there wasn't, and I was tired of this dance, of her constant advances and my constant refusals. "It's not about Rowyn," I said firmly.

Her laugh was bitter and hollow. "You expect me to believe that?" There was a sharpness to her words, a venom I hadn't heard before. "You should know," Ingrid continued, flippantly brushing off an imaginary speck of dust from her dress, "the Byrnes don't raise stupid women."

"Ingrid . . ." I began, but she held up her hand, silencing me.

"I don't know what happened between you and that girl in the Nightlands, and quite frankly, I don't care. You know that your marriage is an alliance, Destrian," she said, her eyes hardening. "And what better alliance against Ayastaren than with Caldeaon to the South? We are wealthy, and as a Byrne, I bring a lot to the table." Ingrid leaned closer, her voice now a whisper. "Stop messing around and propose a suit already."

"I'm not messing around," I said, my voice steady. "I don't have the time or the patience for your games. Another alliance between our houses may benefit Caldeaon, but it does not benefit me."

She flinched as if I'd struck her, but her expression quickly hardened. "You're a fool, Destrian," she spat. "You and your bizarre affection for that savage. She'll be the downfall of you."

Her words hung between us, heavy and final. I wasn't entirely convinced that she wasn't correct.

Rowyn could very well be the ruin of me. But that's what I was choosing. I couldn't imagine hurtling myself anywhere if it wasn't toward her.

"You overstep your bounds, Ingrid." My words were sharp and unyielding. "You need to understand something; I'm not interested."

Ingrid, however, didn't flinch. Instead, she coolly looked me up and down, her anger hardening in determination. "When you're ready to come to your senses, Destrian, I'll be waiting. But don't keep me waiting too long."

I watched as she turned on her heel and left me in the deafening silence. Her words echoed in my mind. Was I a fool? Was my faith in Rowyn misplaced? I didn't know. All I knew was that I had a city to rebuild and people to protect. And I couldn't afford to be distracted by Ingrid's petty jealousy or her selfish opinions. I had to remain focused. For the sake of Helena and for the sake of my sanity.

But in the silence of the room, I was confronted with the gnawing doubt that had begun to take root in my heart. Would it all be enough? Would she even care?

The truth was, I was terrified. Terrified of the day when I'd finally see her again, only to discover that she had moved on. Terrified of the look of indifference, or worse, disgust, in her eyes. The idea of Rowyn with someone like the Butcher . . . it was unbearable.

Yet what could I do? I had already set my course and made my promises. But the possibility that all my efforts, all my sacrifices, would be for naught . . . it was chilling.

My heart felt like a lump of lead in my chest. The sense of hopelessness was almost overpowering. The things I wanted to do and the changes I wanted to bring all suddenly seemed insignificant. Would anything ever be enough to make her choose me over the life she was building in the capital?

THAT NIGHT, I FOUND MYSELF still at my desk, the ink barely dry on the parchment I was working on. The girls were leaving in the morning, and I was distinctly relieved. I was over the distractions. I needed to focus on bringing Morgania into a new era.

The door opened and Ilisa walked in. Her tall, statuesque figure seemed to fill the room, her gaze as cutting as a winter wind.

"Why haven't you written to the lord of Caldeaon yet?" She cut to the chase without preamble, her voice cold.

I set down my quill and looked at her directly. "I have no intention of doing that, Ilisa," I said, my tone matching hers.

She scoffed, crossing her arms over her chest. "And why is that?"

"I am not pursuing a suit with Ingrid."

Her eyes narrowed. "She's in love with you, Destrian, and you are leading her on."

"I have done no such thing," I defended myself, anger simmering beneath my calm exterior. "I've made it clear that I have no romantic interest in her."

"You rejected her?" Ilisa's voice rose a notch.

"I will not be guilted into something I do not wish for, nor does it further my agenda with Morgania," I snapped.

The room filled with silence, a chasm seeming to form between us. Ilisa's eyes were icy, her lips set in a thin line.

"You brought her to Morgania," I went on. "This is all on you."

Ilisa's gaze hardened further. "And why do you think I did that, Destrian?" she countered, her voice barely above a whisper. "Why would I want to bring a lady of Caldeaon to Morgania?"

"To further ally us with Caldeaon, I presume?"

Ilisa nodded. "Exactly. It's in the best interest of Morgania."

"But why, Ilisa?" I asked, genuinely curious now, my anger giving way to confusion. "Why Caldeaon? They pour their wealth into the arts, pageants, and plays. They don't have a standing army or navy to speak of."

"Exactly, Destrian." Her voice was steely. "Their investment in arts . . . culture . . . it attracts people—brings trade and prosperity. Their lack of military is not a weakness but a testament to their strength. They don't need swords when they wield influence."

"But we are already allied with Caldeaon through your match," I countered, unconvinced. "It makes more sense to expand our allies. This . . . obsession with Caldeaon, it's not helping anyone."

Ilisa fell silent. It was as if a veil had fallen between us, obscuring any glimpse into her thoughts. I could only guess at the impact of my words, hoping that perhaps they had made some dent in her stubborn resolve. But as she stood there, still as a statue, her silence seemed to echo in the room, a grim reminder of the divide that lay between us.

Chapter 5

S LEEP REMAINED ELUSIVE, a distant hope chased away by the shadows that haunted my mind. I tossed and turned in the sheets, the stars taunting me with a memory of Rowyn bathed in moonlight and darkness. I remembered it vividly—the way the air shimmered around us, dotted with millions of twinkling stars that arced across the dark velvet sky like an artist's careful brush strokes. Lying next to Rowyn, our bodies touching and sharing warmth in the chilly night air, I was completely at peace. The sky above us seemed to fold in like a quilt that cast our worries into the shadows.

Her hair fanned out across my chest and tickled my nose. I inhaled the scent of rain and wildflowers that clung to her and sent my heart beating wildly. It was addicting, as though she was a part of the elements, an embodiment of earth and water, existing just for me to cherish. It felt beautifully intimate, just us beneath the endless night, bound together by an unseen thread.

"Do you see that cluster of stars?" Rowyn broke the silence, reaching up to trace an invisible pattern in the sky. I followed her gaze.

"Yes, I do."

Her voice was smooth, a comforting melody in the quiet of the night.

"See how they tend to follow the moon," she continued, her fingers moving to another set of stars. "That's the man who tried to reach Imor. His daughter had been taken by the god. In his grief, the man used a rainbow to climb to the heavens. But Imor, fearing retribution, hid the daughter among the stars."

She pointed toward another group of stars, her hand shaking slightly. "See, that is the man's daughter, eternally out of reach."

I pulled Rowyn closer, taking comfort in her warmth—in her presence. Underneath the star-studded sky, we existed in our own world.

My heart clenched, a dull ache spreading through my chest. The longing, guilt, and frustration all kept sleep just out of reach. I would give anything just to be back.

With a deep sigh, I sank back into the pillows, closing my eyes to shut out the moon's relentless glare. But the darkness didn't bring respite, only the stirring of deeper memories.

The silky smoothness of her hair as it slipped through my fingers, the feeling of her skin against mine. The heat of her was intoxicating. Rowyn's

542

cheeks flushed a rosy pink as she stood before me in the soft glow of the fire. The look in her eyes, the uncertainty and anticipation, mirrored my own.

Her voice, soft and breathless, whispering my name. "Destrian," she had said, each syllable laden with emotion. I could still recall the taste of her lips, the soft sighs that escaped her, and the way her body responded to mine.

Yet, as the memory faded, I was left with an overwhelming sense of emptiness, a void that echoed with her absence. My heart ached with longing for what was lost—for the girl who had once, even fleetingly, been my entire world. With a bitter sigh, I turned onto my side.

With every breath, I was haunted by the what-ifs. What if I had been honest? What if I had given her the chance to confront her heritage on her own terms?

The guilt, once a dull ache, was now a sharp, insistent stab. The image of her face when she finally learned the truth replayed in my mind: a silent show of shock, betrayal, and sorrow. I couldn't escape the pained look in her eyes, nor the quiver in her voice.

I'd thought I was shielding her, but instead, I cast a shadow on our relationship, a shadow of distrust and deception. I took from her the right to her own past, identity, and choices. And the guilt, it seemed, was my just punishment.

THE MORNING ROOM was blessedly empty when the girls left at dawn for Eslin. I spent most of the morning being more productive than I'd been in a week's time before Aunt Maureen entered, carrying a tray laden with freshly steeped tea and assorted biscuits. With a motherly smile, she placed the tray on the low table before me and settled into the plush chair opposite mine.

"I'm surprised you didn't go with the others to Eslin," I muttered, my eyes on my cup.

"I am needed here," Aunt Maureen said, reaching for her own cup of tea, taking a moment to savor its warmth before she shifted the conversation. "I've had your parents' rooms cleared out, as you ordered." Her voice carried a hint of nostalgia. "If you wish, I can have them redecorated."

I glanced toward the hallway leading to the rooms that once belonged to my parents, a lump forming in my throat. "Leave them plain," I instructed, my voice unsteady. "Just the normal furnishings. Whoever takes charge of the rooms should be able to decorate it themselves."

A moment of silence passed as Aunt Maureen observed me, her gaze softened by understanding. "Will you be moving into your father's room, then?" she asked. "Now that you are consul . . ."

I shrugged, the weight of the new title still a strange, unfamiliar feeling. "I'm not ready for that yet, Aunt," I admitted, swirling the untouched tea in my cup. "I've always liked my room best anyway."

She chuckled.

When I thought of a mother's laugh, I always thought of Aunt Maureen's.

"Your father would be proud, Destrian. In his own way, he, too, longed for peace."

I shrugged. "Perhaps," I managed to murmur, my voice barely audible. "I truly hope so."

Aunt Maureen set her teacup down, her fingers curling around the porcelain handle, her gaze thoughtful. "Ingrid noticed that you cleared out your mother's room," she began, her voice careful. "She had some suggestions . . ."

I stiffened, my fingers tightening around the teacup. "Ingrid thinks a lot of things," I retorted a bit more harshly than I intended. "She thinks we should marry, and Ilisa would force the match if she could."

Aunt Maureen sighed. "And what do you want, Destrian?"

I focused on the swirling contents of my teacup. "What I want doesn't seem to matter."

Aunt Maureen remained quiet for a long moment. She reached across the table, her hand closing over mine in a warm, comforting squeeze. "What you want always matters, my sweet," she said quietly. "You just need to find the courage to voice it . . . and the strength to fight for it."

The memory of my journey to Yliria, the violent conflict I had witnessed there, and the striking resemblance it bore to the infighting at home all flooded back to me. "I want peace, Aunt Maureen," I confessed, my voice heavy with years of concealed despair. "I'm tired of the bloodshed. I want it to end, no matter the cost."

The room fell into a hushed silence. The only sounds were the distant twittering of birds and the rustling of the morning breeze through the drapes. Aunt Maureen contemplated my confession, her gaze softening with understanding.

"Doubt and guilt are heavy burdens to carry, Destrian," she began. "But they won't change the past. They can, however, guide your future actions. To strive for peace, that's a noble pursuit."

With that, she rose and left me alone to mull over her words. I glanced over at the sideboard, my father's bottle of old liquor catching my eye.

My legs carried me over to the bottle as if they had a mind of their own. I hesitated for a moment before grabbing a nearby glass and pouring myself a generous measure. Then I went to my desk, pulled out a blank piece of parchment, and got to work.

I WORKED WELL into the afternoon before calling the council together. In the middle of my request for an arms report from the Consul of Rudin, the door to my study creaked open and Sir Bernard stepped inside. "They are ready, Consul," he informed me.

I looked at him, taking a moment to process his words. Slipping the small journal back into my pocket, I rose from my desk, giving the city one last glance before facing Bernard. Nodding, I followed him out of the room.

We journeyed down the sprawling corridors of the citadel, finally arriving at the grand council room. The councilmen were already assembled. I'd remembered them all growing up. Then, they were my heroes. Now they looked old . . . and tired.

I lowered myself into the seat at the head, the weight of responsibility seeming heavier with every passing second. I clenched the arms of the chair, the cool, polished wood grounding me. I drew a deep breath, and as I exhaled, I met the expectant gazes of the council members.

"Good afternoon," I began, my voice steady despite everything. "I would like updates on the initiatives I sent you."

I turned my attention to the captain of the city guard, an old Lyrican man with iron-gray hair and a severe countenance. "How is the recruitment of Morganite soldiers going?" I inquired, trying to maintain an even tone.

His response did little to calm my mounting irritation. "We've had some . . . difficulty, Consul," he confessed, reluctance staining his words. "Managed to convince a few to join, but none stuck around. Can't handle the training—lack the fortitude."

I clenched my jaw, feeling the heat of my anger licking at my restraint with the captain's casual dismissal of the Morganites' potential.

As I surveyed the room, my gaze lingering on the lined faces of my advisers, realization dawned. I needed new voices. Voices that would speak for a united Morgania and not just echo the mistakes of the past.

The captain, and quite a few others, would have to be replaced. The thought filled me with an odd mix of relief and trepidation. Aunt Maureen was right. I could do this—if I got my act together.

Continuing to navigate the agenda, I addressed the next item on my list. "What's the status on the rebuilding of the Temple of Imor?" I asked, my eyes finding Bernard's steady gaze.

"Gale accepted our offer," Bernard reported. "The work will progress soon."

His update sparked a wave of murmurs at the table as the men exchanged uneasy glances. "What seems to be the problem?" I asked, ending their whispers.

The room fell silent once more before an adviser spoke up, his words laced with thinly veiled superiority. "If we are to unify our city, it would be more beneficial for the Morganites to adopt our worship—to embrace the Temple of Sol."

His words sparked a chorus of agreement from the rest of the table. "It's about assimilation, Consul," another added, "showing them the right path."

I felt a surge of anger. "No," I said with finality. "That is no longer our answer."

With a curt nod, I moved on, hearing updates from

the other council members. The information varied: some mundane, others alarmingly insufficient. The lower district needed a new judge. The Solston tasked with building a school system couldn't find a willing teacher. Each piece of information, each stumbling block, painted a clearer picture of the mammoth task that lay ahead.

Throughout the discussions, my mind strayed, constantly returning to the thought of replacements. There was a dire need for change. I couldn't help but think that Bernard was perhaps the only one who stood with me. I had him and my aunt Maureen.

It wouldn't be enough. I would need more, many more, if I were to steer Helena toward a future where peace wasn't merely a far-fetched dream.

Chapter 6

THE LOW-HANGING SUN PAINTED the sky in a soft hue of crimson as I rode along the road to Caymir's Rook, the tower and fertile valley near DarkPort that the empire had given to the Morganites. Beside me rode one of my oldest friends at home, Sir Alexo, with a steel glint in his dark eyes and wariness radiating from him. Our retinue of guards, equally vigilant, scanned the area for any signs of danger.

Within the few weeks that had passed since the Morganites received the deed, they'd been hard at work with fall planting. Entire families were bent to their tasks, seeding, pulling weeds, and clearing the fields. We skirted around a group of massive warhorses dragging large trees along the road where a group of Morganites were stripping them of their branches.

As we passed, the Morganites stopped, their imorets wrinkling as they narrowed their eyes warily. I supposed it was not often that they saw Lyrican guards who came in peace. I set my gaze forward. We needed this.

A group of Morganite warriors came riding into

view. The man in front immediately caught my attention. I'd seen him before and recognized the black hair and blue eyes of Rowyn's kin. Her cousin, I thought. Ferris. The man who'd taken issue with Rowyn and me in the market at SeaPort months ago.

Our groups slowed, approaching each other cautiously, each measuring the other. I held up my hand, stopping my guards, while Ferris followed suit with his own men. Nudging Valor forward, I approached, stopping in the middle between the two groups. One of the Morganites, with large markings completely covering his left arm, leaned toward Ferris, murmuring and gesturing angrily. Ferris shook his head and motioned the man back. He nudged his own mount forward and met me halfway.

Leaning against the pommel of his saddle, he studied me, his jaw set, his eyes narrowed in mistrust. "Consul Destrian. To what do we owe this unexpected visit?"

I gritted my teeth, my eyes on the fields bordering the road where Morganites watched us. I'd sent Bernard to Caymir's Rook once or twice, just to check things out, but had yet to visit myself. "I'm just seeing how the move has treated you," I replied, meeting his gaze with an even one of my own.

"Well enough," Ferris said, his stance casual,

though his voice was guarded. "Are you here to monitor us—to see if we're falling in line?"

"Not at all," I admitted. "I wish to speak to whomever has taken charge here."

Ferris was silent for a moment, studying me as the Morganite soldiers behind him glared over his shoulders with contempt. "Why?" he asked finally.

I shrugged, trying to appear nonchalant, as though it were nothing important. As though I hadn't traveled the many miles. As though my entire world wasn't dependent on the answer he gave me. "My rule has started, and I find myself needing . . . help."

Ferris's brows rose. "What kind of help?"

I shook my head. "I'd prefer to discuss this with whomever is in charge."

Ferris continued to stare at me for a moment. Finally, he spoke. "I didn't think she'd ever love another after Luc," he said, his voice soft. "Least of all you."

My breath grew shallow. I didn't know what to say to that.

Ferris went on as though he'd been wishing for the chance to speak with me for a while and refused to let this one slip by. "I was sure that you'd fooled her somehow. That you were manipulating her to reach us where it hurt most."

The irony was almost laughable. That's what I'd

thought of Rowyn when I'd first met her. I'd thought she was trying to get into my good graces, gaining my trust before she sank a dagger in my back. It didn't take long until I realized my mistake.

Still, something about Ferris's words drew my anger. "You claim that gaining Rowyn's trust would harm you in some way? Yet you all were quick enough to sell her when it benefited you." I swept my hand out, motioning to the valley, the tower, everything the Morganites had gained by giving away the freedom of their brightest star.

A muscle in Ferris's jaw tensed and he looked away. "I was surprised that you showed up . . . the day of the battle. We were fortunate that you came when you did."

Again, I chose not to respond. Yes, I'd shown up . . . drawn by Rowyn's need. The price of my loyalty to love had been my father's life.

Ferris sat up, turning his horse and motioning me with his head. "Come along then." Ferris's voice was bitter. "I suppose if Rowyn trusted you, I might as well honor it . . . given everything. The others will be at the tower."

I couldn't help but wonder how he felt about his father's deal with the Lyricans, the sacrifice of Rowyn for land. Everything Rowyn had told me of Ferris made me think that they were close friends, if not like brother and sister. Rowyn had no other siblings, and she'd said that her cousins and she were close.

I nodded to the men behind me, who followed as Ferris led us down the winding road. I exchanged a quick glance with Sir Alexo. He was usually composed, but his brows were furrowed with worry and unease. The Morganites weren't much better. They were openly hostile.

I sighed.

There was so much work to do.

We arrived at Caymir's Rook soon enough. Though the tower was large, it was relatively simple, with the ability to house about a hundred men, give or take. It was well-placed strategically, especially for the Morganites. The shroud lay but a day's ride away to the west. A day's ride to the east would take them to Dark-Port.

Ferris paused at the entrance. "Wait here," he told me as I dismounted. Sir Alexo and I looked at each other and found a place to stand in the shade. The rest of our guard remained mounted, their eyes traveling over the defenses of the tower. Alexo shifted uneasily beside me, his hand straying subconsciously toward the hilt of his sword.

"Are you sure we should be doing this?" Alexo

hissed, turning his face away from the Morganite guards who'd also stayed behind.

I nodded. "I have to speak with them, and I don't think they would've responded if I'd asked them to come to Helena."

"I guess I just don't understand what we're doing here. What do you need them for?" Alexo asked.

"You'll see," I said, turning away. I didn't need Alexo going off and starting unnecessary rumors within the men before I said my piece. There was too much riding on it.

After what seemed an eternity, Ferris finally returned to escort us within the fortress. Our footfalls echoed off the worn stones as we were led into the depths of the tower. Our destination was a simple room adorned with rustic decor and lit by the warm glow of a fire crackling in the hearth.

"Wait outside," I murmured to Alexo, who nodded and slipped back out as I shut the doors.

Two figures sat around a heavy wooden table. One was a man of middle age, his hair black with silver patches threaded through and his face weathered. I recognized him immediately as Rowyn's uncle and my heart hardened to stone. The man who'd sold out his niece to the Lyricans.

Ferris strode in front of me and stopped at the

table. "Consul Destrian, this is my father, Chief Baylin, and his wife, Urdua. You asked to speak with them."

"I will not treat with him," I stated coldly. "Not after what he did to Rowyn."

Baylin bristled, rising to his feet with a huff. "I am the chief. You have no say in whom you will or will not treat with when you come seeking aid from Morganites."

I turned to the woman sitting next to him. Her hair was so faded, it was nearly white. She seemed older than her husband, more calculating and less given to rage. She wore breeches, and a smudge of dirt had been overlooked on the sleeve of her tunic. I remembered Rowyn briefly speaking of her.

"Are you not also a chief?"

Urdua raised one brow. "Yes."

"Then it is with you that I wish to speak."

A hush fell over the room. Baylin's face twisted into a scowl. "This is preposterous—"

I glared at Baylin. "I will treat with no one else. And I'm going to bet that you want to hear what I have to say."

Baylin's hands clenched. "You don't frighten me, boy. The deed is clear. You have no power over us anymore. Not here."

"That's not true," I scoffed. "I still rule over the

largest consulship in Morgania. I am still in charge of exports and fulfilling the region's duty to the duchy of Ayastaren and the empire across the sea. But I'm not here to talk about Caymir's Rook," I said simply.

"Well, we don't give quarter to—"

"I think we should hear what he has to say," Ferris interrupted, his eyes on his father.

Urdua was nodding. She rose with an imposing air, growing in consequence, if not stature. "Ferris is right. We should hear the young lord out."

"Shouldn't we discuss . . ." Baylin began, but Urdua was already shaking her head.

"I've made my decision. There is no harm in listening to what he has to offer. I didn't say I would agree to anything."

"And if he asks you to make an agreement?" Baylin blustered.

Urdua raised her brows even farther. "Then I shall do as my conscience dictates. Do you not *trust* me, husband?"

Baylin shot a venomous glare at his wife, but after a tense moment, he conceded, grumbling under his breath as he strode out of the room.

"You are welcome to a seat, my lord," Urdua said, sinking back to her chair. She motioned to one across the table. "Ferris, please pour his lordship a drink. If he came all the way from Helena, then he is travel-worn."

I nodded, grateful to feel the tension ease from the room. I accepted the cup Ferris offered and took a sip of the cool water while mulling over my next words. Ferris lowered himself into the seat that had been occupied by his father, his hand resting lazily on his sword hilt.

"Now," Urdua said, folding her hands in front of her as she scrutinized me with a frown. "What brings you calling?"

I set the goblet on the table. "As you all know, I've come into the consulship rather unexpectedly." Urdua didn't flinch, but Ferris did. "Despite that, I'd been keeping a long list of things that I wished to accomplish when I gained my seat, and I'm finding myself struggling to complete those that are most dire. I come seeking aid."

Urdua's lips pursed as she glanced at Ferris. "What kind of aid would that be?"

I clenched my fist under the table. The first request wasn't even the hardest, yet I was already losing courage. "My father let the Helenian military languish over the years, and now all we have is a skeleton crew's worth of men to cover the castle and the city, but not much more. What happened with Ayastaren was a lesson. We need to rebuild our defenses—"

"We?" Ferris scoffed. "*We* are doing just fine with our soldiers, thank you very much. We withstood Ayastaren, and if all else fails, we can retreat to the shroud if Morgania is invaded again. This isn't a *we* problem at all . . . This is a *you* problem."

"Except now you have all this to lose," I said, motioning to the window overlooking fields that were being sown as we spoke.

Ferris opened his mouth to speak, but Urdua raised her hand, silencing him.

"By my count, we've already provided you with enough stolen men from conscription." Urdua's eyes hardened. "Though, I will admit, yours is a kinder approach than your grandfather's."

I had enough honor to lower my eyes.

Father had preyed on the men.

Grandfather, the women.

I took a deep breath. I met Urdua's eyes, then Ferris's. "I am fully aware of what we did," I said, wishing the waver in my voice would go away. "It was wrong. I am acknowledging that . . . here and now . . . and am offering you my apology. I am ashamed for any part I might have played in the history of the last hundred years when it comes to the Lyricans' treatment of the Morganites." I met both their eyes again. "But I ask you this . . . what now? What do we do now that a hundred years have passed, and the majority of the population in Morgania is Lyrican? What is your grand goal? Retribution? Are you demanding that we give you the reins and then you go burning our families in the streets?"

Ferris smashed his hand against the table. "That's exactly what you all did!"

I glared at him. "I'm aware of that; I'm making a point. Is that really what you want out of all of this? More bloodshed? More divides? Another war, perhaps. Let's kill each other off so Ayastaren can swoop in and plant one of his demented sons on the seat. Why not just make it easy for him?"

Ferris glanced uneasily at Urdua who didn't appear surprised by my words. I found myself glad that I was speaking to her and not one of the Blythes. I loved Rowyn, I really did, but the Blythes as a whole tended to struggle with seeing the big-picture consequences. Urdua, on the other hand, looked as though she had thought about what I'd said before and considered the dangers. If the Morganites thought the Everetts were bad, wait until the Lyons managed to slaughter their way to the consulship.

"Some of the Lyrican families have been here a hundred years or more . . ." I went on. "It's all they know. It's all they have. Who takes charge of Morgania if not me? Chief Baylin? Who's going to run Helena? We need to rebuild the army, and soon, otherwise it will be more than Ayastaren who comes testing our borders, and woe to us if they find Morgania defenseless."

Urdua cleared her throat, effectively silencing Ferris again before he could speak. "Be clear. What exactly do you wish of us?"

I sighed. Too much probably.

"First, I need good, *willing* soldiers for the Helenian Army."

"We have two battalions we can send," Urdua said. "They will join your fight whenever you need."

"I'm not talking about a militia. I have money and a host of resources I'm making available to complete this task. The men would be paid soldiers if they joined. They could move their families to the city."

Urdua tilted her head to the side. "It is known that the cities are not safe for us."

I remembered back to Rowyn, when she was supposed to meet me in Helena before we left for the Last Dusk. She'd been falsely accused and attacked in the streets. She'd told me of that Morganite boy she was supposed to marry. He'd been conscripted while attending a festival in Helena. They were wise to be cautious.

"I am also recruiting and reoutfitting the city guardsmen. I want the streets to be safe for everyone, not just Lyricans. I'm also rebuilding the Temple of Imor in Helena."

Ferris scoffed.

"I will encourage our men to sign up for your army," Urdua said, shrugging her shoulders. "It is their choice, not mine. That can't be all you're here for though. You send a call for soldiers in a letter."

I nodded. "That brings me to my second request. I need a Morganite captain. Someone to oversee the guard and plan defense. I figure, who better than someone who grew up in these woods."

"Did you have someone in mind?" Urdua asked, her brows furrowed.

I started laughing at myself. "Honestly? No. You all are the foremost fighters in the empire. I figured you had some good minds among you who were attuned to trainings and battles that you could point my way or something. I mean . . . is he any good?" I directed the question to Urdua while pointing at Ferris.

Urdua chuckled, looking Ferris over. "He's got the potential for it, I'd say. He's not had much of a chance to spread his wings though."

I turned to Ferris. "Would you like to make some

money?"

"Why are you so dead set on a Morganite?" Ferris asked. "Won't your own soldiers get pissy about it?"

I knew the question was coming. Why was I going to all the trouble? I sighed, my hands on my knees. "When I was making plans for changing Morgania, I . . ." I shook my head, unwilling to meet their eyes. "I foolishly thought that Rowyn would be there to help me champion these causes that she opened my eyes to . . . that we could work on them together. I don't know enough about your ways, and I don't know where to turn to gain trust, even with my intent to make things better. No one has cause to believe me . . . no one yet anyway. But, I can't hold off on this any longer. Things have to change. I need *someone* to help me."

"So, you are giving us all this opportunity for our people . . . for what? I think you came here for more than that." Urdua leaned forward. "Tell us now."

I glared at her. "I want that Imorati. He needs to be arrested and answer for the murder of my father."

Ferris rose. "You ask us to give up one of our own? How dare you."

I refused to look intimidated by him. After all, even though Urdua and Ferris were formidable fighters, I was a sorcerer. I could easily kill them both and escape if need be. I was pretty sure they knew it too.

"I demand it if we are to work together to rebuild Morgania into a fair home for all. Justice must be met."

I glared at Ferris. "Furthermore, I find it patently ridiculous that you would give up the realm's most powerful sorceress for the 'good of your people,' yet not a simple man."

"What would you do with Conal when you have him?" Urdua asked, her voice giving away nothing.

"*When* I find him, I will make sure he is tried and sentenced."

"To death?" Urdua prodded.

I shook my head. "Rowyn wouldn't have wanted that. Imprisonment is enough for me."

Something flickered in Ferris's eyes. "Are you going to try to bring her back?" he asked.

Urdua glanced from Ferris to me, waiting.

"In time," I admitted. "I can't just sneak into her room in the palace and kidnap her from a duke. If we want to help her, we have to use the right opportunity."

"You already have a plan," Urdua accused.

I nodded. "The quinquennial is in the summer, and I will have to deliver my first vows. This can only be done at the capital."

"A year," Ferris said. "You're going to leave her

there for a year?"

"She told me to stay," I said icily. "I'm not happy about it, either, but that means a year is all I have to make things ready."

"Ready for what?" Urdua asked.

I met Urdua's eyes. "Her."

Chapter 7

A MONTH LATER, the clash of steel reverberated through Helena's new training yard as I stood with Captain Ferris, watching the new city guards being put through their paces.

Ferris was detailing the training regimen he had implemented. He had taken the old captain's place on my council—a decision that was met with skepticism by some, the old captain included.

But as I watched the guards—men who had once been at odds now training side by side—I knew I made the right choice. Ferris was very friendly and affable as long as you were on his good side. He'd been tasked with ensuring that everyone, Lyrican and Morganite alike, trained fairly in the guard fields.

"They are coming along well," I commented, my eyes still on the field.

"We'll have to work the softness out of some of them," Ferris said, watching two young men from the city whose father owned a bakery. They were out of breath while a couple of Morganites ran circles around them.

"What about the changes to the defenses?"

"I sent a notice to Caymir's Rook and the clans to the west, asking for additional men. I figured we might get more takers if I requested it."

I nodded. "Wise of you."

Suddenly, one of the baker's sons lunged at the Morganite running next to him. He grabbed him by the shoulders and shoved him. The Morganite came back swiftly, landing a punch to the nose before another grabbed him and held him away.

A blast of fire exploded above them. I glared as the men looked around, their eyes wide with fear.

"See, lads?" Ferris called out to the men, gesturing grandly toward me. "Best mind your manners, or the Dragon will roast you for breakfast!"

One or two of the men chuckled. Most threw wary glances my way.

In spite of everything, I felt a spark of satisfaction ignite in my chest.

IN THE MORNING ROOM that evening, the warmth of the fireplace cast a mellow glow on the figure seated across from me. Ferris had claimed to have found me an Imorati, Kaelan, a man whose outward appearance contrasted sharply with his spiritual calling. His body was a canvas of markings. They wound around his bald head, the patterns containing some hidden meaning. Both arms were covered, and I could see another one crawling up his neck. I judged him to be about late middle age, but it was clear that he'd been a soldier or warrior at some point. Weapons were strapped to every inch of him, a somewhat disarming trait for a holy man. Despite the blades strapped to his body, there was a calm serenity about him. As though nothing could provoke him.

"Ferris tells me you've been congregating in your home," I began, leaning back in my chair and observing him. Kaelan nodded, his fingers idly tracing the hilt of the knife at his belt.

"Ever since Imor started speaking to me as a boy, I have shared his words with others."

"Imor . . . speaks to you?" I asked, intrigued. Kaelan nodded again, his gaze distant.

"His voice comes to me in my dreams."

I glanced at Ferris, who was watching the exchange with keen interest, his blue eyes, so like Rowyn's, shooting between me and the Imorati to gauge our reactions to each other. His respect for the man was evident. Ferris heard of him from a Morganite who'd enlisted from the lower city. He'd brought Kaelan to my attention, seeing potential in the Imorati's fierce dedication and the influence he held over his small congregation.

I leaned forward, catching Kaelan's eye. "The Temple of Imor is being rebuilt," I told him. "We need someone to lead it and join my council here in Helena."

Kaelan looked taken aback, his eyes darting between me and Ferris. "What do you mean, on your council?" he asked, folding his arms as he leaned back in the chair.

"You would give me advice, essentially, and ideas on ways to improve things. You might need to be the voice of Helena to those at the temple."

"I don't fancy a Lyrican telling me what to say," Kaelan said with a shrug. "You've fed us poison cake before. What makes now any different?"

"I can vouch for him," Ferris said, straightening.

Kaelan harrumphed and looked to the side. "I'm glad the temple's being rebuilt, don't get me wrong." He ran his hand over a tattoo on the back of his neck. "But who's to say all this intent doesn't disappear when you lose interest in the Morganite girl."

I gritted my teeth. "*This* has nothing to do with Rowyn and everything to do with the right course of action."

I could tell that Kaelan wanted to believe me with the way he was watching me. He looked closely for a reason to say no, but I wasn't giving him any. The Morganites had Caymir's Rook and were a part of the guard. The temple was being rebuilt. I was making strides, and I could begin to reap the rewards. Kaelan wanted to trust me.

"What is Imor saying now?" I asked, leaning back in my chair. Solston Ignace had been very vocal about the fact that unrest was coming.

"To be honest?" Kaelan said. "I don't really understand it, but it's giving me a feeling of fear. War is coming, I think. War and change."

I gritted my teeth. I didn't like the sound of that. My mind went again to the issues I'd had of rebuilding the army. Where would I find men?

"So, about the offer?" I asked, raising my brow.

Kaelan didn't even look at me. He was meeting Ferris's eye. "I suppose I should be honored," Kaelan said after a significant pause. "If I can man the temple how I see fit, o' course."

I let out a breath. "Sure, let us know what you need. I'll have a guard take you to the site so you can speak to our master builder and go over the plans."

Our conversation was interrupted by Bernard's abrupt entrance. The elderly man rarely wore his concern so plainly, but it was evident now, written in the creases of his weathered face and the restless tapping of his fingers on the parchment he held.

"News from the capital," he announced, his tone grave and serious. This wasn't the usual gossip. Something was different. Something was wrong.

I shared a quick glance with Ferris before nodding toward Kaelan. He rose from his seat without protest and excused himself with a quick nod, leaving the room in eerie silence.

"Well?" I prompted Bernard once Kaelan had left, my heart pounding against my ribs. His hesitation was unusual, even in the most dire of circumstances. He swallowed hard, gripping the parchment tighter.

"There's been an attack."

My gut twisted, a sudden wave of dread washing over me.

"Rowyn . . ." he continued, and I felt my world screech to a halt. "She was the target. Several people died in the incident."

My breath hitched, the room around me blurring.

"Is Rowyn all right?" Ferris asked, rising.

Bernard shook his head. "She was burned . . . badly. She's on the mend, but . . ."

A sickening silence filled the room following Bernard's announcement. The words hit like a hammer blow, echoes of them rebounding in my mind. How could I have abandoned her to the capital?

I dismissed Ferris and Bernard and turned to grip the mantel, sending a stream of magic to draw the fire higher.

I should have been there.

My eyes drifted to the dancing flames. How ironic that the very element that had shaped me, that had made me who I am, was wielded as a weapon against someone I cared for. I could have prevented it had I been by her side. I could have shielded her from *fire*.

I'd made a mistake letting her go. I just hoped it wasn't too late to get her back.

With a sudden surge of purpose, I left the morning room behind. The news of Rowyn's condition had sparked a sense of urgency in me, and I intended to act on it immediately.

As I shut the door behind me, I noticed Ferris and Bernard just up ahead. They were huddled together, deep in conversation. Their heads snapped up at the sound of the door. I didn't stop, didn't even break stride, and headed straight for my quarters at a determined pace. I could feel their gazes on me as I passed, and without a word, they fell in step behind me.

Ignoring their whispered conversation, I pushed open the door to my room and made straight for the large mahogany wardrobe at the far end. I began pulling out clothes and armor, tossing them onto the bed. I threw a pack open on the bedspread, my intentions clear.

"What are you doing, Lord Destrian?" Ferris asked, finally breaking the silence. I didn't look at them, my focus solely on the task at hand.

"Going to Somme," I stated simply, the words falling from my lips with an unwavering resolve. I knew it was the right decision, even if it was a difficult one. There was no doubt, no hesitation. Rowyn needed me, and I would be there.

"Consul, you can't just leave," Ferris began, his voice laced with a rare urgency. "All the work you've done here, bringing the Morganites into the fold—it will crumble the moment you're not here to keep everyone in line."

I opened my mouth to protest, but Bernard quickly chimed in, his tone firm and steady. "He's right, lad. The only reason they listen to me is because they know my orders come straight from you."

A flicker of frustration ignited within me. Couldn't they see how important this was?

"Aunt Maureen can rule in my absence," I retorted, my words laced with impatience.

The suggestion was met with a scoff from Bernard,

his lips curling into a sour expression. "And what do you think Ayastaren would do, hearing that Maureen Everett was taking charge of Helena in your absence?"

His words hung in the air, and a wave of sobering realization washed over me. I knew he was right, even if I didn't want to admit it.

"Fuck!" I roared as anger surged and magic swelled within—a raw and uncontrollable force. The fireplace erupted in a fierce blaze. I flung open the window so the oxygen wouldn't get sucked from the room.

They were right. My place was in Morgania, working toward the peace we all longed for. But it felt as though I was sacrificing my heart knowing that Rowyn was in danger and I was helpless to protect her.

"Get out," I demanded, my voice low and dangerous. Ferris and Bernard exchanged a worried glance.

"I will leave if you promise to stay," Bernard said, taking a step forward. "On your honor as a consul, you will stay and see this through. She has an entire capital of trained sorcerers to help her. We only have you."

"I'll stay," I confirmed, my voice strangled. No sooner had they left the room than I hurled the satchel I'd been packing against the wall.

Sweat trickled down my brow as I worked off the excess magic, the fire roaring and dancing under my influence. But I couldn't calm the fire raging within, unhindered and all-consuming.

I walked over to my side table and pulled out one of my father's bottles that I'd taken out of his room. I poured myself a glass to calm my nerves and took a sip.

I couldn't just do nothing.

The yearning grew stronger, an ache that seemed to fill every fiber of my being. My heart called out for her, a desperate plea echoing in the empty room. But there was no answer. Only the crackling of the fire and the haunting silence.

I took another swig of liquor. I thought back to who I knew in the capital. I had no allies to speak of . . . unless . . .

The fleeting friendship seemed like forever ago, but I hoped I could count on an honorable person not to change too much.

I strode purposefully to my desk and yanked out a fresh piece of parchment. The quill danced across the page as I wrote, my mind spinning with thoughts and questions. The script was hurried, almost frantic. I held the quill tight, forcing the tremors to stop as I poured all my frustration and worry onto the parchment.

The letter finished, I sat back in the chair, a sense of relief washing over me as I finished the glass and poured another. With one last look at the words I had written, I folded the parchment, sealing my resolve within.

Chapter 8

S TANDING AT THE CREST of the hill, I looked down at the construction site of the Temple of Imor. The rebuilding was a monumental task, one that both the city's builders and tradesmen had initially approached with skepticism. Yet, here they were, toiling under the midday sun, their hammers and chisels ringing out in the streets of Helena.

Workers called out to each other, their voices a steady drone beneath the cacophony of construction. Every so often, I would catch snippets of conversation—updates on progress, concerns about the day's tasks, and quiet discussions on the intricate details of the temple's original design.

As the men labored, their earlier skepticism seemed to melt away. Even though there were fewer Morganites in the city than in the fields beyond, more were moving in with the burgeoning guard.

I lingered a moment longer, watching as a block of stone was painstakingly hoisted onto the rising walls of the temple. A gust ruffled my hair, carrying with it the scent of freshly cut timber and stone dust.

Reaching the temple's foundation, I studied the

intricate blueprints sprawled out on a makeshift table.

"How goes the work?" I asked, turning to the master builder, a grizzled veteran of the trades named Gale.

He removed his cap and wiped the sweat off his forehead with the back of his hand. "Better than we initially thought, sir. We're finding more of the original stone that can be reused than we expected."

I nodded, pleased with the news. "Good, very good. I would like to maintain as much of the original structure as possible."

He returned the nod. "We'll do our best, my lord. That Imorati you sent, Kaelan, he showed us where to rebuild the altar and the seats."

I nodded, running my fingers over the notes that various people had made.

Staring back at the construction site, my eyes moved across the temple's skeletal structure. The last remnants of sunlight were cast over its stones, highlighting the inlaid crescent moon motifs scattered all over the walls.

As I headed back to the castle through the bustling marketplace, the murmur of the crowd was a constant hum in my ears. The air was filled with the scent of fresh produce and the heated discussions of the townsfolk, their voices rising and falling.

"The master said it will be done by midwinter,"

Bernard said next to me. I nodded, smiling at a group of children who were performing feats in a little alley-way.

"We should mark it with a celebration," I said, re-calling a conversation I'd had with Rowyn in the Nightlands.

Bernard was nodding. "We could, if we had time to plan it."

"Leave it to me," I replied.

INGRID AND ILISA HAD JUST RETURNED from Eslin, so I joined them in the grand dining hall for dinner, along with Aunt Maureen.

The smell of freshly cooked food wafted in the air, mingling with the low hum of conversation. The fall harvest was proving to be plentiful, and though much was shipped across the sea, there was still plenty to be had. I'd wondered if Morgania would continue to be fruitful in Rowyn's absence, but so far we'd been lucky.

". . . and little Galvin," Ilisa was saying, her eyes sparkling with delight. "He's the cutest little boy, I swear. And so smart!" She sighed dreamily, a hand ab-sentmindedly moving to her stomach. "I can't wait to have one of my own," she confessed, a faint blush coloring her cheeks.

Aunt Maureen glanced at Ilisa, her eyes bright. "Give it time, dear," she advised kindly. "There's no need to rush into things. Babies come when they're meant to. Just enjoy your time with your husband. Early years of marriage are precious."

I glanced at Ingrid out of the corner of my eye. Her gaze kept drifting toward me. Her dark eyes were inquisitive and oddly intense. It was clear that she was trying to gauge whether I'd missed her. Her glances were subtle, almost imperceptible, but they were definitely there, and definitely for me. There was a glimmer of expectation in her eyes, like she was waiting for some sort of recognition or acknowledgment.

But I didn't have the heart to give her the satisfaction. My mind was elsewhere, preoccupied with thoughts of Rowyn and the letter I'd sent to the capital.

But, for now, I had to play my part. I had to maintain the façade of a content, unconcerned consul, even as my heart waged a silent war within. I raised my glass in a mock toast to Ilisa's future family, my lips stretching into a forced smile, and all the while, my gaze remained carefully, deliberately averted from Ingrid.

"How long do you ladies plan to stay in Helena?" I asked before taking a sip of wine. Ilisa turned her gaze to me, immediately hardening to stone.

"Are you so ready to be rid of us, brother?" she asked icily.

Aunt Maureen sighed, her head in her hands.

"Not at all," I said, trying to appear nonchalant. "I'd just been down to see the progress on the Temple of Imor, and the master builder was saying that it will probably be ready by around midwinter. I was thinking about how much the people of the city would enjoy a Winter Solstice celebration to bless the new temple, though, of course, I've no time to plan such a thing." I shrugged. "But, it's nearing, and it could mark a turning point from our period of mourning and also bring the city together, Lyrican and Morganites alike."

A hushed silence followed my words. Then, slowly, a glimmer of excitement began to surface. It was Ilisa who broke the silence. "A celebration?"

"That sounds wonderful, Destrian!" Ingrid's face softened into a smile. She'd been telling me for two years how Helena would benefit from the celebrations and galas that they threw in Caldeaon for their populace. I hoped she wouldn't read too much into the fact that I was essentially asking her to plan one. I was just trying to keep them busy while getting something meaningful out of it.

"We can take care of it, Destrian," Ilisa was quick

to reassure me, determination clear in her voice.

"Now, that's only if you ladies wish to stay," I said, holding up my hands while ignoring Aunt Maureen's pointed look. Perhaps I was laying it on a bit thick, but they were both nodding their heads.

"I don't think we're in that much of a hurry to return to the way of things," Ilisa said, her eyes on Ingrid.

Ingrid smiled. "My parents have allowed me to be finished at Solridge, so I'm at your disposal until the quinquennial," Ingrid said, shooting me another hopeful smile.

A wave of relief washed over me, not just at the prospect of having the Winter Solstice celebration handled, but at the hope that this diversion might allow me some much-needed space from them while, at the same time, maintaining our alliance with Caldeaon.

"I have a few . . . stipulations, though, if you are willing to take on the event."

Both women turned their gazes to me with raised eyebrows, awaiting my conditions.

"Firstly," I began, "the party must coincide with the opening of the Temple of Imor."

There were nods of agreement.

"Second," I continued, drawing in a deep breath, "the celebration must incorporate both Morganite and Lyrican traditions. This isn't just a party; it's a statement—an acknowledgment that we are one city, one people."

This particular decree was met with a more pronounced silence. I watched as the women exchanged uncertain glances. I could almost see the cogs turning in their minds, their excitement momentarily dampened.

Finally, Ilisa broke the silence. "If that's what you really want, we will do our best to make it happen."

Ingrid finally nodded, her initial hesitations replaced by determination. My heart pounded with relief.

"You will need to speak to Solston Ignace and Imorati Kaelan to figure out how to incorporate the different traditions. Let me know when you plan to meet with them, and I would like to sit in. I'll give Aunt Maureen a budget," I said, nodding to my aunt. "Go through the particulars with her and make sure to stay within reason when it comes to expense." My voice was a little softer now. Their willingness to support my vision for the celebration was reassuring. I leaned back in my chair, the tension easing from my shoulders.

"We'll need to allocate funds for food and drink, decorations, entertainment . . . We might need to hire additional staff for the day . . ." Ilisa said while Aunt Maureen and Ingrid nodded.

"I'll leave you to figure out the specifics," I told

them, a knot of anxiety easing in my stomach. "And check in with you regularly about how preparations are coming along."

They all nodded. "Of course, Destrian," Ingrid assured me, her gaze holding a spark of excitement. "You'll be kept informed about every detail."

As they began chattering among themselves, diving headfirst into planning, I rose from the table. A sigh of relief escaped my lips as I walked down the hall. For now, at least, they were distracted and helping, leaving me to focus on the other challenges ahead.

Chapter 9

T HE WALLS OF THE MEETING ROOM held a strange, uncomfortable quiet as I looked upon the new council. There was an undercurrent of unease, a lingering tension that refused to dissipate.

Sir Bernard sat at my right hand. Sage Rasmus sat at my left. Rasmus still held the position that he'd held for my father as the head of the treasury. The old man was an expert in handling Helena's coffers and our staggering wealth. I'd worried that he would give up his seat on the council if I replaced a few key figures, but Rasmus seemed unchanged by it.

Ferris and Imorati Kaelan sat beside each other on Rasmus's other side. Kaelan was still dressed in knives from head to toe, glaring around the table suspiciously at the others, still concerned that I was implementing a convoluted plan to turn on the Morganites. Still, I was glad he was there, staring at Solston Ignace who sat opposite him.

"So, Imorati Kaelan," I began, leaning back in my chair and folding my arms over my chest, "how are the plans for the temple progressing?"

Kaelan ran a hand over the back of his bald head.

"The walls are going up," he reported, "and workers have dug in the foundation for a pool out front to reflect the light of Imor."

"And what of the people? How are they reacting to the temple being rebuilt?"

Kaelan shrugged. "They are cautiously optimistic, Consul. Several more Imorati have come to me asking if it's true. They're eager, filled with ideas for the temple."

I nodded. With the temple going up, more Morganites might return to Helena.

Just as I was about to respond, Solston Ignace cut in. His voice was sharp, the underlying worry clear as day. "The Lyricans at my temple are highly concerned. Are we turning our eye from Sol? Are you prepared to risk his wrath?"

The room fell silent, his words echoing in the heavy silence. Ferris and Kaelan were glaring at Ignace, then me.

I leaned forward, meeting Ignace's eyes. "The gods need not be rivals," I stated firmly, "and neither do we."

Ignace frowned, clearly not the answer he was hoping for.

I turned to Rasmus. His gray eyes met mine. "How are we doing with the compensation for the soldiers?"

I asked.

Rasmus rubbed his chin thoughtfully before answering, "I have the figures and funds ready, Lord Destrian. However, our primary challenge isn't finances. There's a lack of individuals stepping forward to take up the post."

Ferris chimed in, his voice a low rumble. "We're still having trouble finding willing men, my lord, especially among the Morganites."

My brows furrowed in thought, my fingers drumming on the armrest of my chair. I had suspected that would be an issue, which was why I asked to raise the wage. We'd gotten plenty of Lyricans to join up, but I still hoped to have more Morganites to bolster our forces and expand our knowledge of the area.

Imorati Kaelan was nodding. "Many still harbor anger about the forced conscription, Consul," he said, his deep voice filling the room. "And far too many were sent overseas to Yliria."

I sighed. "Let us then focus on rebuilding trust here at home. We need to show the Morganites that serving in the guard isn't a punishment or a chore, but an honorable duty that pays well."

I shifted my gaze to Ferris, his tall, muscular form clad in the uniform of our guard. "Captain Ferris," I said, leaning forward. "Tell us about the new recruits.

How are they doing? And how are the rotations shaping up?"

Ferris straightened. "We've bolstered the patrols," he began. "We've sent additional men to the border near Ayastaren as well."

"Excellent," I said. "Now, what's the status of the search for the Imorati who killed my father?"

Ferris's shoulders tensed, his face hardened, and he swallowed visibly. I knew this was a topic that neither of us liked to revisit, yet it was impossible to avoid.

"I went into Espiria myself to get him, Consul," Ferris began, his deep voice tinged with frustration. "But he had already fled. We've been searching for him in the surrounding cities, but so far, no sign."

My fists clenched. Anger and frustration boiled inside me, memories of my father clouding my mind.

"He better not leave Morgania," I said, my voice low. "And I trust you're not protecting him, Ferris."

Ferris raised his brows. "Of course not, Consul."

I forced myself to take a deep breath. Getting angry would not help, I reminded myself.

A knock sounded at the door.

"Come in," Sir Bernard shouted as we all turned toward the sound.

A servant stepped in, his eyes wide when he noticed everyone's attention on him.

"Consul Destrian," he said, taking a tittering step forward. "There is an urgent message from the guard at the gate. Lady Vianne of Solridge is here and requests an immediate audience with you."

My brows furrowed. I was taken aback by this unexpected visit. What would bring one of the instructors at Solridge to Morgania? And why Lady Vianne of all people?

"Thank you," I said to the guard. He nodded and left the room.

"I must see to this," I said, turning to the men. "Sir Bernard has further orders for a couple of you, otherwise, I would like to meet again next week to check on our progress." They nodded and I left them to check with Bernard on new plans.

With a deep breath, I hurried down the hall toward the entrance of the citadel, my mind racing with possibilities. What could Lady Vianne want?

Chapter 10

A S I NEARED THE ENTRANCE, the imposing figure of Lady Vianne of Solridge came into view. She wore a dress that wrapped around her figure, and the amethyst at the center of her brow emitted its violet aura as Vianne read the minds of those around her.

"Lady Vianne," I greeted her, maintaining my composure. "I was not expecting your visit. To what do I owe this honor?"

Lady Vianne did not waste any time on pleasantries. "I would speak to you in private."

"Follow me." I led Vianne through the halls toward the morning room. The ladies would be out and about now, off to the market to check out vendors for the solstice celebration or planning in Ilisa's room.

I held the door open for her as Vianne walked in, looking around the room with a studied air. I motioned her to a seat in front of my desk.

"Is there a problem?" I asked. I'd achieved mastery by shepherding Rowyn through the Nightlands, so I wondered why Solridge would send Vianne . . . unless they were unhappy with how I completed my task.

I gritted my teeth.

Lady Vianne sat, smoothing her skirt beneath her. "I'm not here on Solridge's errand," she began, extinguishing my thoughts. "I am here on my own calling."

It was about Rowyn. I could feel it. "What can I help you with?" I asked, trying not to sound as nervous as I felt. Was something wrong? Had something happened with Rowyn that I'd not heard about?

"I have heard that you are making changes to Morgania. Is this true?" Lady Vianne asked, her brow raised.

I didn't know why I bothered to speak. Lady Vianne's gem was glowing a bright violet, which meant she was poring over every decision I'd made since becoming consul and finding out why I'd done it. Since she already had all the answers she needed, I shrugged. "I'm making necessary changes to ensure that Morgania is able to house and protect Rowyn, if she chooses to return."

Lady Vianne laughed. "You think she will have a choice in the matter?"

I gritted my teeth. "I think Rowyn will be powerful enough to make her own choices."

Lady Vianne sighed. "If only that were true. Duke Agramon doesn't let his possessions go until he's done with them."

I stared at her for a moment. "What are you doing here?" I asked again. Surely, she didn't travel all the way to Helena just to lecture me on the evils of her old mentor.

"You need to prepare to see him at the quinquennial," Vianne said, sweeping her dark hair off her shoulder.

Agramon. He was a formidable figure within the empire and a renowned mind reader. It was said he could peer into the deepest recesses of one's thoughts with just a glance.

"Prepare for what, exactly?" I asked, my mind racing with thoughts of potential threats and alliances.

"He'll see you as a threat," she said, her tone grave. "You hold sway over Rowyn, and that makes you an adversary."

A threat to Agramon? Me? The idea seemed ludicrous, yet the urgency in Lady Vianne's voice suggested otherwise.

"You need to learn to shield your thoughts, Destrian," she continued. "If you wish to protect Rowyn, and yourself, you must keep Agramon from accessing your true intentions."

"And why are you helping me?" I asked. "Why put yourself out?"

Lady Vianne narrowed her eyes. "I've known for

quite some time that Duke Agramon's been planning something against the empire, and it seems that Rowyn is one of the keys he's using for success. If he manages to fulfill his plan, I will need a place to go."

"Solridge won't be safe for you? Lord Alexander is a Marendesly. I would think Agramon would be slow to anger the most formidable family in the realm."

"Agramon didn't take my defect lightly," Vianne said in a tone that sounded as though she was severely understating the issue.

I eyed her warily. There was something in the way she presented her fears, in her quiet conviction, that made me take her warning seriously. Agramon was powerful—that was no secret—and his connections within the empire were vast. But I hadn't truly considered the risk he posed until Vianne laid it bare.

Lady Vianne continued, her voice dropping to a whisper. "And he's ruthless. He'll stop at nothing to get what he wants. If he sees Rowyn as a key to his plans, then you, Consul Destrian, are in his way if you give her hope for a world where she isn't tied to his side."

"Then I need to be prepared."

The look in her eyes was serious, perhaps more serious than I had ever seen it. "You will. Morgania is sorely lacking in sorcerers, but that doesn't mean you're alone. There are those in the empire who would stand against Agramon if given the chance. If he truly does make a play against the empire."

"Who would dare to stand against him? He's one of the most powerful men in the realm."

Vianne gave a grim smile. "There are more of us than you might think. Some are within the empire, others in distant lands. We are scattered, silenced, but not powerless."

"I'm just trying to protect my city, my people," I protested, but my words felt hollow. "And Rowyn."

"You care. You're willing to risk everything for those you love. That's the kind of person people will follow."

"Very well," I said, my voice steady. "In exchange for your training, Helena is prepared to shield you, should the time come that you feel unsafe."

Lady Vianne nodded. "Now's a good enough time to start. You remember when we worked on this at Solridge, yes? The wall that you build around a secret?"

I nodded.

"Let's practice that exercise again," Vianne urged. "Fixate on a single thought or image. Let it be simple, devoid of any emotional ties."

I closed my eyes, breathing in slowly. I focused on a simple, mundane image—a single flicker of a flame in the darkness. I held on to the image, trying to banish every other thought from my mind.

"Good," Lady Vianne said. "Now you need to erect a wall around that thought. It should be impenetrable—unyielding."

Again, I followed her instruction, visualizing a tall, imposing wall that encircled my flame. It was challenging. Every noise and sensation threatened to shatter my concentration. Yet, I held on, my determination fueling my efforts.

Lady Vianne was silent for a while, her eyes closed as if trying to penetrate my mental barrier. Then, she nodded approvingly. "Good. I could not see beyond your wall. But you have to maintain this at all times, especially in Agramon's presence."

It was harder than I thought, this act of constant vigilance.

"The more you practice, the easier it becomes," she said. "It has to become as natural as breathing. Only then will you be safe." She rose from her chair. "Just remember, this is not a battle you can afford to lose. Agramon is cunning, more so than any you've faced before."

I watched her leave, curious by the turn of events. It was lucky, I supposed, to have another sorcerer in Morgania. Rowyn and I were the only sorcerers from within the region's borders that I knew of.

I opened the drawer to my desk and pulled out the bottle of liquor that had been my father's, as well as his glass. Pouring myself some, I took a sip of the bitter drink and rubbed my hand over my face, my thoughts wandering back to Rowyn. I wondered how she was doing, surrounded by the opulence of the capital and scrutiny of the empire. I hoped that, in the end, everything we've done would be worth it.

Chapter 11

THE MORNING ROOM WAS FILLED with a pleasant warmth, sunlight streaming through the tall, arched windows. I sat across from Aunt Maureen, her hand moving deftly over the parchment as she sketched out potential plans for the Winter Solstice. Ingrid and Ilisa sat beside me, their gazes alternating between the parchment and each other, occasional smiles punctuating their quiet collaboration.

Aunt Maureen looked up at me from time to time, seeking my approval, while Ingrid watched me out of the corner of her eye, a silent question in her gaze. Would I be pleased with their work?

"A grand feast in the market square," Aunt Maureen was saying, tapping a spot on the parchment with her quill, "followed by a dance. We'll need to organize musicians, decorations, and discuss menus with the vendors."

Ilisa nodded, her brows furrowed in thought. "And we must ensure to send invitations to the foremost people of Morgania," she added, a note of haughtiness creeping into her tone. "We can't overlook any of the prominent families."

My lips curved into a smile. Ilisa had grown into her role quite well, embracing her newfound responsibilities with an admirable level of determination. It also kept her off my back.

"Yes, we must," I agreed. "Do we have a draft of the invitation yet?"

Ingrid, who'd been watching me so far, nodded and pulled out a piece of parchment from the pile before her. "Yes," she said, offering it to me with a small, hopeful smile. "I drafted one last night."

I took it from her, scanning over the beautifully penned words. "This is excellent, Ingrid." Her face lit up with a broad, relieved smile.

Our planning was abruptly interrupted as the heavy oak doors to the morning room swung open. Captain Ferris and Sir Bernard stood in the entrance, a look of urgency on their faces.

"Ladies," Ferris greeted when their eyes fell upon him.

Aunt Maureen's lips tightened slightly, but she gave Ferris a brief nod of acknowledgment. Both Ilisa and Ingrid paused in their chatter, their attention lingering on the Morganite captain. There was a reluctant admiration in their gazes as their eyes swept over the markings around his eyes and on his arms.

"I'm sorry to interrupt, Lord Destrian," Sir Bernard

began, stepping farther into the room. "We have urgent news."

"Of course." My pulse quickened in anticipation. I turned to Ingrid and Ilisa. "Ladies, if you'll excuse us."

They looked at me, their faces filled with a mix of concern and curiosity, but they nodded their assent. Aunt Maureen, her expression inscrutable, gave a curt nod before standing.

"I will meet with you later," Aunt Maureen told the girls before ushering Ingrid and Ilisa out and shutting the door behind them.

She turned and came back to my side as Ferris sank into the chair across from me, his expression grave. "What's happened?" I asked.

The room was silent for a moment, save for the faint crackle of the fire in the hearth. Ferris drew a deep breath, meeting my gaze with a look of fury.

"It's about Caymir's Rook," he began, his voice harsh and grim. "A couple of the old Lyrican families who used to reside there managed to sneak past our guards and set fire to a cluster of houses that the Morganites were occupying."

Aunt Maureen gasped as I gritted my teeth, trying to keep my heart calm and steady. "Was anyone hurt?"

"There were a few injuries," Ferris replied, his voice steady despite the anger evident on his face. "The

600

houses were mostly empty, as everyone was out for the day's work. However, the damage to the homes is significant."

I clenched my fists, struggling to rein in my anger. It was a challenge, and I would not let it go unanswered.

"Take a squadron of men and find those responsible," I demanded icily. "I want them brought to me. And tighten the security around Caymir's Rook. This can't happen again."

Ferris nodded. "I'll see to it, Consul."

Sir Bernard cleared his throat, drawing my attention back to him. "Lord Destrian, we also need to consider who will preside over the trial once the perpetrators are captured. The position of judge has been vacant for far too long. It's crucial to find someone to mete out sentences."

I nodded, pinching the bridge of my nose. Yet another matter I needed to resolve urgently. The issue had been on my list for a while now, but other matters had somehow always pushed it to the side. No longer.

"You're right, Sir Bernard," I conceded. "I will make it a priority to review the list the council provided. Set up meetings with potential candidates."

The old knight gave me a nod, his stern expression easing a bit.

Ferris got up, bowing slightly before excusing himself to pack for his journey to Caymir's Rook, along with a squadron of men. Sir Bernard also stood, giving me a respectful nod before leaving the room.

I turned to Aunt Maureen, who'd remained silent throughout most of the meeting. She laid her hand on my shoulder. "It's a terrible thing that happened, truly."

I nodded, my gaze fixed on the flames dancing in the hearth. "I just wish the others wished for peace as much as I do."

She took the seat across from me, studying my brooding expression. "Well, the selection of a judge is critical if you want to be taken seriously by the Morganites. They've long railed that they are judged harshly in Helena."

"They will want blood, though," I said, rubbing my eyes with my fingers.

"Who?"

I raised my eyes to hers. "The Morganites." I shook my head. "We've come so far, and now this." I leaned my face into my hands. "I feel as though I'll never get this place up to where it needs to be."

"What are you trying to prove, nephew?" Aunt Maureen asked, leaning forward with her hand on my arm.

"That I'll be able to keep her safe." I sighed.

"Nephew, you've been bending over backward for this girl, but isn't she the most powerful sorcerer in the world? She can keep herself safe. You just have to show her you love her."

"I don't think it will be enough," I admitted.

Aunt Maureen gave me a scrutinizing look before finally releasing a heavy sigh. "Destrian, you've been working tirelessly. That in itself is a testament to the person you are. You don't need to prove your worth to anyone, especially not to the woman you love."

I met her gaze, hearing the truth in her words but still struggling with my insecurities. "I just worry that . . . that it won't be enough. That I won't be enough. I mean, look who I have to contend with . . . the Butcher of Bruin? Duke Agramon? Even Mellan Lyon is probably more desirable of a match than me."

"Love isn't about being enough, dear nephew," she said softly. "It's about who you want to spend your days with for the rest of your life. Most importantly, it's about trust."

I mulled over her words, my heart heavy with a multitude of feelings.

"You'll figure it out, nephew. I'm sure of it," Aunt Maureen said, patting my arm and rising. "Now find a judge."

"Yes," I agreed, rising from my chair. Sir Bernard had given me the first candidate on his list. I decided to visit his home. I couldn't afford to look ill-prepared.

Chapter 12

S IR MORWEN CAME WITH GLOWING recommendations from the old captain of the guard. Sitting across from him in his receiving room, I mulled over his references. He was known to be experienced and fair, but that was when he'd worked with strictly Lyrican soldiers. I needed someone to preside over trials for everyone, and I refused to mess up the choice. I needed someone who was measured and balanced.

"Lord Destrian," Morwen greeted me with an affable smile. "I'm gratified to see you so committed to justice."

I returned his nod, grateful for his apparent understanding. "Sir Morwen, it's imperative that all trials are conducted without reproach. I demand consistency. The tension between us and the Morganites is already high."

"Pah," he replied, his smile never waning. "The Morganites have never been anything to worry about. I don't know why you've put such stock into them. They will turn on us in the end. It is their way."

I stood. "Thank you for your time, Sir Morwen, but

I will not be offering you this position."

Sir Morwen looked surprised before he frowned, his eyes hardened on me. "You really are that lovesick puppy, yapping at the feet of the Morganites. To think, the consulship of Helena reduced to such levels. Your grandfather is turning over in his grave right now."

Despite my effort to shove my anger down, I felt my fingertips warm. I didn't have time for any of this.

"I will see myself out," I said, turning and striding from the room, not even waiting for a servant to lead me out.

Fuck.

He was awful, and I had a feeling most people on the list were awful. I needed a Morganite judge because that person would also sit on my council. I needed someone who I knew myself. Someone who *I* trusted.

I rode past the citadel and into the guard's living area. Ferris had rather nice rooms there, I thought. The captain's quarters were a ground-level apartment with a trim little porch. I didn't even have a balcony.

I knocked on the door. Ferris answered with a bag already slung over his shoulder.

"I'm going with you to the Rook," I said, nodding to the pack.

"Why? Do you not trust me to do this on my own?" Ferris asked, his brows raised.

I shook my head. "It has nothing to do with that. I need a judge."

"Who are you thinking?"

"You'll find out when I ask them," I replied with a smile.

I turned on my heel and swung back onto Valor's back. "I will be ready shortly. *Don't* leave without me," I said, turning Valor toward the citadel. I rode off, finally feeling a sense of hope for the day.

Of course, Lady Vianne intercepted me in the halls of the castle.

"I was hoping you would find time to train today," she said, falling into step beside me. I could tell she read my thoughts from the way her gem glowed. I tried to shove her out with little success. Her mouth flattened into a grim line.

Point. Taken.

"I'm sorry. I am heading for Caymir's Rook, but I'll be back in a few days."

"I will go with you," Lady Vianne said, turning back toward her rooms. "Don't leave without me!"

Gods be all. I shook my head and packed as fast as I could. I'd hoped to evade Lady Vianne on my way out, but she was already prepared, wearing a riding dress and carrying a perfectly packed saddlebag.

"I would've thought you'd be more interested in

staying and helping Ingrid and Ilisa with the festival."

Lady Vianne shot me an appraising look. "Not at all. I'm far more curious to meet Rowyn's kin. You are the only one who has."

"Why do you care?" I asked with a frown.

"When we are hedging our bets on people, we want to be sure."

I strode past her. "I don't know what any of that even means."

AS THE CITY GATES FELL BEHIND US, Lady Vianne slowed, forcing me to keep pace beside her and let the guard ride ahead with Ferris and Kaelan, since the Imorati wanted to see Caymir's Rook for himself.

It was just Lady Vianne and me then, riding through the sprawling forest that stretched toward Caymir's Rook. The muted sounds of our horses' hooves against the dirt path filled the silence, and I could hear the soft rustling of wind against the leaves.

"Lord Destrian," she began, her amethyst gem glowing in the morning light, the gleam in her eyes matching it. "Is it true? The stories of you and Rowyn in the Nightlands?"

My heart skipped a beat, and I fought to keep my expression unreadable. She was clever; I had to give her that. The perfect question to test me, to see if I could truly keep my thoughts hidden.

I focused my mind, channeling my attention to a single point, just as she had taught me. It was like trying to hold back a river with my bare hands, but I was determined. I would not give her the satisfaction of reading my mind.

"Stories tend to exaggerate the truth, Lady Vianne," I replied, my voice calm and steady.

There was a pause and then a chuckle escaped her lips. "Indeed," she said, "they certainly have a knack for spinning tales."

Her gem glowed less intensely, as if she had hit a wall in my mind, unable to push past. The corners of my lips twitched upward. Perhaps I was making progress after all.

"What kind of queen do you think Rowyn would make?" she asked next, her voice carrying a hint of something that sounded strangely like curiosity.

A frown etched its way onto my face, my heart lurching uncomfortably. That was a sensitive subject, and one I hadn't allowed myself to dwell on too much. How did she know about it?

Trying to keep my focus, I let my mind wander to a

peaceful image, a serene waterfall gushing with calm, rhythmic tranquility. "We do not have kings and queens in Lyrica," I responded, my voice steady despite the trepidation thrumming in my veins. "Everyone knows the emperor rules all."

Lady Vianne hummed thoughtfully, her amethyst shining brightly.

The road to Caymir's Rook suddenly seemed a lot longer.

Lady Vianne's question stirred a contemplative silence within me as we journeyed onward. My mind was drawn back to Rowyn, her eyes alight with the fire of determination, her spirit wild and untamed, yet full of compassion.

Yes, she lacked the finesse of a seasoned diplomat. Yes, her straightforwardness might be viewed as a weakness. But Rowyn's strength wasn't cloaked behind manipulative charm or guileful politics. It was raw and unfiltered, a beacon that others could rally around.

She cared deeply about her people, often putting their needs above her own. Her compassionate nature could win hearts, and her empathy could build bridges where there were walls. A queen didn't necessarily need to be charming to be loved, and Rowyn, I knew, would be loved.

The contrast between our approaches to leadership

was stark. While I viewed leadership as a responsibility, something that was thrust upon me, Rowyn saw it as an opportunity. An opportunity to bring about change, to fight for justice, to create a better world. And that, I realized, was what made Rowyn truly remarkable.

AS THE IMPOSING TOWERS of Caymir's Rook rose to meet us, the flurry of activity within its walls was evident. Awaiting our arrival, the Rook's men were stirring, a wave of anxiety rippling through their ranks.

Ferris nodded to me before directing his men toward the soldiers from the Rook who enveloped the squadron with angry expressions and harsh words. I turned my eyes back to the tower. I figured Ferris was the best person to deal with unrest between the warriors of the Rook and the Helenian guards.

The entrance of the tower creaked open, and out strode Baylin, his demeanor as self-important as ever. His eyes narrowed in disapproval as they fell on me, but I held my ground, directing my attention to Urdua, who stepped up to stand beside him. Raising a hand, I signaled my intention to speak solely with her.

"What is this?" Baylin growled, his face contorted

in a scowl. "You dare disrespect me in my own do-main?"

"I am here for a civil discussion," I replied evenly, "with Urdua."

"This is a matter concerning the Rook, Consul," Baylin hissed. "You cannot exclude me."

My gaze held steady on Urdua in a silent plea for her understanding. This wasn't an act of disrespect but a necessary move. Baylin had sold out his own kin; his judgment could not be trusted. Urdua, on the other hand, held the impartiality and strength we needed in Helena.

"Very well," she said, nodding toward the door. "I suppose you'd best come inside, Consul." Her eyes drifted to Vianne who'd dismounted beside me.

"Chief Urdua," I said, motioning beside me. "May I introduce, Lady Vianne of Solridge."

"What are your powers, sorceress?" Urdua asked, her brow raised.

"I'm a mind reader," Vianne said stiffly.

Urdua's eyes narrowed.

"I understand that the Morganites are distrustful of sorcerers," Vianne commented. "But I assure you that I am merely here to observe, and we have a mutual ac-quaintance in Rowyn the Morganite."

"Did she trust you?" Urdua asked.

"No," Vianne replied. "But regardless, I am here to aid Lord Destrian in ensuring that Morgania is able to weather the storm of the capital, should the whisperings be proven correct."

Urdua harrumphed but led us into the tower. Baylin's cheeks flamed a crimson hue and he sputtered, unable to articulate his outrage. I ignored his ire.

"I have a proposal," I said as I took a seat in her receiving room, my gaze unwavering from Urdua's. "Helena is in need of judges—fair, impartial voices."

Urdua sat back, her eyes shifting between Lady Vianne and myself. "You wish me to nominate someone?"

Beside me, I sensed Lady Vianne's curiosity, her amethyst gem pulsing rapidly.

"No," I replied, my voice firm. "There are no women on the council as it stands."

Urdua's lips pursed, a wordless question in her gaze. "That is the norm."

"Rowyn, if she chooses to return," I went on, "should come home to a city where she can trust the people in power. People like you. Would you consider serving as a judge in Helena?"

I could see the surprise in Urdua's eyes. But there was also something else—a glint of interest, perhaps. I held my breath, waiting for her response.

Lady Vianne remained conspicuously silent, her gem pulsating rhythmically against her skin, casting eerie violet shadows across her face. Even as she remained physically quiet, I knew she was engaging with every thought crossing our minds.

"Baylin would also be a fair judge," Urdua offered. "You've been risking his anger lately, and it would put me in a position to pick a side, more so than I already have."

"Baylin is a small man," Lady Vianne said, her voice a calm contrast to the tension hanging thickly in the air. "And he carries a lot of anger."

"The Morganites, like most people, have a history of selling their daughters for profit. It is a disconcerting practice but hardly an unusual one," Urdua scoffed.

"I need *you*," I insisted. "The people in Helena need you. Wouldn't you want to be involved in ensuring that Morganites are given justice? Wouldn't you want to help enact changes to the very laws that plague your people? I imagine you probably have ideas."

"You can legalize divorce when requested from a woman," Urdua said, her mouth crooked to the side.

Lady Vianne tried to stifle her laughter, but she didn't do a very good job of it.

"Put it to the council," I offered.

In the silence that followed, I couldn't tell what was

going through Urdua's mind. I only knew that I felt like I needed her. Honestly, she reminded me of my aunt Maureen, who would probably leave soon to return to Eslin with Onora and leave me without someone to get advice from.

"Let me think on it, and I'll give you an answer tomorrow," Urdua said, rising from her seat. "I'll see what my people here in Caymir's Rook think."

"I would be grateful to have you," I replied with a bow.

Lady Vianne followed me out into the corridor. "You did well," she murmured, adjusting the blue wrap that crossed her shoulders and was held fast by her belt. "Her thoughts were hopeful about the opportunities."

I let out a sigh of relief. Finally, something was going right.

THE DAWN OF A NEW DAY brought Ferris's return and an answer to the question I had proposed to Urdua.

Urdua accepted my offer, and a large group of Morganites from her tribe insisted on accompanying her to Helena to make their homes, where I assured they would be welcome.

It wasn't long afterward that Ferris emerged from the tree line with two barred wagons following him. I studied them uneasily. The people within were tired and beaten, but alive.

News of Ferris's success swept through the encampment like a wild gust of wind, bringing a sense of victory but also a sense of foreboding. As Ferris approached, the air thick with accomplishment, he reported an unexpected find.

Conal. The name sent a shiver of anger down my spine. The face of the man who had killed my father swam into focus, an image I had spent countless nights burning into memory. Revenge, so long an elusive whisper, was suddenly within my grasp.

I made my way to the makeshift cages, my heart pounding. There, amid the caged Lyricans, sat the wilted holy man. His figure was smaller than I remembered, his body showing signs of age and hardship. But his eyes caught me off guard. They held a weariness that seemed to echo my own, carrying a sense of being poisoned by a lifetime of anger and vengeance.

Chains clinked around his wrists, his lips twisted in a snarl as he spewed a stream of vitriol at Ferris and the Morganite guards surrounding him.

"Traitors of Imor!" he spat. His light eyes blazed

with the same defiance that I remembered, even as he pulled against his restraints.

"Consul." Ferris acknowledged my presence with a nod. I took in the scene, the chaotic mixture of relief, apprehension, and rage settling heavily in my chest. Conal's capture was a significant victory, but his presence here threatened to unearth old wounds and ignite fresh conflicts.

His burning gaze turned on me, a challenge in the depths of his defiant eyes. A part of me wanted to return the stare, to engage him in conversation, to make him see the futility of his actions. But I steeled myself against it. He was a prisoner now, and I was his captor.

I stepped closer to the cage, meeting Conal's scowl with a level gaze. The silence stretched on between us, so thick that it seemed to choke the very air. Finally, the older man spat a curse in my direction, his voice a rasping growl. "May you rot in the fires of the Abyss, boy."

I watched him, his hatred a palpable entity between us. I had anticipated a surge of rage in response, an answering hatred, but instead, all I felt was an oddly detached pity. Here was a man so consumed by his desire for revenge that he'd become a shell of his former self, his spirit corroded by bitterness.

"I don't wish for your death, Imorati," I found

myself saying. "I wish for justice."

"Justice?" he snarled, the word a sharp bark of bitter laughter. "What would you know of justice, boy?"

I had imagined this moment countless times—envisioned the satisfaction of seeing Conal pay for his crimes. But now that it was here, I felt . . . empty.

His capture didn't erase the pain. It didn't bring my father back. It didn't erase the mistakes I'd made, the lies I'd told, the trust I'd lost. Capturing Conal was supposed to be a victory, but it felt hollow.

"You'll get a fair trial. And you'll face the consequences of your actions, as we all must."

Silently, I turned away, striding toward Urdua who was studying me from the door of the tower as I left Conal to his fate. I had my own demons to face and a kingdom to mend. This was only the beginning.

Vengeance was not justice, I realized. And justice was what I would strive for, for both my father's memory and for the future of Morgania.

With the Lyricans confined to their makeshift cages, a heavy silence fell over the encampment. Around me, the Morganian soldiers wore their success in the square set of their shoulders and the grim satisfaction in their eyes. The mission had not been an easy one, but Ferris and his men had surpassed my expectations.

As the sun began to wane, we prepared for our journey back to Helena. The wagons were loaded up, the horses tethered, and orders were given in terse, efficient commands. Despite the turmoil of emotions coursing through me, I couldn't help but feel triumphant.

Chapter 13

THE COUNCIL CHAMBER was brimming with an unfamiliar tension, as though the bubbles within a boiling cauldron were just kissing the lid of the pot. The usual hum of idle chatter had been replaced by urgent murmuring between pairs of worried eyes. I looked at the woman sitting opposite me—Urdua. Her eyes reflected the flicker of torchlight, her lips a tight, straight line, and she sat tall, her posture not betraying any sign of her apprehension. She wore a traditional Morganite dress, black with silver crescents and stars with all sorts of magical beasts and people embroidered into the wool around the collar of her throat and stretching down the front to her feet. I wondered if she'd done the embroidery herself.

"Chief Urdua," I addressed her, our voices the only ones daring to break the silence. "It's your first time conducting a trial of this magnitude, isn't it?"

She nodded as if not trusting her voice to keep steady. The weight of her responsibility bore heavily on her, and I couldn't help but feel a pang of sympathy.

"You'll do fine," I assured her. "Ferris and the guard will be there to protect you and justice will be served, for *all* the people of Morgania."

We made our way toward the grand doors of the castle. They creaked open, revealing the courtyard filled with people bustling about, many with anger alight in their eyes as they turned to glare at me or the guardsmen posted on horseback. The wealthier merchants had found spots on the ramparts, while the commoners from the market and city beyond crowded together, pushing and shoving to see the consul's brand of justice.

My gaze swept over the crowd, settling briefly on the stationed guards. Each of them stood tall, alert, and ready, their armored presence providing a sense of security in the tense environment. Ferris met my gaze with a reassuring nod.

The Lyricans were ushered onto the platform, their faces wrought with anxiety and defiance, and Conal was stoic despite the heavy chains weighing him down. The sight of the man who had murdered my father was a raw reminder of the personal nature of this trial. But my role demanded impartiality.

As I ascended the steps to the top of the landing, the crowd fell into an even deeper silence. The weight of the moment seemed to press down upon us all. As I settled into my seat, my gaze locked onto Urdua.

"Let the trial commence," I declared.

Conal was tried for his heinous act of murdering Consul Colman. As the trial began, I found myself struggling to keep my personal feelings at bay. The desire for revenge was potent, gnawing at the edges of my composure. But this was not about revenge; it was about justice. And as the consul, it was my duty to ensure that justice was served impartially.

As the testimonies died down, Urdua rose from her seat. She took a deep breath, scanning the crowd one last time before she began to deliver her judgment.

The air in the courtyard seemed to thicken as she recounted his crime—the murder of my father. A murmur rippled through the crowd, quickly hushed as Urdua raised her hand for silence. She then declared Conal's sentence: "For the crime of murdering the lord of Helena, Conal Butler of Espiria is sentenced to imprisonment until Imor has deemed it be the end of his days."

Her words echoed in the silence that followed. Conal himself showed no reaction. He stood there, his face a mask of indifference, showing neither fear nor remorse.

As the guards escorted Conal off of the platform, I could hear the whispers starting up again, a mix of relief and anxiety humming in the undercurrents.

Then Chief Urdua stepped forward once more,

drawing the attention of every person in the yard. As she began to speak, outlining the charges against the Lyricans for the attack on the Morganite houses, the city remained silent.

She straightened in front of the host of people, her eyes hard. "The families involved in the attack are found guilty. As no one was seriously hurt, you are ordered to pay restitution and must help rebuild the community that you preyed upon."

The guilty verdict was barely out of Urdua's mouth when the cries of bias began to fill the air. My heart sank as I saw the faces of the Lyricans in the crowd harden, their eyes gleaming with accusation and bitterness. The shouts of injustice grew louder, coalescing into a cacophony of outrage that drowned out Urdua's final words.

As the verdict was relayed throughout the city, the streets of Helena came alive with the sound of dissent. A call that grew louder and more fervent with each passing moment. I could see the path this anger was taking, and my blood ran cold.

They were angry. Some of the families who had been turned out of the Rook to make room for the Morganites had lived there for generations. I could understand their anger. I had paid them for their lands to make up for the loss.

"Captain Ferris!" I shouted, waving him toward me. "Get the counselors inside, then I want all of the squadrons we have on the streets. Try your best not to injure anybody, and above all, maintain order!"

My heart pounded in my chest at the thought of the mob running throughout the city. Without a second thought, I called for my horse and pulled on my riding gloves. Alexo was at my side instantly. I leaped onto Valor's back and led Alexo and a group of guardsmen through the streets as the mob began to riot.

Fuck.

They were heading to the Temple of Imor standing silent and serene and unaware of the danger that lurked at its steps. Nearly finished, the marble gleamed in the sun, glass panes of deep blue with white stars and crescent moons lining the entryway, ready to welcome worshippers.

The throng of people, now fueled by anger and blinded by hate, stood at the foot of the temple, their faces twisted and ugly. Someone threw a stone and I heard the sound of breaking glass.

Absolutely fucking not.

Not happening on my watch.

I kicked Valor into the crowd, not caring if I was stepping on toes or if someone was jostled more forcefully than intended. I had to save the temple. It had become about saving the city. It was about saving Rowyn.

I finally reached the entrance and waited half a beat more for Alexo to draw reins beside me, along with the rest of the guard who had ridden into the city. Alan was there, a guard who'd gone through training while I'd still been home at Helena. Standing next to him was Polic, a Morganite man who'd been in the first batch of sign-ups from Caymir's Rook. He was hoping to have enough money to get married soon.

"Stop!" I cried out.

The crowd began to direct their shouts towards me. I could see men picking up more rocks.

I faced the mob and called a wall of fire, which stretched from the ground to the top of the temple. I'd never made a ward that large before.

"I will not let you destroy this temple," I declared, my voice resonating with a force that even surprised me. The magic within was burning through me, but instead of draining me, I felt even stronger.

The crowd backed away from the temple, the flames of my barrier reflecting off its marble façade, creating a halo of fire. Most looked stunned. Rocks fell from hands. You did not often see magic in Morgania. Many might go their entire lives without seeing it.

The retreat was slow, reluctant, the crowd seeming

to unravel at the edges first. There were sullen faces and downcast eyes, but the temple stood untouched behind its shield of flame. The tense atmosphere lingered, an echo of the fury that had so recently filled the air, but the imminent threat had been quelled.

My heart pounded in my chest, the adrenaline of the confrontation slowly ebbing, leaving me with a feeling of exhaustion and a sense of relief. The city guard followed me as we rode through the crowd, their eyes scanning the people warily. Alexo rode beside me, his usually jovial face drawn in a tight line. Ferris was silent as well, his gaze flickering over the dispersing crowd with a troubled expression.

"I didn't want it to come to this," I admitted, watching a mother tuck her children behind her as we rode past.

"Sometimes, it's necessary to show strength, Consul," Ferris replied. "Especially when the peace is at stake."

THAT NIGHT, I SAT ALONE in the council room, drinking from my father's glass, the events of the day weighing on me. The quiet was broken only by the crackling fire in the hearth, its light casting dancing shadows on the walls. A city in turmoil, a trial, a riot, a near catastrophe at the temple, and the strain of holding it all together beat me until I felt as though I had nothing more to give.

Chapter 14

THE WINTER MORNING WAS CRISP, a chill clinging to the air. The usual bustle and hum of the castle were absent, replaced with the rhythmic clanging of steel and the grunts of effort as the new recruits started their day with training. I stood among the men, feeling the satisfying pull of my muscles as I swung my sword in well-practiced arcs.

For the first time in a long while, I felt good. The taste of regret was fading, replaced by the sharp tang of progress. Despite the challenges and adversities, we were moving forward, growing stronger each day.

When we took a break, I noticed something new. Several of the Lyrican guardsmen, their armor shed for the moment, sported fresh markings on their arms. The designs were intricate and hinted at some deeper significance. Curiosity piqued, I approached them for a closer look.

"Where did you get these?" I asked, turning to the closest Lyrican guard who had a band around his arm that looked woven.

Captain Ferris, standing nearby, answered before the man could speak. "Kaelan and his sister do them.

They're a kind of blessing to ward off ill luck." His eyes gleamed with amusement.

I frowned at his explanation, scanning the other markings. The others took note of our conversation and grinned. "Why not get one yourself, Dragon?" one of them called.

The moniker "Dragon" had initially been a jest. A nod to my fire magic, the fact that I'd helped defeat a dragon, and my temper. But it had stuck, becoming something akin to a badge of honor, a reluctant acceptance of my power and a testament to the fire in my veins.

I'd always admired the Morganite markings. Rowyn had a shadow falcon on her back that she said she'd earned for bravery. I counted myself lucky that I was one of a few who'd seen it. I never imagined myself with one though. I wasn't a Morganite, after all, and wasn't sure what went into choosing a marking. Rowyn made it seem like an Imorati chose it.

Before I could ponder it further, one of the men had already run off to fetch Kaelan. When he arrived, there was a surge of activity, the men jostling me playfully toward him. With a good-natured roll of my eyes, I allowed them to guide me to a bench as Kaelan prepared his tools.

"Where do you want it?" Kaelan asked.

I shrugged. "Wherever is best," I said, feeling excitement build in my stomach. What would Rowyn think?

The pain was sharp, the needle a constant sting, but I bore it silently. There was a strange sense of camaraderie in this shared experience, a unity forged in pain and laughter.

Kaelan worked with meticulous precision for several hours, the needle scratching into my skin, a trail of dark ink left in its wake. A dragon took form, its wings spread wide, its tail spiraling around my forearm. It hurt like hell.

When it was over, Kaelan stepped back and gave me a respectful nod as he packed his tools. I turned my arm, studying the black tattoo. Despite the lingering sting, I found myself grinning.

I stared at it, even hours later, as the fire crackled and the night drew its cloak over the castle. I had to stifle a laugh. The Dragon, indeed.

OVER THE WEEKS, my mental shielding had grown stronger. At first, I struggled to keep my mind guarded for more than a few minutes at a time, but with

Vianne's guidance and relentless training sessions, I had begun to sustain the shield for hours. It was far from perfect, but it was progress.

"Your control is improving," Vianne noted as we wrapped up for the day. "Keep at it, and you'll have a solid shield before you know it."

I might not have enjoyed every aspect of being a consul, but at least I was getting better at the parts that mattered. I nodded at Vianne, a small smile playing on my lips. I still had a long way to go, but for the first time in a while, I felt ready for it.

"The ladies are waiting outside to corner you," Vianne warned me as she rose, her tone serious. "And frankly, they've been working hard. You should let them."

Staring at the table in the council room, I took a deep breath and prepared myself to face the formidable force that was my sister, aunt, and Lady Ingrid. "All right," I nodded.

They filed in, their faces expectant as they took a seat across from me. Ilisa had lost her irritation with me in the throes of this new pursuit and looked as though she were ready to bounce out of her seat with excitement. Ingrid was calmer, her fingers flipping through pages of parchment and notes, getting everything in order.

"Let's hear what you've got," I said, drumming my fingers on the table.

Ingrid glanced at the others before starting. "I've contacted several performers," she said. "Bards and musicians. Sir Bernard told me of a man in Rudin who was rumored to know all the traditional Morganite ballads. I wrote to him, and he has accepted an invitation to play at the celebration for the opening of the temple."

I couldn't help but smile. "That sounds perfect," I said, unable to keep the admiration from my voice. Ingrid's smile widened and I had to look away. I hoped she didn't read too much into my tone. I was grateful for her help in planning the festival, and they'd really been doing a good job of it, but that was as far as my admiration went.

Next was Ilisa. "I've been sampling the local fare," she started, earning a few chuckles around the room. "One Morganite vendor makes these mooncakes that are absolutely divine," she continued, her eyes practically sparkling. "The family chef says he can make enough sunbuns for the masses as well, and all the vendors are clamoring for a spot on Temple Row for the opening. I've also found several seamstresses to work on our banners."

Ilisa handed me a little triangle of cloth. One side

was gold with a black sun sewn into the fabric. The other side was black with a golden crescent moon stitched within.

"Who designed this?" I asked, my brows raised.

"I did," Aunt Maureen said. "We plan to string these along Temple Row. I've also spoken to Solston Ignace and Imorati Kaelan about the temple services. Solston Ignace's will kick off the festivities at sunrise with his service, while Imorati Kaelan's will continue the festivities at sunset. That way people can attend both if they desire."

"Excellent idea, Aunt Maureen," I agreed. "It's important to remember the purpose of this event amid all the celebrations."

As the meeting concluded, I felt a sense of relief and anticipation. The solstice was shaping up to be a memorable one. I was grateful for Ingrid, Ilisa, Aunt Maureen, and everyone else working tirelessly to bring it all together. I only wished Rowyn was here to see it.

I rose as the others left. Ingrid lingered behind, glancing at me with an unreadable expression. She hadn't really been putting herself in my way as much, which I was thankful for, but the look in her eyes made me uneasy.

"Ingrid," I started, "I'm glad you're here. I wanted to tell you how happy I am with all your work on the festival. You, Ilisa, Aunt Maureen . . . You've all out-done yourselves."

A blush tinged her cheeks as she smiled. "Thank you, Destrian," she said. "It means a lot to hear you say that."

I was about to say something else when Ingrid leaned forward, her eyes closing as she moved toward me. Her intentions became clear, and a jolt of surprise ran through me.

"Ingrid," I said, stepping back before her lips could reach mine. Her eyes fluttered open, confusion swirling in them.

"I . . ." she started, her cheeks growing even redder, "I thought . . ."

"Ingrid, I've told you . . ." I started, but she held up a hand to silence me.

"You are still mooning after her?" Ingrid snapped suddenly. "Even after all these months?"

I raised my brows. "I was clear with you before . . . I'm in love with Rowyn. It is she who I see a future with, not you."

Ingrid stepped closer, her eyes sharp with anger. "I have been patient. I have waited and waited for you to come to your senses and fulfill your duty to your seat."

"You didn't have to be here!" I said, throwing my arm out, completely fed up with the situation. I

634

appreciated her help with the Winter Solstice, I really did, but it seemed that the end result was what I'd been worried about all along. It seemed that Ingrid had taken it to mean I wanted her around, and it was far from the truth. She insisted on being around, and I was just keeping her busy and out of my hair.

"What do you even think of yourself, Ingrid?" I snapped, unable to contain my irritation. "I am in love with someone else. Doesn't that matter at all to you? Where is your dignity?"

She recoiled as if I'd slapped her, the sting of my words landing like barbs. Her expression faltered, the confident veneer wavering as doubt crept into her gaze. For the first time since I had known her, Ingrid seemed unsure of herself.

Then, Ingrid straightened her back, her eyes shining with a new sense of resolve. "I will be honest with you, Destrian," she began, her voice steady, "since apparently no one else will." She paused for a moment, searching my gaze.

"Rowyn will never come back. I've heard stories from the capital already. The nobles are falling over themselves for her."

Each word was like a blow, every sentence a stab at my heart.

Ingrid continued, a cruel smile curling her lips.

"They say the Butcher of Bruin can't keep his hands off her. He's tripping over himself to get a moment of her attention. And the duke . . . he dotes on her, showering her with the finest clothes and food the east has to offer."

Her words hung heavily in the room, the silence deafening as the implications of what she said settled in. "Tell me, Destrian," she continued, her gaze piercing mine, "what woman in her right mind would leave all that behind?"

I felt a hollow feeling settle in my chest, the images that Ingrid's words painted gnawing at my insides. She strode to the door. "I'm sorry you have to hear it from me, but that's the way of our world. You keep thinking that you need to rescue her . . . but what if she doesn't want to be rescued? We both know Rowyn. If she really wanted to be here, she would've returned already."

With that, she turned on her heel, leaving me alone with my thoughts. I could do nothing but stare at the closed door, my heart heavy with a fear that was slowly taking root: the fear of losing Rowyn forever.

Sighing heavily, I poured myself a generous drink from my father's old liquor bottle, the amber liquid shimmering in the dim light. I took a gulp, the harsh taste familiar yet offering no comfort.

Chapter 15

INSIDE THE HALLOWED WALLS of the Temple of Sol, the air vibrated with an energy I hadn't felt before. Stained glass windows framed the room, bathing it in a multitude of hues as the first rays of sunlight pierced through them.

The grand space was filled to the brim with people, and despite the bitter chill outside, the warmth radiating from the gathered bodies made the large room comfortable. I glanced at Aunt Maureen who'd seemed to be waiting for my reaction the entire morning. I smiled at her, pleased with how the festival was going so far.

Ingrid had been watching me, looking resplendent in a pure white cloak, her blonde hair tumbling over her shoulders in curls. She turned away and ignored me when I tried to meet her gaze, still angry about my refusals. Ilisa was analyzing everyone with a discerning eye, as though trying to find fault with her own planning.

I glanced at the crowd, a mixture of faces I recognized and those I didn't. A couple of them were Morganites, their presence in the Temple of Sol catching me by surprise. They stood out, their markings dark against their pale skin. Their faces held a respectful solemnity, their attention focused on the sermon.

Solston Ignace, his golden robe radiant under the early morning light, stood at the altar. His voice filled the temple with his call for light to dispel the darkness.

Ignace's eyes swept across the crowd, locking onto the few Morganites present. There was a moment of hesitation, a stutter in his words. But then he continued, his voice rising above the whispered confusion.

As I watched the crowd, I felt a surge of hope. The mood was warm and friendly, an unusual calmness that spread through the congregation. Perhaps I'd been too harsh on Ingrid before when I'd dismissed her talk of parties and festivals being good for people. I'd thought it merely a frivolity. But now I realized that giving everyone a reason to celebrate together could do more for unity than shoving it down their throats and forcing them to swallow the changes whether they liked it or not. The past was behind us, and the future, though uncertain, was full of potential.

Solston Ignace finished the sermon and the music rose, echoing within the stone walls and streaming out to the streets as those who'd come to the morning service left the temple.

The ladies piled into the open carriage waiting

outside, while I swung myself onto Valor and we began to make our way through the streets.

The city was alive, festooned with black and gold banners fluttering from buildings and stretching across the streets. The snow from last night's fall shimmered under the bright sun, adding to the festive spirit. Among the revelers, I noticed groups of Morganites. They kept to the shadows, wary as they observed the patrolling guards. Yet, they were here, participating and mingling, somewhat.

I found Urdua standing among a group of Morganites from Caymir's Rook. A thin smile tugged at her lips when she caught my eye.

Ilisa's voice drew me back, her finger pointing at a pair of Morganites adorned in brightly colored, richly embroidered clothing. They were performing on a raised platform. The man skillfully manipulated a drum, each beat synchronized perfectly with the woman's movements. She was decorated in intricate markings, dancing with a pair of gleaming knives that spun and twisted in her skilled hands. Occasionally, she threw a knife toward her partner, who, without missing a beat, incorporated the blade into the rhythm of the drum.

We watched, munching on sunbuns—sweet bread filled with a bright-orange fruit preserve, the traditional treat of the solstice. The sugary flavor complemented the spiced wine, and the warmth was a welcome reprieve from the winter chill.

Performances punctuated the city at every corner—music and dance, fire-breathers, jugglers, and puppet shows for the children. Vendors hawked their wares—everything from food, to trinkets and toys, to clothes, to rare herbs. I shopped with Aunt Maureen and Ilisa, haggling over baubles and purchasing small trinkets as mementos. The day was filled with laughter and hope, and I felt as though finally, I'd made ready for Rowyn to come home.

As THE SUN BEGAN TO DIP toward the horizon, marking the end of the day and the onset of the long night, we made our way to the Temple of Imor. The new stone façade took on a softer hue under the gathering dusk. Inside, the air was heavy with anticipation.

Imorati Kaelan led the service, his voice strong and reassuring. He spoke of darkness not as an enemy, but as a counterpart to light, a necessary balance. He preached acceptance of our fears and encouraged us to harness our insecurities, turning them into strengths.

I glanced around, noting the larger number of Lyricans present than there had been Morganites at the Temple of Sol. There was a sense of openness, a willingness to understand and accept that made my chest swell with pride.

Once Kaelan's words fell into a resonating silence, we stepped out into the city, transformed by the early night. The Morganite pines that lined Temple Row were adorned with tiny candles, their flickering light casting a glow on the snow. It was a beacon in the darkness.

Smoke and the tempting aroma of roasting meats wafted through the air, mingling with the sweet scent of mooncakes. People crowded around fires, sharing food and stories. Music filled the air, strings and drums setting a rhythmic backdrop to the lyrical melody of flutes and pipes.

Looking around, it felt like a dream and a sudden impulse taking hold. Without a word, I lifted my hands, feeling the familiar energy gather and then released it upward. Balls of fire shot into the air, each one exploding in a shower of vibrant hues—crimson, azure, emerald, and more.

Down below, the crowd gasped, all chatter dying as they turned their gazes skyward. Faces lit up in the colors of my magic, children pointed excitedly, their laughter filling the air.

"Show-off," Ilisa said, shaking her head at my antics, her lips curling in a rueful smile. I caught the spark in her eyes, though.

Ingrid crossed her arms over her chest, her displeasure clear. Yet, I couldn't bring myself to regret the impulsive act. For the first time in a long while, I was genuinely, exuberantly happy.

As the applause and cheers from the crowd died down, my mind wandered to Rowyn. I imagined her standing beside me, her eyes alight with the same enthusiasm that coursed through my veins. How she would've laughed and teased me as she joined in the applause.

"I wish you could see this," I murmured to myself, my gaze shifting from the crowd to the moonlit sky. But as I stood amid the laughter and cheers, the music and dancing, the warmth and light, I realized that she was there. Not in person, but in spirit. The Winter Solstice marked not just the longest night, but the promise of a new dawn. And for Helena, that new dawn was nigh.

AS WE MADE OUR WAY back to the castle, I couldn't help but be overwhelmed by a sense of gratitude for the family that surrounded me. Despite our differences and the tension that occasionally boiled over, we had pulled together when it mattered, and it had paid off.

"Wait," I called, stopping them in the hall as they began to head to their rooms. They all turned to me, their expressions questioning.

"I just wanted to say . . ." I started, unsure exactly how to phrase it. "You all did a tremendous job today. The solstice celebration was nothing short of magnificent. I couldn't have done it without each of you."

There was a moment of silence. Then, Ingrid and Ilisa exchanged glances before nodding.

Aunt Maureen looked like she was on the verge of tears. "Thank you, nephew," she said, her voice thick with emotion. "It means a lot to hear that."

Before I could respond, a servant appeared at my side, a letter in his hand. "A message for you, my lord," he said, bowing respectfully.

"Thank you." I took the letter from him. With a nod to the women, I excused myself, feeling a twinge of anxiety when I noticed the seal of Ayastaren on the letter. It was the news I'd been waiting for.

In the quiet of the morning room, I sparked a fire

with a flick of my fingers, the magic crackling to life and casting a warm, inviting glow. Settling down into a comfortable chair, I broke the seal and started to read, the words in front of me holding the power to change everything.

His Lordship
Consul Destrian Everett of Helena,

I trust this letter finds you well. I have received your correspondence and can appreciate your concerns regarding Lady Rowyn's welfare after the recent fire. It is my pleasure to assure you that although the injuries were grave, she is now healed well. The resilience of her spirit continues to inspire us all.

Lady Rowyn has left on a tour around the Eastern Empire. This decision came as a bit of a surprise, considering her recent injuries, but Agramon was adamant about the urgency of her mission—to bring rain to the parched lands of the East. Duke Agramon and Commander Samael of Bruin are accompanying her on this journey. A peculiar company, to say the least, but they've proven effective in providing her protection.

Now to address the rumor you've heard, and I regret to write this, but I cannot deny its veracity. Whispers about Lady Rowyn and the Butcher of Bruin have become louder, and the word is that he will likely ask for her hand. Understandably, this news may disconcert you. However, I assure you, these are yet rumors, and we know well how quickly gossip can twist the truth.

I hope this response provides some solace, even if it carries news you might not have hoped to receive. I urge you, in the spirit of friendship and respect, to remain patient and let time reveal the truth.

Yours faithfully,
Sir Mellan Lyon
A Third Son

As my eyes lingered on Mellan's last sentence, the letter slipped from my grasp, floating gently onto stone floor. My heart pounded against my ribs, each thud echoing the cruel, undeniable words—Rowyn and the Butcher of Bruin. The edges of my vision blurred, and the ornate patterns of the room's carpet seemed to sway beneath me.

I didn't want to believe it. I couldn't. But Mellan wouldn't have written it if there weren't some truth to the matter. A lump formed in my throat, stubborn and persistent as I attempted to swallow it down. I stumbled backward until my knees hit the cushioned arm-chair behind me. Sinking into it, I allowed my gaze to drift toward the dancing flames in the fireplace.

Rowyn and the Butcher of Bruin. The thought was as alien as it was unbearable. A sharp, bitter taste filled my mouth, and I struggled to push the image out of my mind. The Butcher of Bruin, the man I'd learned to despise. Could she really find something worthy in such a man? And why him, when she'd chosen to leave me?

The bottle of my father's liquor sat on the desk. I snatched it up, hoping to drown the pain welling within me, only to find it empty. Rage flared within, as raw and blistering as the wound in my heart. With a roar, I hurled the empty bottle at the stone wall of the fireplace.

As the echoes of the shattered glass faded, I was left in silence with the resounding truth. No matter what I did, it would never be enough. For all my efforts, all my dreams of a better future, I was still losing her. To him. The knowledge cut deeper than any blade.

Chapter 16

THE HEAT FROM THE FORGE surrounded me, yet I was comfortably settled in its familiar embrace. The rhythmic clanging of my hammer against metal formed a steady heartbeat within the echoing chamber of my workspace. Sparks erupted with each strike, casting fleeting shadows that danced across my focused countenance.

As I worked, my mind began to wander back—back to the darkness and uncertainty of the Nightlands. The memories were vivid, still fresh in my mind. I could feel the chill of the perpetual night on my skin, the unknown dangers lurking at every turn, and the constant fear that clung like an unwanted cloak. But within all that fear and danger, there was also her, Rowyn.

She had been my guiding light, my beacon in that darkness. It was her courage, her conviction that kept me going, kept me fighting. I could see her, standing defiantly against the inky blackness, her spirit untamed and unyielding. She was a force of nature, a tempest of fiery determination and enduring hope.

Rekindling my focus, I lifted the hammer once again. Rowyn . . . with the Butcher of Bruin. The mere thought was enough to send shards of ice stabbing my heart. The man was known for his cruelty, a merciless warrior who reveled in the pain and suffering of others. To think of her with him . . . it was an unthinkable, unbearable thought.

How had it come to this? I'd been so sure of her feelings, so certain that the bond we'd been nurturing was strong and true. Had I been fooling myself? Was I merely a safe harbor until she found someone more powerful and compelling?

No. I refused to let that thought take root. I knew Rowyn. I knew her kindness, her courage, and her unwavering sense of justice. There was no way she'd willingly align herself with a man like the Butcher. But if she did, if she felt that she had no other choice . . .

The hammer fell harder, the sound echoing throughout the empty courtyard, drowning out the harsh whispers of my thoughts. The suitors at the capital . . . they'd be more than ready to offer her the world. But would they offer their hearts? Their loyalty?

Rowyn deserved more than wealth and power. She deserved love, respect, and a home where she was cherished and protected. And I was more than willing to give it all to her.

Despite the heavy weight of disappointment, I felt a spark ignite within me. A refusal to succumb or let regret and despair dictate my path. I had not come this far to crumble now. Helena needed me, and I wouldn't fail them. I wouldn't fail myself.

I was not my father. I would not drown my regrets. Instead, I would face them, learn from them, and rise above them. I ordered the servants to keep my father's bottles empty and to put them in storage. I didn't have time to lose myself in what-ifs. I could only press forward. All I had was the future, and I realized, if I wanted a future with Rowyn, I had to give her everything.

Everything that was within my power to give.

The red glow of the forge illuminated my surroundings, reflecting off the polished surfaces of my tools and casting long, distorted shadows. Sweat trickled down my face, disappearing into the collar of my rough-spun tunic, but I paid it no mind. My focus was solely on my tribute.

As the sparks flew around me, I poured my heartache, my hope, and my love into each strike, shaping the metal and giving form to my unspoken feelings. Rowyn may have been lost to me now, but I wasn't about to give up.

Not on her. Not on us.

As the first light of dawn began to peek over the horizon, I made a silent vow. No matter what, no matter who stood in my way, I would fight for her the way I fought for our future.

The End

STEEL AND FURY

Tempest Rising 4.5

Sam's Story

Elliott VanDruff

Belle Rose Press

Dedication

This book is dedicated to the hidden evil in all of us.

Map of Lyrica

Chapter 1

THE IMAGE OF ROWYN stared back at me from the confines of its ornate frame, her eyes fixed, a dark-blue sea captured in the stillness of the painted canvas. I stared at the portrait, my fingers tracing the intricate details of the imorets around her eyes and the inked roses that bloomed on her neck.

I studied her face, just as I had the first time Agramon presented her image to the council. An anomaly within the empire. He'd claimed she could change the world. He'd claimed we needed to save her life.

Agramon didn't warn that she was like a drug. Once you had a taste; you would crave more and more until the desire to surround yourself with her began to consume you.

The seer had already seen her, and one thing the seer hated most was change.

"This Morganite girl could be our weapon against the revolutions and uprisings plaguing the empire. She could possibly end the drought as we know it. Think of what that could do for your reign," Agramon told the emperor, clutching his staff. I always recognized when he used his powers in the council room, though few of us went unprotected against him. I'd forced the habit of holding my sword pommel and focusing on everything else that plagued my thoughts. But the news of the Morganite had caught my attention, drawing me out of my stupor.

Out of everyone in the council, I knew Morganites best. Most came to the East as fighters on the field of battle. Sure, there were some Morganite slaves at various noble houses, but they were just one of the many different clans of people that dotted Lyrica and the lands around us.

"It is a sign of hope after years of hardship," Agramon finished.

"So, you've taken charge of her then?" the emperor asked, his chin resting on his fist, bored.

Agramon nodded. "She's at Solridge now. But I plan to retrieve her after her Trial by Stone."

"Why Solridge and not here?" Captain Diardo had asked, glancing at the little portrait before passing it to me. "Where we can ensure she is safe."

"The girl is skittish, prone to distrust. Especially with us Lyricans, given her upbringing. Gillius has said that he's worried about her running away. We would be fools to let her sneak off in the middle of the night when her presence here could do so much good," Agramon said silkily, his eyes on other council members.

I grinned ruefully. Wise girl. I ran my finger along the side of the little gilt frame, her blue eyes glaring at me from the confines of canvas and paint.

I forgot to breathe for a moment, unprepared for how beautiful she was. Her black hair hung in curls over her shoulders, a little pert nose, turned up just a bit at the end. I recognized the markings around her eyes and another on her neck. Roses . . . fitting. She certainly had the look of a Morganite. I'd had a fair few of them to command over the years, and I always preferred to have them at my side.

She looked ruthless, those brilliant eyes holding a challenge. My heart stirred with an emotion I couldn't name. Was it affection? No, too soon for that. Curiosity then? Yes, that was a safer bet. Curiosity and a hint of something else—anticipation, perhaps.

The fortune teller's words floated into my mind. She had gazed into the distance. "As the sun bows to the moon, a girl comes. Her heart, a wellspring of tears. With her, the rain shall return, washing away the stains of old sins. From the ashes of the past, a new dawn shall rise. And you, son of Lyrica, you shall find redemption in her tears."

My hand had clenched around the small portrait as the others began to argue. The debate raged on—whether Rowyn should be housed at the capital, under the eyes of the council, or continue training at Solridge.

Agramon was calm amid the flurry of dissenting voices. In my silence during these meetings, I'd always noticed that Agramon relished when the others argued. Dissent in the council meant only good for him. He loved to disrupt, to catch off guard, to fill with doubt. Most of the time. I tried not to speak too much around him, avoiding his notice as much as possible. Since I was usually away during wartime anyway, my plan had so far worked.

"We must tread carefully," Agramon advised, twisting his staff. "Rowyn must be willing. I have already sent a letter to the Morganite leader in Espiria, asking for her guardianship. It would be wise to grant the Espirians pardons and several tracts of Morganian land to ensure Rowyn's future lies in Somme."

So, he was going to trap her as though she were some wild thing to be brought down and tamed. Already I was feeling sorry for the girl. We'd been doing it to the clans for years. The men were forced into the military, the women into servitude.

I glanced back at the portrait. That girl didn't look

like she could be slave to anyone. I looked up at Agramon. I loathed the thought of him breaking her.

I felt oddly protective of the girl. I was sure it had to do with the fortune-teller's words. The nightmares were back, and only a stiff drink before bed held them at bay.

The ghosts...the ghosts were always there. Sometimes it was a noise that brought them back. A smell. The sight of blood, the taste of ash.

I looked to the corner of the room. The weeping woman was huddled there, her body peppered with arrows. A yawning slit visible in her throat. Her children lay before her, their bodies pierced through. The woman held her hands out, blood dribbling down her front.

A wine stain that had appeared on the corner rug was what had first brought her back. The outline of the stain had reminded me of the blood pooling beneath her when we came upon the sight while passing through an Ylirian camp. The household had changed the rug out, but the weeping woman had stayed behind, haunting me through every council meeting. She wasn't the only one.

I couldn't shake the ghosts. I couldn't forget my guilt and regrets. My life had turned into a joyless existence. Yet, the fortune teller had promised that a girl would take it all away. She had given me hope that I would redeem myself.

I would've given anything to make the hauntings disappear.

The emperor, who had been silent until then, nodded. "The land grants and pardons are approved. Solston, you will talk to the seer. Make her stop her attempts on the girl's life. It is paramount that the girl is unharmed."

"Where would she go?" I asked suddenly, looking up from the portrait to Agramon. "When you'd mentioned her before, you said that Gillius had come across her running away, and now you claim that she's thinking of sneaking from the school. Where is she planning to go when she runs?" I asked, more out of curiosity than anything.

Agramon turned his attention to me, a furrow in his brow, probably because I so rarely spoke. I gripped the pommel of my sword when his eyes centered on mine, daring him to try to reach into my mind.

"Gillius said that she mentioned Horan," Agramon said.

"She wouldn't have survived long." The emperor laughed, then nodded at Agramon again. "Excellent work, though I hope Your Grace reconsiders bringing the little Morganite witch to the eastern shore sooner.

The Earl of Nordow is having a gods of a time quelling the discontent there."

As the council began to disperse, I slipped the portrait into my pocket. My heart felt heavier, the weight of the fortune teller's words and the girl's stare overburdening the already weak muscle.

As the day gave way to night, I'd retreated to the solitude of my quarters, the painted image of Rowyn offering silent company, along with the ghosts who dwelled there. I ignored the phantom boy in the corner, his white eyes and misty face unrecognizable, with his head cleaved nearly in two, right down the middle. He'd followed me from my first battle. I ignored him, as I always did, and sat on the bed, my elbows on my knees, observing the portrait once more. The Morganite girl's blue eyes met mine with an intensity that seemed misplaced in her youthful features.

There was something about Agramon's involvement in this that didn't sit well with me. Sorcerers, I'd always maintained, were a necessary evil, especially during war. Their immense power was also dangerously unpredictable, a force that was as likely to harm its wielder as much as its intended target. And Agramon was, in my opinion, the worst of them all.

There was many a moment, as I listened to the Duke of Solin weave tales and lies within the shadows of truth, that I'd wondered why the other nobles abided his company. They knew how devious he was, they simply did not care.

I learned early on that it was best to steer clear of Agramon's games. I followed orders and participated in the council meetings, but I'd always been careful not to get engaged in the power plays. My life in the fields, leading men into battle, was complex enough without adding the nuances of noble squabbles to it.

I ran my fingers over the painted image of Rowyn, my mind filled with thoughts of her. The girl who could bring rain. The girl who, according to the fortune teller, could wash away my past sins. The girl who was now under the "protection" of Agramon.

I'd propped the picture next to the bowl and mirror that sat at the corner of the room, next to my wardrobe and window. I half hoped Agramon didn't have another one. If she did run away, I might just go after her myself. I was the commander of the army, after all, and it was not unheard of for us to go rooting out people for the crown.

It was mere months after that day when Agramon announced his departure to retrieve Rowyn. It was marked vividly in my memory, a reminder of the worry and unease that had seized me.

Driven by concern and a sense of duty, I had

attempted to join Agramon's mission. I recalled pacing the marble floors of the chamber, my mind racing to come up with convincing arguments.

"You might need a squadron of men. If Ayastaren is planning to attack, you shouldn't face it alone."

I had hoped he would see the logic in my proposition, but Agramon, being as stubborn as he was, rejected my offer. His casual dismissal had irritated me, but the underlying fear for Rowyn's safety made me press on. I'd stood my ground, my fists clenched in determination. "You can't take any chances, Agramon. You don't know what you might encounter."

Agramon had stopped, staring at me with narrowed eyes. Belatedly, I placed my hand on the pommel of my sword.

"Why are you obsessing over the girl?" Agramon asked quietly, his head tilted to the side.

He knew. He knew every thought I'd had of Rowyn, seeing her face each morning as I got ready for the day and every night as I got ready for bed. I knew it was stupid and silly, an infatuation that I'd allowed to grow despite never even meeting the girl, but there was something about her. The way she glared at the world as though she could banish us all to the depths.

I cursed myself for being so careless. "The emperor is spending a lot of money . . ."

"You don't care about any of that," Agramon said, stepping closer. "I'm warning you now, Butcher. You better keep your distance from that girl. I'll not have you sniffing around, distracting her."

"It is the Emperor's Council who is taking charge of her welfare. I'm only trying to do my part," I insisted, turning away. If I made it into a bigger deal, then Agramon would press harder, and that's not how to win a battle with him.

I left him standing in the hall and returned to my rooms where I paced . . . for weeks . . . until I heard that they'd returned. I'd called some men and made my way to the docks immediately. I could wait no longer.

I had to see her.

It was raining before we even made it there. I quickened my pace at the sound of thunder. My eyes found her despite the crowd. A figure in white sitting atop a horse with another Morganite girl clutching her back. The rain had drenched the sorceress, soaking her gown, revealing the outline of her corset and legs while she straddled the horse. Her hair clung to her thin arms and pale shoulders as she brandished the sword, shouting at Agramon. Then she turned that hardened gaze to me, and it took everything I had not to sweep her up on the spot.

She looked so small. The bones in her cheeks and

on her chest seemed sharper than her portrait. My breath hitched in my throat. The Nightlands seemed to have ravaged her form.

I hated the fact that the others could see so much of her. They shouldn't get to ogle. I took off my cloak and covered her, making sure that she and her maid were taken care of before I took charge of bringing them back to the castle.

I glanced over my shoulder. Rowyn was taking in the views of the city, her eyes curious as they swept over the buildings and turrets. The clouds dissipated quickly and the eye of Sol returned, warming the puddles into clouds of steam.

Despite the warmth, she continued to wear my cloak. My mind played with the idea of her wrapped in something of mine. When I watched for her at the feast that night, I'd half hoped she brought it with her . . . or even wore it. Of course, Agramon would've never allowed that . . . no. She was wearing something far too revealing that she looked uncomfortable in. Jealousy seemed to whisper in my ear as I glared at the other eyes that followed her throughout the room.

She walked with Del around the hall, and I lost sight of her between nobility as she tried to smile. It didn't look natural. It didn't look like the picture at all, in fact. The hardened gaze from the market was gone, replaced by something much more humbling . . . fear.

But then, as the night grew late, she'd found my hiding spot, as though my mind had called to her. A gift from the gods. She'd come to the balcony and seen *me*.

I dedicated weeks to getting close to her, trying to show her that she could trust me. Sometimes I even doubted myself. Why should I drag her into the darkness with me? Why should I share the burden of my name and what I'd done with her?

But the ghosts had all but gone, her presence seemingly repelling them. No longer did the man with the missing legs drag himself towards me in the banquet hall. No longer did the drowned child lurk at the edge of my bathwater. Rowyn had chased them all away.

And the way she made me feel . . . it was intoxicating.

I stirred just thinking about our time in Bruin, where I had Rowyn all to myself, sinking into her every night, hearing her beg, her dewy skin trembling beneath my hands. I could never seem to get enough. The thirst for more plagued me as I went about my day, counting down the minutes until I could have her in my arms once again. It felt as though nothing could dim my joy.

Of course, it was too good to last. Duty, as always,

got in the way of my happiness. I had to be firm with how I ran Bruin, otherwise the soldiers and fieldmen would take advantage. Now that the threat of war was over, I planned to turn my focus back on farming, and I needed the fields to work smoothly.

Rowyn had a soft heart. It was sweet, really, one of the things I loved most about her. She was soft and kind-hearted despite her hard exterior. But I had to do my job, and I knew, over time, it was just something she would get used to. I knew plenty of women who'd balked at what their husbands did at first until it just became part of their lives. Rowyn just needed more time. Time Agramon refused to give me.

But she'd agreed to marry me.

She'd agreed to marry *me*.

And though her agreement had felt like a victory, a triumphant validation of my feelings, in the midst of my elation, there lay a cruel twist—the knowledge that her heart might belong to someone else.

I understood, then, how love could be both a blessing and a curse, a source of joy and a wellspring of sorrow. I had won her hand, yes, but I desired more.

With Rowyn, I wanted everything.

Chapter 2

THE TAILOR'S QUARTERS were a flurry of activity, the air thick with the scent of fresh fabric and hot iron. I stood still, my body draped in the black-and-red overcoat that would serve as my wedding attire. The rich fabric was smooth and plush, strewn with intricate red decorations that were the result of hours of careful craftsmanship. The most impressive part was the symbol of the bear proudly displayed on the chest. It wasn't easy to rise from meager beginnings and join the class of nobility, but by the gods I'd done it.

I smoothed the coat over my chest.

I was the one who conquered Yliria.

I was the one who protected Rowyn from the machinations of the most power-hungry man at court.

I was the one who she said yes to. Her young crush might be back to make things difficult for me, but it was me who she envisioned a future with. Otherwise, she wouldn't have said yes. I was sure of it.

I wished I could've shown that Everett boy my memories of Bruin. The sounds that Rowyn made when I had her sprawled beneath me in a gasping, writhing mess. She'd told me one night, wrapped in *my* arms, about how they'd both been their first times. At first, I refused to believe it. Her, sure, but a consul's son? Not likely. Still, the Western Empire was more conservative. I supposed it could've been possible.

What was more likely was that the honorable Destrian Everett lied to her. Rowyn's presence in Morgania would make him great if he could ensnare her to return to the wilds of the North. But no, that's not where she belonged. She belonged with *me* in comfort and wealth, where I could worship her as the goddess she fucking was.

I wished the quinquennial wasn't so gods-damned long. I supposed it was too much to ask to have her old lover out of Somme by the time we made our vows. I hoped fervently that he would leave on the morrow, with the rest of the Morganians who were being returned to their homeland. Perhaps he expected her to run to him, to go back on her word.

But Lord Destrian didn't know Rowyn as well as he thought he did. I wished I could tell him what I really thought. Or rather, show him the memories of how much she needed me in Bruin. How happy it made her to warm *my* bed. I wanted her with such longing, there was no way that I would let a little boy from the West snatch her from my hands. She was *mine*.

Around me, the tailor fussed. His nimble fingers tweaked a seam here, adjusted a cuff there, his eyes appraising. I tried to keep as still as possible, though my mind was anything but. It was filled with thoughts of Rowyn, my soon-to-be wife.

For a year I had half a hope that Agramon would find a reason to get rid of the new Consul of Helena. Imagine my surprise and fucking delight that he never saw a reason to. So *I* was the one who had to watch them dance at the masquerade as he mooned all over her. He was a good actor, I'd give him that, but I saw right through him. It was the way he looked at Rowyn, with greed in his eyes.

The same way Agramon looked at her.

The same way I probably did.

But Rowyn didn't have to insult me over it. Everyone in the entire room knew who they were. I felt everyone looking at me, some with pity, others in jest.

Leaning on a cane, Captain Diardo stumped toward me, his eyes on the tailor who was pinning the back of the coat. Diardo was a good man, a loyal friend, and one of the few who knew of the storm brewing within me. Our eyes met, and he raised an eyebrow, a silent question. I simply nodded.

"Are you sure this is what you want, Sam?" Diardo asked, his tone soft.

I swallowed, my eyes drifting to the bear emblem on my chest. I'd fought for my title. I'd fought for my country. Now, I was going to fight for her.

"I want her," I replied. "That's enough for me."

But even as I spoke the words, I couldn't silence the nagging voice in the back of my mind. The image of Rowyn with Destrian haunted me—the way she gazed up at him as they danced. The seeds of doubt were sown, threatening to shatter the façade of calm I was desperately clinging to.

"Baron," Diardo began, his tone shifting into one of seriousness, "why have the wedding so soon? I just don't understand the rush."

"The emperor requested it," I said with a shrug. "The sooner the better, in my mind."

"I don't trust her, Sam," he insisted. "Would it be so hard just to let her go?"

His words trailed off as he caught my glare. I was anything but lovesick. I was furious. I was . . . jealous. A sentiment I'd never truly understood until now.

I kept seeing them together, Rowyn and Destrian. Their stolen moments seared into my mind, sparking a resentment that burned within, little embers that warmed my insides. I wanted her back. I wanted her to look at me the way she used to, with that glint of love and warmth, not the fear that had replaced it.

Rowyn had nothing to fear from me.

I would protect her.

Diardo sighed, leaning heavily on his cane as he watched me. "You're taking this too far, Sam. We've fought battles together—seen things that most people would never dare to dream of. You're strong—capable. You don't need to trap her to prove that. This . . . this is beneath you."

I frowned, the weight of his words hitting harder than I expected. He was right. This was beneath me, but I was past thinking. I just wanted her to be mine, fully.

"I can handle my own affairs, Diardo," I growled, jerking my arm away from the old tailor who flinched in surprise. "I don't need your approval or your pity. Especially considering the shambles your own love life is in."

It was an unnecessary cruelty, but Diardo knew well that I wasn't the only member of the Emperor's Council prone to obsession. He'd been in love with the empress for years. As far as I could tell, it was unrequited, but I never quite knew what to think of her. She seemed so clever and prone to deviousness. Even if she did pursue Captain Diardo, I would question her feelings about him. She played the game too well for me to trust her.

Silence blanketed the room, Diardo's gaze never wavering. He sighed, a weary, resigned sound. "Is this really who you wish to become?"

My grip tightened around the fabric of my coat. I wanted to dismiss his words, to tell him he was wrong, but the truth of his statement rang in my ears. This wasn't me. The fear, the uncertainty, the anger . . . they were all consuming me.

"She's changed you," Diardo said gruffly, "and not for the better, my friend."

My gaze fell on the bear emblem once more, the symbol of my status and strength. I was losing myself in this battle for her. I was becoming the very thing I swore I'd never become: a man controlled by his emotions.

"Perhaps you're right," I said quietly, "but it's too late now."

Diardo sighed again, a sad look in his eyes. "It's never too late, Sam. Remember that."

Perhaps, Diardo was right. Perhaps, it wasn't too late.

My hands balled into fists, the white of my knuckles stark against the black of the overcoat. The feeling of powerlessness was suffocating. It gnawed at me, filling me with a sense of helplessness that was all too familiar.

I felt a rush of anger and resentment. Why did it have to be this way? Why did it have to be him? I was offering her everything—a title, power, protection . . . love. Wasn't that enough? What did he have that I didn't?

The questions tormented me, gnawing at my sanity, pushing me to the brink of despair. I was trapped in a tempest of doubt and insecurity, one that threatened to consume me.

The day after tomorrow, I would marry the girl of my dreams, even though her heart belonged to another. But it didn't have to be that way.

I just had to win her back.

Chapter 3

T HE EMPEROR'S BANQUET was a whirl of color and sound, but amid the splendor and the laughter, only one figure caught my eye. Rowyn stood like a beacon in the room, wearing a red silk dress that clung to her form, leaving nothing to the imagination. Her loose, wild curls tumbled down her shoulders, the way I had always loved them. The room was buzzing with activity, but my attention was solely hers, my gaze drifting to the familiar shadow falcon marking on her bare back. Agramon liked to show it off every chance he got, as though bragging that he'd tamed some wild thing.

A pang of another memory hit me as I recalled how that tattoo looked beneath me in my bed at Bruin, the faint light of dawn illuminating the inked bird on her pale skin. The sight of her arching under my touch . . . I shook my head, pushing the memories away. This was not the time or place to get lost in the past.

I refocused on her, and I noticed Mellan Lyon, her faux lover whom she used to placate Agramon and Duke Roland Lyon of Ayastaren, her sworn enemy. The sight of them talking, his lean frame bending toward her, sparked a fire of jealousy. I knew Mellan was nothing more than a friend to her, but his sudden closeness with Everett ever since the quinquennial began was enough to put me on edge. I'd been surprised when Mellan stood up with Destrian to present his sword to the emperor. Was he now acting as intermediary? Mellan and I had been somewhat friendly before, but now? No longer. He'd clearly chosen a side.

I watched as he gestured animatedly, his face a picture of seriousness. She listened intently, her brow furrowed as she nodded. It sent a prickle of irritation along my spine.

I clenched my fist, my jaw setting. I'd already won. Rowyn was going to be mine, legally and in every other way that mattered. I just needed to hold on. To be patient.

Drawing in a deep breath, I picked up my glass and took a sip, my gaze never leaving her. My beautiful, tantalizing, infuriatingly stubborn Rowyn.

I thought of my past marriage proposals to her— the first one had been too abrupt and unplanned. I hadn't given her time to think or adjust. Then, there was the second proposal, which was interrupted by duty. It was like fate was laughing in my face. But this time, I had planned everything meticulously. And for the first time, everything seemed to be falling into place.

I would let nothing get in the way.

"Did Agramon choose that gown?" I asked, coming up behind Rowyn as I glared at Mellan's retreating figure from over her shoulder.

"Of course," was the reply.

"I like the color," I admitted, trying to hide the intensity of my feelings. I let my eyes travel down the length of her body, a faint smile on my lips. Just a few more days.

I'd half expected to have to rip her out of Lord Destrian's arms once more. I was happy to be wrong. "I know the night is young, but I would be honored if you would come with me. There are things I wish to say."

"Of course, my lord," she replied, accepting my hand with grace. My heart thundered through my chest as I led her through the hall, those tiny fingers encased in mine. I could feel the power from her stone thrumming on the back of her hand. I resisted the urge to caress the stone along with her fingers. I tried to avoid touching her stones altogether, well aware of the power within.

Eyes followed us throughout the hall. I began to understand Agramon's enjoyment of seeing other noblemen grow envious of you. They were jealous because she was *mine*. There was no question about it anymore. I couldn't help the pride that seemed to stiffen my spine.

I saw a flash of movement from the corner of my eyes. Destrian Everett stepped out from an alcove to glare at me. But I didn't let it get to me, not this time. I tightened my grip on her hand and led her out of the banquet hall and through the maze of corridors toward my quarters.

I had done it right this time. I could feel it. It was my turn to make her happy—to show her that I could be the man she needed. It was my turn to win.

I unlocked the doors, revealing the room beyond, which had been painstakingly arranged for the perfect proposal. I'd prepared everything down to the last detail, from the flickering candles to the freshly picked roses from the empress's garden.

I hoped to gift her with a memory that would replace the old ones—the ones filled with hurt and doubt. I yearned to see the smile that always managed to take my breath away.

"Come in," I called, opening the door wider.

"What is this?" Rowyn asked, her stunningly blue eyes taking in the dimly lit room adorned with flickering candles and strewn with rose petals. As her gaze swept over candlelight, there was no spark of surprise, no softening of her eyes. Her face remained unreadable. The knot of anticipation in my stomach twisted into a bitter sting of disappointment. Had I misjudged? Misread what she would like?

I couldn't falter. I had to see it through. Gathering my courage, I let go of her hand and dropped to one knee. A wave of memories rushed at me—the failed attempts, the heartbreaks, the missteps. This was my chance to rewrite it all. "I told you that one of these times, I would get it right," I murmured, my voice thick with emotion. "Rowyn of Morgania, will you marry me?"

Rowyn tried to smile. How I wished it had been a genuine one. It had never been easy to make Rowyn smile, but if I could manage it before, I could manage it again.

"I already told you I would."

"I know," I replied, my voice rougher than I had intended. My hand fumbled in my pocket, pulling out the signet ring—a bear rearing on a red field. A part of my lineage now, my life that I wanted to build with her. "But we need this if we are to start again." With trembling hands, I grasped hers, sliding the ring onto her finger. As she looked down at it my heart pounded anxiously in my chest.

"It is lovely," she commented, her voice lacking the warmth I yearned for. Her hand dropped back to her side, the ring catching the candlelight. "Thank you for the gift."

A sharp pain tore through me at her restrained response. "You are not pleased," I concluded, my chest tightening. I was a fool to think it would be so easy.

"It isn't that." She bit her lip, a habit I had come to associate with her contemplation. "The problems between us, they remain."

I was wound too tight. The anger came far too quickly. "How?" I demanded, rising to my feet. "The Morganites are gone from Bruin. That was the bargain. I refuse to be forever punished for doing my job."

"That's just it," she countered, her voice holding a hint of accusation. "It was the same with the war and the conscripted men running away and putting the weakest on the front lines."

"What would you have me do?" I asked, my hands outstretched in desperation. "What more can I do to get you to trust me again?"

Her answer came quickly. "Relinquish command as general."

"If that is what my emperor wishes, then I will gladly step down," I managed to say, my voice guarded. A part of me recoiled at the thought, my desperation to win her back warring with my duty. How could she ask my life's work, everything I've strived for, to be thrown away?

"The soldiers hate me, and war has already turned you into a villain once," she added, her words stabbing me like knives. "I ask that it not turn you into a villain again."

"And what of your Lord Destrian?" The words slipped out before I could stop them. I hadn't wanted her to think of him while with me, and here I was bringing him up. I must be a glutton for punishment. "Would you ask this of him?" It was a cheap shot, and I knew it.

The sight of Rowyn in that red gown, like a goddess brought to life, was driving me to the brink. I *needed* her. She had to see that.

"No," Rowyn replied, her look hardened. "But I'm not marrying him."

Her words offered a small glimmer of hope, but I was far too wrapped up in my emotions to fully grasp it. My mind filled with thoughts of Destrian, of the way he looked at Rowyn, of how she reacted to him. I could taste the sour note of jealousy. He had no cause to speak to her anymore. No reason to touch her. It was bad enough he got to look at her.

I brushed a lock of hair off Rowyn's cheek, the soft strands whispering against my fingertips. "After the quinquennial, we will return to Bruin, and everything will return to normal. I promise."

I was excited to create a life for her in Bruin. Hugh and Winnie already loved her. She could hire her own maid, study combat as much as she desired. Even if another war was called, Rowyn could go with me...her potential for battle magic was great, and I already knew that she fought well on the battlefield.

It would work for a time, before we had children, at least. I could wait a few years more, if that was what she wanted. Then, perhaps, we could settle more at home.

It was all planned out and I was sure it was a life Rowyn would love.

"Where you hid my eyes from everything I would hate to see about what you do and how Bruin works?" she questioned, lifting the miniature portrait of her from between the candles and running her fingers over the familiar features.

I couldn't resist the urge to wrap my arms around her, the warmth of her body seeping through the thin fabric of her dress. I rested my chin on her shoulder, trying to ignore the fluttering in my chest. "I love you. At least give me a chance to make you happy."

"I am," she said, her voice barely above a whisper. "I will give you that chance, but I'm telling you what would make me happy."

"That's all I ask." I tightened my hold on her. "Until that day comes," I whispered, my breath fanning against her neck, "my love will be enough for the both of us."

Everything in my body begged Rowyn to stay as she walked out of the door. She left me there, amongst the perfume of the candles and rose petals, mourning the loss of her warmth. As I snuffed out the candles, I startled, seeing the boy with the ax wound in his skull lurking in the corner, his form barely visible through the wafting smoke.

It had been months since I'd seen any of my ghosts. Months of blessed respite from the phantoms who followed me. But they still lurked within the shadows, watching me warily and waiting for their chance to return.

Chapter 4

THE DOCK WAS A CACOPHONY of noise and movement. Soldiers milled around, coordinating the loading of the navy boats. Morganians, forcibly conscripted and now being repatriated, were boarding, their faces a mix of relief and wariness. Rowyn was watching the crowds below, looking for Arden, her pet shadow falcon that she'd given to Luc.

As the Morganians filed onto the boat, I tried to let Rowyn have her moment of acceptance. Destrian's oath's gift was an allowance to take Rowyn's clansmen back home, and away from Bruin. Though I secretly mourned the loss of some of my strongest fighters, Rowyn's hand was far more precious to me. It was a blessing really. There would be no reason for her to balk at living in Bruin now.

I had naively thought Lord Destrian would ask for Rowyn, given his obsession with her. That was what everyone else seemed to want at the palace, despite the emperor's refusal to entertain such a demand. I had almost wished Everett would make the request, to see him humiliated in front of the court. But when he asked for the return of all of Morgania's conscripted men, I was taken aback.

I'd watched Rowyn's eyes shimmer, her gaze fixed on Destrian as he stood before the emperor. My heart tightened in my chest as painful jealousy bubbled within. I hated how she responded to him. Even her body seemed to lean towards the Consul of Helena, as though her very blood sought him out.

Rowyn, my Rowyn, had been slipping away slowly and inevitably. I'd seen it in her gaze, felt it in the growing distance between us, sensed it in her words. My chest constricted with each passing moment, my heart yearning for what seemed to slowly slip through my fingers.

"Do you really think it's a good idea to send an entire host of angry and seasoned warriors to Morgania? We know nothing of the boy's loyalties," Agramon had spat when we'd convened in the council's chambers.

Finally, the decision was placed on me. Of course I would refuse. I had to farm my own land. I needed the recruits for the army. Most importantly, I desperately needed Rowyn to have no cause to return to that damned boy. I couldn't afford to gamble my armed force.

But then *she* begged me to reconsider.

"You asked me to marry you," Rowyn had said. "If you gift me this, I will accept."

A flicker of hope ignited within me. My mind had raced with a flurry of emotions. A pledge. A promise. A chance. I found myself staring at her, my mind swimming with possibilities of a future I'd been sure was lost.

Rowyn's voice was quiet, but it rang in my ears as clear as a battle cry. A marriage proposal. An acceptance. The world seemed to stop, my heart hammering in my chest. I could barely comprehend what was happening—the enormity of it. But there had been one thing that came through loud and clear—Rowyn, my Rowyn, would finally be mine.

I clenched my jaw, looking at her with newfound hope. The disappointment, the jealousy, the despair . . . it all seemed to fade away, replaced by a rising tide of elation. "If I let your countrymen go, you would pledge yourself to me?" I asked, just to confirm. I needed to hear it again, to be sure I'd heard correctly.

Her eyes met mine, and I could see the truth in her gaze. "You need only name the date." Her voice was a soft whisper, but it was the most powerful thing I'd ever heard.

Suddenly, my world was no longer crumbling. My hope, which I'd thought was hanging by a thread, surged with newfound strength.

I had an answer for the emperor, my mind made

up. "Send the men home," I declared, my eyes lingering on Rowyn. A sense of victory had washed over me, the sweetest I'd ever tasted. I was going to win her, after all. Against all odds, in spite of everything, I had won.

Agramon was protesting, but his words were a distant murmur. Nothing mattered anymore except for Rowyn and the future we would build together. I had a purpose now, a goal. It was as if I was awaking from a long slumber, renewed vigor pulsing through my veins.

With every fiber of my being, I was ready to fight for her. I would face any enemy, overcome any obstacle, and endure any hardship. In that moment, I knew without a doubt that nothing could stand in our way. Rowyn was going to be mine, and I was going to be hers. No one, not even Destrian Everett, could take that away from me.

I stole another glance at her on the dock, her eyes somber. My jaw clenched as the familiar stab of jealousy wracked me. But buried underneath the pain was a stubborn resolution. I would win her back. I had to. And if it took every last breath in my body, I would fight for her—for us.

THE THREE OF US—Agramon, Rowyn, and I—made our way back toward the palace after the Morganite's ships disappeared over the horizon. When we reached their quarters, I took a deep breath, bracing myself for what was sure to be a fucking torment of a conversation.

"I think it's time we moved Rowyn's things to my rooms," I announced, trying to keep my voice steady. I could already anticipate the objections and the disdain in Agramon's tone, but I was past caring. I would stand my ground. She was to be my wife.

Mine.

Agramon's expression curdled. "Do you think that's necessary?" he drawled, oozing condescension. "You're not married yet."

I set my jaw, my gaze meeting his with a challenging glint. "She will be by this time tomorrow," I retorted. I wouldn't let Agramon's snide remarks get to me. This was not about his endless ego.

"Sam's right," Rowyn said, striding into the receiving room before opening the door to her bedroom. "Let's do this now so I don't have to worry about it tomorrow."

I hoped she wasn't worried about tomorrow. If she really wanted to wait, I would order a host of servants to march in and grab all of her things whenever she required. It was no matter to me. I just . . . I wanted an excuse to stay by her side in that moment. I wanted to feel as though she cared about what was about to happen and thought of it not with pain, but with the excitement that I felt.

With a grunt of displeasure, Agramon backed off. There was no denying the impending wedding. He might not like it, but I didn't think he could stop it.

Gree, Rowyn's handmaid, entered at that moment. She'd never liked me. In Bruin, she'd always shot me the most hateful looks. But it didn't matter because as soon as the quinquennial was over, Rowyn was coming home to Bruin with me. She could choose a new handmaid.

"This couldn't have waited until after the wedding?" Gree grumbled, her wrinkled face set in a permanent frown. She glared at me with distaste as she began shuffling through Rowyn's things, her movements rigid and curt.

Rowyn shot me a quick, apologetic glance before she joined Gree, carefully sorting through her belongings. She seemed quieter, more restrained, around me. Her guarded demeanor puzzled me. I wished she would look at me, really look at me, like she used to. I wished she would let me in again.

Gree huffed, muttering under her breath as she worked, her displeasure evident in every move. I tried to ignore her, focusing my attention on Rowyn instead. She moved with an elegance that took my breath away, every gesture exuding a grace that seemed to be woven into her very being. Yet her eyes . . . they were different, filled with a caution that had never been there before. I frowned, my heart sinking a little.

Once we'd gathered enough, the three of us made our way to my quarters, Rowyn's arms filled with her dresses and Gree trailing behind us. As we walked through the hallways, the stony silence was interrupted only by Gree's incessant huffing. It was almost comical, but the tension hanging over us was too tight to laugh.

Entering my room felt different this time. The usual sense of solitude was gone, replaced by a heady mix of anticipation and nervousness. As Gree began to hang dresses in the wardrobe that I'd emptied, I found myself watching Rowyn, my gaze lingering on her. There was an undeniable beauty to this moment, a sense of rightness that washed over me.

After Gree left, the silence in the room seemed to deepen. It was just Rowyn and me. She looked around, her gaze flitting across the walls, her fingers trailing along the top of my wash table.

I studied her, as if memorizing her every gesture, every soft curve, and every expression. I noticed how her eyes lit up when she caught sight of the vase of roses on her side of the bed. I'd hoped she'd like them. I'd gone out of my way to make the room welcoming for her, to make it a place she could call home.

I had cleared the weapons off the walls. The bed linens were new. The room was cleaner than it had ever been. It wasn't just mine anymore. It was ours.

"Rowyn," I began, my voice soft. She turned to look at me, her blue eyes meeting mine. Her expression was guarded, cautious, but I saw a hint of something else there. A glimmer of hope, maybe. Or was it acceptance?

"I want you to feel comfortable here," I said, gesturing around the room. "Make any changes you want."

Rowyn was silent for a moment before giving me a small nod. "Thank you, Sam," she murmured. "I appreciate that."

She was still cold, though. Far too cold.

I stepped toward her, my hands on her shoulders. "Don't worry about tomorrow," I murmured, studying her eyes. "We'll do the ceremony, then as soon as the quinquennial is over, we'll leave for Bruin."

"Bruin?" she asked, resigned.

"Is that not what you want?" The words slipped from my lips before I could stop them, catching me off guard. I had assumed, perhaps wrongly, that she would want to go back there, where we had been happiest. She hated court.

"I . . ." She trailed off, her gaze falling to the floor. "I'm not sure," she confessed after a moment. Not sure? How could she not be sure?

I opened my mouth to ask her what she meant, to question her about her reservations, but then I saw it. The hesitant tremor in her lips.

I wanted to ask her then if she really wanted to do this. If she wanted to marry me—to tie herself to me.

The words teetered on the tip of my tongue, begging to be released. But I couldn't. I couldn't risk it. I wanted her too much. Needed her too much. I couldn't bear to hear her say she had doubts, that she might not want this as much as I did.

So, I swallowed the words, burying them deep within me. Instead, I tightened my grip on her shoulders and offered her a reassuring smile. "We'll figure it out," I promised.

It was all I could do. All I could offer her in that moment. Hope and reassurance. A promise of a future, of a life, together.

Feeling a surge of desperation, I found myself tilting her chin upward, my lips closing over hers in a heated kiss. She was taken aback at first, stiffening in my arms, but then she relaxed, her lips tentatively moving against mine. It was a familiar dance, one that we'd performed countless times, yet it held an almost painful intensity.

I deepened the kiss, drinking her in as my hand threading through her hair, her soft curls tangling around my fingers. The taste of her, the smell of her, like rain and flowers and darkness—it was intoxicating. It filled me with a yearning that drowned out everything else.

Rowyn tried to back away but I followed, my body pressing against hers. But just as my hands began to travel down her hips, she pushed my arms gently away, a flush coloring her cheeks.

"Sam," she breathed out, her chest rising and falling rapidly. Her eyes were wide, full of surprise . . . and something else. Was that fear? That couldn't be fear. I wasn't Agramon. I would never hurt her. I *could never* hurt her. She had to know that.

A knot formed in my stomach, my heart beating wildly against my chest. "Rowyn," I pleaded, my voice rough. "Stay. Stay the night."

"No, Sam," she replied firmly, her gaze refusing to meet mine. "You will have me every other night . . . please just leave me this one."

I nodded, forcing a smile. "Of course. I understand."

As she left, my smile faded, replaced by a grimace. I could taste the bitterness of defeat as the ghost of the boy stepped closer, drawn by Rowyn's absence.

Chapter 5

I SUPPOSED IT WAS AN HONOR to have my wedding as the grand opening of the Crystal Temple. Delise of Marion had done well, for it was a pretty enough place. Shafts of sunlight streamed through the towering crystalline windows, rainbows reaching across the temple floor in a luminescent dance. The altar was draped in fragrant summer blossoms, and Miyu had ensured that flowers burst from every corner, their blooms bright and cheerful, perfuming the air with their heady, calming scent.

The highborns had turned up, looking like peacocks with their silks and gems. They chattered like birds, too, filling the temple with a constant buzz. Outside, the city folks were making a racket, waving whatever they could get their hands on.

The Sons of Sol, the cult that had taken a disliking to Rowyn and the empress, were out there, too, spouting their nonsense, but I wasn't going to let them spoil the day.

This was our day. My wedding day. And despite the yammering nobles, the overly perfumed temple, the cheers from the city, and the damned cult shouting in the distance, I was ready.

They could all watch as I made my vows. I was a rock in the face of a storm.

Let them come.

Let them see.

Let them talk.

Then, the sight of Lord Destrian standing defiantly at the periphery cemented my boots to the entrance. A surge of ire and envy snaked around my heart, sudden and uninvited.

Not today.

"Captain Diardo," I spat, severing the silence with the accuracy of a masterfully sharpened sword. "Escort the Consul of Helena out."

Diardo swiveled his gaze to meet mine. A thick brow hitched in surprise before his eyes traced my stare toward the source of my anger. For a beat, Diardo held his peace, his gaze dissecting Destrian. "Such a move may backfire," he cautioned in a muted grumble.

"Backfire?" I echoed. A cynical snort escaped my control. "And when have we started to tread lightly around noble sensibilities, Captain?"

A soft clinking resonated as Diardo adjusted his position, the sound of armor scraping against armor. "Expel Everett now, and it's akin to announcing to this crowd that you suspect lingering sentiments between him and Rowyn."

Heat prickled my skin as I remembered Everett's scathing words from our last encounter. "How could a monster like you seriously expect her to love you back?" he'd asked.

"How can a boy like you know what love is?" I'd fired back, eyes burning into his. My chest tightened even now at the recollection. "How can someone like you seriously think you can protect her? You've already failed multiple times by my count. Me? I've never failed her. I *won't* fail her."

I'd saved her at the capital when Agramon was attempting to bend Rowyn to his will.

I was the one who ensured she continued weapons training.

I was the one who rescued her from those raiders near Bruin.

I was the one who made her feel safe when the world was ready to turn against her.

Where was her Lord Destrian when the vultures had come?

No, he'd abandoned her to the empire. He had no right to pretend he actually cared for the girl.

I shook the memory off, pushing back the vestiges of the past. Today was about Rowyn and me. Today was about us. Not Lord Destrian's unfounded accusations on my honor, nor his foolish hopes.

And yet, as I stood there, under the arch of summer blooms at the altar, unease slithered within me. I couldn't help but be assailed by a cruel thought, a haunting whisper of "what if."

What if she didn't come?

What if Agramon had found a way to ensnare her once more?

What if Lord Destrian managed to spirit her away?

My fingers clenched at my side. The cool metal of my blade pressed against my palm. I had let her go last night, had given her the space she needed and respected her request for solitude. But the worry lingered like a gnawing pestilence.

I should've been more insistent on her staying the night. I should've done more to ensure that she would be ready for our wedding day. My desire for her trust may well have led to my undoing. My jaw tightened as the whispers of the crowd reached my ears, their hushed tones and speculative glances breeding a storm of paranoia.

Yet in this swirling tempest of anxiety, Destrian's presence was an odd anchor, a backhanded solace. It was proof that he was not out there trying to pull Rowyn away, not whispering sweet nothings or tempting her with the promise of another life.

Rowyn would come. She had to.

She promised.

I drew a long breath, tasted the intoxicating perfume of the flowers, and swallowed my fears. The whispers of the crowd turned into a muted hum as my focus crystallized on the archway, waiting for her arrival.

Let them come.

Let them see.

Let them talk.

Rowyn would be here. And together, we would silence them all.

With the hushed reverence only royalty could command, the emperor and his family paraded through the temple, their magnificence cloaked in the radiant sunlight that painted the altar. With each step, their jeweled attire shimmered, casting an array of light around them. The emperor's gaze met mine, a firm nod and a smile of encouragement washing over his golden features. I tried to mirror his warmth, my lips pulling into a strained smile.

The doors swung open again, and a hush fell over the congregation. My breath hitched when Agramon appeared, but it was the figure beside him that stole my breath away.

Rowyn.

She was a vision, the embodiment of my dreams. White roses nestled in her black hair, reminding me of the night that she'd slept in my bed, leaving a stream of rose petals in her wake. I'd practically rolled in the sheets after, burying my face in the pillow and inhaling the perfume of her, drinking her in.

And then, I noticed the sword, Iranoct. A gift from Lord Destrian. I tried to smother the jealousy. It was her weapon, a part of her past and her strength. I would give her another sword, one from me, as soon as we returned to Bruin.

As the ceremonial music swelled, Agramon offered his arm to Rowyn. Each step she took was a promise, a step closer to our shared future. Her eyes roved over the crowd.

I could tell the moment Rowyn saw him. Lord Destrian. Her gaze lingered, and my heart dropped. "Don't," I silently pleaded. "Look back at me."

Finally, her gaze slid away from Lord Destrian, and as if guided by invisible threads, her eyes met mine. As she continued her walk toward me, toward the altar and our waiting future, I knew, deep in my bones, that despite the whispers, the lingering doubts, and the mistakes of our pasts, she was mine.

Excitement, a vibrancy I'd never before felt, throbbed in my veins when Rowyn finally reached me.

Her dainty fingers slipped into mine, grounding me. She looked anxious, her eyes wide and her breathing shallow. But I knew it wasn't me who unsettled her; it was the crowd, the expectation, the glaring spotlight of attention.

I could see it—sense it—the unease that rippled through her like waves crashing against a rocky shore. But it didn't matter. Soon it would be just us. No pomp. No prying eyes. Just Rowyn and me. The way it was supposed to be. The way we were best.

"Love," I whispered, gently squeezing her tiny hand, careful not to hurt it against the black opal embedded in the back of her palm. "Look at me." She raised her head, gazing up at me with those blue eyes that seemed to melt me every fucking time.

As Solston Gowther raised his arms, a heavy and profound silence fell over the congregation. His words echoed through the temple, a declaration of our union before the eye of Sol. I stood rigid as the Solston traced the symbol of blessing on my forehead.

The ceremony unfolded in a rhythm, each step methodically performed and echoing with significance. We stepped to a pedestal filled with water, the soothing words of blessing resonating in my ears as the Solston traced another symbol on my forehead.

Once the blessings ended, Solston Gowther turned

to Rowyn, and her vows echoed in the temple. I held her hand tighter, reassuring her with the squeeze. She responded with a vow that rang clear and resolute.

Then it was my turn, and I choked like an idiot, a lump forming in my throat. I swallowed and reaffirmed my vows louder. From this day forward, Rowyn was mine, and I was hers.

A hum of excitement surged through the hall. Solston Gowther's raised hands fell like a curtain, the murmur quickly amplifying into a deafening roar. I frowned, perplexed, as I saw the attention of the nobles shift from us, their gazes riveted on the sky. We were in the middle of the ceremony. What had drawn their attention?

I followed their gaze upward, and the sight that met my eyes sent a chill through me. The moon was drifting across the sun. The temple's light waned, casting us all in eerie half-darkness.

Around me, voices whispered in fear with questions of curses and forsaken gods. A momentary panic welled up inside me. I looked down at Rowyn, my hand wrapping around hers tighter.

Her eyes were panicked, staring behind the Solston. I twisted, one hand clenched in hers, the other going to the pommel of my sword.

A scream. I think it was Empress Lesedi as she

pulled away from her husband, grabbing her children as Mem drew both curved blades, her dark eyes wide and frantic. The emperor was slumped in his seat, an arrow lodged in his throat.

I drew my sword, turning my gaze back to the crowd.

The beautiful crystal walls exploded in a shower of glimmering shards. I felt the grip on my hand loosen and then . . . emptiness. Rowyn was gone.

Chapter 6

PANIC SEIZED ME, a mad, frenzied terror that stole my breath. I struggled to my feet, shielding my face from the raining glass fragments, my eyes desperately scanning the chaos.

By the gods, if she was hurt, there would be no end to the depravity I would sow on whoever the fuck did this. Where was she?

The glass and smoke masked my view. I shielded my eyes. Where was she? Didn't she know that the safest place to be was at my side? Had someone taken her?

The memory of finding her gone after the road skirmish in Bruin tore through me.

The panic.

The terror.

The absolute fucking world ending rage. I made sure that we killed every last one of those men. I fucking enjoyed it too. Rowyn was there, so I wasn't able to fulfill all my fantasies about ripping them open and leaving them spread out for the carrion. I'd had to hold myself back. But this?

There would be no end to my rage until I was

bathed in blood.

Through the dust of the explosions, I squinted, searching for Rowyn. My heart pounded in my chest like a desperate hammer as I moved through the rubble. I stumbled upon Solston Gowther's body, a gory sword wound declaring his fate. Cold dread lanced through me. This wasn't just an assassination; it was an attack. Panic clawed at me.

"Rowyn!" I yelled, my voice hoarse. I swatted at the choking smoke, my eyes watering—stinging. Every breath was its own battle, but I pushed through, fueled by my desperation to find her.

Then, through the smoky veil, she appeared—in Lord Destrian's arms. Fury scorched through my veins and devoured my fear. I bellowed, the blood roaring in my ears.

But then, amid the turmoil, Rowyn pushed Lord Destrian away.

She was *mine*.

But the moment was fleeting. My heart lurched as I saw her turn, her gaze set on Agramon. The realization of her intentions dawned on me, and with a newfound surge of determination, I sprang into action.

Discarding my fear, my anger, my jealousy, I pushed through the panicked throng. Debris and desperate nobles, frantic soldiers . . . none of them mattered. All that mattered was reaching Rowyn.

Every step was a battle, every breath a triumph. I shoved through the crowd. I had to reach Rowyn. I had to reach her. I had to protect her.

"Rowyn!" My voice was desperate, a yearning call that ripped through me as I shouldered nobles aside. She was so close, yet a field of rubble and flames stood between us. I stretched towards her, pleading. "We need to get out of here!"

Rowyn looked over her shoulder at me. Her brows furrowed, as if she couldn't decide.

But there was only one right choice.

I was Rowyn's future.

Not Agramon.

Not Everett.

Not Mordog.

Not even the emperor could come between us now.

Rowyn's life was *mine* to cherish and protect.

My eyes locked onto her again. "You are my wife!" I roared, fury clawing at my words. My hands latched onto a Solin soldier who dared step in my path, and I hurled him aside. "He doesn't control you anymore!"

But Rowyn's gaze kept moving from me to Agramon, a little boy's hand clutched in hers. Rowyn raised her hands and the wind began to swirl, kicking up more dust and more debris.

No.

Not this.

The wind swept her and the little boy up, a vortex of power lifting them high above the throng.

"Rowyn!" I screamed her name, my voice a desperate plea in the churning smoke. The last thing I saw was her eyes, full of determination, before she was swept away.

Around me, the temple lay in ruins, nobility strewn across the floor, crying out or groaning in pain. Many were still in shock, staring wide-eyed at the devastation, the sky above visible through the shattered remains of the glass ceiling. But I barely noticed them. My entire focus was above, on the place where Rowyn had been.

I slipped over glass, clutching my sword, as I pushed past guards trying to maintain some semblance of order. They were shouting something at me, but I couldn't hear them over the ringing in my ears—over the desperate pounding of my heart.

I needed to find her, to make sure she was safe. But the temple was vast and in turmoil, and Rowyn was gone.

Desperation fueled me, pushing me into a wild sprint over the wreckage. My heart pounded, a rhythm of fear and anguish matching the strides I took and the obstacles I leaped over. When I emerged from the smoke-ridden temple, I scanned the sky. I had to find her, to protect her, to plead for her. I just needed her by my side once more.

"Rowyn!" I called again, my voice echoing off the ruined temple walls. But all I saw were dust and despair and the echo of her name in the wind. I didn't even know which direction she'd gone.

Fuck.

My heart sank as the realization set in. Rowyn was gone, whisked away into the smoke. And I was left alone in the ruins of our wedding day, surrounded by death and destruction, with nothing but the cold dread of uncertainty clutching my heart.

With smoke still choking the air, I stumbled from the wreckage of the temple, its grand architecture reduced to a grotesque parody of what it once was. My heart pounded like a war drum in my chest, the taste of panic bitter on my tongue.

My eyes fell to the lifeless form of my horse, Hale, strewn just a few yards away from the temple entrance. The horse had served me faithfully, and his undeserved end added fuel to the fire already burning within me.

"Dammit!" I hissed, clenching my fists at my sides. No time for mourning. Not yet.

Nearby, a nobleman was clumsily trying to mount a terrified horse. He was some lesser lord from the West, a parasite living off the hard work of others. I didn't even remember his damned name.

Burning anger twisted my features as I stormed toward him. He turned at my approach, stammering something about decency, but I was beyond caring. I drew back my fist and slammed it into his face. He reeled back, clutching his nose.

"Sorry," I growled, but there was no remorse in my voice. He had a horse; I needed a horse. I yanked the reins from him, launched myself into the saddle, and dug my heels into the horse's sides.

The city was spiraling into madness, but it all blurred into insignificance. My sole focus was on the open sky, scanning for a trace of Rowyn. But the heavens remained stubbornly empty.

I let out a guttural roar of frustration, the sound tearing from my throat as the horse pounded down the cobblestone streets. Each hoofbeat was a cruel reminder of the seconds slipping away, of the widening distance between Rowyn and me.

People screamed and scattered as I rode through, but their fear was nothing compared to the rage boiling within me. I was a tempest, a hurricane of fury and despair tearing through the city.

"*ROWYN!*" I bellowed again, but the wind carried my voice away and swallowed it whole.

I would find her.

I would tear the world apart to get her back.

Nothing and no one would stand in my way.

When I turned a corner, I met with Bald Walden, the captain of the city guard, ordering around a bunch of soldiers.

"Commander!" Walden shouted. "I'm thankful to see you're not hurt. What happened in there?"

"I don't know," I admitted. My eyes crawled through the throng, hoping I could see a glimpse of my bride in white.

"What are your orders, Commander?"

I took a moment to gather my thoughts, battling the gut-wrenching despair that coiled in my stomach.

"Secure the city," I ordered, my voice ringing out with newfound authority. "Let no one in or out until we can sort through this mess." There was a flicker of agreement in Bald Walden's eyes as he nodded. "Send word to my captains outside of the city where the army is camped. Have them ring the wall. They should keep their eyes on the sky. I want barricades at every gate. Anyone wanting in or out has to be thoroughly inspected."

"Who are we looking for?" Walden asked with a frown.

"The man who shot the emperor," I said. "He knew

to wait for the eclipse. We need to find out who shot the arrow and whether or not someone else paid them."

"Aye, Commander," Walden said.

"And Captain," I added, swinging up. "We need to find my wife."

Bald Walden huffed and shook his head. He and Diardo had tried to warn me about her. They'd told me she was more trouble than she was worth, but they were wrong. If she ran, it was because she was frightened.

As I tore through the city, flanked by Bald Walden and his men, I realized this search wasn't just out of duty; it was a desperate manifestation of my fear of losing her. Every street we scoured, every corner we turned, every face we scrutinized only served to amplify my worry. It felt like an unending nightmare, but every passing second—every failed attempt—only intensified my resolve.

The first sign we found of her was a grim spectacle. Several soldiers lay sprawled across the streets, their bodies lifeless and eyes staring blankly into nothingness. Each wore Solin's coat of arms. Bolts had found their mark, brutally cutting short their lives. I felt a cold knot form in my stomach.

As I dismounted, my boots landing with a dull thud

on the cobbled street, I spotted something that made my heart wrench painfully. A small spray of white roses, their delicate petals marred by dust and blood. The same roses she'd worn in her hair.

I bent down to pick up one of the crushed blossoms with a trembling hand, the delicate petals bruised and torn.

"I need all the men scouring the city for her," I ordered Bald Walden, my voice catching in my throat. "Leave no stone unturned, no alley unexplored. I want her found."

Bald Walden gave a curt nod, then rallied his men with a booming shout. A group of them approached us. They had a survivor of the skirmish. Hope swelled at the news. This man could have information—could know where Rowyn was.

We made our way to a healer's house, filled with the stench of blood and sickness. Inside, the survivor lay on a cot, his face a pallet of pain and fear. His eyes met mine and I saw a flicker of recognition. Agramon's men knew who I was.

The man's tale at first seemed to be a wild flurry of half memories and fear-driven hallucinations. A bird turned into some wild, naked girl. I'd never heard of anything so mad in my life.

But then, I recognized his description of her. It

matched the portrait that Rowyn carried around with her all through our tour of the empire. Her friend, Fin, who'd gone missing.

I felt a surge of hot and blinding anger. Rowyn's pet bird, the falcon that had been with her the entire time she'd been at the capital, was her sorceress friend? Rowyn had lied. She knew Fin was in Somme, and she hadn't told me.

A million questions swirled in my head, each more confusing than the last. Who was Fin really? Was she friend or foe? And why would Rowyn keep her presence a secret?

I turned my attention back to the wounded man. "Tell me everything," I growled, my mind a whirl of worry and anger.

Rowyn had run with the child prince. It was as if the ground beneath me had given way, plunging me into a dark abyss of fear and confusion. My heart pounded in my chest, each beat echoing the gnawing dread in my gut.

The rest of the journey back to the palace was a blur. My thoughts were consumed by Rowyn, by my desperate need to find her. To hold her, to reassure myself that she was safe—that she was still mine.

But my mind was not kind to me. Instead, nagging questions seemed to pester me as we rode. Had she planned it all along? Given that the soldiers littering the road were from Solin, it appeared that she was not, in fact, working with Agramon on ruining her own wedding day.

The image of her in Destrian Everett's arms swirled back to my consciousness.

No, she had given me her word. She'd been scared, frightened. I just needed to make it clear to Rowyn that I would protect her. That she needn't fear Agramon anymore.

As Bald Walden and I approached the palace, the sight of Solin guards lining the gates sent a shiver down my spine. We were halted at the castle entrance by Elgar the Swift, a sorcerer known for his ability to traverse great distances in the blink of an eye.

"Commander," Elgar greeted me, his voice resonating in the crisp air. "You are summoned to the Emperor's Council chamber."

Bald Walden and I exchanged a glance before following Elgar into the heart of the citadel. It was then, in the eerie silence of the halls, that the truth hit me.

The emperor was dead.

Chapter 7

STILL REELING FROM THE CHASE that had proved fruitless, I shoved the double doors to the council chamber wide, making them slam into the walls on either side. The room fell silent as every eye turned to me. My anger was a living entity, clawing and surging, fueled by my desperate need to find *her*.

Striding across the marble floor, I bore the weight of their gazes and the murmur of questions. But I didn't have time for their petty curiosities. I had a singular mission.

At the head of the room, Agramon rose. As poised and pristine as ever, he looked as if the chaos of the day hadn't touched him. He watched me approach with a dispassionate gaze, a slight frown creasing his brow.

"Agramon!" I roared, my voice echoing off the vaulted ceilings. I ignored the other council members. Sage Bromwell was there, along with Captain Diardo, standing across from Agramon. The room was ringed with guardsmen, some in Solin's colors, others in the emperor's. Owain the Warder stood near the window. Elgar the Swift went to stand at his side.

"You know where she is!" I accused, lunging toward him, a primal urge to shake the truth out of him driving me forward.

But when I reached for him, a shimmering field of magic threw me back. The room spun, but I quickly regained my footing. Safety spells. Damn him.

I turned back to Agramon, my gaze burning with a dangerous promise. "Where. Is. She?" I growled, my words seething between gritted teeth.

Agramon looked at me, his gaze as icy as ever. "I don't know."

"Bullshit!" I snarled, slamming my fist onto the table. "Stop feeding me your fucking lies!"

"She kidnapped the heir," Agramon said, throwing his hand out. "The emperor is dead! We have more important things to worry about than your wounded pride!"

"He's a child!" I retorted, my voice booming through the chamber. "The attack at the temple wasn't a simple assassination. It was an attack!" I turned, locking gazes with each of the council members. "I found Solston Gowther murdered as well."

The room fell into stunned silence, the shock palpable. Solston Gowther, the head Solston of Somme—a force to be reckoned with in his own right—was now reduced to a mere memory. The implications of his murder were clear. This was not just about the emperor's death.

Captain Diardo's gaze met mine. "I saw it," he admitted. "I saw Rowyn slay Solston Gowther herself. He grabbed her—threatened her."

Each word was a hammer beating down on my mounting frustration. I should have been there. I should have protected her. Was this why she had run? Because of the Sons of Sol?

By Sol above…were they responsible for this mess?

In the midst of my anger, Bald Walden's deep voice pulled me back to the moment. "I have the city guard scouring the streets," he informed us, his gaze sweeping over the council. "We're looking for the assassin, Rowyn, and Prince Artian."

My hands clenched. All that mattered was finding Rowyn. Finding the woman I loved and bringing her home. I took a deep breath, forcing myself to calm down. My anger wouldn't help me here.

The council chamber was filled with subtle tension as discussion continued, voices murmuring facts and speculations about the attack. The words, however, were only a faint buzz in my ears. My mind was elsewhere, piecing together the disjointed puzzle before me.

Agramon had been too composed, too ready to take

charge. I looked around at the room, at the guardsmen dressed in the golden eagle livery of Solin, their presence a harsh reminder of the shifting power dynamics. Their numbers far exceeded what a noble would typically bring for the quinquennial.

A cold knot formed in the pit of my stomach. Had Agramon played a part in this? I always hated this shit. Though I wasn't a huge fan of the emperor myself, I wasn't entirely sure I knew a good man to run the empire. As far as I was concerned, one man was as good as any other.

I glanced over at Bald Walden. The burly captain was in Agramon's pocket. I had seen him giving orders to the Solin guardsmen earlier, proof of his allegiance.

My gaze slid over to Owain and Elgar the Swift. Loyal as ever. The sorcerers would side with Agramon, regardless of the circumstances. This was always going to be a losing battle for me.

Agramon's influence was growing, his hand gripping the council with an iron fist. My mind raced, thoughts tumbling over each other as I grappled with the implications. How much control did he already have? How much more was he planning to seize?

As the council room swirled with speculation and thinly veiled accusations, I found my thoughts wandering to any other options. With the emperor dead, who would retain power then? The Marendesly family? The emperor's kin, hailing from the grand city of Maryse, second only to Somme, were among the wealthiest nobles and held the highest political status in the realm. For being the most powerful family in the empire, there wasn't a single one sitting at the council table discussing the emperor's death and what to do next.

Where the fuck was Duke Eldred? They would certainly try to retain control of the empire through the empress, another outsider in the people's eyes.

I glared at Agramon. He had the empress. The only way for Maryse to retain control of the throne was to have the heir. The heir who was currently missing beside my fucking wife who ran off on my wedding day. I leaned my face into my hands.

I respected the empress, despite everything. People called her the most stunning woman in the world, and it was true. I'd never seen someone with such perfect bone structure. She always carried herself like a goddess among men, and I didn't blame Diardo for falling completely head over heels for her. She'd drive any man crazy if they were around her long enough.

Lesedi the Peerless was a woman of resolve, of strength. She was kind and had a good heart. She made an excellent empress, but ruling as emperor was a ruthless business, and she didn't have enough backbone for that. She was also a stranger to the people, an outsider trying to implement changes that were not always well received. The common folk, the soldiers—there were whispers of discontent and distrust. And the Sons of Sol, they despised her. Without the support of the people, without loyalty from her soldiers, could she truly stake a claim to the throne?

Maryse and the Marendeslys might stand by her, but without Prince Artian, their influence would wane. The child was the true heir, the emblem of hope and continuity for the people.

Yet, my interactions with them had been anything but cordial. Memories of my time in Maryse began to unfold—the way the duke and his entourage treated Agramon and me. We were outsiders to them, mere dirt under their pristine shoes. Their snobbish demeanor, their veiled insults—it left a bitter taste in my mouth. Their complete disrespect and disregard for Rowyn took them off the table for me. Fuck the Marendeslys. I wasn't siding with them just to be treated like shit.

The problem was, that took away General Ivar's troops. I did some calculations in my head. I wished I hadn't given the men the option to return home. I sighed, trying to think of how many remained. Calla's forces would still be there. The mercenaries gifted by

Ardent had shown up, their commander a stern, graying man with blood in his eyes. Perth had stayed, along with the deadened prisoners from Solin who weren't good for much other than as pack mules who could set up and break down camp.

Which meant that, even without Maryse, I still had enough men to make a decent move if I needed to.

The problem was that I didn't know where to go. The next hours were going to be crucial. I needed to get to Rowyn. If I could get ahold of the child emperor, we could decide where he went together.

"Where is the empress?" Diardo asked. "The royal family must be protected until we get this figured out."

Agramon glared at him. "I've already had her escorted to her quarters and put under guard."

"You expect us to trust her with Solin guardsmen? Not likely!"

"What if the traitor in our midst is in one of the emperor's guards?" Agramon asked, his voice silky as he looked around the room. "The empress isn't being cooperative." Agramon continued, "Without her help, locating the prince will be difficult. We need to strategize accordingly."

Agramon was hiding something; I could feel it. Yet, what it was, I couldn't tell. His involvement in the attack was as obscure as ever.

"I am the captain of the royal guard," Diardo shouted. "It is my duty to protect the royal family."

"Then find the child!" Agramon snarled. It was the first time I'd actually seen him lose his temper. "For no one can claim rule without him!"

He was right. The fate of the empire hinged on the whereabouts of the young prince.

The room was once again filled with murmurs, the council members leaning in closer to discuss among themselves. As they did, I stole a glance at Agramon, my gaze narrowing slightly.

The only man who would oppose Agramon in the room was Captain Diardo. But I knew his opposition was driven by concern for the empress, rather than any real political alignment. Diardo was glaring at me, waiting for what I would choose to do. Bald Walden had cleared the city for Agramon—it was clear that he was in the sorcerer's pocket—and Owain and Elgar were overseeing the meeting for a reason. To make sure that none of us made a false move.

"My men are looking everywhere they can," Bald Walden said, pulling out a chair and taking a seat at the table, beside Bromwell. "Commander Samael has pulled the army in to help. If they are in the city, we will find them."

Agramon nodded, his fingers tapping on the

wooden armrest of his chair. "I wouldn't be surprised if this wasn't the work of Lu Shen. You know how they are when their honor is called into question. The use of black powder, the timing—it all adds up."

"But should we go to war over it?" Sage Bromwell wondered aloud, his usually bright eyes clouded with concern.

Owain scoffed, shaking his head. "That's foolish talk, Bromwell," he argued, his gaze hard. "We can't afford another war. If we do, we risk losing the empire for good."

Agramon cleared his throat, bringing the room back to a tense quiet. "While we consider the possibility of war," he began, his voice resonating with authority, "we cannot lose sight of our immediate task. The emperor is missing, and his absence creates a void that threatens the very stability of our empire."

The council members around the room turned their attention to him, their conversations tapering off. Agramon stood tall.

"The council of lords will need to convene," he continued, his gaze sweeping across the room. "Someone will have to oversee the search for the emperor and manage the capital in the interim. We need a leader who can make the hard decisions, who can bring order in these troubled times."

Agramon paused, letting his words sink in. Then, he straightened up, puffing out his chest. "I am willing to take on this role." His voice rang with determination.

A low murmur swept through the room as the council members digested his words. Agramon, in charge? The idea was not surprising. As a powerful sorcerer, respected and feared in equal measure, he'd expertly maneuvered himself into the position.

Diardo shot me a challenging look from across the room. But my mind was spinning. Agramon in power was a dangerous prospect, yet without an immediate solution, it seemed inevitable.

Bald Walden, who had already proved his allegiance to Agramon, nodded in agreement. "We'll find them, Agramon. You have our support."

I could see Agramon's lips curl into a smug smile as he nodded back. "I'm grateful for your voice, Walden."

My gut churned with unease. The game of power was shifting rapidly, the board being rearranged. With every passing moment, the stakes were growing higher. And in the heart of it all was Rowyn, a constant presence, a lingering obsession.

I stood abruptly, the sudden movement drawing the council's attention. "I have to go," I announced, feeling their gaze on me as I strode toward the exit. I could almost hear the murmurs—the whispers. Let them talk.

Before I reached the doorway, a figure moved to intercept me. Bald Walden. I scowled. He was likely spying on me for Agramon. But there was no time for confrontation. Let him follow if he wanted. I had nothing to hide.

Bald Walden fell into step beside me, his towering frame creating an imposing shadow in the dimly lit corridor. His presence was as welcome as a thorn in my side, but for now, I had to tolerate him.

As we exited the council chamber, I felt my resolve harden within me. Rowyn . . . She was out there somewhere, and she was in danger. Agramon, the council, the politics . . . it all seemed inconsequential compared to finding her.

Chapter 8

THE NIGHT AIR was cool and crisp, a welcome respite from the stifling atmosphere of the council chambers. The rhythmic clatter of hooves against cobblestone filled the night as Bald Walden and I made our way toward the city gates.

As we rode, I could sense Walden's eyes on me. His behavior had been off since we left the council chambers, a fact that didn't go unnoticed. I knew better than to brush it off as mere paranoia. I had known Bald Walden for a while, and something about him tonight was . . . different. I could feel it.

My thoughts were interrupted by the sound of galloping echoing in the distance. A man came into view, riding in the direction of the castle. A city guard, from the looks of his uniform. His wide-eyed expression suggested he was bearing news of some urgency.

"Halt!" I called out, bringing my horse to a standstill. The guard skidded to a stop, panting heavily as he saluted.

"Commander. Captain," he acknowledged, trying to catch his breath. "We . . . We've found him. The emperor's assassin."

"Take us to him," I ordered, turning my horse around. "And not a word to the council until we've seen him."

"Yes, sir." The guard nodded, leading the way as we followed him deeper into the city.

Upon reaching the site, we found a Lu Shen man sprawled on the ground, a crossbow still clutched in his cold, dead hand. His sightless eyes stared up at the night sky, a testament to his fate.

I dismounted. The man's death, while vindicating for some, only bred more questions in my mind. Questions I feared the answers to. Walden remained oddly silent, his eyes flitting over the scene with an almost calculating gaze. His suspicious behavior only deepened my unease.

I kneeled beside the dead man, inspecting his attire and the crossbow in his grip. He'd come from Cheapside. His fingers were dyed blue, like many of the impoverished who worked in textiles and other manual work, his clothing colorful but threadbare. Why would a man like that kill the emperor? As the pieces fell into place, I felt a chill run down my spine. The night had just begun, and already, it was turning out to be one of the longest I had ever faced.

"How did he die?" I asked, my eyes never leaving the lifeless figure before me.

"He . . . he tried to run, sir," the guard stammered, nervously shifting his weight from one foot to the other. "We shot him."

I turned to glare at the guard. "You shot him? Why didn't you think to keep him alive for questioning?"

The guard shrugged, his face impassive. "We were told he was dangerous and to take no chances. Who knows what he might have done if we'd let him live."

I turned to Bald Walden. "Your orders were to kill on sight?"

Bald Walden didn't respond.

Walden's nonchalance was unsettling, but my frustrations had to wait.

"Have the body taken to the castle," I ordered, turning back to the guard.

"Yes, Commander." The guard nodded, saluting before he moved to fulfill my order.

With a final, lingering glance at the body, I mounted my borrowed horse. The night was far from over, and I had more pressing matters to attend to. The council meeting had left me with a sour taste in my mouth, and the sudden appearance of the assassin only served to heighten my suspicion.

My mind was awash with a torrent of thoughts as I urged my horse into a canter, leading Walden and the guards toward the city gates. Agramon was making his move, and the empire was teetering on the edge of collapse.

The night air was crisp against my skin, the city of Somme sprawling beneath a sky peppered with stars. I rode alongside Bald Walden, a constant reminder of Agramon's insidious influence. His presence was as unsettling as the situation we found ourselves in.

It wasn't at all how I'd planned to be spending the evening. I took a moment to grieve what would've been my wedding night if my bride had decided to stick around. I thought of her as I looked into the darkened windows of the city street. She'd been scared, that much was clear. She'd been frightened of the blast, of Agramon, of the eclipse foretelling some ancient prophecy no doubt.

I sighed, rubbing my eyes with my fingers. I remembered the feeling of Rowyn in my arms when I'd rescued her from the raiders outside of Maryse. How she trembled, her skin clammy and pale, her eyes wide and glassy. She'd been so frightened. Agramon always put too much stock in how much Rowyn could withstand.

No wonder she'd run. It wasn't from me. It was the moment. Her fear for the boy and what Agramon would do to her if he got his hands on her. I just needed Rowyn to see me looking, trying to find her, and then she would come back. I was sure of it. Just like in Maryse, I would keep her safe from Agramon's cruel schemes.

The clopping of horse hooves echoed on the cobblestones as we neared the city gates. A group of military captains waited for us, their uniforms crisp, faces hardened by years of battle. My loyal men. They straightened at my approach, salutes sharp.

"Commander," the first of them greeted me, his voice strained. He had the look of a man who had seen the worst of what the world could offer and still chose to stand firm.

"Captain." I nodded in return, dismounting my horse. "What's the situation?"

"We have our men securing the gates," another replied. "All incoming and outgoing traffic has stopped."

"Good," I said, my mind running over the next steps. "We'll need to coordinate with the city guard as well."

The captains shared a glance, and the air seemed to grow tense. Bald Walden cleared his throat, drawing our attention. "The city guard and the Solin men are under my command, Baron," Walden answered, his tone deceptively calm. "They are following my orders."

That's when the planning began under the starlit sky with the city in turmoil, an emperor dead, and a kingdom at stake.

"Here." I pointed at a spot on the map of Somme spread across the wooden table. "I want Ardent's mercenaries to secure the harbor and docks."

Bald Walden bristled slightly at the command, his expression a careful mask of neutrality. "The Solin guards are already holding the docks, Commander," he explained, a hint of steel in his voice. "They've been searching the ships for any signs of the prince or Morganite sorceress."

"Call them back to the castle," I ordered, my gaze not leaving the map. "I want every Solin guard within the castle walls by nightfall."

A flicker of satisfaction passed over Walden's face at the mention of the castle. He must have liked the plan, since it meant keeping Agramon's loyal men close.

"Tell me about the nobles," I said, shifting the topic.

"The Marysian nobles were escorted out of the city by General Ivar," one of the captains responded, his tone laced with uncertainty. "They are headed back to Maryse. They plan to fortify themselves there. They have their own port in Lark Harbor outside Somme."

I nodded, taking note of the information.

"Most of the western nobles have retreated to their ships," Bald Walden added, pointing to the map.

"They're waiting it out until they can safely leave."

My gaze darkened. "Post our camp at the harbor, directly in front of Lord Destrian's ships. I want him under constant watch. If he even thinks of slipping away, I want to know about it."

"Yes, Commander," the captain acknowledged with a salute.

"I'll personally pay Lord Destrian a visit," I declared, rising from the table.

With that, I swung onto my horse. I looked out at the city once more, its streets illuminated by flickering torches, its future hanging by a thread.

The moon hung over the city of Somme, casting an eerie light on its streets. An unsettling quiet ruled, the usual hustle and bustle swallowed by the shroud of fear that gripped the city.

I sat astride my horse, heart pounding, scanning every shadow and corner. Bald Walden rode beside me, matching my pace. We ripped through the silence of the night, an emblem of the turmoil that had seized Somme.

We pounded on innkeepers' doors, questioning the few souls still wandering the streets. Every scrap of information, every hint, every possibility, we grabbed at them like drowning men clutching at straws.

My fury was a storm filling the air around us. Yet

beneath the anger, beneath the frantic urgency, a fear curled, cold and terrifying. With each passing minute, dread settled deeper into my guts. She was out there, my Rowyn, possibly in danger, possibly . . .

The thought was like a dagger twisting in me, adding to the blaze of my fury. I spurred my horse forward, the echo of hooves against the cobblestones punctuating my desperate plea to the gods to keep her safe.

Red-hot fury washed over me as I heard the derisive laughter cutting through the eerie quiet of the night. Turning around, my eyes fell upon the source—one of Bald Walden's men, a sneer etched on his face.

"It's only what you'd expect." His voice dripped with malice. "Who's to say the sorceress didn't have a hand in the emperor's death? I'm aiming to kill on sight."

I was off my horse and charging toward him, the edges of my vision tinged red as raw anger overpowered everything else. My fist connected with his face with a satisfying crunch, sending him sprawling onto the cobblestones, his surprised yelp quickly followed by groans of pain.

This man, this insignificant speck, had no right to judge Rowyn—to declare her guilt or innocence—and his mockery of my pain was more than I could bear.

Again and again, my fists found their mark on his face and his body. Each punch, each drop of his blood, was an outlet for the storm of emotions raging inside me.

"Enough, Commander!" Walden's voice broke through my rage-induced haze, his hands grabbing my shoulders and yanking me away. I stumbled back, my chest heaving, the taste of fury bitter on my tongue.

In the shadows I saw her. A little girl, her skin translucent in the moonlight, crawling towards me, her broken limbs scrabbling awkwardly across the cobblestones as she studied me.

My breath caught in my throat. It didn't take long for Rowyn's absence to bring the phantoms back.

Wordlessly, I turned away, remounting my horse. I was a man possessed, possessed by a fear I couldn't put into words, possessed by an anger I couldn't contain.

Destrian Everett was my only lead, my only hope of finding Rowyn. If she was with him, he was going to pay dearly.

Chapter 9

T HE BITING SEA AIR was a harsh slap against my face as I approached the harbor alone. The ships stood tall, silhouetted against the morning sky like a row of silent guardians.

My boots clipped over the cobblestones, breaking the silence of the twilight hour as I stormed toward the docks. Gulls cawed overhead, their cries echoing eerily off the abandoned warehouses. I scanned the darkened horizon, searching for the familiar silhouette of the fleet's flagship.

There it was. The *Sea Serpent*, its vast masts reaching toward the heavens, its silhouette a looming shadow against the dwindling sunset. I moved with purpose, my rage propelling me forward. My nostrils flared with the familiar scent of brine and seaweed, the noises of dock workers fading into a distant hum.

Admiral Abelard, the fleet's commander, was standing at the helm, barking orders at his crew, with Duke Agramon next to him. As I clambered up the boarding ramp, they paused to look down at me.

"Commander," Admiral Abelard greeted. "I am sorry for how your wedding has turned out. I know you were looking forward to a happier conclusion."

I nodded at the admiral, then turned my gaze to Agramon. "What are you doing here?"

Agramon smiled. "You did not hear? The council of lords met, even without Maryse, and voted for me to oversee the empire until we can locate the prince."

Of course they did. Of course he would have them meet without me there. I didn't mince words. Time was a luxury I couldn't afford. "Have you searched all the ships?"

Abelard's eyebrows rose at the harshness of my tone. "We've already let several go," he admitted, his voice cautious. "Maryse refused to stay."

Anger flared in my chest at the admiral's words, but Agramon was nodding. "I searched the ships myself. She wasn't there."

"I thought you couldn't hear her mind," I growled. I wouldn't take any chances with her.

Agramon met my glare. "I still know when someone's there," he said. "So enough, Butcher." He shot me a pointed look. "We can't afford to antagonize Maryse now. They have their own ports, and I don't think I'm wrong to think that Maryse would be last on the list of places Rowyn would go for help."

I turned back to the admiral. "I want to search Helena's first."

740

Under the light of the rising sun, Destrian's ship, *The Avalon*, bobbed gently on the calm sea. I watched him from a distance as he lounged on the deck with his crew, the rattling of dice heard across the water.

I beckoned my mercenaries who'd camped exactly where I told them to. Their stolid faces hardened further under the evening glow, their hands instinctively reaching for the weapons at their sides. I could feel their collective anticipation, a fine line of tension that vibrated through the still air.

Swallowing the bitter taste of rage, the sound of Lord Destrian's laughter grated against my senses, sparking a dangerous flare of anger that threatened to consume my sanity.

We strode onto the ship, our boots thumping ominously against the wooden planks. Everett's laughter died down, his eyes flicking up to meet mine. A smug grin spread across his face as he leaned back, a die still twirling between his fingers as his guards, some Lyrican, some Morganite, sat beside him, palming their swords.

"Duke Agramon. Commander Samael," Lord Destrian drawled. The die in his hand stilled, his gaze meeting mine with unmasked amusement. "To what do I owe the pleasure?"

"We are searching every ship, Lord Destrian," I

said, my gaze unyielding. The tension in the air tightened like a bowstring, as if one wrong move could shatter the fragile peace into a thousand shards. The mercenaries tensed behind me, their silent presence an unspoken threat.

Destrian looked at me, a glint of amusement flashing in his eyes as he crossed his arms over his chest. "You can search away," he said, "but she isn't here. Why do you think she would come running to me on your wedding night?"

I took one step closer, my hand on my hilt as I stared him down. I didn't need his fucking impertinence. But before I could get any closer, Destrian's men rose beside their lord as a wall of fire roared up to shield him.

A humorless laugh echoed from behind the flaming barrier. "You eastern nobles always seem to forget that there is still power in the West." Destrian's voice held an edge of warning. "You are free to search the ship, but Rowyn is not here."

His cavalier attitude stoked my anger. "You claim to love her," I spat out, "but you do not care what danger she is in?"

The flames reflected in his eyes, his voice carrying a quiet conviction as he met my gaze. "I have always thought that Rowyn was more than a match for you all. She doesn't need me. I have no doubt she can take care of herself."

As the sun slowly began to rise, casting long shadows over the ship, Agramon turned his gaze back to Destrian, a calculated look in his eyes. "And what about in the future, Consul?" he asked, his voice barely more than a whisper.

Destrian let out a bitter laugh that echoed in the still morning air. "I will always welcome Rowyn, and you can damn well try to stop me. But remember this, your grace." His voice dropped, his words carrying a heavy warning. "The other nobles are watching. This little power play of yours, they see it for what it is—a coup for the throne."

He paused, his gaze meeting mine with a knowing smirk. "If they see you or your *Butcher*"—the last word dripped with contempt—"antagonize me without any provocation, you'll lose any shred of loyalty you have left."

A sharp jolt of resentment coursed through me as that title slipped past Destrian's lips like an ugly brand. To the world, it seemed as though I'd made my choice, aligning myself with Agramon in this twisted game of power. Yet within me, a war raged, a tumultuous battle between loyalty and instinct.

As Agramon and I followed the mercenaries deeper

into the vessel, our every move shadowed by the vigilant Helenian guards, I could feel the unsettling tension coiling around us like a deadly serpent.

Every empty cabin, every deserted hallway twisted the knot of dread tighter in my stomach. The fear that had been gnawing at me since Rowyn's disappearance was threatening to overwhelm me, fueling my rage even more.

With each passing moment, the chances of finding Rowyn aboard seemed to dwindle.

After what felt like an eternity, Agramon finally called off the search. "She isn't here," he said, walking beside me as we returned to shore. I refused to look over my shoulder at Lord Destrian who was surely watching. But as I walked away, I couldn't escape the harsh reality of his words, a bitter reminder of the love I'd selfishly claimed but could never truly have.

The ride back to the castle was steeped in silence, punctuated by the clopping of the horse hooves on the cobblestone road. A heavy gloom settled over us, an invisible shroud woven with the threads of defeat.

Agramon rode beside me, the usually confident and shrewd duke reduced to a silent, brooding figure. It seemed our collective failure had pushed us into an unwanted truce.

"Where could she have gone?" My voice was a rasp,

strained under the weight of the dread and sorrow. I shook my head, raking my fingers through my hair, my gaze flitting over the city lights.

"I don't know," Agramon admitted. "I do know that she's too smart to take the emperor to Morgania though."

"Why would you say that? Her Lord Destrian just said that he would offer her quarter if she came."

Agramon sighed. "She wouldn't put him in danger like that. The whole reason she agreed to come east with me was to keep him safe."

"Then where?" The desperate plea in my voice was undeniable.

Agramon's gaze met mine again. "She would go to someone for help," he said, certainty tingeing his words. "Especially with the child. She knows she can't handle it alone. But who? Who does she trust enough to . . ."

His voice trailed off, his gaze distant as his words hung in the air, a beacon of hope amid the churning sea of despair. It was something, at least. A lead. Something to hold on to in this whirlpool of uncertainty.

"Who does she trust enough?" I repeated. But the road gave me no answers. Only silence. Only echoes. Only the question reverberating back at me.

"The empress," I murmured, the realization a sharp

sting. "Rowyn trusts the empress."

Agramon frowned. "The empress?" he echoed. "I did not take them for being close at all."

"I suspected they colluded during our tour of the empire," I admitted. "Rowyn was spying for the empress. She all but admitted it to me. It was what made me doubt her."

Agramon was silent, his face a canvas of simmering anger at the realization. "That means . . ." He trailed off, the implications of my revelation sinking in.

"The empress must have sent the prince to Rowyn deliberately?" I mused aloud. "You say she's been barricaded in her rooms the entire time. Have you asked where Rowyn might have gone?"

"She wouldn't speak to me. She's rebuffed every attempt I've made," Agramon admitted. "But she might speak to you."

The silence stretched, my mind a battleground of conflicting emotions. But as I looked at Agramon, as I considered the possibility of finding Rowyn, I knew there was only one answer I could give.

"You want my help," I said, glaring at Agramon. It had been a day. An entire day and Rowyn was still missing. Despite the city being under lockdown, despite the mobilization of all the troops, despite every measure I'd taken to bring her back to me, she was still gone. Desperation clawed at my heart as if with talons, reaching into the darkest parts of me and drawing out the demons that always seemed to be teetering on the edge of being unleashed.

Agramon glanced at me. "You know who the players are? I do not think that you are so dense that you can't see the choices in front of you."

I gritted my teeth. "You are the one who did this," I said, my anger swelling. "You are the reason she is gone. Do you think me such a fool that I don't know the blasts at the temple were not you?"

Agramon didn't respond for a moment. It's not like it mattered anymore. After all, the emperor was dead, the heir was missing, and the city had descended into pandemonium. What would a few words do?

"Everything I've done, I've only done for the betterment of the empire," Agramon said, his voice filled with conviction. "Before you try to cast judgment, ask yourself if you can say the same."

I shook my head, trying to push the fury back. "You nobles are all the same," I spat. "No matter if you came from gilded beds or the dirt on the street. Always certain that you are the better man, if only you had more power."

"The emperor was a fool, and you know it," Agramon hissed sharply. "What's more, he's gone now, and the commander of the Lyrican forces is love-sick, trying to find a girl who never returned his feelings."

I pulled the reins to my horse, stopping it in the street before turning my fury onto Agramon, my hand on the pommel of my sword. "This is how you try to get me to join your side? Insults? You ruined my wedding day. You made her *run* from me."

"I might've ruined the wedding," Agramon admitted, "but I had no idea she would get away. I'd thought to keep her here and use her to appease the common folk as I solidified my hold on the throne and guardianship of the young prince. There, happy now? You know what my plan was . . . the plan that didn't fucking work."

"So your little ward got the best of you, did she?" I scoffed.

Agramon glared at me. "Do you want her back or not?" he asked, his voice silky. "Because by my count, you only have two options. You can try to ally with the empress, whom you've already said is partial to Rowyn, and try to get her to return your bride to you. How do you think that will go, I wonder? Does the empress often push unwilling women into marriage? Is that the alliance that would get you what you want? Will the army stand by your side if that is what you choose? Are you prepared to have only Maryse back you?"

"And you are the other choice?" I spat. "You tried to keep her from me from the start."

"And now I'm offering her to you," Agramon said, his eyes sharp. "If you help me, you can have the girl. Just leave her available to call the rain when we need it."

I knew Agramon had his own motives, his own sinister agenda that was as veiled and complex as the man himself. But for now, our interests aligned. However twisted the circumstances, he was offering me a chance to get Rowyn back.

My obsession with Rowyn had made me ruthless, blinded me to the extent that I was now straddling the thin line between rescue and coercion. I was becoming reckless, willing to do anything to bring her back, even if it meant going against her will.

"Let me see the empress first," I said, turning my eyes back to the castle. "Let me see if I can get any information from her."

Agramon laughed. "You are free to see her, and I hope your visit goes better than mine. If you think she will waste breath drawing you to her side, you'd be wrong. She has never liked you."

"She's always liked you less, though," I replied, spurring my horse on.

The ride to the castle was a blur, the cobblestones rushing beneath my horse in a steady rhythm that did little to quiet the unease of my mind. The city was normally loud and busy, but now it was quiet, a ghastly sheen lurking over the deserted streets as everyone cowered within their homes. The emperor was dead and the world was in chaos. I clenched my teeth.

The Solin guards at the gate shot me suspicious looks as Agramon and I rode through, their hands ready at their weapons.

Despite the early hour, the halls were teeming with life. Courtiers huddled in corners, their whispers echoing eerily in the grand hall. Guards stood tall at every turn, their faces stern and alert.

The air was thick with tension, the invisible thread of uncertainty weaving its way around every corner. It seemed the whole empire held its breath, waiting for what would come next.

Elgar the Swift was waiting for us in the council chambers, a map of the city spread out before him on the table. He barely acknowledged my presence, his eyes suspiciously darting between Agramon and me. But Agramon silenced his unspoken questions with a curt nod, giving Elgar leave to speak in front of me.

"The city is under lock and key," Elgar reported, his gaze hardening as he began his report. "We've been searching everyone who tries to pass through the gates. Few have been able to get through, causing unrest among those kept inside the capital. People who came for the quinquennial celebration are clamoring to leave, claiming the city is unsafe."

"And Rowyn?" I asked impatiently, my voice a low growl. "Any sight of her and the prince?"

Elgar shook his head, his features drawn into a grimace. "No sign of them, even in the lower city. The city gangs have been keeping their eyes out, but they've seen nothing."

"And Pythia Golden-Eyes?" Agramon interjected, a flicker of concern crossing his usually stoic features. "What is she doing?"

"Waiting for orders," Elgar answered, shifting uncomfortably under Agramon's sharp gaze. "And Tristam is seeing to the wounded at the temple."

"He did not go with Maryse?" I frowned, looking back at Elgar. "That's unexpected."

Elgar shrugged, rubbing his eyes wearily. "Tristam won't leave without Pythia, and Pythia refuses to leave the castle."

I blinked, taken aback. I had no idea there was anything going on between Tristam and Pythia, but then again, my focus had been singularly on Rowyn for the longest time. Perhaps I'd been blind to more than I'd realized.

Ignoring the surprise on my face, Agramon continued the conversation. "I want Edmund the Bright watched," he commanded, his gaze steely. "We need eyes on the university. Make sure none of the younger sorcerers get any bright ideas or try heroics."

"Understood." Elgar nodded. He hesitated for a moment before adding, "Del was injured in the blast. She's shaken up, but she'll recover."

Agramon's usually stoic face flashed with surprise, then worry, before resettling into its usual mask of indifference. "She'll be fine," he muttered, almost more to himself than to Elgar. "She's strong."

Elgar nodded, watching Agramon with a mixture of concern and suspicion. "Any other orders?"

My attention was drawn to a list of the nobles being harbored in the castle. "What about here? Have the rooms been searched?"

Agramon turned his attention to the list, nodding. "The Solin guard was charged with that, although Bald Walden's men might have better luck getting the nobles to comply."

"Search the castle again," I interjected. "After I speak with the empress, I want his grace to read Mellan Lyon's mind. He was her closest friend at the palace."

"Good point," Elgar said, glancing up and meeting

Agramon's eye.

When Elgar disappeared, I turned back to Agramon. "I am going to see the empress."

He chuckled, the sound as cold as ice. "By all means," he said. "But don't expect her to be of much help."

Ignoring him, I exited the council chamber, my heart pounding with a renewed sense of hope. If Mellan Lyon didn't know where Rowyn was, I wasn't sure anybody did. Was she already well outside the city? What about Calla and her friend Araceli? What about the Tores? The quinquennial had brought all manner of people to the capital, and we would need to search them all. As I made my way toward the empress's quarters, I couldn't help but feel that I was one step closer to finding the woman I'd lost.

Chapter 10

THE ENTRANCE TO THE empress's quarters was heavily guarded. Teams of Solin guardsmen stood at attention, their weapons glinting ominously in the sunlight that came in through the arched windows that looked out to the city beyond. The guards regarded me with suspicious eyes, but at my approach, they simply nodded and unlocked the massive double doors.

I ignored the lavish furnishings, focusing instead on the impressive woman sitting on the plush couch in the center of the room. Lesedi the Peerless. Her dark eyes, once full of life, were weary and filled with an undeniable sadness. The room was stuffy despite the summer breeze attempting to wisp in through the heavily barred windows. The colorful birds in their cages were strangely silent.

To her sides were the two young princesses, Eladia and Lesedi the Younger. Their eyes were swollen, clear indicators of their grief. Behind them stood Mem, the empress's bodyguard. Her formidable form towered over the young princesses, her dark head gleaming under the chamber's light. She bore an air of protective fierceness, her hand twitching toward the place where her blades used to be.

The empress looked up at me, her black eyes ablaze. She had scrubbed her face clean of any paints, revealing raw, unguarded fury beneath. "So, you've come," she spat, her voice filled with venom. "I hope you're happy, turning my home into a prison."

"Empress Lesedi," I began, bowing in respect. She looked at me with an odd glimmer in her eyes. "I'm sorry," I said sincerely. "It wasn't supposed to be this way. You should never be a prisoner in your own home."

A dry laugh escaped her lips, the sound filled with bitterness. "And yet, here I am," she retorted, gesturing to the room around her. Her eyes bore into mine, unyielding. "And for what? For a throne that's no longer mine, for a people who look to a child for leadership. It's a mockery—a charade. So save your platitudes. You are part of this, whether you admit it or not."

"I had no part in the emperor's death, Your Highness," I replied, my patience already wearing thin. "I am here to keep order, and to find my wife. I need your help. There are things you might know—"

"My help?" She laughed, a bitter sound that echoed through the room. "You have taken everything from me. My husband, my freedom, my peace. And now you want my help? My help in finding my son so that you Lyricans can turn him against me, as you all turned my husband?"

I swallowed hard. This was not the woman I'd known. This was a mother mourning the loss of her husband, her son, and her power.

"I need to find Rowyn," I said, meeting her fiery gaze. "We need to find the prince. How else can we keep him safe? Rowyn took him away to protect him, but I need to find them. Can you . . ." I stumbled, my voice pleading. "Can you tell me where you think she might have gone?"

The question hung in the air like a heavy fog before Empress Lesedi's laughter echoed once again, the sound bitter, yet filled with a strange sense of amusement.

"Do you think me a fool, Samael?" she asked, her voice soft but cutting. "Do you think I would place my son in the council's hands after what has occurred? Do you believe I would trust the very men who planned my husband's death?"

The rage in her eyes was searing. I swallowed hard as I approached, trying to keep my composure.

"Empress," I started, but before I could continue, Lesedi spat in my face.

The surprise, the raw disrespect . . . It stung. I wiped the spit off my cheek, my fist clenching at my side. "Why would you do that?" I asked, struggling to keep my voice steady.

"Because I know a traitor when I see one, *Butcher*," she hissed through clenched teeth, emphasizing my hated name with a sneer. "And I see one standing right in front of me."

I stared at her, gritting my teeth. "Why would you call me a traitor?"

She let out a harsh laugh, void of any mirth. "Isn't it obvious?" Her voice dripped with disdain. "You're standing on the other side of the bars."

There it was. A knife forged from words, and it cut deeper than any blade ever could. I looked at her, my anger mingling with a sense of defeat. "I did not put you here, Empress," I said quietly. "I am not your enemy."

"But you are not my ally either, Commander," she retorted, her gaze hard as steel. "You are here with the council, with Agramon. You may not have put me here, but you are complicit in my imprisonment."

The room fell silent. The only sound was the soft whimper of the young princesses huddled behind their mother. My gaze flitted to them, a pang of guilt twisting in my chest. The seeds of doubt planted by the empress started to sprout in my mind. I desperately tried to figure out my options to find Rowyn as they dwindled away. Was Agramon capable of reading the princesses' minds?

And what about Empress Lesedi? Would she break if her daughters were taken away? I looked at the woman in front of me, her regal visage marred by grief and defiance. Even in her weakened state, there was a fierce strength in her eyes. But how long would she be able to hold on?

How cruel was I to even think such things? It was far too easy, reclaiming the mantle of brutality. My grip on the situation was slipping. My single-minded obsession with finding Rowyn was starting to feel more like a mad dash into hell. The line between right and wrong was getting blurrier by the second, and I was striding without hesitation into morally ambiguous territory. I'd been there before. Was there a limit to what I would do to find her?

I startled, my eyes on the hanging cages of birds who still studied me, oddly somber. Within the gilded cages were others, shadows of iron, the whisps of ethereal spirits. A small child, no more than two, clawing at his mother's robes, so thirsty he could no longer even cry tears. The mother's head lolled onto her shoulder, her body barely more than a faded husk.

I ripped my gaze away from the ghostly memory and left the empress's chamber, the echo of her bitter laughter ringing in my ears. I knew now that Lesedi would not help me, not willingly. Agramon was right to keep her under watch, as twisted as his motives might be.

As I walked away, I could feel the weight of my choices bearing down on me. The choices that were slowly taking me down a path I wasn't sure I could return from. The ghosts seemed to be coming back, even stronger, more numerous than before. My desire to find Rowyn was now taking me to the edge of sanity, and I was teetering dangerously on the precipice, ready to plunge into the abyss at any moment.

My gaze fell on the barred door of the empress's chamber one last time before I turned away. If this was the price I had to pay to find Rowyn, then I would become the villain.

THE RAGE THAT BURNED in my chest was still hot and raw as I stormed into the council chambers.

At the heart of it was Mellan Lyon, bound and seated in a chair, a defiant look in his eyes. The sight

of him, tied up and vulnerable, brought a surge of unwanted emotions to the surface.

Agramon stood before Mellan, his hand on his forehead, the gem on his forehead glowing a rosy pink as
he probed Mellan's mind for answers. Captain Diardo
glowered in a seat near the end of the table, watching
Agramon. Bald Walden and Elgar the Swift stood
nearby, their faces grim.

"Imprisoning the empress in her room?" Diardo
asked as I walked in, his voice laced with disbelief.
"Questioning nobles like they're criminals? This is a
dangerous precedent we're setting here."

"We're doing what's necessary," Agramon shot
back firmly. "These aren't normal times."

I let them argue, my gaze fixating on Mellan. His
presence stirred a deep-rooted anger in me, a jealousy
that had been there since the first day I saw him together with my future wife.

Mellan and Rowyn. That combination had always
been a source of irritation for me. Their closeness,
their easy company and jokes—it all ate at me in ways
I hadn't admitted even to myself. The lines of their relationship were blurred in my eyes—allies, confidants,
friends. To my jealousy-fueled mind, it was all a threat.

Agramon suddenly released Mellan and stepped
back. "He knows nothing," Agramon announced, his

voice echoing ominously in the chamber. His eyes, however, told a different story. There was something, a spark of interest that lingered even as he moved away from Mellan.

Mellan spat at Agramon's retreating figure, a display of defiance that earned him a sharp glare. "I told you, Agramon," he snarled, his voice filled with venom. "I don't know where she went. The only lead I can give you is the one you already know. Destrian Everett is your best bet…aside from that? I know nothing."

My eyes moved from Mellan to Agramon, my heart pounding in my chest. Could Agramon be lying? Could he have found something and was keeping it from us?

There was no way to know. Agramon was a master of deception, his true intentions as elusive as a wisp of smoke. I swallowed hard, a strange sense of anticipation settling within me.

My gaze met Mellan's, and for a moment, I saw my reflection in his eyes—and for the first time, I was afraid of what I saw.

"No!" I snarled. I didn't bother to keep the rage from my voice, my glare focused on Mellan as I marched toward him and slammed my fist into his cheek. "He's hiding something. He has to be."

Agramon turned to look at me, his eyebrows raised in shock. "I've searched him, Butcher. There's nothing."

"You've said before that his mind was hard to read," I shot back, my voice laced with bitterness. "What if he's been fooling you all this time? What if he's learned to guard his thoughts from you?"

I saw a flicker of doubt cross Agramon's eyes, but he remained silent.

"Rowyn got away right under your nose," I spat, my hands balled into fists. "It should have taught you to be more cautious, but you're so used to being the most powerful one in the room that you can't even consider the possibility of being outmaneuvered." I stepped toward Mellan again, but Diardo grabbed my arm and shoved me into the wall.

"Sam," Captain Diardo said, cutting through the argument. "This isn't you."

I shifted my gaze to him, his usually firm stance sagging with fatigue from his old injury. Vivid memories filled my mind. We'd been comrades in arms during the council meetings, built on the shared objective of serving the empire rather than getting embroiled in the petty power games of the nobility.

"Sam, we've been friends for years," Diardo grunted, his voice softer. "I don't recognize you anymore."

There it was, the truth laid out bare for all to hear.

I saw the concern on Diardo's face, in Agramon's watchful gaze, and in Mellan's defiant stare.

We were soldiers, not courtiers. We didn't have the taste for political squabbles and manipulations. We found contentment in our duty, and it was this common ground that had anchored our friendship. Whether in decisions of war or peace, in disputes of law or duty, we had always found ourselves on the same side of the coin.

"When you look in the mirror, do you even recognize the man staring back at you?" Diardo implored.

The unity shattered. The shared ideals that once bound us together seemed to be drifting apart, and I found myself staring at the divide that had grown between us. He didn't understand. None of them did.

The ghosts were back. The gods were punishing me for my sins of war. My sins brought on through the emperor's conquests. Rowyn was the only cure. The only remedy for the madness.

My breath hitched. A harsh laugh broke free from my throat. "What I see," I said, my voice trembling, "is a man who will stop at nothing to rescue the woman he loves. Can you say the same?"

The silence that followed was heavy. I turned back to Mellan, my resolve hardened. "You're lying," I hissed, stepping closer to him. "You know something.

I can see it in your eyes."

"Butcher," Agramon warned, but I didn't let him deter me.

"I don't care what you found in his mind," I snarled, my blood boiling. "I want to hear it from him. I want to hear him say where Rowyn is. And if he won't tell us . . . then maybe we need to persuade him."

Ignoring the shocked expressions of the others, I lunged at Mellan, my fist connecting with his jaw. He let out a cry of pain, but I didn't care. I had never been more determined in my life. For Rowyn, I was ready to cross every line I once thought uncrossable.

"Tell us where she is!" I grunted, landing another blow.

Agramon was yelling at me and Elgar was trying to pull me off, but I was lost to my rage. Mellan's face was a bloody mess, his eyes swollen shut, but still, he remained silent.

"Enough, Butcher!" Agramon bellowed, but I ignored him. Mellan was hiding something. I just needed to break him.

Elgar was on me, his grip like iron bands around my arms. "Enough!" he barked. I tried to wrench out of his grip. A violent lurch seemed to pull at my stomach as the world careened sideways. When I finally steadied myself, I was outside in the streets. I blinked in the sudden brightness, my mind whirling as the cool air hit my hot, rage-filled face.

"No!" I roared, turning on Elgar. "Take me back! He knows something! I know he does!"

It was clear that something was brewing in the castle, a whirlpool of plots and schemes that threatened to pull us all under. And as much as I wanted to deny it, I was caught in its deadly pull.

Chapter 11

I HADN'T SLEPT, but my rooms felt suffocating, the stone walls closing in as if to match the unbearable weight pressing on my chest. My hand trembled around the neck of the bottle, the amber liquid inside sloshing as my mind churned with a tempest of tormenting thoughts.

Her broken promise echoed around me, the whispers of her words fueling my anger, driving me to confront the bitter truth. She was gone. I had lost her, and it felt like I was slowly losing myself in the process.

Her belongings, meticulously moved into my room in anticipation of our wedding night, were a stark reminder of the future we were meant to have. I found myself being drawn to them, as though they were a lifeline to the woman I loved.

I stumbled toward the wardrobe and flung open the doors, a wave of her smell enveloping me in a cloud. Rowyn. My wife, my life, was now a dream in the wind.

The clothes hung like sentinels, bright dresses she'd once worn, their colors as vibrant as her spirit, guarding the room in wait for her return. My fingers caressed them and eventually I pulled out a familiar green one.

I brought it to my face, inhaling her scent, my heart throbbing painfully.

I could almost see her in it, could almost feel her lips on mine as she gasped into me on that night in Maryse. It was the night I felt something shift within her. The night when she actually seemed to let me in.

With a shaky breath, I pulled the dress close to my face, clutching the soft fabric as I buried my face in it. The faint scent of her perfume still clung to it—floral and sweet with a hint of something uniquely Rowyn. I breathed in deeply, as though trying to fill the void she'd left behind.

As if her presence were suddenly tangible, my gaze fell upon her portrait set against my mirror. Her painted eyes seemed to watch me, the delicate arch of her brows and the curve of her lips taunting me, feeding my torment. The anger surged in my veins, boiling beneath the surface as I stared at her likeness, her painted smile mocking my pain.

The face in the mirror stared at me, unrecognizable, twisted by the bitterness of jealousy and the sting of abandonment. The words of Diardo taunted me, his accusation sharp and clear. "When you look in the mirror, do you even recognize the man staring back at you?"

I didn't. I saw a man crumbling under the weight of

his fears and insecurities. A man drowning in his jealousy, ready to sell his soul for a glimpse of hope. A man who let his only hope slip away.

The ghosts seemed to relish my misery. They crawled ever closer, through the windows, creeping under the door, dragging themselves to the bed.

The mirror met its fate against the unforgiving stone wall. My rage was an uncontrollable beast, gnashing and clawing at the remnants of my sanity.

Another surge of anger propelled the bottle towards the phantoms. The sound of shattering glass echoed my breaking heart, shards scattering across the floor like fragments of my sanity. The portrait seemed to mock me further, her painted visage forever preserved, forever out of reach.

Clinging to the remnants of my self-control, I staggered back to my bed, the portrait of Rowyn and her green dress in hand. As I sank into the cold sheets, my fingers brushed over the fabric, a poor substitute for the woman I'd lost. The room spun around me, Rowyn's glaring eyes in the painting the only constant, watching as I succumbed to the waves of despair, fear, and betrayal coursing through me.

The ghosts crept closer to the bed.

Was she with Lord Destrian now? Images of her with him intruded, their laughter intertwining, their bodies too close for comfort, and his arms offering her the sanctuary that should have been mine.

The phantoms rose, their spectral fingers reaching towards my flesh leaving icy feeling in their wake as they tried, in vain, to seek their vengeance. The gods must've heard their cries for I couldn't bear it—the thought of her with him, of his touch replacing mine, his voice drowning mine out. It was unbearable—unthinkable. I was being devoured by my own jealousy, my heart torn apart piece by piece.

Every second that passed was a jab in my heart, a reminder that he could be with her, holding her, loving her. And there I was, trapped in this gods-forsaken place, consumed by my powerlessness.

I STOOD AT THE PORT, my gaze sweeping over the sea of vessels, a labyrinth of potential hideouts. Admiral Abelard was there too, a stern presence overseeing the tedious search process. His face was lined with the same worry that mirrored my own. What would happen to the empire if the prince was lost?

I watched as the admiral let another ship go. The sailors shouted in relief, their cries a jarring contrast to the heavy silence that hung over me. I turned my gaze back to the water, the waves lapping at the wooden docks.

The days had blurred into nights as I led the search, fueled by unending determination. I interrogated people ruthlessly, their pleas for mercy falling on deaf ears as my need to find Rowyn overrode any sense of empathy I once possessed. The city was once a vibrant heart of culture and beauty. Now it was a maze of potential hideouts for me, each one more menacing than the last.

The relentless search for Rowyn and the young emperor seemed to be an infinite loop of disappointment and mounting dread. Each passing hour, I felt the grip of fear tightening around my heart and the demon of doubt gnawing at my resolve.

I felt a pang of fear at the thought that Rowyn may have left the city. It was a possibility I had not allowed myself to consider until now. I clenched my jaw, feeling the familiar surge of desperation wash over me. The woman I loved and the heir to the throne were missing, and there was nothing I could do.

"Another one clear, Butcher." Abelard's gruff voice cut through my thoughts, bringing me back to reality. He was a few paces away, his gaze trained on the ship that was disappearing on the horizon. "We can't keep holding them back forever. The nobles need to return to their consulships. We've done what we can."

He didn't need to say it. His message was clear. We were running out of time and, more terrifyingly, out of options.

"What will you do now that the ships are leaving?" I asked the admiral, my eyes drawn west.

Admiral Abelard sighed heavily with resignation. He turned his gaze from the disappearing ship to look at me. "I'm sailing home to Iora," he said, his voice carrying the faintest tremor of concern. "I'll make sure all's well there before combing the western shore for Rowyn and the prince. Many of my men have contacts in the West—people who hear things—and it is the most likely place for her to turn up. A girl with that much power isn't going to run for long. Eventually, she'll wise up and choose a place to make a stand. We just have to look for wherever she pops up."

"Did you search Helena's ship again before it left?" I asked, trying to calm the blood that was beginning to heat.

Admiral Abelard nodded, scratching at the blonde hair growing over his chin. We'd all been running ourselves ragged, trying to save a dying empire. "Duke Agramon and I looked together. She'd not been there, I assure you. Duke Agramon even said that he thought it unlikely she would escape on a ship. He said that she absolutely abhors traveling by sea."

His plan was sound, reflecting his seasoned command and clear-headed judgment. But it did little to quell the worry.

"Do me a favor, Abelard," I said, my tone taking on a desperate edge. He nodded, urging me to continue. I took a deep breath, mustering my courage before I made my request. "Keep a close watch on Morgania's waters for any ships that haven't been vetted. If they have not been cleared by the royal guard, board them. Search them. She may be aboard."

Admiral Abelard's eyes flickered with understanding, his expression somber. He nodded, placing a firm hand on my shoulder. "I will, Commander," he promised. His reassurance felt like a life raft in the midst of a stormy sea.

Chapter 12

"A LITTLE TO THE LEFT, Rowyn. There. Now, hook your foot around mine," I murmured, my voice low, soothing, like a river gently caressing its banks. A memory surfaced in my mind, a vision from an era long past, painted in hues of joy and shared warmth.

We were in Bruin, in the privacy of my quarters. Rowyn was radiant in the soft light, dressed only in my tunic, her hair a disheveled raven halo. The room had been transformed into a makeshift arena, the floors covered with soft furs to cushion our playful skirmishes.

I was teaching her the same move I'd shown her in Somme. The mere suggestion of her doing weapons training had sent Agramon into a fit of rage. But Rowyn had wanted it, and I couldn't deny her the joy that came with the graceful dance of a fight.

"Like this?" Her voice cut through my reminiscing, a lilt of concentration present in her question. She moved like a warrior, and I nodded approvingly, feeling a swell of pride. She'd always been a quick learner.

I underestimated her though. With a surprising

burst of energy, she executed the hip throw flawlessly, sending me flying through the air to land with a hard thud on the plush furs. A grunt escaped my lips and echoed off the stone walls, mixing with our fading laughter.

"Sam!" Rowyn was beside me in an instant, her eyes wide with worry. "I didn't mean to throw you that hard. Are you all right?"

I couldn't help but laugh at her concern. "I'm fine, sweet," I assured her, reaching up to tangle my fingers in her black locks. Her breath hitched when I pulled her down, aligning her body with mine. "You're a natural, you know that?"

She blushed. The rosy hue dusting her cheeks made her look even more endearing. "You're not so bad yourself, soldier," she whispered, her gaze flicking to my lips.

I bridged the distance between us, capturing her lips in a tender kiss. Our little world faded away, replaced by the sweet sensation of her soft lips moving against mine. It was a slice of heaven I didn't realize I'd been yearning for until it was taken away from me.

The memory faded, leaving me alone in the grim reality of the present. My laughter was replaced by a grimace, the blissful silence now a painful void. The taste of her lips, the sound of her laughter—they were echoes of a past I feared I'd lost forever.

THE BICKERING VOICES of traitors ricocheted off the council chamber walls. The long table bore witness to the power struggle at play, with Agramon at the head, his hawkish gaze surveying the scene.

The heavy tapestries were silent and still, drinking in the sharp, biting words thrown back and forth across the room. My fingers drummed on the table, each tap a sharp rebuke to my own impatience.

The ghostly woman in the corner seemed to have come back for good.

I tried to ignore her, scanning the room, taking in the expressions of the council members. But one face was conspicuously missing. Captain Diardo.

My gaze darted to his vacant seat, the absence of his sturdy, reliable presence only adding to the discord in the room. Diardo and I had often found common ground, our shared sense of duty and the will to serve our country binding us together. But recently, our paths seemed to have diverged, particularly over the handling of the empress.

Was he avoiding the council meeting out of protest?

Or was his anger still brewing, waiting to spill over? I understood his sentiments—even respected them. But my duty came first, above friendships and alliances.

The voices cut through my thoughts, pulling me back to the urgent matters at hand. But the worry lingered, an unwelcome guest lurking in the back of my mind.

"Maybe she's at Solridge," suggested Sage Bromwell. "That's where she'd gone to school, after all. I would think she'd be used to relying on their council and teachings."

Agramon shook his head, twisting his staff in his hand as he stared at the table, deep in thought. "She hated the teachers at Solridge ... especially Gillius. And she'd already tried to run from them before."

"The Nightlands?" suggested Bald Walden. "Remote, disconnected, hard to access without the right ships ..."

That stirred a murmur of interest around the room. The Nightlands, the wild lands where she'd quested for her gem ... where it had been a miracle that she'd survived ... It made a strange kind of sense.

I swallowed, feeling a cold dread settle in my stomach. It wasn't a pleasant thought, Rowyn alone in those wild lands. But it was better than the alternatives. It was better than thinking she might be with Lord

Destrian.

"We can't just pack up and head for the Nightlands without confirmation," Elgar the Swift protested. "The journey itself is treacherous, even for someone like me."

Agramon raised an eyebrow, leaning back in his chair. "She wouldn't take a child to the Nightlands. Let alone the heir to the throne."

"Admiral Abelard thinks she's heading west," I said. "What does it matter where she is now, if we can predict where she is going?"

Agramon glared at me. "I haven't entirely ruled out her finding a way to get to Maryse. Duke Eldred hasn't responded to any of my requests, and the Marysian soldiers have defected. They are planning to put the child emperor on the throne with Duke Eldred overseeing him."

"You know she wouldn't go there," I said, speaking just to Agramon. "She's not going to use the emperor as a bargaining chip. She's going to protect the boy, just like she did with Nirah."

"You think she'll take the boy to Morgania?" Agramon asked.

I shrugged. "She'd go to where she knows . . . where she could feel safest. I already directed the admiral to search the Morganian shore after he visits home."

We were deep in discussion when the heavy doors of the council chambers burst open, slamming against the stone walls with a thunderous crash. All heads turned as a Solin guard, panting and wide-eyed, stumbled into the room in a state of panic.

"The empress is gone!" he stammered, breathless.

Agramon's eyes widened, and he was on his feet in an instant. "What do you mean, *gone!*"

The guard gulped, trying to regain his composure. "The empress and the princesses . . . they've escaped their rooms."

Chaos erupted in the room as council members began shouting over one another. I remained rooted to my spot, the reality of the news washing over me like a bucket of cold water.

Agramon was barking orders at the guard. "Lock down the castle, send out search parties, alert the city watch!" His gaze moved to me, a spark of accusation in his eyes. I shook my head, denying any involvement. As much as I was ready to confront him, helping the empress and her children escape was beyond my capabilities.

THE AIR IN THE PALACE was thick with tension and uncertainty as I rushed through its grand corridors with Elgar the Swift by my side. We'd worked together before. Even though the league leaper was mostly Agramon's man, there was an odd sort of honest deviousness to him that I'd grown to appreciate.

"I need you to coordinate with the palace guard," I said. "Get to every gate, every exit point. I want the city locked down immediately. No one leaves, no one enters without thorough verification."

Without a word, he vanished, his form dissipating into thin air only to reappear elsewhere. I hoped he would thread through the city with an urgency that matched my own.

When I turned the corner to the royal family's quarters, I found the hallway eerily silent. Standing amid the cold stone and flickering torchlight was a figure as imposing as the surroundings. Pythia Golden-Eyes stood over the lifeless forms strewn across the floor.

Her dark hair was pulled into a long braid that tumbled down her back. Her eyes were pools of hardened amber shimmering under the glow of the torchlight. A gem, the color of clotted blood, sat nestled within her dark skin between her brows.

We'd spent quite a bit of time together in Yliria as

Pythia was one of Lyrica's foremost war sorcerers. It's always lonely in the army, and Pythia had her choice of lovers from the pretty men who marched off to battle and hoped for some moment of pleasure before they died. Her clothes, far from the silken dresses and lavish embellishments of court ladies, were utilitarian, designed for a life far removed from delicate dances and whispered courtship.

As the gem embedded in her forehead glowed a rust red, a palpable energy filled the grand hall. The air itself seemed to shudder as the lifeless bodies around her stirred, rising in obedience to the power she commanded.

"Who attacked you?" Her voice imbued with inherent authority. The deceased guards' mouths opened, their voices emerging as harsh rasps from beyond the veil of death.

"Castle guard," came the guttural reply from a fallen man. Pythia's eyes met mine, a flash of understanding passing between us.

All I could do was plunge forward.

I strode purposefully toward the castle entrance. The stone walls echoed with the banter of Solin guards and Bald Walden's men, their armor gleaming in the pale light.

As I approached the gathering, their conversations

dimmed, their attention shifting to me. Before I could engage, a blur of motion caught my eye. Elgar the Swift materialized beside me, his eyes reflecting an urgency that sent a jolt of adrenaline coursing through my veins.

"Commander," he grunted, a bead of sweat trickling from his silver-white hair and down his weathered face. "Agramon needs to speak with you."

Without waiting for a response, he grabbed my arm, his fingers closing around my wrist in a grip as sure as iron. In a blink, we leaped, a dizzying feeling of pressure crushing us before spitting us out into the grim depths of the castle dungeons.

The dank, cold air of the underground cells hit me like a wave until it felt as though I was drowning in anguish. The ghosts had all followed me into the darkness. They took full advantage of the grisly surroundings and began to surge towards me.

I took a breath, trying to push them from my mind.

What did Agramon want? I could only hope it was not a portent of more dire times ahead.

As I stepped into the dimly lit hall, my eyes fell upon a scene that shook me to my core. Captain Diardo, a man who I had considered a friend and ally, sat hunched in a narrow cell, his body bearing the cruel marks of a recent fight. He looked up at my approach, his gaze hard and angry. I faltered under the weight of his stare, feeling as if I were looking at a mirror reflecting my own discontent.

"Diardo . . ." My voice trailed off, the sight of him in such a state a brutal blow. The captain had always stood as a bulwark of duty and dedication, unwavering in his service. I hated to see him reduced to an injured and incarcerated criminal.

Agramon's voice cut through the heavy silence, his words echoing off the cold stone walls. "He betrayed his duties, Butcher. He helped the empress to escape."

Chapter 13

THE VERY STONES of the dungeon seemed to whisper tales of treachery and torment as I stepped forward. Before me, Agramon's menacing silhouette was cast in the eerie glow of the single torch illuminating the oppressive darkness. On the opposite side, separated by the unforgiving iron bars, sat Diardo, his glare the embodiment of resilient defiance.

Diardo had been the emperor's best friend once.

Agramon's fingers drifted over a piece of parchment, his hawkish gaze locked on the captain. "This," he began, his voice resonating in the stony silence, "proves Diardo's treason." The parchment was flung toward me.

Hesitantly, I picked up the ragged document. I recognized the words in the spidery script of Duke Eldred of Maryse. Each sentence was a dagger, each revelation a twist of the blade in the festering wound of disbelief.

"Diardo—ensure the escape of the empress . . . rewarded with nobility and a home in Maryse . . ."

I cast a glance at Diardo. He looked far from regretful. He glowered at me, as though to challenge *my* honor with his own treason.

My grip on the parchment tightened, the edges biting into my skin. I moved closer to the bars of the cell, my hands white-knuckled against the cold iron, my eyes never leaving his. The dungeon's air was thick with unspoken words, a suffocating silence that was somehow louder than any battle cry.

"Speak, Diardo," I growled, my voice echoing ominously in the stone chamber. "What have you done?"

His gaze held steady as he broke the silence, the acoustics of the dungeon amplifying his voice into a haunting echo. "It isn't treason if you haven't won yet," he snarled, his words filled with anger. "And you . . . you are no better than him." Diardo pointed to Agramon.

Agramon's words were steady and unyielding. "This traitor cannot go unpunished, Butcher. Order must be maintained, else we risk more betrayals."

I clenched my jaw, my gaze flickering to Diardo. His once vibrant eyes were now clouded with resignation, almost unrecognizable to the handsome man I had known. It felt as though I were looking at the hollow shell of my friend, his essence having faded away.

"He's always been loyal," I retorted.

"Friendship does not erase treason, Butcher," Agramon snapped, his eyes going back to glare at Diardo. "He assisted the empress in her escape. He was last seen in her company."

"But . . ."

Agramon was unrelenting. "There are witnesses. There is evidence." His gaze bore into me. "Denying the truth will not change it, Butcher. Diardo must be punished. And the punishment for treason—"

"Is death," I finished, the words tasting sour in my mouth.

Agramon nodded, a victorious gleam in his eyes. "Exactly."

THE COUNCIL CHAMBER was silent as we contemplated the fate of Captain Diardo. The question was not whether he was guilty. He'd admitted as much himself, stating proudly that he'd helped the empress escape.

"He has betrayed us," Agramon said in a low rumble. "If he is willing to aid the enemy, then he is an enemy himself."

"I would not say the empress is an enemy," Sage Bromwell said, his brows furrowed in consternation. "A liability, sure, but she is no enemy."

"She is who Maryse seeks to put into power. She and Duke Eldred," Agramon said, his gem beginning to glow.

"I agree with the duke," Elgar the Swift cut in, his voice cold and unyielding. "The captain knows too much about the palace to be trusted."

"We could keep him in prison," Bald Walden suggested with hesitation.

Diardo was a friend. But he had chosen his side. And rotting in a prison was the last thing Diardo would want.

"Or perhaps he will escape and bring the empress to power," Agramon countered, his eyes glinting dangerously. "You've seen the support she has. If she claims the throne, the empire will be torn apart, and I am not fond of the idea of keeping a viper so close."

"And I agree," Elgar added, his gaze hard. "It must be execution."

Agramon turned to me, his gaze expectant. "And you, Butcher? What say you?"

I glanced at the corner. The ghosts seemed to grow bolder day by day, not content to exist in the confines of the shadows. They'd begun to reach closer to the light. They'd begun to whisper curses.

Rowyn had been the only presence to keep them at bay. I'd even asked Pythia to banish them back to the veil, but she'd said she couldn't sense the spirits at all. I'd almost cursed our friendship right then and there, sure that the necromancer was lying to me. It's hard to accept when you're the one whom the gods have cursed.

And what had I gained for my loyalty?

No, I refused to think of it. I found a way to lift the curse. I found the way to make the ghosts of the past disappear. It was as the fortune-teller had said.

Rowyn was key to my redemption.

Rowyn was the only future I had left.

If the empress succeeded in gaining power, I might as well kiss my hopes for the future goodbye.

"He will not fail to try to help her," I said finally, my voice steady. "He won't give up, and if he is imprisoned, those who remain loyal to him at the castle will try to free him. It is better to be safe."

There was a cold finality in the words that spilled from my lips, a grim indicator of the path I had chosen to tread. A path where my desires and obsessions overrode the bonds of friendship and loyalty.

Agramon nodded, a look of satisfaction crossing his face. "Then it is settled," he said, pulling a piece of parchment toward him. "The council has spoken."

One by one, we signed the order of execution. Agramon, Elgar, Sage Bromwell, Bald Walden, and then me. It was done. We had made our choice, for better or worse. The reality of our decision weighed heavily on me. But there was no going back. We had chosen our path, and now we could only move forward.

The council room felt cold, colder than it had ever been. I ran my fingers over the worn engravings on the table, memories of the countless hours spent around it gnawing at the edges of my consciousness.

"I'm heading west," I declared, my voice resonating in the room. "To Morgania."

The ensuing silence was deafening. The mere mention of Morgania was enough to elicit uneasy stares from the others, but Abelard's words had remained in my ears long after his departure—he believed that Rowyn, or rather the young prince, would emerge in Morgania.

"I do not wish for Everett or anyone else to have the emperor," I lied, folding my hands on the table, staring at each of them in turn. I had to make them believe my intentions were noble, that it was for the betterment of the kingdom. The truth, though, was a bitter poison I dared not spill.

Agramon was the first to break the silence. "Are you sure this is the wisest course of action?"

"I am," I responded firmly. "I'm not leaving the prince to his fate."

Elgar frowned, crossing his arms. "But we have more pressing issues here. Leaving for Morgania now seems . . . irresponsible."

The others murmured their agreement, their expressions dubious. I understood their skepticism—it was a bold move, one that could tip the scales of power unfavorably. But I had to do this. I had to find her.

"I am aware of the risks," I admitted, holding their gazes, "but this is something that I must do. For the sake of the empire, and for all of us."

"No." Agramon's tone was stern. "We cannot afford to leave Somme undefended."

I tried to quell the fury that was beginning to cloud my mind. "What are you suggesting, Agramon?"

"We need the forces here, where they can do the most good. If Maryse sees an opportunity, they won't hesitate to put Duke Eldred on the throne."

"That's why we have to—"

"No," he cut me off sharply. "I won't allow it. If you're going to Morgania, you won't take the army with you. You have your mercenaries from Ardent and the soldiers of Bruin."

"You can't just—"

"I can, and I will." Agramon's eyes were hard, his determination evident. "Bald Walden will assume command here. The forces within the city will stay and defend it."

The tension in the air thickened. I glanced at Bald

Walden. He met my gaze, an ambitious glint in his eyes. I knew then that Agramon's decision was final.

Anger bubbled within me, fueled by the frustration of my plans falling apart. I knew Agramon was right. I knew it in my gut. Yet, I couldn't help the wave of resentment that surged within me.

I turned to leave. I felt stripped of my power, my command reduced to a handful of men. But I wouldn't let that stop me.

Rowyn was out there, and I would move heaven and earth to find her. The cost didn't matter. Not anymore. I had lost too much already.

Chapter 14

GAINST THE BACKDROP of the inky darkness, almost hidden from the curtain of rain falling on the stone parapet, stood a figure whose beauty held me in a spell. Opal gems embedded in her skin glowed, their multifaceted light glimmering between the raindrops.

Rowyn.

Her arms were raised to the skies as they answered her command. I watched from the doorway a moment, unable to tear my gaze away until every instinct screamed at me to reach out.

"I'll take it from here," I murmured to the guard, motioning him away. I made sure he'd disappeared into the bowels of the castle before I stepped through the door and shut it behind me, blocking out the light from inside.

Taking a deep breath, I moved forward, every step echoing the pounding of my heart as rain streamed from the sky. She turned her gaze toward me, the glow of the opals reflecting in her eyes. For a moment, her gaze faltered, as though she struggled to truly see me. Little rivers of black hair marbled her pale skin, the dress she'd donned that morning clinging to her as she bathed in her own power.

It was breathtaking.

It was intoxicating.

It was fucking addicting.

My heart thundered in my chest, threatening to match the rhythm of the rain. The words tumbled out in an avalanche of emotion that I could no longer contain. "I love you." The confession felt raw, exposing a vulnerability I had never allowed myself to express. "Since the moment we met . . . I've loved you."

I still remembered her smile. The sadness that lurked in its depths as she reached, her touch as soothing as the rain against my fevered skin. Her lips met mine in a kiss that tasted like a promise and a plea. Love spilled between us, her impossibly blue eyes pleading with me to make her forget every torment that had plagued her life, and I did. I kneeled before her like the goddess she was and drank her in.

It was only afterward, when we'd slipped into my bed, naked and soaked, that I realized she'd never said it back.

The morning was a somber serenade, the world awaking to the symphony of life, while inside the castle walls, death held its dark vigil. The harsh scrape of metal against stone broke the unsettling silence that permeated the castle, a chilling reminder of the gruesome spectacle that was to follow.

I found myself in the castle's armory, the familiar scent of oiled leather and cold steel offering a bitter comfort. My reflection stared back at me from the polished surface of my sword—an unrecognizable figure with hollow eyes and a hardened set to his jaw.

The weight of the blade felt heavier today, the balance skewed by the guilt that gnawed at my conscience. Each pass of whetstone over the steel echoed in the otherwise silent room, a haunting melody to accompany the turmoil within—a distant echo of a friendship lost to the cruel clutches of duty and ambition.

Today, I was to be the harbinger of his end. A friend turned executioner.

Yet, in the midst of the remorse, another voice rang in my thoughts, and a new feeling began to emerge. Fucking Rowyn. Why the hell was she still gone? I was prepared to give her everything, and she was throwing it all away. I shook my head, angry at what she reduced me to. It was for her that I'd truly turned into a monster. When I had my hands on her, I would let her know exactly what she burdened me with. Naked fury began shooting through my fists.

Agramon was an unlikely ally, but an ally nonetheless, because at least I knew he could get the job done. I didn't have to like him to see that he was good at what he set out to do—and damnably efficient about it. Being tasked with taking charge of someone like Rowyn came with a lot of burdens in and of itself. Despite his questionable methods, she did a great deal of learning under him. She'd been spoiled for it, quite frankly. I'd trained her myself in combat, and she'd grown well in fighting without weapons, thanks to me. She'd learned how to fly, she'd learned manners from the emperor's sister—the princess as her companion. She'd been shown the best the lands in the East could offer her, and she completely took it for granted.

She took *me* for granted.

I felt like such a fool.

The first few days of her disappearance, I'd thought maybe she was frightened. The temple literally exploded as though we were at war. That would frighten everyone, and she used her magic to get herself out. At first I'd thought she'd been in shock and that she was just making sure it was all clear before she returned.

But she'd stayed away, and I began to consider the situation.

Rowyn didn't fucking freeze in a fight. She didn't run from battle.

She knew she was taking the prince and leaving, and I wondered again about the empress. We should have never let her get away. Did Rowyn help her escape?

Probably.

They were probably laughing at us, the Lyrican fools who trusted the words of women.

I gritted my teeth.

Agramon would get me what I needed, and I needed her back.

The words of the fortune teller echoed in my mind.

"When the sun bows to the moon, a girl will come. Her heart, a wellspring of tears. With her, the rain shall return, washing away the stains of old sins. From the ashes of the past, a new dawn shall arise. And you, son of Lyrica, you shall find redemption in her tears."

I would find her, and I would make sure she never got away again. The fact that she'd kept away from me—didn't even *try* to communicate—was a fucking slap in the face.

I was going to be her husband. It's not like I forced her. She was the one who insisted on it. Then she made a spectacle of me in front of the entire empire and thought she could just disappear?

Not. Fucking. Likely.

When I got my hands on her . . .

My fingers tightened around the hilt of my sword, the cool metal a stark contrast to the burning determination within me. I had to find her. For every friend lost, every alliance shattered, and every part of my soul that was slowly decaying, there was no turning back now.

I would find her.

Suppressing the guilt welling up within me, I sheathed my sword and exited the armory. The stone corridor leading to the prisons stretched before me. The morning light spilled through the barred windows and fell on the stone floor, casting shadows that seemed to lengthen with each step I took.

The guards wouldn't meet my eyes when I walked through; they looked down at their shoes as the cursed man walked past. It was really bad when we'd returned from Yliria, with the whispers and veiled disrespect. But this was a hundred times worse because they had been around to watch it all.

Captain Diardo sat on a worn-out wooden bench in the farthest cell, his back against the stone wall. His usually vibrant eyes were dull, his cheerful demeanor replaced by a solemn stillness. He looked up as I approached, a bitter smile twisting his lips.

"Never thought I'd see the day when you would be

on the other side of these bars," Diardo's voice echoed through the dank cell, a hollow laugh following his words.

"Diardo . . ." I began, but he raised a hand, silencing me.

"No need for pleasantries, Sam," he said. "I'm well aware of my situation. But tell me, how does it feel? To be the lapdog of the man who once was our enemy?"

His words cut deep, but I couldn't argue. He was right, wasn't he? Agramon had become an ally out of necessity, but the price of that alliance was Diardo's life.

"I didn't want this . . ." I started, but Diardo cut me off.

"But you let it happen, didn't you?" he spat, his eyes burning with accusation. "You could've defended me—fought for me. But instead, you chose Agramon. You chose to believe that . . . monster."

"I didn't have a choice," I argued, but my voice was feeble and filled with doubt.

"Everyone has a choice, Butcher," Diardo retorted, a bitter chuckle escaping him. "You made yours."

"I'm sorry, but I was outnumbered."

"You're sorry?" His laughter echoed in the cell, a harsh, cold sound. "Your apologies won't save me."

His words echoed in the silence that followed, each one a harsh reminder of the decision I had made. I was out of words, my apologies hollow in the face of his imminent death.

THE MORNING AIR WAS CRISP, tinged with the scent of impending doom. The square, usually bustling with activity, was eerily quiet save for the somber murmur of the gathered crowd. A grim gallows stage had been erected at its center so the crowd could witness the spectacle of a man who'd given everything to the empire, only for us to turn around and betray him for it.

I stood at a distance, feeling the icy grip of regret strangle my resolve.

Agramon stood by my side. A solemn look on his face belied the satisfaction I knew he must be feeling. He turned to me, his lips parting as if to speak, but I cut him off with a glare. There was no comfort he could offer, no words that would absolve me of this guilt.

Clad in the stony gray of a prisoner's garb, Diardo was led to the block. The metallic scent of fear hung heavily in the air as he passed. He'd been devilishly handsome before, vibrant and filled with charm. Now his face was marked by the weary lines of a life lived in pain and hardship.

Diardo turned to the crowd, his eyes scanning the sea of faces. I saw the hurt there, a raw, visceral pain. My throat tightened. My heart pounded against my ribs. What the fuck was I doing?

The executioner drew a sharp, gleaming sword from a scabbard. It glinted menacingly under the early morning light. Diardo straightened, squaring his shoulders, the picture of dignity even in the face of death. He looked up at the sky, peaceful resignation in his eyes.

I was held in place by a monstrous duty and an all-consuming obsession. I swallowed hard, the lump in my throat a painful reminder of the price I was willing to pay to find Rowyn. The need to find her, the relentless pull, forced me to push down the wave of despair, to lock it away in the darkest recesses of my heart.

The ghosts had accompanied me to view death. They didn't watch me now, transfixed as they were by the executioner's blade as it arced through the air. Time seemed to crawl, a spectacle drawn in horrifying slow motion. The sun reflected off the metal of the blade. The breath of the assembly hitched in unison, eyes wide with morbid fascination.

The blade fell true, and Diardo slumped onto the platform as the crowd began to roar. People pushed against each other to dip their sleeves in his blood. "Saint Diardo," they were already chanting.

The ghosts turned as one, their phantom eyes boring into mine, and stepped closer.

I looked away.

I had sacrificed everything, betrayed my closest friend, forsaken my honor—all for her.

As Diardo's life had been extinguished, so, too, had the remnants of my old self. What remained was a twisted version of the man I once was—driven by desperation, fueled by resentment, and teetering on the precipice.

When I found Rowyn, she would face the tempest she had stirred. She would bear the cost of her choices. She would know the depth of the chaos she had sown, and I would make sure that she *felt* my fury.

Acknowledgments

Writing alternate point of view novellas for the Tempest Rising series and universe was something I'd kicked around for a while as I released each book. With the help of family and friends, I am happy that I was able to go on this adventure with the readers, because it was something I'd dreamed of, but didn't think it would come to reality so soon. For that I have to thank my huge support system.

My husband Bryan, who has assisted with giving time for the deadline and high-pressure weeks. He has always been my biggest cheerleader.

To my sister Olivia, and my parents, Joe and Rachel, who have always harbored my writing and given me a quiet place to work.

To Mom and Debbie, who helped out with the kiddos when I needed days to write and get work done.

To my editor, Cayce Berryman, who was such a good sport about fitting in several extra projects on short notice. As always, she was a pleasure to work with.

Finally, to my children, who have been patient with me as I multi-task, and who bring me so much joy each day.